A TALE OF TWO ISLANDS

The Last Prince of Kalymnos

Dominic Koulianos

Dominic Koulianos

First Edition

ISBN: 979-8-218-73069-7

Edited by Jim and Sandy Dorman

Printed in the United States of America

A TALE OF TWO ISLANDS

Chapter 1

PROLOGUE - CARTHAGE 533 AD

Tzazo loomed over the deck of his magnificent vessel, *The Cleopatra*, as he reflected on everything he was leaving behind. The scent of the sea filled the air; the briny tang mingled with the exotic aromas wafting from the market stalls—cumin, cinnamon, and something sweet he couldn't quite place. He surveyed the stunning Carthaginian harbor, admiring its elegant buildings and intricate architecture. In the distance stood the grand Agora marketplace, evidence of the city's wealth and success.

The sounds of the waterfront enveloped him: the rhythmic creaking of moored ships, distant calls of merchants, and the occasional cry of a seagull overhead. His gaze drifted to the cothon, the circular inner harbor at the heart of Carthage, once the pride of the city and now the stronghold of the Vandal fleet. At its center lay an island, crowned by a towering structure where the Vandal admiral stood watch, surveying the maneuvers of his ships.

Tzazo commanded an intimidating presence from the prow of *The Cleopatra*, overseeing a diverse fleet. Three formidable triremes with towering masts and fifty sturdy cargo ships with broad, robust timber frames were anchored in the cothon. The ships groaned and grated, their wood bearing the tales of countless voyages. The constant hustle of the wharf rang out, creating a symphony that mingled with the shouts and the jostling of equipment from the vessels' bowels. *The Cleopatra* stood majestically at the fleet's helm, ready to spearhead the charge.

Waiting within the ships' holds were Tzazo's five thousand battle-hardened soldiers, ready to face any foe, along with all the necessary provisions and equipment to conduct an efficient campaign. Every element was in place, like meticulously arranged pieces on a grand chessboard, each poised to play its part in the battles to come.

Tzazo's calloused hand traced the smooth wood of the rail that lined the ship's prow. He paused at the point where it converged to form a bronze-capped ram. He recalled the days when naval battles were decided by strength, not maneuverability, and the sight of a battering ram striking true with all the might of a thunderbolt filled his heart with pride. Memories of past sea battles in the Mediterranean flooded his mind: the screams, the clash of iron, and the taste of blood and salt. But those days were gone, replaced by the swifter, more agile dromons of the Byzantine navy, rendering battering rams nearly obsolete. Yet, Tzazo stood firm, proud of the heritage of his people and confident in the strength of his ships and his men.

Tzazo's skin remained pale despite the scorching heat of this accursed land. It never relented; even now, it caused rivulets of sweat to stream down his brow. Yet, he would not remove his iron-banded helm, for it shielded his skin from the merciless mid-morning sun of Africa. He strode the deck of his war galley, clothed in his battle attire. His mail, a masterfully crafted lamellar armor of interlocking plates, clinked softly with every movement, its design evidence of the Vandal blacksmiths' ingenuity. His sword, a traditional spatha, hung at his side, its blade a mirror of polished steel. Though the armor pressed heavily on his shoulders, he bore it with pride, knowing he must present an imposing figure—a beacon to inspire his men to victory.

In his right hand, he held his spear, its tip honed to a gleaming point, while in his left, he held his oak shield, emblazoned with the emblem of the white horse on a scarlet field—the sigil of his elder brother Gelimer. Craftsmen had used layers of indigo and madder dye to tint the scarlet background, and once dry, a white horse's head was overlaid with a mixture of limestone and crushed shells.

King Gelimer, Tzazo's brother, had granted him the command of a mighty host, charging him with the task of quelling the rebels who had risen in Sardinia. Tzazo and his fleet had prepared to depart at dawn to spare their rowers the toil of straining at the oars under the scorching African noontide. Despite this, it was past mid-morning before King Gelimer's messenger hastened toward them.

Tzazo was in a foul mood as he set aside his shield and plucked the scroll from the messenger's hands. He was unsure of the letter's contents and despised last-minute changes to his battle plans. It had been fourteen days since the tidings reached him that his cousin, the governor of Sardinia, Godas, had rebelled against the realm. Though blood-related, Tzazo had always deemed his cousin Godas a craven, short-sighted fool, groveling to anyone who would grant him greater power. And now, his cousin sought the favor of Emperor Justinian by offering all of Sardinia to the Byzantine Empire.

Tzazo broke the waxen seal and unfurled the parchment. The frantic script declared, "*We have fallen upon evil times. Skylla has cast her runes and believes she has discovered a way for us to avoid a dark fate. Wait for my arrival. I have a task for you that may alter the outcome of this conflict.*" He sneered and handed the scroll back to the trembling messenger. "My brother, with his misguided faith, clings to God with his words while heeding the counsel of a pagan sorceress with his ears. He will lead us to ruin." With a hint of sarcasm, he added, "Inform the king I eagerly await his arrival."

The haunting, low bellow of a horn resonated from the far end of the cothon, drawing Tzazo's attention toward the distant assembly ground. He exhaled in frustration, knowing the delay he feared was now inevitable. The deafening clamor grew closer, unmistakably indicating his brother's approach. From his vantage point, Tzazo watched as the royal procession began. His patience, already thin, stretched to the breaking point.

A chariot of gilded bronze carried King Gelimer along the broad paths encircling the harbor. Four steeds, as white as snow, drew the chariot slowly into view of each ship. As the procession glided by, the soldiers stood at attention. They were adorned with iron-rimmed helms and red cloaks, their spears pointing skyward. As the king passed each ship, the soldiers raised their spears and struck their shields with a clang that echoed like the beat of a war drum, matching the rhythmic thud of the horses' hooves. Each ship flew the standard of the white horse on a red flag, the symbol of King Gelimer.

The king appeared resplendent in his tunic, white as bone, with a crimson cloak at his neck. A simple circlet of ivory crowned his ruffled hair. Though not in the best spirits, he understood the importance of maintaining a regal appearance. As the ruler of his kingdom, Gelimer's demeanor could shape the mood of his subjects. If the sorceress was correct, he would need all the support he could muster. He inhaled deeply, steeling himself against the nauseating smell that pervaded the enclosed end of the cothon. The basin's circular design trapped the stagnant water. Filth from countless workers and soldiers clung to the algae-stained porticos, filling the air with an inescapable stench.

The king's elite guard, the Vult, led the regal parade. They advanced in two columns, marching in perfect unison. Each of their shields bore King Gelimer's emblem, centered by a gleaming bronze knob. Their armor shone in the light, made of polished mail, with a blue tunic beneath. Their bronze domed helmets were topped with plumes of golden horsehair, and bronze gladiuses hung at their waists. In their right hand, they gripped staves, their heads crowned in bronze, fashioned like dragons. Conical banners, shaped like dragon bodies, flapped in the breeze, conjuring the semblance of a horde of dragons flying above the men.

A group of Arian priests, robed in white and wearing embroidered hoods, followed close behind. They swung bronze censers, filling the air with the sweet aroma of frankincense. Behind them, the royal heralds, trumpets in hand, made way for the king's chariot. At King Gelimer's side stood a woman draped in black dog pelts, her ghostly pale hands clutching a coffer wrapped in black linen. She stood tall and proud, radiating an aura of mystery. Not a single inch of flesh was visible from head to foot, except her hands. They stood in stark contrast to her dark attire, casting them in an otherworldly glow.

The Vult came to an abrupt halt, and the two columns stepped back, opening a clear path for the king's chariot to pass. It continued toward the end of the cothon, where *The Cleopatra* stood ready. As the king approached, his elite guard slammed their shields together in salute, creating a thunderous sound. Then, the heralds announced the king's arrival with three triumphant blasts from their trumpets. King Gelimer rose from his chariot and walked toward

Tzazo, who trudged down the gangplank and muttered, "What a tedious day. I should be halfway to Sardinia by now."

The king paused as he felt a sudden chill on his shoulder, and he turned to see the pale hand of the sorceress upon his cloak. He shuddered as she leaned close to him, whispering in his ear. She drew nearer still, pressing the coffer into his hands, which he cautiously accepted with a nod of acknowledgment. Many priests in the procession averted their eyes as the king stepped back from the sorceress, her dark nature a conflict to their faith.

Tzazo watched as his brother, the king, drew near. Gelimer's once-proud figure now seemed diminished, his vigor sapped by the haunting company of his sorceress. "So, this is how kingship wears on you, brother?" Tzazo spoke with a dry edge in his voice, the butt of his spear tapping the ground as he knelt.

Gelimer placed a hand on his helm, the gesture heavy as though trying to impart a strength he no longer possessed. "We have no time for mockery," Gelimer replied, his voice cracking with unspoken dread. "This rebellion must be crushed before it spreads like a sickness. If Sardinia falls, Carthage may not stand for long."

Tzazo straightened, his armor gleaming in the noon sun. "The strength of our fleet will accomplish more than Skylla's visions," he answered bluntly. "I need soldiers, not riddles."

Gelimer's eyes darkened at the mention of his trusted sorceress. "Do not dismiss her so lightly," he warned, his voice dropping to a dangerous low. "She has foreseen our doom unless we act swiftly. Godas holds a child—a girl—who must die. If she lives, Skylla says my crown will fall."

Tzazo's appearance stiffened. "A child?" His voice was cold but curious. "You trust the fate of our kingdom to the death of a child?"

"She is not just any child!" Gelimer's voice grew sharp, his hands tightening around the coffer. "Skylla says the girl's bloodline is cursed, destined to undo everything we've built. You must kill her, Tzazo. Only then can we avoid the ruin foretold."

Tzazo's eyes narrowed. "And you place your trust in a sorceress over your men? Over me?"

"Hold your tongue," Gelimer snapped, stepping closer, his tone cold as iron. "This is not about trust, brother. It is about survival. Do you think I enjoy this? It must be done. Skylla has never erred in her visions—not in war, not in famine."

Tzazo's eyes shifted to the harbor where the sails of his fleet flapped in the wind, their strength tangible, real. "And if she's wrong this time?" His voice, quieter now but no less defiant, drifted on the breeze.

Gelimer's anger surged, and he leaned in, his voice a venomous slither. "There will be no more debate. You will do this, Tzazo. The girl must die...and by your hand."

Tzazo hesitated, then finally spoke, his voice quieter now. "My King, I cannot obey this... this is no ordinary request. To kill a child—"

Gelimer's eyes flashed. "If this child stands in the way of my kingdom, then she must die. Skylla believes she is a threat to the crown." He looked directly into Tzazo's eyes. "You are my brother, but more than that, you are my sword. This is not a request. It is a command."

"I am your sword, but not your butcher," replied Tzazo, his voice taut with restrained emotion.

Gelimer's expression twisted, and a slow, wry smile curled on his lips. "But remember your family, brother. Your wife... your son." His smile faded into a sneer. "You wouldn't want any harm to come to them, would you? Skylla has promised their safety while you're away... for now."

Tzazo's face darkened, his pulse quickening with an unspoken fury. His words came out hard, almost spat. "I will see it done," he said, realizing the veiled threat. "But remember this, brother—history will not call us strong for this. They will call us cowards."

"History remembers the victors, not the hesitant," he declared. "Do this, and we will make the world kneel at our feet."

Tzazo fought to contain his rising disgust as he glanced at the distant figure of Skylla, her silhouette looming like a shadow over the king. The sorceress was always there, her presence heavy, as though she was more than mortal. Gelimer's eyes flickered toward her, his voice growing bold once again. "Skylla's visions leave no room for doubt. The child must die Tzazo. You are the only one I can trust with this."

Gelimer pressed the coffer into Tzazo's hands as his voice dripped with suspicion: "Beware of our cousin Godas. I do not trust him. He knows that I am seeking this child. He may have already hidden her. When you find the girl, check for a strange birthmark on the nape of her neck. We must be certain you kill the right child."

Tzazo nodded, the king's command like a curse upon him. The king continued, his words striking like venom. "Make sure the child dies in the Necropolis of the Vipers. It was foretold in Skylla's runes that she must die there."

Tzazo had heard of the Necropolis of the Vipers—an ancient burial ground steeped in dark legends. Rumors abound that those who died there had their souls claimed by the earth, never to find peace. Skylla believed that the child's death in such a cursed place would not only end her life but sever her spirit from the world, preventing her from seeking vengeance in the afterlife. Duty and honor clashed violently in Tzazo's heart as he wrestled to agree to such a command.

Gelimer leaned in so close that Tzazo could feel the heat of his breath, the menace curling in each word. "In this coffer is a vial," Gelimer hissed, his voice cold. "It must be filled with the child's blood—freshly drawn, while her heart still beats. Seal it at once and deliver it to Skylla. Her body… bring that to me. No one else is to see it. Do you understand?"

Tzazo stiffened, his pulse quickening as the implications of the order sank in. He gave a sharp nod, but his mind spun, grappling with the enormity of what was being asked.

"And what of the assault on Sardinia?" Tzazo ventured, his voice quieter than he intended.

"That is no longer our priority, Tzazo," the king retorted, his eyes narrowing. "Now, swear on your sword and the lives of your family that you will carry out everything as I have instructed."

Tzazo's fingers tightened around the coffer, the cold metal biting into his skin. 'To kill a child,' he thought, the words resounding in his mind like a curse. 'Is this who I am now? What have I become?' Once a shield of pride, his armor now felt like a prison of iron. Each link seemed to weigh heavier than the last, a chain binding him to a fate he could no longer escape.

With the lives of his family on the line, Tzazo forced himself to reply, "By my sword and the blood of our kin, I swear it, my king. I swear upon my honor and my loyalty to the crown."

King Gelimer abruptly turned on his heels, a burden seemingly lifted and scuttled back to Skylla. Tzazo remained steadfast, his face unflinching until the king returned to his chariot. The heralds' horns blared one last time, signaling Gelimer's departure.

Once the procession began its slow march back to the palace, Tzazo turned away, his heart heavy with what lay ahead. He marched back up the gangplank to *The Cleopatra*, where his host awaited orders. His men were disciplined, ready to set sail at his command, but Tzazo felt only the pressure of his grim task.

He took his place at the ship's stern, his voice booming as he shouted, "Rema!" The oarsmen responded, pulling back and plunging their oars into the water. With each shout of "Rema!" the ship inched forward. Finally, *The Cleopatra* was underway, cutting through the water.

Once the Carthaginian coast faded entirely from view, Tzazo allowed himself a moment of respite. The relentless heat, which had plagued him earlier, finally settled into a dull discomfort. He removed his helmet, feeling the rush of warm air against his sweat-slicked brow. He looked toward the horizon, trying to quell the unease that churned within him.

Beneath the deck, the rhythmic chant of the rowers, pulling in time with the command of "Rema," filled the air. The oars sliced through the water like a machine built for war. With its towering masts and sleek design, *The Cleopatra* moved with the prowess of a beast, a symbol of the strength Tzazo had always trusted. But now, the ship's progress felt ominous, as if it carried him further from the man he used to be.

As Tzazo stood in the silence of the open sea, his thoughts inevitably drifted back to the king's words. 'Kill the girl.' He clenched his fists, remembering the coldness in Gelimer's eyes as he uttered the command. The notion felt profoundly wrong, yet the threat to his family's safety loomed over him like an axe. Could he really defy the king—his own brother—and protect those he loved?

He absently stared at the coffer at his side. Inside, a vial lay coiled like a venomous serpent, a promise of death. The ghostly green glass seemed to pulse as if it anticipated the blood it was meant to hold. 'It must be filled with the child's blood—fresh, drawn while her heart still beats,' Gelimer had said. Tzazo could still hear his brother's voice, as sharp as a blade in the back of his mind.

He snapped the coffer shut, his jaw tightening. It was as though the mere sight of the cursed vial had tainted him. He straightened and walked toward the ship's edge, watching the waves crash and foam against the hull. The open sea, usually a source of solace, now felt like a prison without walls.

An uneasy silence hung over *The Cleopatra*. Tzazo's men were disciplined, but even they seemed to sense a grim purpose to this voyage. The typical banter and camaraderie of soldiers preparing for war had vanished, replaced by a nervous tension that clung to the air. They knew nothing of the specifics of his orders, but soldiers could always sense when something was amiss. War was one thing but an order like this felt like a descent into something darker.

Suddenly, a voice broke through the silence. It was Sigisvault, his second-in-command, who had approached from behind. "My lord, the fleet is assembled and ready to proceed. We await your orders."

Tzazo didn't turn to look at him immediately. He stared at the horizon for a moment longer, then spoke. "Continue on to Sardinia."

Sigisvault hesitated. "And after we reach it? Will we attack?"

The usual certainty in Tzazo's commands faltered. He finally turned, meeting Sigisvault's eyes. "There will be a change of plans once we arrive." His voice was steady, but the uncertainty within those words was noticeable.

Sigisvault nodded, sensing something unsaid but knowing better than to ask questions. He offered a salute and made his way to the rest of the crew, barking orders to keep the men busy.

Left alone again, Tzazo turned his thoughts back to the mission. Sardinia was still many days away, but he already felt the pressure of the decision he was destined to make. The Necropolis of the Vipers awaited him there, an ancient, cursed place that had long been spoken about in fearful tones. The sorceress Skylla had claimed it was essential—that the child's blood must spill upon the cursed soil for the threat to end.

But could he believe in such things? A sorceress's runes, predictions of doom tied to the life of a single child. Tzazo was a man of battle, blood, and steel. He trusted in what he could see and feel, not the words of a witch who whispered to his brother like a serpent coiled around his ear. And yet, there was something about Skylla's presence, something unnerving. He had felt it when she touched Gelimer. Something unholy.

Tzazo's thoughts were interrupted by the soft sound of footsteps behind him. He turned to see Wulfric, his most trusted warrior and a man who had been at his side through countless battles. Unlike Sigisvault, Wulfric rarely hesitated to speak his mind.

"My lord," Wulfric said, his voice low. "I can see something troubles you."

Tzazo studied Wulfric for a moment, debating whether to share his burden. The man was loyal, but even loyalty had its limits. "There are things in motion that none of us can control," Tzazo said, choosing his words carefully.

Wulfric frowned, his sharp eyes narrowing. "Aye. But we can still choose how to act. I trust your judgment, my lord."

Tzazo gave a curt nod, appreciating the words but knowing that Wulfric didn't entirely understand the situation. How could he? No one on this ship could.

As Wulfric returned to his post, Tzazo's mind wandered again. If he failed to obey Gelimer's command, the consequences could be dire—not just for him, but also for his wife and son. Gelimer had made the threat clear enough, even if he hadn't spoken it outright. And yet, the thought of killing a child, of spilling innocent blood in the name of a vision—was that something he could live with?

He placed a hand on the coffer once more. It was cold, unnaturally so, even under the blistering sun. Sardinia would come soon enough, and with it, the necropolis, and the girl. He closed his eyes and prayed under his breath, barely audible over the sound of the waves. "God help me."

Chapter 2

PROLOGUE - SARDINIA

The wind whistled across the parapets, carrying with it the scent of salt and damp stone. Michaēl stood with his arms crossed over his chest, his gaze fixed on the horizon where the sea shimmered beneath the early morning light. Beside him, Calias leaned forward slightly, gripping the weathered edge of the stone battlement as he narrowed his eyes.

"They're coming," Calias grumbled.

Michaēl said nothing at first, merely watching as the distant Byzantine dromon cut through the water with effortless grace. Its oars moved in unison, the great sail catching the wind as it neared the coastline. He exhaled, his breath visible in the crisp morning air.

"It took them long enough," he finally said.

Calias shifted uncomfortably. "Do you think it will be enough?"

Michaēl scoffed, though there was little humor in it. "We prayed for an army and Emperor Justinian sent us a single ship." He shook his head. "Tzazo landed weeks ago, and in that time, he has cut us off from the rest of Sardinia. The city of Caralis has fallen without much of a fight. We are alone, Calias."

Calias clenched his jaw. "I prayed Justinian would send more ships."

Michaēl turned to him, his smile fading. "Perhaps he has, but if so, they are not here now. We sent messengers, but no word ever returned. Either they were captured, or…" He let the thought hang between them.

Calias exhaled sharply, running a hand through his graying hair. "And if this dromon carries only a few men?"

Michaēl glanced at the ship again. He could barely make out the silhouettes of armored men on the deck. At this distance, he couldn't be sure, but it looked like there were far fewer soldiers than he had wished for.

"Then we will make do," he said grimly. "We cannot afford to turn away any help."

They stood in silence as the dromon cut through the sea spray, the oars and sails working in perfect harmony. This marvel of ancient engineering, designed to endure the sea's unpredictable moods, had a streamlined design ideal for navigating jagged coastlines and perilous crags.

The Byzantine Clebanarii stood clad in sturdy leather armor on the deck of the dromon, the sigil of the Chi-Rho prominently emblazoned on their chest. They were the empire's renowned shock troops, always the first to infiltrate enemy lines.

Their leader, Longinus, once a member of the elite Praetorian Guard under Emperor Justinian, stood at the ship's stern. He scoured the waters for hidden shoals or unforgiving currents as the dromon carried its crew steadily toward Sardinia.

As Sardinia's rugged coastline rose into view, the crew marveled at the sheer cliffs and outcroppings jutting defiantly from the sea. The scent of salt and seaweed filled the air, punctuated by the thunderous crash of waves against the rocks.

Amidst this untamed landscape, even the most experienced sailors found their attention drawn to the solitary stone tower, rising from the green hills like a skeletal finger pointing toward the heavens. Its thick, weathered walls and the ancient parapet spoke of an age long past. At last, they arrived at Nuraghe Porto Pirastu.

Longinus shouted over the commotion, "Hold fast! Drop anchor! We will wait for the tide before moving in."

The men, weary from their long voyage, welcomed the rest. Amongst the oarsmen were fourteen Clebanarii, Longinus being one of them. With the wind at their backs, they had made good time, reaching Sardinia before nightfall on the twentieth day. Their muscles ached from the relentless rowing, but the sight of land had lifted their spirits. The sailors trimmed the sails and dropped the anchor as they waited for a signal from the ancient tower to ensure safe passage through the shoals.

Longinus glanced over his men, noting the weariness upon their faces. "Stay sharp. We're not safe yet." His tone, more that of a soldier than commander, cut through their fatigue.

The lines on Longinus's face, marked by years of service, softened as he turned back to face the sea. The setting sun blazed its deep hues across his battle-scarred armor. He stood tall, a leader fortified by the knowledge that this particular corner of Sardinia remained loyal to Godas and the Byzantine cause.

Longinus stood silhouetted against the horizon, his thoughts drifting to the strategic importance of their position. As he waited for the tower's signal to guide them through the shallows, his mind turned to the perils ahead. "There is too much at stake," he complained to himself. "We have no room for error."

Suddenly, the lookout's cry rang out as he pointed toward a small boat emerging from the waves, its oars manned by two weathered men. Their skin, toughened and cracked by years of salt and sun, matched their sun-bleached hair and rough-hewn, threadbare clothes, well-suited for a life of toil at sea. Between them sat a third man, his bearing unmistakably noble. Draped in shimmering silk, his neatly groomed hair and calm demeanor radiated wealth, an image out of place in this rugged scene.

As the boat drew near, sailors tossed a rope ladder over the side. The nobleman climbed aboard quickly, his movements steady and sure. The rowers, their job done, turned their boat back toward the mainland, their attention returned to the distant shore.

Longinus extended his hand. "Welcome aboard. I am Longinus, once a Praetorian under Emperor Justinian, now commander of the Clebanarii. Emperor Justinian assures me we can count on your help."

The nobleman nodded, grasping Longinus's hand. "Well met, commander. I am Michaēl, nephew of Godas and regent of Sarrabus-Gerrei. Sardinia stands with Emperor Justinian. We will do all we can to help you drive the Vandals out of our lands."

Longinus spoke bluntly. "You realize fourteen men cannot stand against the Vandal armies."

Michaēl replied, "It is a means to an end, is it not?"

Longinus agreed, "Indeed, it is."

"Good," Michaēl said with a nod. "Once the watchtower gives the signal, I will guide us through the shoals."

The minutes passed as the dromon rocked gently on the flowing tide. The men rested but remained vigilant. Then, as dusk settled, a flaming arrow streaked through the dimming sky—a signal.

The crew erupted into a flurry of activity. Michaēl took the helm and directed one of the oarsmen to lower a depth gauge from the vessel's bow. The rhythmic pull of the oars resumed, propelling the ship smoothly toward the shore.

The silhouette of a once-mighty fortress appeared in the gloom, flanked by smaller fortifications and defensive walls. The crew marveled at the skill and ingenuity of the builders who had created such a formidable stronghold. They were confident it could withstand any assault from land or sea.

As the island's cliffs loomed ever nearer, the water became more tumultuous. The oarsman called out the depths while the sails were deftly adjusted. Michaēl barked sharp orders to navigate the dangerous coastal shallows with accuracy. The hull grazed the seabed only a handful of times, but under his guidance and the crew's skilled handling, the dromon reached the shores just as daylight faded.

Upon reaching the fortress, the men sighed in relief. They had braved rough waters and unpredictable weather, and their resilience finally paid off. With supplies safely unloaded, they embraced the chance to rest and recover.

The weary travelers were ushered into a modest barracks where a simple meal awaited them. Salted meats, dried fish, freshly baked bread, and the nutty tang of Pecorino Sardo cheese rejuvenated their spirits. Though the food was briny and the wine a bit vinegary, they ate heartily, feeling their strength gradually return.

Longinus and Michaēl left the bustling barracks behind, seeking the solitude of the stone tower. They climbed to an upper chamber, dining quietly by the dim glow of rushlights. Their low conversation echoed in the ancient tower, words spiraling upwards into shadowed arches.

The meal before them was lavish: braised wild boar and the exotic Casu Marzu cheese. While Longinus relished the boar, he eyed the notorious cheese, infamous for its live maggots, with clear apprehension. Despite his curiosity, the wriggling bugs deterred him from trying it. Michaēl chuckled softly, noting Longinus's hesitation. "An acquired taste," he said, popping a small bite into his mouth without a second thought. "We Sardinians take pride in it, but I admit—it is not for everyone."

Longinus offered a thin smile but said nothing, his mind already on the task ahead. Wiping his hands on a cloth, he shifted in his chair, his tone turning serious. "Tell me friend, what are the latest happenings in Sardinia? When we disembarked from Constantinople, word had just reached us that Tzazo and his forces landed near Caralis."

Michaēl responded, "Your messengers travel slowly, my friend. Since his landing, he has overtaken most of the island. He has had little resistance to his advances. Especially in Caralis."

Longinus asked, "Do you have spies in the city?"

Michaēl jested, "What kind of Sardinian would I be if I did not employ spies?"

Longinus pressed, "Then what do your spies tell you? What are Tzazo's plans?"

"We know he hunts a child. He has employed every means to find her," responded Michaēl before continuing, "and strangely enough, he set up his command in the Grotta della Vipera."

"And how far is this grotto?" asked Longinus.

"It is deep in the city of Caralis," Michaēl said, his voice laced with worry. "Tzazo has complete control of the city. I am now fearful for my uncle's life."

"How far?", Longinus pressed.

"Twenty-one leagues by the southern pass, fifteen as the crow flies," Michaēl explained. "The direct route is risky—foot travel only. We can send a guide through the Monte de Sette Fratelli to help you ford the rivers, but it will take at least two days—longer on the return."

Longinus leaned forward, elbows on the table. "Two days there, and two days back if all goes well… We need speed and discretion." He rubbed his temple thoughtfully. "Is there a faster way?"

"The Via Romana is faster, but it's crawling with spies. The closer you get to Caralis, the more dangerous it becomes. We can give you Sardinian horses and a guide, but they'll stop at Quartu Sant'Elena. From there, it's on foot."

After Longinus weighed the options, he finally asked, "And how do we return?"

Michaël replied, "The guide and horses will wait at Quartu Sant'Elena for your return."

"How far is it from Quartu Sant'Elena to the Grotta della Vipera?"

"Three leagues, but the area is watched closely. The northern forest path is quieter. Less likely to be guarded."

Longinus frowned. "And Tzazo's forces—how many?"

"Five thousand soldiers. Plus, servants and sailors," Michaël said with a heavy exhale. "They have locked down the city—every road, every gate. Last I heard, my uncle was confined to his chambers… I'm sure his days are numbered."

Silence hung between them. Longinus's features hardened. "And the girl?" he asked quietly. "Is she still alive?"

"My uncle hid her before the attack," Michaël said, concern in his voice. "My contacts say she is still safe, but Tzazo is closing in. His cruelty… it knows no bounds. Her guardian was taken— beheaded in the piazza. His head is on a pike now, a grim warning to anyone who dares resist."

Upon hearing these developments, Longinus stiffened. "All this bloodshed… it could have been avoided," he began. "For five centuries, the name Longinus has passed to the eldest son in my lineage. Each of us swore an oath to guard a legacy as old as

Christianity itself." His countenance shifted slightly. "It began with the first Longinus—the centurion who pierced Christ's side and was forever changed."

He paused to clear his throat and sip some wine. "To me, Longinus is much more than just a name. It is a destiny which tied my family to an ancient prophecy that reaches back to Egypt's last pharaohs. A prophecy that speaks of a child descended from Cleopatra herself. A child destined to reignite the lineage of a forgotten age."

Longinus's voice deepened. "This girl—she is the last of the Ptolemies. Her bloodline can be traced back to Cleopatra and Marc Antony. They had three children, two of whom died as adolescents. Their third child was named Cleopatra Selene. She in turn had one son named Ptolomy of Mauretania. He had only one legitimate child. A daughter, who married a Roman soldier. That soldier's name was Longinus, the very man who etched his name into history as the centurion who pierced the side of Christ."

The mood in the room grew somber as Longinus went on. "The child Tzazo hunts is the last living descendant of this line. She is believed to be the key to powers more dangerous than we can imagine."

Michaēl let out a disbelieving chuckle. "Surely you jest."

Longinus shook his head, "Do you believe that Emperor Justinian would send me to Sardinia in jest? This is no jest my friend."

Michaēl asked, "So you believe this prophecy to be true?"

Longinus retorted, "True or not, those who hunt her believe the tale."

Longinus pressed on, his voice lowering to shield his words from unseen ears. "A woman with considerable influence has now risen to power in Gelimer's court. She is rumored to be a graeae."

"A graeae? I am not familiar with this word," replied Michaēl.

Longinus nodded. "A graeae is witch of terrible power. This one has named herself Skylla… after the beast in Homer's stories."

At the mention of Skylla, Michaēl crossed himself nervously. "And you believe this witch has set her sights on the child?"

Longinus's expression darkened. "I am sure of it. Skylla has convinced those in power that the girl is the key to finding a relic."

"What does this child have to do with a relic?" Michaēl asked quizzically.

Longinus continued, "The girl carries a strange mark—a birthmark. Few know of its significance, but those that do believe it is tied to an artifact of immense power."

Michaēl raised an eyebrow, his voice skeptical. "What is this artifact?"

Longinus gave a slight nod. "An object… which kings and emperors would kill to possess. Skylla knows how to dangle that in front of those with power. But it's not the relic she's after." His eyes narrowing. "She wants the girl… not for the relic, but for her blood."

Michaēl blinked, confusion giving way to a deeper concern. "Her blood? Why?"

Longinus hesitated, then spoke cautiously. "Skylla believes that the child's blood holds the secret to eternal youth—to achieving immortality. She has spent decades delving into the arcane which has twisted her soul and her mind."

Seeing the cynical look on Michaēl's face, he continued hesitantly. "There's a legend… that the blood of Cleopatra's line holds a secret. Some say it can cure illness. Others said it grants eternal youth. Skylla believes in the latter. She's spent decades chasing rumors of immortality and she is convinced the girl's blood is the key."

Michaēl sat back, processing this. "So, she is using the legend of the relic as a ploy. A lure for those who seek power."

Longinus nodded gravely. "Exactly. She's letting the story of the artifact spread, fueling the ambitions of kings and generals so they'll bring the girl to her. Meanwhile, she waits, planning to take what she truly wants: the girl's blood."

As the night wore on, the crackle of the dying rushlights filled the room. Michael rubbed his chin thoughtfully. "And the birthmark… is that legend as well?"

Longinus hesitated for the briefest of moments, then acquiesced. "The mark is said to be a map, a clue that leads to the artifact's resting place."

Michaēl's eyes widened. "Then anyone who learns of this mark…"

"Will stop at nothing to capture her," Longinus finished grimly. "That's why I've told almost no one about it. The fewer who know, the better."

Michaēl grimaced, "And if they find her?"

Tears glistened in Longinus's eyes. "If they find her, they will deliver her to Skylla. My family has sworn for generations to prevent this power from getting into the wrong hands. But in my loyalty to the Emperor, I failed. I left the child unguarded, vulnerable to those who do not understand what she is."

Michaēl's voice tightened. "So, you've come to rescue a child. But what of my country? My people are also at risk. Tzazo and his men will wreak havoc upon our land. We do not have the strength to stop them. We prayed that Emperor Justinian would send you with an army."

"My first duty is to protect the child," Longinus said firmly. "But have faith. Tzazo does not know it, but Emperor Justinian has already launched an assault on Carthage."

A glimmer of hope crossed Michaël's face. "Carthage will be left nearly undefended. The full force of the Byzantine Empire will leave Tzazo with nothing to return to."

Longinus emphatically said, "Belisarius himself was sent to lead the attack at Carthage. He set sail from Constantinople just hours before we did. They may have already landed, and the assault on Carthage could already be underway."

Realizing the implications, Michaël protested, "But Sardinia will be lost. Are we just a pawn in their game of thrones?"

"No, my friend," Longinus replied. "When Tzazo learns of this danger, he will abandon Sardinia, and our fleet will be poised to strike."

"I pray that is true," Michaël said.

A momentary silence settled over the room, broken only by the distant rumble of the surf crashing against the shore. Longinus stood abruptly. "That's why we must act now. We cannot leave anything to chance. We leave at dawn. The Via Romana awaits."

Michaël rose from the table, speaking, "At dawn, the horses will be ready. Two of my best men will go with you— Christianus, a master rider, will stay with the horses outside Quartu Sant'Elena, and Calias, an expert tracker, will guide you through the forest to the grotto. Pack light for a quick retreat. We will ensure your ship is ready to sail back to Egypt when you return with the child."

A thick haze enshrouded the valley as the morning sun peeked over the Tyrrhenian Sea. The men worked diligently to finalize their preparations, meticulously checking the saddles and provisions of their steeds. The mission called for speed and secrecy; therefore, they traveled light.

Longinus, admiring their Sardinian horses' sturdy and noble bearing, was impressed by their responsiveness to the slightest pressure of his knees upon their flanks. Calias, the group leader, reviewed the final instructions with Michaēl and Longinus, ensuring that every detail was committed to memory. He handed each man a drab tunic to cover their leather armor, concealing the sigil of the Chi-Rho from travelers.

As the men completed their final preparations, Calias felt a deep unease as he noticed storm clouds looming on the horizon. "I fear we may be riding into a heavy storm," he said gravely, gesturing at the dark clouds gathering in the distance.

Michaēl stared at the accumulation, saying, "I would be more comfortable if you delayed another day or two. The wet season is upon us, and rain at this time of year could be catastrophic."

But Longinus shook his head, his mind set on the task. "That is no longer an option. The life of this child is in my hands. I will not fail."

Calias knew the urgency of their mission but also recognized the risks. "Then we must make haste. The longer we delay, the closer Tzazo comes to achieving his goals."

With a nod in Michaēl's direction, he added, "My Lord, with your leave."

Michaēl nodded in assent. "Go! May Christ watch over you and return you safely with the child in hand."

With Michaēl's final blessing, the party set off. Christianus and Calias led the men, their horses trotting briskly through verdant fields and scattered woodlands. The morning air was cool, the dampness clinging to their cloaks as they rode. As they ventured further from the coast, the surrounding flora thickened into a lush tapestry, and the scent of earth and greenery grew richer.

Majestic holm oaks towered above, their grandeur complemented by the fragrant lentisk shrubs dotting the forest floor. The horses kicked up clumps of hard earth as they wove through the ancient landscape, their pace steady.

Emerging from the dense woodland, they found themselves in a serene valley cradling a meandering river. Calias reined in his horse, approaching the riverbank with caution. He turned to his men, his voice resonating through the valley, "Behold, the Rio Sa Figu! Our progress is swift. Just downriver lies a shallower crossing."

Calias led the way to a more manageable crossing by gently steering his horse downstream. At the ford, their mounts moved through the water with practiced ease, barely disturbing the glassy surface.

As Longinus reached a steep, winding trail, he discovered that Calias and Christianus were already at the ridge's summit, waiting patiently for the others. They regrouped and took a moment to admire the panoramic view, their gazes sweeping from the dense forest behind them to the distant coastline, then westward to the formidable Monte de Sette Fratelli mountains. Beneath them, the well-trodden Via Romana snaked southward through the valley like a stone serpent.

Calias gestured northwest, his tone laced with respect for the landscape. "Those peaks are the Monte de Sette Fratelli, a challenging journey even under the best conditions. The road below, the Via Romana, will lead us south to the only safe passage through the mountains."

After a brief rest, they urged their horses onward. The descent through the foothills was hazardous; the rocky trails were slick with moisture and loose stone. But the Sardinian horses, bred for such terrain, navigated the path with ease, their hooves finding purchase on even the most uncertain ground.

As they reached the other side of the ridge, the horsemen made their way to the Via Romana. Christianus cautioned, "From here on, our journey should be smooth. But we must remain aware of our surroundings and avoid drawing attention to ourselves."

The rhythmic clacking of the horses' hooves clanged on the large limestone blocks paving the ancient road. Only a few travelers crossed their path, each casting fleeting, curious glances at the swift-moving team of horsemen. But as the trail narrowed and the mountains cast their towering shadows ever nearer, the occasional passersby became increasingly rare until there were none.

With each passing hour, the stillness in the air grew. What had begun as a calm, steady journey had taken on a more ominous tone. The once-comforting solitude of the road now seemed filled with unseen threats. Even the horses became restless, balking at the path ahead and refusing to press on.

Calias, sensing the change, reined his horse back slightly, surveying the terrain ahead. "This is where unwary travelers often meet their fate at the hands of bandits," he warned the group in a low voice. "The mountain pass ahead is steep and narrow. We will be hemmed in by its ridges and forced to cross a single-span bridge. We must proceed with the utmost caution, my friends. Danger is not merely a possibility here; it is a certainty."

Christianus guided his horse closer to Longinus and Calias. "Movement," he whispered, pointing to a disturbance in the brush. "It is a small group, but they are watching us."

Calias narrowed his eyes. "There are not enough of them to pose a direct threat to us, but…" he trailed off as he noticed two men breaking away from the group, speeding into the forest.

Christianus's instincts sharpened immediately. "It is not their swords that worry me," he said. "It's their tongues."

Without warning, Christianus spurred his horse into a gallop, chasing after the fleeing riders with reckless abandon. His sudden surge of speed left the others scrambling to keep up, but his intent was clear—he would not let the bandits warn their comrades.

The thrill of the chase surged through Christianus as he pressed his mount faster, the wind whipping against his face, the landscape blurring around him. His focus locked on the two men ahead, the terrain beneath him just another obstacle.

Suddenly, the air around him shifted. A sharp whistle rang out, followed by the hiss of arrows cutting through the air. Christianus barely had time to react as a volley of arrows rained down from the cliffs above.

An arrow tore through the leather of his left shoulder, and a searing pain erupted as his armor quickly soaked with blood. His horse reared back in panic, but Christianus fought to regain control. Most of the arrows embedded themselves in the dirt and trees around him.

"AMBUSH!" Christianus bellowed, his voice thundering through the woods. The men behind him reacted instantly, forming a defensive circle, their swords drawn, eyes looking deep into the surrounding trees for their hidden attackers.

Longinus, reacting swiftly, shouted orders above the chaos. "Shields up! Archers, return fire!"

The disciplined Byzantine troops moved with efficiency, some raising their shields and others unleashing a counter-volley of arrows into the dense underbrush. The forest exploded into a cacophony of shouts and flying arrows.

The ambush had been well-planned, but the bandits had underestimated Longinus's men. Under pressure from the return volley, the bandits charged out from their hidden positions. They were a ragged, desperate lot—clad in mismatched armor and wielding crude weapons. But what they lacked in coordination, they made up for in ferocity and their intimate knowledge of the terrain.

Longinus leapt from his horse, unsheathing his sword in a single fluid motion. The blade gleamed in the dim light filtering through the trees, its edge keen and ready. With his back to a towering oak, he observed the advancing enemy, eyes searching for weaknesses.

Longinus barked orders to the men, his voice cutting through the din of battle. "Dismount and hold your ground! Shields up! Do not let them divide us!"

The Clebanarii were no ordinary soldiers—they were trained to face far worse than ambushes in foreign woods. They formed an impenetrable wall, their swords bristling menacingly from behind their shields.

Christianus rode ahead to flank the attackers, signaling to the men. "Push forward!" he shouted. "Force them into the open!"

The bandits, realizing they were outnumbered and outmatched, attempted to fall back. But they were too slow to escape the Byzantine's wrath. Longinus cut down the two nearest attackers with swift, brutal precision—one to the throat, the other to the chest. He spun around, blocking a wild swing from another bandit, then drove his sword into the man's gut, ending the fight with deadly efficiency.

But the bandit leader, a hulking brute wielding a heavy axe, broke through the defensive line, his sights set on Longinus. With a roar, the bandit charged, swinging his axe in a wide, savage arc. Longinus ducked just in time, feeling the blade whistle past his head.

The bandit swung again, this time aiming low. Longinus sidestepped, using the momentum to thrust his sword up and under the man's ribs. The bandit staggered back; his eyes widened in shock as blood gushed from his mouth. He fell to his knees, his axe clattering to the ground, before collapsing completely.

Seeing their leader fall, the bandits hesitated, their courage faltering. The Clebanarii seized the opportunity, pressing their attack with renewed vigor. The remaining bandits, with no chance of victory, began to retreat, disappearing back into the forest where they came.

The sudden silence that followed was almost deafening. Only the distant rustle of leaves and the labored breathing of the men remained. The ambush had been swift and brutal, but the Clebanarii had held their ground.

Calias surveyed the scene, wiping blood from his sword. "Is everyone accounted for?"

Christianus, still mounted, scanned the trees warily. "No casualties, but a few are hurt." His attention was drawn to his own blood-soaked leather, the wound on his left shoulder clearly troubling him.

Longinus frowned. "Can you ride?"

Christianus winced but waved him off, his hands clenched tightly on the reins. "It's nothing—a flesh wound. I'll manage. But we can't afford to linger. This was just a scouting party. If we tarry, more will come."

Calias, already alert, nodded sharply. "Tzazo's spies will know we're here soon enough. We need to move before the word spreads."

Longinus, wasting no time, swung himself back onto his horse. His voice was stern. "We ride now. They will know we are coming, which means more ambushes lie ahead. Speed and caution—nothing else matters."

The sun was setting behind the peaks of the Monte de Sette Fratelli as the men remounted their steeds. Longinus paused to look ahead toward the ridge they needed to cross.

"Do you think we are being followed?" Longinus said quietly to Calias.

Calias gave a short, matter-of-fact nod. "Count on it; bandits like them rarely scatter without sending word ahead."

The path beneath them grew steeper as it twisted higher into the mountains. The scent of rain clung heavily to the air. Longinus looked skyward—dark clouds were gathering, their edges flickering with distant lightning.

"We should find shelter before nightfall," Christianus suggested, his voice filled with urgency. "A storm this high up in the mountains could be disastrous."

Longinus shook his head. "We cannot stop. If Tzazo's scouts find us exposed in the open, the storm will be the least of our worries."

Calias, riding beside Longinus, eyed the approaching storm. "The rain will slow us down. Rivers may flood, and these paths could turn to mud."

"We will deal with that when it happens," Longinus replied, his voice steady. "For now, we ride on."

The path narrowed even more as they approached the ridge, forcing them to slow their pace. The horses struggled with the steep ascent, their hooves slipping on loose gravel. As they crested the summit, they found themselves facing a narrow, rickety wooden bridge spanning a deep ravine.

The sight of the bridge gave everyone pause. The old beams creaked balefully in the wind, and the drop below was nothing short of deadly.

"Is this the only way across?" Longinus asked, frowning as he studied the fragile structure.

Calias nodded grimly. "There is no other way without doubling back for leagues. It should be sturdy enough for a few men at a time but not the entire group at once."

Longinus glanced at the sky again. The storm was nearly upon them. The first drops of rain began to splatter on the ground, and the distant rumble of thunder echoed through the mountains.

"There is no choice," Longinus decided. "Calias, take three men and cross first. Test the bridge. The rest of us will follow in pairs."

Calias nodded, dismounting and signaling three of the lighter-footed Clebanarii to join him. They crossed the bridge cautiously, leading their horses on foot. The wooden planks groaned under the weight of the men and their steeds. The remaining soldiers watched in silence, their hands resting on the hilts of their swords as they scanned the surrounding cliffs for any sign of danger.

As Calias reached the far side and signaled back, Longinus urged the next group forward. The rain began to fall in earnest now, thick droplets soaking through their cloaks and making the ground slick beneath their boots. The storm, it seemed, was unwilling to wait.

As each pair crossed the bridge, the sound of thunder grew louder, the wind rising, whipping the trees into a frenzy. Longinus and Christianus were the last to cross. As they stepped onto the creaking planks, an uneasy feeling crept over the men.

"Move quickly!" Calias shouted from the other side; his voice barely audible over the howling wind.

Just as Longinus and Christianus reached the bridge's midpoint, a sharp crack rang from above. Longinus's instincts flared. He glanced up just in time to see a boulder crashing down the adjacent peak. It picked up steam as it thundered directly toward the bridge they were crossing.

"Go!" Longinus shouted, pushing Christianus forward as the boulder smashed into the bridge behind them, splintering the wooden beams with a deafening crack. The force of the impact sent a violent shudder through the entire structure, causing it to sway dangerously.

The bridge creaked and shivered, but Longinus and Christianus managed to leap onto the far side just as the bridge began to give way behind them. The remaining beams snapped, and with a final deafening crash, the entire structure collapsed into the ravine below, sending splintered wood tumbling into the abyss.

"That was close," Longinus said, his face pale from the near miss.

"Too close," Christianus agreed, his mind already moving ahead to what lay before them.

Gasping heavily, he surveyed the wrecked bridge. "It looks like we may need to find a different route back."

The storm raged above, the rain falling in sheets. The Sardinian wilderness was proving to be as perilous as any battlefield, and the real enemy still waited for them in the shadows.

Chapter 3

PROLOGUE - GROTTO DELLA VIPERA

The fellowship arrived at a small farm on the outskirts of Quartu Sant'Elena, lightning still blazing overhead. After a brief rest at the farm, five of the company set off on foot—Longinus, Marcaus, Calias, Constantine, and Alexios—leaving behind the injured Christianus with the majority of the Clebanarii. With fewer numbers, they could move more swiftly and silently. Calias, well-acquainted with the terrain, led the way. His eyes darted between trees and shadows; every sense heightened in the darkness. The sun had long since slipped below the horizon, and the storm swept across the countryside, battering them with wind and rain.

The narrow track wound its way through an ancient, wooded valley, and their movements became more arduous. As the night deepened, the land, once peaceful, seemed to come to life. In the distance, wolves howled, their cries rebounding between the trees. The rain battered the five men unceasingly, turning their leather armor into dead weight. The once-firm trail had melted into slick mud, with streams of water carving through the dirt, transforming the path into a sucking mire.

By daybreak, the storm still hadn't relented, and the men were soaked through, their armor chafing their skin. Each step felt heavier than the last as the wind gnashed at their faces, but Longinus's determination kept them moving. After what felt like an age, the group finally broke free of the forest and stepped onto a vast plain that stretched endlessly ahead. On the distant horizon, looming like a sentinel carved from stone, stood Caralis—the most impregnable fortress in Sardinia.

Longinus paused momentarily, as he studied the distant fortifications, thoughts turning toward what awaited them inside.

"Stay low," Calias said, his voice barely audible above the rain. "The guards of Caralis have sharp eyes—and sharper arrows. They do not rest."

Longinus squinted toward the stronghold, wiping his eyes as rainwater cascaded down his face. "Perhaps this infernal storm will work in our favor. It might obscure their vision."

Calias shook his head, a faint grin tugging at his lips. "No need to tempt fate. We will not storm the gates like fools. There's another entrance—if you trust me."

Longinus eyed him for a moment before nodding. "Lead on, then."

Calias led them through the dense underbrush, moving like a shade. His short sword briefly caught the morning light as he hacked through the vegetation, but his steps were silent and deliberate. He seemed to know every twist and turn. After a time, he halted, crouching low. He swiftly brushed aside the overgrown foliage, revealing a narrow crevasse hidden beneath. A smile crept across his face. "Here it is," he murmured. "Our way in."

Longinus leaned over, inspecting the crevasse, his expression unreadable. "Not much of an entrance."

Calias chuckled softly. "It doesn't have to be impressive, Commander. It just has to work."

One by one, the men slipped into the narrow fissure, the stone walls pressing in on them like the ribs of some ancient beast. The forest's sounds faded to silence as they descended deeper into the earth. The space was so tight that a few had to shed their leather jerkins to squeeze through. It felt as if the ground itself was swallowing them whole. Gradually, the crack widened, and at last, they found themselves shoulder to shoulder before a small cave entrance.

The air here reeked of rot, the stench infiltrating their lungs. Water dripped from unseen crevices above, each drop echoing through the silence. Calias ran his rough hands along the damp walls, searching for something he knew was there. After a moment, he grunted in satisfaction, his fingers closing around an oil lamp hidden in a hollow. With the ease of long practice, he struck flint to steel. On the third strike, a spark caught, and the oil-soaked wick flared to life, casting a dim, spectral glow upon the cavern walls.

The glow revealed weary, waterlogged faces. Longinus nodded at the lamp, impressed. "How many times have you been to these catacombs?"

"More than I care to remember," Calias said, raising the lamp higher. "But never as deep as we must go today."

Longinus glanced back at his men, then back to Calias. "I hope your memory of this place holds. I do not plan to die here."

The lamp's weak flame danced, throwing eerie shadows across the walls as the men pressed on. Their boots splashed through the puddles, the air growing heavier with every inhalation, laden with dampness and something else—something old and unnatural.

Standing behind Longinus, Marcaus said under his breath, "It feels like the walls are watching us."

"Eyes forward," Longinus replied, though he couldn't shake the feeling either.

At last, they came to a narrow junction. Calias held up the lamp, its unsteady light barely piercing the gloom. His eyes narrowed, looking at something scrawled on the cave wall.

"We have crossed into the city," he spoke softly. "Quiet now."

Longinus stepped closer, his eyes locking onto a faint image of a snake devouring a man painted onto the smooth rock. The crude strokes seemed to writhe in the wavering light. A shiver crawled down his spine. "That's a warning if I've ever seen one," he muttered, almost to himself.

Calias glanced back, his face grim. "It means we're close."

"We need to be careful," Longinus said, his grip tightening around his sword. "Tzazo will not hesitate—he will do whatever it takes to finish this."

The tunnel soon opened into a vast, circular chamber. Calias slowed, his face showed uncertainty as he scanned the walls. "I was afraid of this," he stammered. "This is where my memory of these caverns ends. I've never been this deep in these tunnels."

Longinus growled through clenched teeth. "Perfect."

The chamber walls gleamed, slick and polished, reflecting the dull light from Calias's lamp. Two massive stalactites hung like daggers from the ceiling, their points glinting ominously. Frustration etched lines across Calias's face as he held the lamp higher, sweeping it across the far corners, searching for any sign of a path forward.

"Is this the end of the path?" Longinus snapped, his patience frayed. "If we have to retrace our steps, the child will die!" His voice reverberated off the chamber walls.

Calias whipped his head around. "Keep your voice down! Every sound in this cursed place echoes. We're close, but if they hear us…"

"How can you be sure?" Longinus interrupted. "Every passage looks the same. This place is a maze."

Calias didn't flinch. His voice was low and steady. "I'm sure because we have entered The Grotto della Vipera… We are now standing in the Necropolis of the Vipers."

Longinus stepped back, his eyes tracing the smooth, circular walls that rose around them, tapering upward like the jaws of a massive viper poised to strike. The men huddled together, looked small and vulnerable—like prey caught in the predator's grip. The walls, reflecting the dancing light from Calias's lamp, gave the chamber an unnatural sheen. Above, the two large stalactites were reminiscent of serrated fangs. In the dim light, water dripped from their tips, the drops swirling in pools below like venom. The air was musty and cold. The only sound was the soldiers' labored breathing—soft, like the hiss of a snake.

Suddenly, a soft whimper spread throughout the chamber, faint but unmistakable—the sound of a child. Every man froze, straining to catch the sound again. A moment later, it came again, louder this time.

Longinus's senses sharpened. He motioned for his men to spread out, his voice low. "Find the source."

Constantine, the oldest of the Clebanarii, spotted a narrow opening near the back of the cavern. "Over here Sir!" he whispered, pointing toward the gap. "I see something."

Longinus pressed his ear against the small opening, listening. "The child's through here," he spoke in a hushed tone.

The passage was barely wide enough for a man to crawl through. Without hesitation, Calias stepped forward. "I will go first," he murmured. He shot a glance at Constantine. "Stay behind, cover our rear."

Calias slowly lowered himself to the ground, creeping on his belly through the tight space, his arms outstretched as he squeezed through the narrow, uneven tunnel.

Longinus followed close behind, the rough surface of the cave walls scraping his sides and torso. He felt as though he were crawling through the belly of a serpent—constricting and suffocating. But the child's cries grew louder, cutting through the repressive atmosphere, driving him forward.

Calias spotted it first—a faint glimmer of light at the end of the tunnel. He slithered forward faster, driven by urgency, slowing only when the passage began to widen. Before him, a small rocky chamber opened up, just large enough for four men to stand side by side. Beyond that lay a vast cavern, its walls bathed in an unnatural light that seemed to seep from the rock.

As Calias slid out of the tight passage, he was immediately hit by the odor of death and decay. The smell of it was overwhelming, hanging in the air like a suffocating veil. He paused, letting his eyes adjust to the dim light, and then he saw it: five headless bodies tossed carelessly across the cavern floor, their blood pooling in deep, dark stains. The air whirred with the sickening hum of flies—tiny musca macedda—feasting on the decomposing remains. The wet ground mixed with the red tint of blood. The sickly-sweet smell of death made Calias want to gag, but he swallowed it down, focusing instead on the child's cries ahead.

Calias took in the gruesome scene, but before he could react further, a low, rhythmic chant sounded throughout the cavern, accompanied by the hollow sound of ringing bells. The noise mingled with the hoarse, desperate cries of the child. As the rest of Longinus's men crawled through the passage and entered the chamber, they disturbed the swarming flies, sending a thick black cloud buzzing into the air. The tiny Sardinian flies bit at any exposed flesh, but the hardened Clebanarii—trained to endure worse—didn't flinch. They spread out quickly, taking positions on either side of the cavern entrance.

Longinus caught each man's eye, an understanding passing between them. With only a slight nod of his head, they surged forward in unison, their short swords catching what little light the cavern offered, glinting briefly before vanishing back into shadow. Time seemed to stretch as they moved deeper into the gloom, adrenaline sharpened Longinus's senses. Every movement, every flicker of darkness registered in his mind—a soldier honed for battle, attuned to every threat. There was no hesitation. Only purpose.

As Longinus stepped into the heart of the cavern, his attention locked onto five dark figures draped in rough, black goatskins. They stood scattered around the chamber, their faces obscured by intricately carved wooden masks, each painted with the likeness of a snake. They held staves laden with clinking bells, which wove though their low chanting like an omen when they shook. Near each figure, a severed head impaled on a pike stared blankly toward the room's center, their hollow eyes a witness to the unfolding horror.

In the middle of it all, towering above everything else, stood Tzazo. His massive frame loomed over the marble altar, where the wailing child lay pinned beneath his heavy arm. The altar was engraved with entwined vipers, their serpentine forms curling around the stone—a twisted mockery of what should be sacred. In his other hand, Tzazo held a grotesque dagger, the blade shaped like a serpent's body. It gleamed dangerously in the light of the flickering torches that lined the chamber walls.

Longinus acted swiftly and without mercy. He lunged toward the nearest masked figure, driving a brutal kick into the man's abdomen. The figure uttered a sharp cry and stumbled backward, crashing into a marble pillar that collapsed in a cloud of dust. The sudden commotion made Tzazo pause, his grip on the child loosening for a moment—but it was enough. Calias, moving like lightning, darted forward and yanked the child from Tzazo's grasp. But in the chaos, the dagger in Tzazo's hand lashed out, sinking deep into Calias's left side. Calias grunted, the pain sharp, as the dagger grated against the bone.

The remaining cloaked figures made a frantic dash for the exit, sensing the impending danger. Their movements were wild and uncoordinated, driven by panic. The Byzantine soldiers, trained for such moments, moved with ruthless speed. They intercepted the fleeing figures before they could reach the cavern's mouth, cutting them down with swift, merciless strikes. The skirmish ended almost as soon as it began.

Calias, ignoring the searing pain, forced himself upright. Blood pulsed from his wound, but he held the child firmly. Despite the sudden onset of vertigo, he managed to bolt for the tunnel. Behind him, Tzazo roared in fury, his gigantic form charging after them. But the Clebanarii were quicker, forming a barrier between Tzazo and the tunnel.

"Fools!" Tzazo bellowed, his voice a booming snarl of rage. "What have you done?"

Longinus stood his ground, his voice calm. "We saved an innocent child. And you, Tzazo, once a feared warlord—now reduced to sacrificing babies? How far you've fallen."

The words hit their mark. Tzazo's eyes blazed with fury. He lunged forward, faster than anyone could anticipate, driving his dagger into the chest of Alexios. The man let out a choked gasp, crumpling to the ground with the blade still buried in his heart. The sudden violence sent a ripple of shock through the room, but Longinus didn't flinch.

Standing over the fallen soldier, Tzazo's rage seemed to crack, revealing something deeper underneath—despair. His voice trembled with fury and helplessness. Longinus saw it, even if just for a moment. But there was no room for pity now. "He has my wife, my child!" he shouted. "My brother—the king—he holds them captive. He will kill them if I do not sacrifice this child!" The rawness in his voice cut through the cavern, a moment of weakness amid the violence.

Marcaus, seeing Tzazo unarmed, seized the moment and lunged. But Tzazo was too experienced, too dangerous, even without a weapon. He stepped into the attack, redirecting its force with a practiced deflection. In a savage motion, he grabbed Marcaus by the throat and slammed his head into the cracked marble pillar. The pillar exploded on impact, shards of stone flying as blood sprayed across the cold marble. The soldier collapsed in a heap, his body jerking in its death throes. Tzazo exhaled heavily, a beast cornered but still lethal.

Tzazo spun toward the tunnel, desperation in his eyes as he tried to break free, but Longinus was faster. The commander moved with agility, anticipating every feint, every attempt to escape. Enraged, Tzazo let out a feral howl and wrenched a wooden stake from the ground; the severed head that once sat atop it tumbled to the floor with a sickening thump.

Longinus's eyes widened as the head rolled to a stop. His breath caught. "Marcellus," he rasped, the name heavy with sorrow.

Tzazo reached down and grasped the severed head by its hair, locking eyes with Longinus and sneering. "You recognize him, don't you? Marcellus—pathetic. He begged for mercy like a dog." The edge of his voice cut deeper than a blade.

Longinus bit his words. "He was the child's guardian, a representative of Emperor Justinian."

"A spy and a traitor," Tzazo spat. "And, once I deal with you, nothing will stand between me and the child."

With a contemptuous flick of his wrist, Tzazo flung the severed head at Longinus, catching him off guard. Tzazo seized the opportunity in that split second, hurling the wooden stake savagely. It hit Longinus squarely in the chest with a sickening crack that shattered his ribs beneath the leather jerkin.

Tzazo made for the tunnel, but Longinus, gritting his teeth through the pain, launched himself in a desperate attempt to stop him. He threw his weight against the larger man, trying to drag him down, but Tzazo was a wall of muscle and fury. With a snarl, Tzazo flung Longinus aside like he was nothing, his body crashing hard against the stone floor.

Before Longinus could recover, Tzazo's heavy boot pressed down on his throat, cutting off his air. Longinus's vision blurred, his lungs screaming for oxygen. His hand frantically groped for a weapon, fingers finally brushing against the wooden stake that had struck him. With one final burst of energy, he drove the blunt tip upward, straight into Tzazo's right eye.

Tzazo let out a guttural shriek as he fell to his knees, clutching his ruined eye. Blood poured through his fingers, staining his face in crimson streaks. Longinus gasped for air, his breath coming in ragged, painful bursts as he scrambled to his feet. The agony from his broken ribs flared with every movement, but he couldn't stop now.

Suddenly, the sound of heavy footsteps coursed through the chamber. Vandal guards swarmed in from the opposite end of the cavern, their intent unmistakable.

Wincing with every step, Longinus grabbed one of the decapitated bodies and dragged it toward the narrow crawl space. His chest throbbed with pain, but sheer will and survival instinct drove him forward. He pulled the lifeless form deep into the tunnel, letting it drop to block the passage. It wasn't much, but it would slow them down—at least for a while.

Longinus lurched out of the tunnel, his heart hammering in his chest. The scene before him was dire: Calias lay on the ground, his breaths shallow and labored, while Constantine knelt beside him, desperately trying to staunch the flow of blood. The child, miraculously unharmed, was cradled in the arms of Calias, quiet but staring in silent terror.

Longinus croaked, struggling to catch his breath, "Will they survive?"

Constantine looked up, his face grim and lined with worry. "The child will live." He hesitated, glancing down at Calias. "But him? The wound's deep, and he is slipping in and out of consciousness. I don't know."

The sound of shouted orders rebounded from the tunnel behind them—Vandal reinforcements were close.

"We have to move. Now!" Longinus barked, his voice filled with urgency. "They'll be on us any moment. That body will not slow them for long. Hand me the child and help Calias."

They quickly hoisted Calias to his feet, though his legs shook beneath him. Constantine wrapped a steadying arm around the wounded man, bearing most of his weight. The light from his lamp threw long, trembling shadows along the tunnel walls as they began their frantic retreat. Calias blinked, his mind fogged with pain, struggling to recall their path.

Calias's voice was a rasping whisper, barely louder than a gasp. "The blade... severed something deep inside of me. I can feel it... draining me…draining my life."

Constantine's face was laced with concern, but his voice remained firm. "Come now soldier, don't start talking like that. You are a warrior, Calias. We will get you out."

The words were meant to reassure, but Constantine's eyes betrayed him. He knew the truth—Calias's ashen skin, labored breathing, and cold sweat soaking his brow spoke louder than any encouragement. He was fading fast. The distant clatter of pursuing soldiers followed them through the tunnels. Time was running out.

The labyrinthine tunnels swam in and out of focus in Calias's fevered mind. Each turn seemed the same; every path was another loop that brought them back to where they had started. With each misstep, the Vandal's shouts grew louder, their footsteps sounding through the catacombs, a reminder of the danger closing in on them.

At last, they stumbled upon something familiar—the crude painting of a viper devouring a man, glaring down from the cavern wall. It felt almost mocking, a symbol of the treachery and danger surrounding them. The passage ahead forked into two different directions: the left path veered toward safety beyond the city walls, and the right plunged deeper into Sardinia's ancient necropolis.

Calias's body slackened, a calm settled over him as they stood beneath the viper's warning. "The child..." he stammered, his voice serene despite the chaos around him. "The child will be safe." His eyes, hazed with pain, fixed on Longinus and Constantine. "Take the left path. Go... now."

His legs gave out beneath him, and he collapsed into Constantine's arms, his body heavy and limp. Constantine struggled to hold him up, but there was no strength left in Calias's frame. With a gasp, Calias murmured, "Leave me... Let me buy you time. Take the child to safety."

Constantine tried to pull Calias forward. But the wounded man's body was too heavy, too far gone. After just a few faltering steps, Calias collapsed again, sinking to his knees. He looked up at Constantine, his voice barely a whisper. "Leave me... I'm finished. The end is here... I feel it. Grant me your sword... let me die with honor. Like a warrior, not a coward."

Constantine let out a frustrated sigh. "You really think I'm going to just leave you here to die?"

Calias gave a weak smile, his eyes soft despite the pain. "This is not a death to fear. My faith is strong." He looked to the heavens. "Today, I will be with our Father. Take the child and go. Find safety. Honor my memory."

Longinus looked deep into Calias's eyes, a surge of sorrow welling up within him. For a moment, he hesitated, grappling with the implications of the decision. Leaving a fellow brother-in-arms behind felt like tearing away a piece of himself, but he could see the acceptance in Calias's eyes that left no room for argument. He exhaled slowly, as if releasing the pain with his breath, and spoke with quiet reverence. "We must leave him."

Constantine shifted uncomfortably; his hands clenched at his sides. He glanced at Calias, then back at Longinus, his face twisted with reluctance. "We cannot just leave him here to die," he said. "This does not feel right. I cannot leave a fellow soldier behind." He looked away, hoping for another solution to fight against the inevitable.

Longinus reached out, resting a hand on Constantine's shoulder, grounding them both. "I feel it too," he murmured, a somber understanding passing between them. "But this is what he wants. We must honor his wishes."

Longinus reached for Constantine's sword with a heavy heart, drawing it slowly before placing it in Calias's trembling hands. The dying man's fingers tightened around the hilt, pride briefly lighting his fading eyes. Longinus spoke as he clasped Calias's forearm in a farewell. "May your memory be eternal. God be with you, my friend."

Then, they disappeared into the darkness of the leftward tunnel. Longinus stopped to cast one last glance over his shoulder. Calias had risen, the sword held tight in his hand, his battered body standing defiant in the darkness. Then, without another word, they vanished into the black, leaving their companion behind to face his fate.

Chapter 4

PROLOGUE -TRICAMARUM

On the eve of the Battle of Tricamarum, the Byzantine camp lay under a star-studded sky, teeming with anticipation. Scattered tents rustled softly in the cool breeze. The night air carried the scent of earth and burning wood into the men's sleeping quarters. Every flutter of fabric, each muted step on the grass, seemed to amplify the tension as the camp settled into a restless wait.

In the dim glow of scattered fires, soldiers huddled in groups, their voices a low murmur of nervous chatter. Clad in a patchwork of mail and cotton tunics, their faces flickered in the firelight, revealing both the apprehension of the young and the stoicism of veterans. One seasoned warrior, his face scarred from past battles, sharpened his sword methodically.

A small band of warriors moved with quiet authority among the war-weary men. Their presence commanded respect, drawing the attention of their comrades as they passed through the camp toward the largest tent, its flaps emblazoned with the emblem of the Byzantine Empire.

As they neared the command tent, two guards stepped forward, crossing their spears to bar entry. Moonlight glinted off the spear tips, hinting at the sense of danger. The leader of the band locked eyes with the guards in a silent exchange—a brief nod of recognition. Without a word, the guards raised their spears, allowing them inside the tent.

Inside, General Belisarius conferred with his officers. Maps and scrolls lay strewn across a makeshift table, illuminated by the flickering light of oil lamps. All eyes turned to the men as they entered—except for Belisarius. Without looking up from the splayed battle maps, Belisarius spoke, "Longinus, what tidings do you bring from Sardinia?"

Longinus slowly replied, "The girl has been safely returned to Egypt, but Sardinia has fallen. Tzazo has razed the countryside behind us. He executed Godas and most of his followers."

Belisarius responded, "So, a success."

"Yes, but at a heavy cost."

"No matter. Sardinia is no longer our concern."

Longinus shot a hard glance at Belisarius, who, sensing the tension, finally looked up and met his eyes.

"He is no longer in Sardinia… he is here."

Longinus stared back, confusion clouding his face.

"Tzazo is here," said Belisarius, his attention returning to the battle maps.

"Here? When?" inquired Longinus, his expression wide with shock.

Belisarius replied without glancing up. "He and his crew slipped by our naval blockade about fourteen days ago."

Longinus nodded, his tone grim. "This changes everything. Your victory at Carthage will mean nothing if we are unable to stop them here."

Belisarius looked up slowly, the seriousness of the situation deepening his frown. "Carthage was hard-won. They fought fiercely but without a true leader. Tomorrow, it's Tzazo we face—the one they'll rally behind. He's the real danger."

Longinus leaned in, his voice low. "How did it come to this? Why are we facing them here, at Tricamarum?"

Belisarius leaned back. His eyes grew distant as he recalled the events that took place while Longinus was in Sardinia. "After we defeated them at Carthage, Gelimer fled, gathering whatever remained of his shattered forces. He brought together desperate men scattered across his empire, clinging to a lost cause. Then Tzazo slipped past our blockade, and their numbers swelled. The army we face tomorrow will not be the defeated rabble we crushed before—they are desperate for survival, and Tzazo is their inspiration. But there is division. Our spies tell us Tzazo and Gelimer's witch, Skylla, are at odds. She holds him responsible for the failure in Sardinia. He, in turn, loathes her influence over his brother."

He paused, letting this thought hang in the air. "Still, they have already tasted victory. Tzazo ambushed our vanguard at dusk. They killed many of our men before nightfall forced them to pull back. Thank God for the darkness—it gave us time we would not otherwise have."

Silence settled over the room. Belisarius broke it with a voice that commanded many years of experience. "Tomorrow, we cannot just rely on strength—we need cunning. You and a select group of horsemen will harass Tzazo and his men. Distract him, draw his attention away from the real battle."

Longinus straightened. "He won't know what's happening until it's too late," he said, though he knew well the chaos of war rarely followed any plan.

Belisarius paced slowly. "We fight not just for victory, but for a lasting peace. Remember that our actions tomorrow will be recorded in the annals of history."

Longinus turned on his heels, his men following in lockstep. "If history remembers us, General, let's make sure it remembers us well."

The camp settled into an uneasy quiet as the night deepened. Soldiers checked their weapons, whispered prayers, and tried in vain to find sleep. Longinus, however, remained alone with his thoughts, his eyes lifted toward the stars. He knew the line between glory and disaster was thin, and somewhere out there, Tzazo waited.

As the first light of dawn brushed the shores of Africa, the plain bristled with the preparations for war. High above, carrion crows circled, their raucous caws piercing the morning calm as they squabbled over the few slivers of shade in the barren landscape.

The Byzantine forces took their positions on the battlefield, a sight of imperial discipline. Five thousand cavalry stood poised on one flank, a mix of heavy and light horsemen. The heavy horseman rode powerful steeds that snorted and pawed at the ground, eager for the charge. Interspersed among them were the light cavalry, nimble and fleet-footed, armed with bows and javelins, ready to harry the enemy with hit-and-run tactics.

Adjacent to them, ten thousand Byzantine soldiers stood in tight formations. These men were a combination of professional soldiers and local militia, all trained to fight as a cohesive unit. Their gear varied, reflecting their diverse origins. But each man carried a shield, spear, and sword—the standard equipment of the Byzantine infantry. The front ranks held their shields forward, forming a wall of metal and wood, while the soldiers behind readied their spears, a forest of deadly points.

Behind them, the Byzantine navy had landed its contingent of five thousand sailors. Though accustomed to naval combat, they were strangers to traditional warfare. They were less heavily armed than the infantry, but what they lacked in armor they made up for in agility. Equipped with an assortment of weapons—short swords, axes, and makeshift spears—they formed a sea of determined faces, ready to defend their empire's honor.

Across the field, the Vandals—thirty thousand strong— waited. These were no mere raiders; they were hardened warriors, veterans of countless campaigns. Their armor, plundered from many conquests, shone beneath the morning sun, and their weapons promised swift violence. Their sheer numbers were a fearsome sight.

The early morning sun illuminated the Byzantine army led by the formidable General Belisarius. He surveyed the battlefield, where the Vandals, under the banners of King Gelimer, were arrayed in formation. From his vantage point, the Vandal army was a remarkable sight, their shields shimmering like a sea of flame, spears pointed toward the heavens.

Belisarius rode along the lines of his army, his black warhorse moving with the calm of a veteran campaigner. His men—some grizzled by years of combat, others eager for their first taste of glory—awaited his orders. United under the banner of Byzantium, they stood ready.

On the opposite side of the battlefield, Gelimer stood flanked by two stark figures: his enormous brother, Tzazo, and the wraith-like Skylla. Gelimer's eyes often drifted toward Skylla, whose presence felt more like a shade than flesh. She moved with quiet confidence, her standard of the coiled viper rippling in the wind like a cruel omen. Each subtle gesture, each word, tightened her grip on Gelimer's decisions as if weaving a web of control around the king.

Skylla stared at Tzazo with a hint of satisfaction as she whispered into his brother's ear. Tzazo stood rigid, the black patch over his missing eye a constant reminder of his failure at Sardinia. Though he physically overshadowed her, his strength did little to mask the tension between them. She had gotten her way. It was her plan that was being set in motion.

Tzazo listened as Gelimer relayed Skylla's latest suggestions, and his demeanor filled with doubt. The strategy she had concocted was unorthodox and reckless. Tzazo clenched his fists, the tension in his body betraying his struggle. His instincts screamed against it, but she had enthralled Gelimer. Tzazo could do nothing but obey.

As Skylla uttered another directive to Gelimer, Tzazo's patience frayed. She blamed him for the failed mission in Sardinia, and he knew it. Skylla's smugness only fueled his disdain for her. He loathed her manipulative influence, her cryptic riddles. But Gelimer hung on every word, trusting her visions and dark counsel. Tzazo stood torn between his duty to his brother and the rising frustration at being sidelined by a woman he despised.

Still, duty prevailed. With a booming voice, Tzazo relayed the orders to his men. "Vult, to the left flank!" he commanded, the words a decision he did not fully own.

His men, the elite Vult warriors, begrudgingly moved away from the center of the battlefield. They could feel it too—the glory of being at the heart of the battle slipping from their grasp. Less experienced soldiers, their shields bearing the coiled viper emblem, took their place in the center. Tzazo boiled over with anger, knowing full well that Skylla had orchestrated this shift. She had pushed him to the outskirts, far from the crucial fight.

As the Vandal armies re-formed their lines, shields locking, spears angled forward, Tzazo's men exchanged wary glances. They trusted him, and their respect for him was evident in their disciplined obedience. But they also sensed his irritation. This wasn't his plan. And though they followed without question, a creeping doubt rippled through their ranks, reflecting their leader's inner turmoil.

Skylla watched Tzazo from a distance, her intent unreadable, though satisfaction glimmered faintly in her eyes. She had bent the king to her will, and now Tzazo—her biggest obstacle—was pushed aside. The corner of her lips lifted ever so slightly as her strategy began to unfold.

Tzazo, his chest tight with frustration, could feel Skylla watching him, reveling in her success. But he would not let her win so easily. His men would still fight, and they would fight with the ferocity that had made the Vult feared across empires. Even if her plans threw them into the periphery, Tzazo was determined to leave his mark on this battle.

Above them all, the sky darkened, and a strange stillness fell over the land. And then, with a cry that split the air, the Byzantines surged forward. Flavius, a battle-tested commander led the heavy cavalry into the fray. The ground trembled under the thunderous gallop of their cavalry, and the desert filled with the clamor of rattling armor.

The Vandals, unflinching, met them head-on. Their long spears and shields formed a wall of steel that the Byzantine cavalry bent but could not break. Despite their bravery and strength, the Byzantine cavalry was repelled, forced to retreat to their lines. The brutal clash left the ground strewn with the bodies of fallen men and dying horses, their screams piercing the chaos. The dry land, like a thirsty beast, soaked up the blood of the unfortunate, turning the ground red.

Undeterred, the Byzantine light cavalry charged, leaving no time for the Vandals to recover. They took a different approach, relying on speed and agility. Darting in and out, they loosed arrows and threw javelins, haranguing the center of the Vandal lines. However, the Vandals were prepared. They formed tight shield walls, their archers responding with a hail of arrows that drove the Byzantines back. Though the light cavalry managed to push back part of the Vandal center, they were forced to withdraw under the relentless barrage.

As the Byzantine light cavalry retreated, leaving behind a trail of blood and shattered armor, the Byzantine foot soldiers swiftly reorganized, shifting from traditional ranks into a spearhead phalanx. Heavy warhorses snorted and pawed the earth as they moved to the tip of the formation, ready to strike.

Tzazo sensed the coming decisive blow aimed at the middle of their lines. He made the decision to break from formation and signaled his men with a sharp gesture. Together, they surged back toward the center, pushing forward to brace for the impending strike. But in his haste to fortify the core, Tzazo left the left flank exposed, a widening gap that spread like a crack through their defenses.

In the chaos, Longinus spotted a chance to sow discord. He saw the gap in the Vandal defenses, left vulnerable by Tzazo's advance. Seizing the opportunity, he led his small group of heavy and light cavalry into the third charge, aiming to exploit the breach in their lines.

Tzazo reached the center of the Vandal line just as Belisarius's command to advance rang out. The Byzantine wedge formation surged forward, cutting through the battlefield like a blade. The horsemen shifted from a trot to a gallop while the foot soldiers picked up their pace, their armor clinking in unison. It sounded like a thunderclap when the Byzantines finally crashed into the Vandal defenses. And in the midst of the madness stood Tzazo, unflinching, holding back the onslaught almost single-handedly.

As the Vandal center pressed their advantage against the Byzantine warriors, Longinus led his small band of cavalry out of the main attack and into a sweeping flanking maneuver, using the dust and terrain to conceal their approach. His cavalry tore into the Vandal flank with the force of an unleashed tempest. The ferocity of the charge shattered the left side of the line. The light cavalry darted through the gaps, spreading confusion and disorder. The sudden assault caught the Vandals off guard, their formation buckling under the hooves of the Byzantine cavalry.

Longinus led the charge, his blade cutting through the Vandal ranks. Bodies fell, and the cries of the wounded filled the air. The Byzantines used this advantage to slowly turn the left flank of the Vandals.

Despite the chaos on the flank, the Vandals held firm at the center. Their desperation fueled a savage defense, driving back the Byzantines with relentless force. In the thick of the fray, Tzazo swung his warhammer in wide arcs, crushing skulls with each brutal strike, his face splattered with blood.

As the sun reached its zenith, a harsh light settled over the battlefield. The Vandals, overwhelmed and outflanked, began to faulter. Their formation slowly disintegrated, leaving gaps for the Byzantine infantry to flood in. As the wall of warriors crumbled, the momentum of the battle shifted.

Tzazo, surrounded by his fallen warriors, felt the bitter sting of defeat. With a roar that cut through the chaos, he charged headlong into the Byzantine ranks, a lone titan defying the tide, determined to change the battle's course. His voice thundered,

"Longinus!" as he stepped over the dead, his weapon sweeping aside anyone who dared to stand in his way.

Two Byzantine warriors rushed forward to stop him, but they were no match for Tzazo's raw strength, their armor shattered by his devastating blows. The force of his strikes crushed them from sternum to spine. The nearby soldiers recoiled, horrified by the sight of this blood-drenched giant.

Across the field, Longinus heard his name boom like a war drum. He spotted Tzazo's hulking figure and spurred his horse forward, urging it to its limits. But Tzazo braced himself. As the horse neared, Tzazo sidestepped. In a single, deadly motion, he brought his hammer down, smashing the horse's skull. Longinus was catapulted from his mount, the world spinning in a blur of air and ground.

Darkness closed in around Longinus. When his vision swam back into focus, the sunlight blinded him before a massive shadow eclipsed it. Blinking against the light, he discerned the imposing silhouette of Tzazo, a black eye patch stark where an eye once was.

"You!" Tzazo bellowed, his voice thunderous over the clamor of battle. "You took my eye, Longinus! Today, I take your life!"

Longinus, his face streaming with blood, grinned. "You lost your eye because you were slow, Tzazo. Today, you'll lose more than that."

"And you talk too much for a man about to die," Tzazo snarled, bringing his warhammer down with lethal force.

With no time to react, Longinus curled into a defensive ball. The warhammer came down with a sickening crunch, shattering his left leg. Agony lanced through him as he dropped his sword and reflexively seized the hammer's shaft with both hands. Summoning all his strength, he pulled, using the gore-drenched ground to unbalance Tzazo.

The giant, thrown off balance, toppled like a mighty oak in a storm, crashing to the ground with a deafening thud. Longinus, acting on instinct alone, rolled over the fallen warrior. In one swift, merciless motion, he plunged his dagger into Tzazo's remaining eye socket. He pushed with all his might until the giant's life ebbed away under the relentless pressure. As Tzazo went limp, Longinus struggled to maintain consciousness.

In the poignant stillness that followed, Longinus lay atop Tzazo's lifeless form. The dust of conflict settled around him like a shroud, and the clamor of war faded into chilling silence. Pain wracked his body with every breath as he fought to stave off death's grasp.

As he lay there, Longinus wondered if the price of victory had been worth the cost. The battlefield around him was littered with friends and foes alike, all reduced to still, lifeless figures in the dirt. The sun, now waning, cast its final rays over the land as darkness enveloped him.

Chapter 5

KALYMNOS – 543 A.D.

A thirteen-year-old boy hurried across the scorching sands of a pebbled beach. The blackened stones basked in the blazing Mediterranean sun at the height of summer. The shoreline stretched for nearly two leagues, its northern and southern ends framed by towering rocks and boulders that seemed as old as the island itself. Five of these behemoths were half-submerged in the sea, where ceaseless waves crashed against their foundations. To the boy, they were more than just spots to fish or jump from; they were silent guardians protecting the island from unseen intruders.

Beyond these stone guardians lay a world of adventure, where the boy spent hours playing while his father fished. Jumbled rocks formed tide pools that reached his waist, the water rising and falling with the tide. When the tide rolled in, he would bound from rock to rock, carefully avoiding the chill of the sea. Sometimes, he dangled his feet in the water, hoping to entice shrimp to tickle his toes. And when the tide receded, he waded through the ankle-deep water, searching for petalithes, flat snails that clung stubbornly to the rocks. He plucked them off and savored their tender undersides raw.

The boy's home, tucked among the island's peaks, lay a half-league from this secluded cove—a private paradise where he and his father often traveled. The path to the tranquil shore was steep, with few roads cutting through the arid hills. Yet his father always insisted on returning to this beach, where the waters stayed clear, and the short, choppy waves kept the seaweed at bay. The boy never minded the long trek; it was a chance to escape his daily chores.

As on most mornings when they ventured to this hidden part of the island, Pothitos had dashed ahead of his father, his youthful energy driving him to plunge into the cool waters. The sea's icy touch sent shivers through him while the salty breeze filled his lungs, mingling with the distant cries of the Audouin's Gulls overhead. He frolicked in the shallows, the cold water an intense contrast to the sun's warmth. It wasn't until his father's voice, carried by the wind, echoed across the shore that Pothitos was pulled back to reality.

"Pothitos!" Antonios called, his silhouette stark against the blinding morning sky. "Where are you?"

"Here, Baba!" Pothitos shouted, his voice filled with the excitement of the sea. "I'm already in the water!"

Antonios's tone carried a gentle reproach: "Come now, my son, I need your help. You ran ahead and left me to carry everything."

Pothitos looked up toward the ridge's crest and saw his father burdened with their gear—a trident, a heavy corded net, a jug of water, and a basket of provisions. The sight of Antonios struggling with the unbalanced load made guilt tug at Pothitos's heart. His feet trudged through the sand as he hurried back to the shore. His soaked exomis clung to his skin. The linen tunic, designed for work—especially fishing—left his right shoulder bare, allowing for freedom of movement.

He raced across the scorching sand, his feet burning by the time he reached the base of the goat trail his father was about to descend. The uneven rocks bit into his feet, a familiar pain he barely noticed anymore. He scrambled up the twisting trail and reached for the trident.

But Antonios lifted his head with dissent and pulled the trident back. "No, take this," he said, handing him the jug and the heavy basket. Pothitos pouted briefly, scuffing the dry earth beneath his feet, but he accepted the task with a reluctant nod.

They made their way to the beach amidst the rugged terrain of Kalymnos, an island on the fringe of the Byzantine Empire. Antonios was the archon of the island, akin to a local king, a title passed down for generations. His firstborn son was named Pothitos, meaning "of Pothaion," a nod to their lineage. Though descended from a long line of leaders, Kalymnos had fallen under Byzantine control during the reign of Emperor Constantine two centuries ago. Antonios oversaw the governance of over ten thousand subjects. Even though he remained under imperial rule, Antonios was loyal to some of the older traditions of Kalymnos. He skillfully blended the wisdom of his ancestors with the tenets of the Byzantine faith. In Christianity's embrace, brought by the empire's influence, the people of Kalymnos had found solace, but the transformation had not been without its struggles. Some still clung to the old gods with reverence, seeing Christianity as a betrayal of their heritage.

As they neared the beach, Antonios headed toward a small grove of salt cedar trees that offered some relief from the sun's rising heat. He leaned his trident against the nearest trunk and draped the heavy nets over a low-hanging branch. Then he spread a linen blanket beneath the trees' shade, motioning for Pothitos to place the jug of water and the basket on it.

As they settled into the cool shade of the salt cedars, Pothitos watched his father arrange their fishing gear with deliberate movements honed by years of experience. The air carried the fresh scent of the sea, mingled with the earthy, resinous fragrance of the trees.

Antonios ran his hand over the rough bark of the salt cedar, plucking a tuft of its soft needles. He inhaled deeply, savoring the fresh, sharp aroma. The resilience of these trees always represented a sense of quiet strength—they endured the briny, harsh soil just as his people endured the hardships of island life. Catching Pothitos's inquisitive look, he knew it was the perfect moment to impart a lesson.

"Do you see these trees, Pothitos?" Antonios asked, gesturing to the salt cedars around them. "They thrive where few others could—in salty, arid soil. Yet here they are, giving us shade and shelter."

Pothitos nodded, his eyes following the gnarled branches reaching upward, defying the harshness of their surroundings.

"These trees," Antonios went on, "are like our people. Life here is hard, but like the cedar, we learn to stand firm, drawing strength from our struggles."

Pothitos picked up a small branch, the leaves rustling softly in the breeze as his father continued, "The cedar's roots dig deep into the earth, finding water even in the barren soil. So too must we dig deep within ourselves, finding resilience amid hardship."

Pothitos listened, absorbing his father's words. The cedar's resilience symbolized the strength within their people—and himself.

"And just as these branches come together to offer us shade, our people come together to support one another,"

Antonios said. Pothitos gently laid the branch back down as his father continued. "In unity, there is strength. Remember that my son. Like the cedar, find the strength to face life's challenges and the wisdom to nurture the bonds we share."

Pothitos smiled, a sense of pride swelling within him. "I will, Baba," he promised, looking around at the cedars that shaded their small haven.

The lesson was clear: resilience and unity were great allies in hardship. At this moment, under the shade of those enduring trees, Pothitos felt a deep connection to his island, his people, and the lineage of strength that ran through his veins.

Antonios turned his attention from the shade to the sunlit shore. Lifting the cumbersome net, he said, "Let's see what bounty the ocean offers us today."

He quickly moved the heavy ropes, meticulously arranging the cork floats for optimal buoyancy. Stones, placed at the net's base, were carefully set to ensure an even spread. Together, they dragged the net to the foaming water, and Antonios, a seasoned sailor, tied it securely between two massive rocks that jutted above the surface. The channel between these rocks was a favored breeding ground for gilthead sea bream, easily ensnared in their well-crafted trap.

Antonios stepped back to inspect his work, ensuring the knots would hold against the sea's pull. Satisfied, he returned to the cedar trees, where his trident rested. He took two small circular sponges from the basket, which he dipped into the cool water, pressing each one into his ears to protect his hearing from the sea's depths.

Turning back to Pothitos, he beckoned him over. "Watch the net closely, my boy," he instructed. "Make sure the sea doesn't pull it away."

With the trident in his right hand and a small net in his left, Antonios plunged into the churning Aegean surf and vanished beneath the waves.

Pothitos stood for a moment, then clambered atop one of the rocks he imagined as a guardian of the island. From this height, he commanded a panoramic view of the western shores of Kalymnos. To the north, azure water stretched endlessly, broken only by the distant silhouette of a small uninhabited island. The shoreline curved gently southward, dotted with secluded coves of every shape and size. At its far end, a crescent-shaped beach met the rolling waves while sheer cliffs plunged into the sea beyond. Pothitos watched the ceaseless war as the sea raged against the unyielding mountain. Each crashing wave spawned a new plume of white ocean spray.

As he watched the distant waves, a gleam of sunlight reflecting off metal caught his eye. The source was the ancient watchtower, Patella—a towering pillar of rock topped with a fortification carved from dark mahogany-red stone.

In ancient times, the watchtower stood as a sentinel against maritime raiders. The watchmen would keep their eyes trained on the horizon, ready to alert their comrades to approaching danger with fire and smoke signals despite the ever-present risk of wildfires in the dry, arid landscape.

Now, the Byzantine army occupied the tower, standing guard day and night. A single blast from a horn was all it took to rouse the garrison. Yet, despite the watchmen's vigilance, a sleek Egyptian merchant vessel slid silently toward the watchtower, seemingly unnoticed. These ships, laden with precious grain from the fertile Nile, easily plied the sea routes, heading toward the island's capital.

But today, this Egyptian merchant vessel dared to approach the shallows surrounding Patella. Pothitos watched with interest as a young girl was lifted from the ship's deck into the arms of a waiting Byzantine soldier. Her raven-black hair stood out against her bronze skin, setting her apart from the rough, sunburned men around her. Clearly, she was important, as the commander of the Byzantine garrison himself awaited her at the tower. Pothitos stared across the sunbaked island as the girl rushed to embrace the soldier.

A crashing wave against the rock beneath him snapped him out of his reverie. His attention shifted back to the channel where his father's fishing nets had been set, and he felt a pang of dread— the net was gone.

Pothitos knew too well the difficulty and cost of replacing such nets, which were carefully crafted by skilled hands. His father would surely make him work off the debt if it was lost. Without a second thought, he leapt from his perch into the turbulent sea.

Though he was a skilled swimmer, this part of the sea was extremely treacherous. The relentless waves buffeted him toward the serrated rocks, and the channel's suctioning undertow threatened to drag him under. Still, he dove beneath the frigid water, squinting through the stinging saltwater to search for the net. Through the blur, he finally saw it—a dark web entangled at the base of one of the larger rocks.

Desperate, he reached for it, only to be yanked backward as the undertow surged, pulling him feet-first through the narrow channel. He struggled to the surface, gasping for air, only to be struck by another wave that slammed him against the barnacle-encrusted stone. The saltwater burned his scrapes as another wave pulled him under.

By some stroke of luck, his hand caught hold of the woven rope of the net. He clung to it with all his strength, hauling himself toward the rock and praying it would hold his weight. As he pulled himself up, his foot slipped, sending a sharp pain through his leg as it scraped against a barnacle. Suddenly, the sea stilled as if by miracle, giving him enough time to haul himself onto the rock and out of the water.

Panting, Pothitos pulled the heavy net from the water and dragged it back to shore. A single sea bream was tangled within, its silver scales flashing as it flopped in the sand. Mesmerized, he watched it struggle, its gills opening and closing like a heartbeat. For a moment, he thought of Achilles and the shining armor of the Myrmidons. Though he knew his father would be angry, Pothitos gently freed the fish and tossed it back into the waves. "Today, we both cheated death, my friend," he murmured.

Exhausted, Pothitos collapsed at the edge of the surf, his thoughts drifting back to the silver-scaled fish he had spared. Soon, his mind wandered back to the mysterious Egyptian girl. Who was she, and why had she come to their island? Lost in thought, he lay there until a sudden sound startled him. When he looked up, he saw his father emerging from the waves. For a moment, it was as if Poseidon himself had stepped from the sea. Water streamed from Antonios's dark hair and beard as he strode through the surf, gripping his trident with a large, freshly caught octopus dangling from its prongs.

Antonios tossed a small net filled with dark purple sea urchins onto the shore. He deftly removed the octopus from the trident and tossed it onto the pebbles near Pothitos.

"I see the net has come up empty again," Antonios said, eyeing his son with a raised eyebrow.

Pothitos nodded, trying to keep his face neutral. "Empty, Baba."

"It's curious," Antonios mused, a glimmer of amusement in his eyes. "Every time I leave you with the nets, they come up empty. But when I set them without you, they're full."

Pothitos thought for a moment, then offered a sheepish grin. "Maybe the fish are afraid of me."

Antonios's stern glance softened into a smile. "Maybe. But enough excuses—come, my son, help me clean the catch."

Pothitos lifted the slimy octopus by its tentacles and carried it to the rocks. He marveled at how the suction still clung to his arm, even though the creature was dead. For a moment, he amused himself by pressing the tentacles onto his hands, feeling them cling like a second skin. Then, sneaking a glance at his father, he quickly resumed his task. Carefully, he washed the octopus in a tide pool, scraping coarse salt from the exposed rocks and rubbing it into the creature's skin. Once it was coated with salt, he gripped it by the tentacles and began pounding it against the rocks, softening the flesh for cooking.

When Pothitos returned to the linen blanket under the cedar trees, he saw his father had laid out a simple meal from their provisions: a loaf of bread, dried figs stuffed with almonds, and a small block of feta cheese. Next to these, a dozen sea urchins were arranged, their purple spines glistening in the sun. Antonios took up a knife and began slicing the cheese, glancing up as Pothitos approached with the octopus. "Did you prepare it?" he asked.

Pothitos nodded, offering the octopus with a touch of pride. "Yes, Baba. I washed, salted, and pounded it on the rocks."

Antonios inspected the octopus, prodding it with his fingers before his brow furrowed. "Did you forget something?"

Pothitos's face fell. "I didn't take out the beak. I hate touching it."

With a faint sigh, Antonios took out his small knife, dug into the flesh, and extracted the sharp, bony beak. He tossed it aside, then hung the octopus to dry beside the nets on the cedar tree.

Antonios knelt on the linen to pray, and Pothitos followed. As he did before every meal, Antonios began the prayer: "In the name of the Father, and of the Son, and of the Holy Spirit. Amen.

Our Father, who art in Heaven, hallowed be Thy name. Thy Kingdom come. Thy will be done, on earth as it is in Heaven. Give us this day our daily bread, and forgive us our trespasses, as we forgive those who trespass against us; and lead us not into temptation, but deliver us from evil.

Glory to the Father, and to the Son, and to the Holy Spirit, now and ever and unto ages of ages. Amen.

Lord, have mercy. Lord, have mercy. Lord, have mercy.

O Christ, our God, bless this food, drink, and fellowship of Thy servants, for Thou art holy, always, now and ever, and unto ages of ages. Amen."

After the prayer, Pothitos carefully picked up an urchin, feeling its spiny exterior stiffen under his fingers. He turned it over and skillfully pried out the orange and yellow roe with his father's knife. He savored the sweet, salty flavor, eating several helpings with half a loaf of bread. After their meal, Antonios led a prayer of gratitude, thanking Christ for the blessing of food and asking for salvation in His Heavenly Kingdom.

Pothitos stood and started toward the beckoning sea, but Antonios called out before he could reach its cool shores. "Come, my son, rest here in the shade with me. We need to talk about our family and your future."

Pothitos paused, torn between the call of the sea and the somber tone in his father's voice. He wanted to pretend he hadn't heard, to ignore the words, but he knew better. With a sigh, he turned and walked back to the shade of the cedars, lowering himself onto the blanket beside Antonios.

"Don't be stubborn, Pothitos," Antonios chided gently. "Sit and listen. There's more to life than just swimming and playing."

Pothitos scowled, a touch of defiance flaring up. "Every day is the same, Baba. Chores and lessons—always chores and more lessons. Can't we do something different? Like learning to swim better or fight with a spear?"

Antonios chuckled, amused by his son's impatience. "You're eager for a warrior's life, I see," he said, his eyes twinkling. "But there's more to being a man than wielding a sharp stick. First, you must learn how to lead."

Pothitos shifted uncomfortably, biting back a protest. He was tired of these lessons about duty and manhood, but the look in his father's eyes kept him silent. There was depth there, something Pothitos had only seen a few times before.

Antonios waited for a moment before he began. "Kalymnos has been divided into seven regions, or demes, for as long as our people remember. The regents of these demes are men and women of power and pride: Savvas of Skaliodon, Theodoros of Amphipetron, Vlassios of Peraioton, Halikos of Orkatou, Aristedes of Panormos, your mother Nomiki of Mesos, and of course, I govern Pothaion."

Each name rolled off Antonios's tongue as if they were figures from ancient legends. Pothitos leaned in, caught up in the earnestness of his father's words.

"Each regent rules their deme independently, but together, they oversee the island as the Council of Regents. The archon is selected by the emperor, tasked with ruling over the council and the entire island. The archon is like a king, though he answers to the council and the emperor. Traditionally, this role is passed from father to son, but the council or the emperor can choose a new leader if there is no heir."

Antonios paused, studying his son's face, then spoke in a quieter tone. "One day, you will be archon, Pothitos. You will rule both Pothaion and Mesos and lead the island's other regents when your mother and I are gone."

Pothitos swallowed, feeling a knot tighten in his chest. "Don't talk like that, Baba. You're never going to die. Please, don't say such things."

Tears pricked at the corners of his eyes, but he held them back, determined to be strong like his father. Antonios reached out, lifting his son's chin with a rough but gentle hand, his face softening. "We all return to the earth eventually, my son. Our lives are like the cedar's roots—anchored deeply but bound to the soil. The well-being of our people is our duty, a responsibility that Emperor Justinian bestowed upon us, but he too, answers to God alone. So, you must listen carefully, Pothitos, and learn our history."

"Our family traces its roots back to the legendary Dorians," Antonios continued, his voice taking on the rhythm of an old tale. "After the Trojan War, four ships of Menelaus were blown off course and landed on the shores of Kalymnos, which was then called Kalydna. Six sailors were so enchanted by the island that they stayed, while a seventh—a Trojan captive—managed to escape. These six sailors founded the village of Argos, intermarried with the locals, and became the first rulers of six of the seven demes."

Antonios took a sip from the water jug, letting the silence hang in the air before he went on. "The seventh ruler, the king of Orkatou, was that escaped Trojan. He fled into the mountains and built his own settlement, but the other rulers despised him and his people. They harassed and persecuted them, driving them further into the wilderness. Yet, through their suffering, the people of Orkatou grew strong and resilient, though also bitter and mistrustful."

"Two brothers, Panormitis and Pothaion, claimed descent from Heracles himself. They ruled Panormos and Pothaion fairly, but their demes began to distrust one another over time. Mesos became wealthy and politically powerful, as it sits in the center of the island. The other Dorian demes dwindled, their people turning to simpler lives as shepherds, shipbuilders, and farmers. Meanwhile, the people of Orkatou remained distant and untrusting, living in the valley of Vothini, hidden among olive groves and orchards, separated from the other regions by treacherous mountains, where they still clung to the old gods."

Pothitos listened, entranced by the unfolding history. He could almost see the ancient rulers standing tall and proud against the backdrop of Kalymnos's rugged landscape.

"Then came Emperor Constantine," Antonios continued. "He decreed that all regions be consolidated under a single archon, officially ending the rule of kings and queens on Kalymnos. The Council of Regents remained, but true power was vested in the archon, and our people were forever changed."

Antonios's countenance grew distant as if peering back through the centuries. "Your mother, Nomiki, was like a princess to the people of Mesos. When we married, our union bound together the two great Dorian bloodlines of Kalymnos. That's why you, my son, are so vital. You are the sole heir of these noble lines—the last prince of Kalymnos."

Chapter 6

KASTELLI

As the sun descended beyond the edge of the world, Antonios and Pothitos, weary but content from a long day at the sea, finally returned to their fortress home: Kastelli. In their language, the name meant simply "the castle." Encircled by towering walls of stone carved from the mountain's bones, the stronghold rose like a sentinel atop the narrow summit of a conical isthmus. Sheer slopes dropped away on all sides, plunging down to the churning ocean below and isolating Kastelli from the mainland. Only a single, slender land-bridge connected it to the island, the sole tether to the rest of humanity.

The sky above Kastelli blazed with the hues of twilight—crimson and gold melting into deep blue, generating a warm, celestial light upon the ancient stones. Within these ramparts lay lush gardens—a green oasis flourishing against the starkness of stone. Beyond this sanctuary of nature stood a ring of unadorned, whitewashed buildings, each bearing the marks of age and the skill of those that crafted them. The steep slopes around the castle rose like the earth's hands, cradling the castle walls. Their rough surfaces, bathed in the last fiery light of day, stood as a testament to the enduring craft of the stone masons who had shaped them.

As Antonios and Pothitos crossed the narrow land bridge, which arched high above the sea, Pothitos paused to look into the valley below. There, the sprawling city of Pothaia lay nestled, bearing the name of the ancestor from whom he was descended. From this lofty vantage, he could see the ancient capital in all its bustling glory. The grand theater, with its rows of marble benches, stood out sharply amid the rooftops of countless dwellings and shops. He thought he could even make out actors rehearsing on the stage. The cityscape was a lively tangle of winding alleys and vibrant markets, proof of the city's thriving commerce.

Smoke from the evening fires drifted up from the city, hazing Pothitos's view as he scanned the rugged coastline of Pothaia. He scanned the horizon from the eastern edge, where Kastelli stood watch, to the western cliffs where the Fortress of Agio Konstantinos loomed atop its craggy perch. This fortress sheltered a community of nuns, protected by a Byzantine garrison from raiding pirates.

As his eyes swept over the bustling deepwater harbor, Pothitos's face lit with recognition. Moored among the local boats was the unmistakable silhouette of an Egyptian vessel, the same one he had spotted on the open sea earlier that day. Around it, workers moved in a frenzy, unloading heavy sacks of grain and forming a steady line toward the granaries on the city's outskirts.

As Antonios and Pothitos neared the fortress gates, rushlights flickered to life, ignited by watchful sentinels. Evening descended, cloaking the land in darkness as the gates creaked open to welcome the weary travelers. The path through the courtyard was illuminated by the warm glow of shining lamps, guiding them toward the inner walls.

As they passed through the outer gate, a disturbance along the inner walls caught their attention. A group of soldiers was escorting several unfamiliar faces into the fortress's inner sanctum—a rare sight that hinted at urgent matters.

Curious about the unusual activity, Antonios turned to one of his household guards. "What is this commotion?" he asked.

The guard returned his glance, his appearance somber. "Strange people, my Lord. I assure you they will only bring trouble to our land."

Antonios peered toward the front gate, straining to see into the gloom, his face stern. He quickened his pace, and Pothitos struggled to keep up. They passed gardens where pink bougainvillea spilled over low walls, and fig trees heavy with ripe fruit dotted the path alongside sunburnt-red pomegranate trees. The air was thick with the sweet fragrance of blooms. Overhead, trellises lined with grapevines bore heavy clusters of green grapes, sagging toward the earth. The tranquility of the gardens stood in conflict to the tension at the gates.

Torches along the stone pathways cast a soft glow, illuminating the faces of guards who nodded respectfully as their leader returned. The courtyard, the heart of daily life—buzzed with activity under the fading light. Byzantine soldiers tended to their gear, speaking in low, earnest tones about the day's events.

Amid the cluster of buildings stood a Byzantine church, its modest dome and simple cross visible above the walls. At its entrance, a weathered wooden semantron hung, ready to be struck for the evening prayers. Its doors remained open, inviting anyone to step inside for a moment of peace beneath the soft light of oil lamps against icon-covered walls.

As they crossed the courtyard, Antonios and Pothitos passed the small church, where soft hymns drifted out. The songs faded into the background as they reached the central building used for governance. There was a small group of Byzantine soldiers who stood assembled outside the heavy wooden doors. As Antonios and Pothitos approached, the soldiers snapped to attention. The nearest guard reached for the doors and pushed them open, the wood groaning softly as it swung inward. Warm light spilled out, and a fire roared in the hearth illuminating the assembled faces with a golden glow. As father and son stepped inside, the room fell silent. Antonios placed a hand on his son's shoulder, giving a solemn nod to the assembly.

At the far end of the room, two figures stood silhouetted against the bright flames of the hearth, their backs to the newcomers. The larger figure commanded the scene with an air of unmistaken authority. The iron-bound staff he leaned on was more than support; it symbolized his resilience and command. His left leg, visibly deformed and scarred from an old battle, marked him as a veteran of war. Beside him stood a small, delicate child, her demure frame casting a slight shadow on the stone floor—a figure no one seemed to recognize.

The murmur in the room died as the larger figure slowly turned, his movements deliberate, weighted by years and battles. Firelight caught the contours of his face—etched with experience and old scars—partially obscured by a thick gray beard. His sharp, calculating eyes missed nothing as he faced Antonios and the young boy. His staff clacked against the stone floor with each footstep toward father and son, while the smaller figure remained alone, staring into the fire.

"Ah, Pothitos, growing more like your father each day," he said with gruff warmth, his authoritative voice softened by age.

Antonios gave his son a proud glance and responded warmly. "Yes, he grows every day—and a little too eager to learn from you, Longinus."

"It reminds me of someone else I once knew," said Longinus with a wry smile.

The old warrior allowed a rare smile to soften his stern demeanor as he reached out and ruffled Pothitos's hair. Nearby, the small child who stood by the fire turned slightly, drawn by the conversation but still partly lost in the glow of the flames. Her quiet presence stirred Pothitos's curiosity as he tried to catch a glimpse of her face.

"It's time for bed," Antonios said, gently nudging his son. Pothitos, still brimming with curiosity and reluctant to leave the circle of adults, protested.

"But Baba," Pothitos argued, his voice full of confusion as he pointed to the girl by the hearth. "What about her? She's younger than I am."

Understanding his son's concern, Antonios knelt to meet his eyes. "Pothitos, she must stay because we need to learn who she is. Longinus would not bring just anyone into our home. This is a serious matter that the adults need to discuss," he said with a firm tone.

Longinus, leaning heavily on his staff, added his voice. "Indeed, she stays not because of her age, but because her presence here is a mystery to your father—and we must unravel it tonight. It's important for everyone's safety."

Antonios patted his son's shoulder reassuringly. "Go now and rest. You'll need your strength for tomorrow—and trust that we'll handle things here. On your way out, send for your mother. She'll want to know what's happening in her home."

With a lingering look at the girl and a heavy sigh, Pothitos finally relented. He turned and walked toward the door, his steps slow, his mind churning with questions about the mysterious newcomer. As the door closed behind him, the adults turned their full attention back to the girl, their faces marked with curiosity.

After reluctantly leaving the command hall, Pothitos hurried to find his mother, Nomiki, knowing she'd still be awake, likely immersed in her evening tasks. Nomiki, a tall woman with striking black hair and olive skin that spoke of her Mediterranean heritage, carried herself with the elegance and poise befitting her status. A soft scent of honey lingered in the air around her—a comforting, familiar presence for Pothitos.

Her gown was crafted from fine white linen, which draped elegantly over her form, reflecting her high social status and refined taste. The white fabric, which symbolized purity and prestige, subtly shimmered under the lamplight.

The dress featured long, flowing sleeves—a hallmark of Byzantine attire—that extended nearly to the floor. The edges were embroidered with delicate patterns of golden threads interwoven with tiny pearls, adding a touch of opulence to the otherwise simple garment.

The dress's neckline was adorned with a band of detailed mosaic-like embroidery. Around her waist, Nomiki wore a thin, gilded belt that cinched the dress, highlighting her slender figure and allowing the fabric to billow softly as she moved. This belt was functional, a piece of jewelry decorated with tiny jewels and intricate filigree work that caught the light with every step she took.

Her dark hair, like a raven's wing, was pulled back from her face and woven into an elaborate arrangement of braids and twists, typical of Byzantine noblewomen. Tiny jewels were pinned throughout, twinkling like stars against the dark canvas of her hair. The overall effect was somehow both regal and approachable. She was a woman who could command respect and invite trust—perfectly suited to her role within the community.

Pothitos found her in her private chambers, surrounded by scrolls and small vials of ink and herbs. He didn't hesitate. "Mother," he began, his voice urgent, "they need you in the command hall."

Nomiki looked up, her keen eyes instantly reading the concern on her son's face. She set aside her work and rose smoothly, her dress brushing against the stone floor as she moved. "What's happened, my son?" she asked, her voice calm despite the gravity of his interruption.

"It's the girl they brought in," Pothitos replied, his words quick. "Baba says they need to figure out who she is, and they're all very serious about it."

Nomiki nodded firmly. "Very well, let's go, then. Your father and Longinus must have good reason to be concerned."

As Nomiki and Pothitos approached the command hall, the boy stayed close to his mother, curiosity propelling him forward. The doors creaked open, revealing the assembly gathered around a central table where the dark-haired girl stood, flanked by Antonios and Longinus.

As they entered the chamber, Pothitos caught his father's stern glance—a silent but unmistakable command to leave. Though disappointment flickered across his face, Pothitos knew better than to argue amid such serious proceedings. He turned obediently, his steps shuffling toward the exit, his mind searching for a way to stay connected to what was happening.

Once outside the hall, instead of heading to his chambers, Pothitos moved swiftly and silently around to a large, arched window overlooking the hall. With practiced stealth, he settled into a shallow nook beside the window, concealed by climbing vines and the deep stone sill. From here, he could see the backs of the attendees and hear their voices—muffled but discernible.

He crouched, pressing his back against the cool stone, his eyes fixed on the figures inside—particularly the mysterious girl who seemed to be the center of attention. Pothitos's heart thudded in his chest, not only from the thrill of his hidden position but from the knowledge of the secrets he was about to uncover.

The debate inside intensified as Pothitos listened, clinging to the shadows outside the window. Longinus, his voice firm, argued for the girl to stay within the fortress walls. "We cannot simply turn her away," he said, leaning on his staff. "She is under my charge, and I must ensure her safety."

On the other hand, Antonios expressed a deep-seated concern for the broader implications of harboring the girl. His voice was tense, reflecting his duty to safeguard the community. "I understand her need for protection, Longinus, but we must also consider the peace of our people. The presence of this child—someone we know nothing about—could stir unrest or, worse, attract unwanted attention to Kalymnos. My responsibility is to the welfare of all who live here."

The strain between the two leaders was palpable, their disagreement rooted in their roles—Longinus as the guardian of the girl's safety and Antonios as the protector of his people. Each man held his ground, embodying the dual priorities that had long governed the fortress: defense against outside threats and the management of the fears within.

Pothitos could only catch fragments of their hushed dialogue, but he noted the unease on his father's face. Suddenly, Longinus grasped the girl's shoulders and turned her around. From his vantage point, Pothitos saw her dark hair being lifted, revealing a distinctive birthmark on the back of her neck. Antonios's eyes widened, but he continued his vehement objections. Longinus braced himself for another argument, but Nomiki laid a gentle hand on Antonios's shoulder, speaking softly in his ear.

Antonios gave a subtle nod, gestured westward and said, "Alas, this may bring affliction upon us all, yet we shall not reject her. We will keep her safe. We must call a council meeting to ensure the regents are all in agreement with our decision."

As Longinus nodded slowly in agreement with Antonios's recommendations, the atmosphere in the hall shifted slightly toward resolution. The girl, enigmatic throughout the discussion, seemed to sense the change. With deliberate grace, she turned to face the gathering, her movements reflecting a quiet dignity.

As she raised her head, her eyes—startlingly green and vivid against her tanned face—caught sight of Pothitos through the open window. Their eyes locked, hers clear and piercing, his wide and unblinking. The depth in those eyes, like endless pools of emeralds, seemed to draw him in, holding him spellbound.

In that brief exchange, Pothitos felt a rush of emotions he couldn't name. Her eyes, radiant but carrying an ineffable sadness, spoke of experiences beyond her years, of secrets and sorrows kept close. There was something intriguing yet cautionary about her—a contradiction that drew him in even as it warned him away.

The connection broke as quickly as it had formed; the girl looked away, her eyes dropping as Longinus stepped beside her, ready to lead her away. Guided by the old warrior, she moved with a solemnity that cast a heavy silence over the courtyard.

Still hidden in the shadows, Pothitos found himself momentarily lost, the image of her eyes seared into his memory. As the pair disappeared from view, leaving the hall abuzz with hushed conversations and lingering looks, Pothitos remained at the window, unable to move.

The encounter, though fleeting, had changed something within him. He knew that whatever came next, the mystery of the green-eyed girl would be at the heart of it.

Chapter 7

THE COUNCIL OF KALYMNOS

In Kastelli's gathering hall, an unassuming chamber with low, vaulted ceilings the regents of each deme assembled around a long, rectangular table. Thin beams of sunlight filtered through narrow, arched windows cut high into the stone walls, producing a muted glow that streaked across a mosaic of Christ the Redeemer. The air carried the faint, flowery scent of beeswax candles flickering in iron sconces.

Antonios sat at the head of the table, his authority underscored by the steady way he placed his hands on the table, fingers splayed. Beside him, Nomiki sat tall and poised. A plain bronze fibulae clasped her cloak at her shoulder.

Each regent of Kalymnos brought the concerns of their communities. Savvas, a lean sponge fisherman from Skaliodon, sat with arms crossed, his hands rough and salt-worn from years at sea. Beside him, Theodoros, the elderly aristocrat from Amphipetron, leaned forward with a slight smile, keen-eyed and wreathed in wrinkles from decades of quiet contemplation among his library's scrolls. Vlassios, the stoic shepherd from Peraioton, sat with his shoulders square, his silence needing no words. From Panormos, the ever-boisterous Aristides, whose laughter was as loud as his debates were fiery. At the far end, a little apart from the others, sat Halikos from Orkatou, his hulking form draped in the earthy tones of his ancestors. He was the last adherent of the old gods, his presence a solemn reminder of the island's deep-rooted past.

Today's council demanded a simple majority from the attendants. They had gathered to discuss the protection of a child—a fugitive from the turmoil in Egypt seeking sanctuary on their shores.

Antonios rose to his feet, clearing his throat. "Friends and leaders of Kalymnos," he began, his voice steady. "We gather today not for the usual disputes, but for a higher cause. A young girl seeks our protection from dangers no child should face."

Nomiki stood, her voice calm but filled with conviction. "This child has been entrusted to us. As long as she breathes our air and as long as she walks on our soil, we must defend her as one of our own."

Nomiki continued, "This young girl, brought to us by fate, is now ours to defend. It is our duty and our honor to safeguard her as fiercely as we would our own kin."

Theodoros leaned forward, his voice concerned. "I understand the need for compassion and protection," he began, his attention falling on his fellow council members, "but what makes this child so singularly important? Children across the empire face peril every day. Why does she warrant such extraordinary measures?"

The council murmured with uncertainty. "He's right!" Halikos shouted, pounding a fist on the table.

"Tell us, why should we care?" Aristides said, nodding emphatically.

"Bringing dangers to our shores would be folly," Vlassios said, his voice rising above the others.

At that moment, the heavy doors creaked open, and all eyes turned as Longinus entered. The steady thud of his staff against the flagstone floor punctuated his steps as he limped through the hall. His armor caught the dim light as he neared the center of the assembly.

Longinus paused, surveying the gathered leaders. "Vlassios, you speak a truth we all grapple with—the world is filled with suffering. But this child is not merely fleeing misfortune. She is pursued by forces that threaten the stability of the entire empire."

He let the assembly grasp the gravity of the situation before continuing. "It is said she is the last living heir of an Egyptian dynasty thought to be extinct—a pawn in a struggle for power and vengeance that exceeds her own life. I have been charged with her protection, and I assure you; I will carry out this duty, with or without the council's permission."

Longinus continued, his voice low but firm. "Her presence on this island is still hidden from those who hunt her. If her enemies find her, the consequences for all of us will be dire."

Antonios nodded in agreement and interjected, "Her safety is not merely a personal matter—it touches on the stability of our region. Letting harm come to her while under our protection would invite chaos and draw us into conflicts far beyond our shores."

Nomiki spoke again, her tone soft, "By protecting this child, we defend not only her but ourselves from the repercussions her capture might bring. Compassion here is not weakness; it is strength."

A murmur of assent rippled around the table, though an undercurrent of unease lingered. Breaking the silence, Savvas spoke, his voice rough as the sea. "And what of our defenses? If her pursuers find her here, are we prepared to face what follows?"

Antonios nodded, understanding the sponge diver's concern. "We will increase our patrols, strengthen our port's defenses, and, above all, keep this matter confined within this council. No one beyond these walls can know."

The room tensed as Halikos rose, his imposing figure looming over the table. A known skeptic and staunch advocate of his people's traditions, he scanned the assembly before addressing Longinus directly. "Commander, you speak of dark forces and destabilizing threats," he began, his voice rough. "Yet here we sit, leaders of Kalymnos, in ignorance of the enemy we're to face. If we endanger our people, I demand clarity. Who pursues her? What is the nature of this danger?"

Halikos's request lingered in the air, echoing the unspoken concerns of several council members who nodded in quiet agreement. They leaned forward, their expressions curious, waiting for Longinus's response.

Longinus met Halikos's concern with a nod, acknowledging the matter. "Very well, your caution is well-founded, Halikos," he conceded, his voice steady. "The threats we face stem not from mere bandits or local dissenters but from a cabal steeped in the lore of the ancients. They are remnants of a once-powerful dynasty; they seek to reclaim their lost glory through this child, an Egyptian princess by blood. This cult believes she is the key to their resurgence," Longinus continued. "They claim that her blood will grant them eternal youth and that she is the map to unlocking an ancient power hidden centuries ago. They believe this power will restore them to their former glory."

Skeptically, Halikos leaned over the table. "Name this cult then," he demanded with a scoff. "Perhaps my people will find their cause more compelling than yours."

Longinus responded unflinchingly, "The ones who pursue this girl are no mere zealots; they are as cunning as they are ruthless. They operate in the shadows, using deception and force to achieve their goals. Their agents are embedded deep within our society, usually where least expected."

He ensured he commanded the full attention of every council member before continuing, "They are known as The Cult of Skylla, a name meant to create fear, like the monster in Homer's tales. Just as Skylla was feared for her insatiable hunger, so too does this cult hunger for power and immortality, driven by beliefs rooted in the darkest magic of the old gods."

"They are not bound by the moral codes that govern civilized peoples. They seek to use this child, believing her blood and very being are keys to unlocking a power that has been hidden since the time of the Apostles." Longinus's tone hardened with each word, conveying the seriousness of the threat. "Joining with them would bring not alliance but subjugation under their ambitions."

Aristides stood, his voice booming through the hall, a contrast to the tones of the earlier discussion. He slapped his palm against the sturdy oak table, making the goblets and scrolls jump. "Like it or not, this task has fallen to us," he declared, his eyes flashing with excitement. "But I say, let us accept our fate with the courage of our forefathers!"

He opened his arms wide, as if to encompass the entire room. "We are the light of our people, the beacons of our proud island!" Aristides continued, his voice rising in passion. "Should we cower because the days darken, and ancient threats rekindle? No! We stand firmer; we shine brighter!"

"Let this girl find not just refuge but a fortress in our care. Let those who chase her find not prey, but the iron will of the people of Kalymnos!" He pounded the table again, his broad smile infectious, igniting a spark in the room.

"This is not merely our duty but our honor. Let the Cult of Skylla come. They will find us ready and waiting, not with fear, but with defiance in our hearts!" His voice rang, not just in the hall but through the very stones of Kastelli.

The room filled with a rising murmur of agreement, buoyed by Aristides's spirited oration. Council members nodded, their faces showing a sense of solidarity.

Yet, amidst this consensus, Halikos stood silent, gripping the edge of the table. "While the fervor of your words stirs the heart, Aristides," Halikos began, his voice cutting through the room, "I find myself unswayed by your passion."

"It is not fear that governs my caution nor lack of resolve," Halikos continued. "It is prudence—and the need for more than stirring speeches if we face an enemy as sinister as this so-called Cult of Skylla."

He paused, letting his attention rest across the face of each council member. "We must not be blinded by our zeal to protect, lest our actions lead us into folly. If we are to shield this girl and, by extension, our island, let it be with eyes wide open, aware of the true costs and consequences—not just swept along by the tide of eloquent words."

Halikos's final words hung with a chilling finality through the hall. "I, for one, reject this proposal." He sat once again crossing his arms across his chest. "I know nothing of this girl nor care to. Her death would be meaningless to me."

The room fell silent after Halikos's blunt rejection. Eyes shifted around the table as Antonios cleared his throat and called for the vote. "All in favor of granting sanctuary to the child under our protection signify by raising your hand."

One by one, hands rose—each more confidently than the last. Only Halikos's hand remained defiantly down, his expression impassive.

"The decision is unanimous, save for one," Antonios noted. He stared at Halikos for a moment, then turned to the others. "The decision stands: we have pledged to protect her from those who pursue her."

Turning to Longinus, Antonios continued, "The girl must enter the convent at the Monastery of Agio Konstantinos. There, the abbess, Gerontisa Angeliki will raise her and teach her the tenets of our Lord. Longinus, you already have the Ierí Frourá within the walls of Agio Konstantinos. Keep it secure as you know how."

Longinus nodded solemnly. "It will be done. We will protect her with our lives, if necessary," he affirmed.

Halikos scoffed, shoving back his chair as he rose. The wooden legs scraped harshly against the floor. "If this brings trouble upon my people, may your Lord help you," he declared bitterly. Without another word, he turned and strode out of the hall, his exit as turbulent as his presence.

The remaining council members exchanged uneasy looks, Halikos's ominous parting words hanging over them like a shadow.

Antonios looked around the table. "Let Halikos go. We have made our decision, and now we bear the consequences together. Our unity in this matter is essential if we are to face whatever trials come our way."

Longinus turned to the remaining council members and offered a nod of respect. "I will keep you informed of her safety. This I swear."

Chapter 8

AGIO KONSTANTINOS

Cradled on the craggy shore of Kalymnos, overlooking the western bank of Pothaia, the Monastery of Agio Konstantinos stood within the fortress bearing its name. Its silhouette cast an imposing figure against the backdrop of the sapphire Aegean Sea. Built in the Byzantine style, its heavy stone walls rose stoically, an earthly manifestation of the faith it represented.

The outer walls, hewn from the island's native limestone, absorbed the warm hues of the Mediterranean sun—a palette of ochre and beige that glowed at dawn and dusk. The monastery's formidable main gate, accented with ironwork that had withstood years of salt and storm, served as the sole entrance.

The gate led to a path which meandered through a courtyard that was the monastery's lifeline, a serene garden where ancient and gnarled olive trees shifted in the breeze and roses bloomed.

Central to the courtyard was a fountain, its flowing waters offering a soothing melody and a promise of renewal. Around this central area, the monastery passages wound through cloisters and corridors, leading to various chambers for worship and work.

With its simple dome, the main chapel embodied the simplicity of the monastic aesthetic. Its heavy wooden door, carved with scenes from the life of Christ, opened to the narthex, a place for quiet reflection before entering the sacred inner sanctum. The interior of the sanctuary was resplendent with iconography. Frescoes of vibrant azure, gold, and crimson depicted saints and scenes from Holy Scripture. The golden flicker of oil lamps illuminated the simple iconostasis—a screen dividing the nave from the altar area, which only ordained clergy may enter.

The living quarters formed a humble complex along the northern wall, each cell offering only the essentials: a narrow bed and a desk where a nun might study scripture or contemplate divine mysteries. The cells' austerity reflected the community's dedication to simplicity and humility, imbuing the rooms with a quiet sense of peace.

The refectory, where the nuns gathered for communal meals, was a long, vaulted hall with a single elongated table. Adorned only with wooden crosses and tapestries depicting the life of Saint Konstantinos, the space was humble but warm. The aroma of fresh bread often mingled with the fragrance of incense from the chapel, producing a comforting familiarity.

The scriptorium was a quiet chamber of study; its walls lined with shelves holding valuable scrolls and codices. Here, the nuns carefully transcribed texts, preserving knowledge for future generations—a rare task on an island like Kalymnos but essential to their devotion. Their work was slow and meditative; each brushstroke of ink was a way to conserve the words of their forefathers.

Beneath the main structures lay the crypt, a place of reverence for relics and the remains of pious predecessors. The cool air and quiet within reminded the sisters of their heavenly promises.

Around the periphery of Agio Konstantinos, utilitarian features—workshops, herb gardens, and fruit trees—were tucked into the rocky landscape, the scents of thrymbi and thyme wafting through the air. The nuns cultivated these gardens to sustain themselves and provide food to the poor.

A narrow path led to a small hermitage carved from the rock high on the cliffs behind the monastery. This retreat was a place of solitude and extreme asceticism, where a nun might spend days or weeks in isolated communion with God. Such solitary devotion was rare, a calling answered only by those prepared to embrace its challenges.

The monastery was not merely a defense against Mediterranean pirates but also a fortress of the soul. It was a microcosm of divine order, a sliver of heaven on earth. Amid the tranquil cloisters, a community of nuns lived a life devoted to prayer and service, their peace seldom disturbed except for the quiet chant of hymns and the vigilant watch of the Ierí Frourá.

That night, as the sea raged against the land, Sister Maria peered out from her small cell, the dim light creating shadows on her wrinkled face. The tempest outside matched a restlessness she felt as she clutched her wooden cross.

"Sister Despina," she called softly into the dark corridor, her voice barely rising above the storm. "Did you hear that?"

Sister Despina, a younger nun with calming eyes, joined her at the window. "It is only the wind, Sister," she replied, though her eyes darted nervously toward the window.

Suddenly, a pounding at the gate broke through the roar of the storm—a desperate sound that cleaved the night. The two nuns exchanged a quick, fearful glance before hurrying down the stone corridors to rouse the abbess, Angeliki.

The Ierí Frourá, a small group of handpicked guards, gathered at the gates, their hands tense on their sword hilts, ready to repel any threat that might intrude on holy ground. The abbess, flanked by her sisters, stepped through their ranks with a presence that commanded respect from the soldiers.

"Open the gates," Gerontisa Angeliki commanded, her voice steady.

Captain Theophilos hesitated for a moment, then signaled his men to comply.

The gate groaned open to reveal a shadowy figure bent against the blustery night wind with a child by his side. The girl, no more than ten, looked ghostly in the darkness, her eyes wide with a fear beyond her years, her clothing marking her a foreigner.

"Who goes there? Speak!" demanded Theophilos, stepping forward, his hand still on his sword.

But Gerontisa Angeliki approached first, her hand raised in a welcoming gesture. "Captain Theophilos, let us not greet our guests with steel but with the grace of Christ," she said, turning her attention to the figure. "You are safe here. What is it you seek?"

The figure, cloaked by darkness, stepped through the monastery's threshold, presenting the child before the abbess. As candlelight illuminated his features, the monastery's inhabitants could make out the weary face of Longinus. He encouraged the child forward into the light, where she stood shivering and sprayed with seawater.

"Longinus…" the abbess murmured, a softness touching her eyes as she looked down at the child. She then turned to the figure and asked, "What brings you here on a night like this?"

The bent figure of Longinus, leaning his weight onto his staff, peeled off his soaking cloak that clung to his frame. He shifted slightly as he nudged the child closer to the warmth of the hearth.

"I have brought this child here under Antonios's direction. She is to seek sanctuary, not just from this storm, but from the perils that pursue her," Longinus replied, his voice deep.

"She," he continued, gesturing to the small figure beside him, "bears a burden too great for her alone. She needs your guidance and your protection."

Gerontisa Angeliki nodded, her face set with a look of understanding. She knelt down to the child's level, her all-black habit rustling softly. "You are under the mantle of the Lord here," she assured the child, her tone gentle yet firm. She then rose and faced Longinus with an air of confidence.

"We will provide the refuge you seek. This monastery has stood as a sanctuary for many. So it shall remain."

She motioned to a sister nearby, who quickly approached with blankets and warm broth. The monastery, a stronghold of compassion, buzzed into action as the community gathered to assist their unexpected guest.

Turning back to Longinus, the abbess's eyes caught his, searching for the unspoken truths behind his urgent journey. "Tell me what pursues her, Longinus. To protect this child properly, I must know what shadows must be cast into the light."

His gaze flickered briefly toward the shivering child, and Longinus seemed to be choosing his next words carefully. The room paused; the only sounds were the crackling of the fire and the storm's roar outside.

Before he could utter a word, a voice interrupted him. "An Egyptian amulet?" Sister Despina murmured, her eyes lingering on an ankh secured around the child's neck.

The girl stood alone, a diminutive figure framed by the gateway. The ankh pendant at her neck reflected dully in the firelight. She looked up at the abbess and the nuns surrounding her; their faces were a tapestry of curiosity and concern.

"A child of the old gods," Sister Despina added, her voice filled with apprehension.

Gerontisa Angeliki's eyes lingered on the ankh. After a moment's pause, she spoke firmly. "The Lord works through all. Tonight, we welcome this child to live under God's grace. Tomorrow, we begin the work He has laid out for us."

Gerontisa Angeliki turned toward Longinus. "We shall continue this conversation in private. These are not matters to discuss openly."

With that, the other nuns gently led the girl to a quieter part of the monastery. Their steps were soft against the ancient stone floors, swishing lightly through the halls. They brought her to a small chamber warmed by a fire crackling in a hearth. Though sparsely furnished, the room was filled with a comforting sense of peace and security.

The sisters provided her with a simple robe to replace her damp, sea-sprayed garments and offered soothing herbal tea to calm her nerves.

After the young girl changed, Sister Despina carefully reached for the clasp of the ankh around the girl's neck, but the child pulled away, clutching it tightly to her chest. Her emerald eyes were wide with fear and confusion. Sister Despina offered a gentle smile and handed her a black rope necklace, knotted into the form of a cross at one end.

She quietly said, "Put it on when you're ready."

The girl held the cross with uncertainty and murmured something in a language unfamiliar to the nuns nearby. She tried again, this time in a more guttural dialect, but her words were lost on the sisters.

Sister Maria, observing quietly from the doorway, stepped forward. Recognizing the cadence and structure of the girl's words, her eyes widened slightly in realization.

"Coptic?" she murmured, before addressing the child directly. Clearing her throat, she spoke in a soft, steady voice, the syllables flowing in the ancient Egyptian Christian language. "*Everēnē, piran. Mē tarebooulé*," she said gently. (Peace, child. Do not be afraid.)

The girl's eyes darted to Sister Maria, a flicker of recognition and relief crossing her features as she heard the familiar sounds. Her grip on the ankh loosened slightly, though her other hand still clutched the rope cross.

"*Ari tekran?*" Sister Maria asked with a gentle smile, encouraging the girl to share her name. (What is your name?)

There was a hesitant pause as the child seemed to weigh her trust in this unfamiliar environment. Finally, she spoke in a whisper. "Delenda."

"Delenda," she repeated, turning to the other nuns who waited in quiet curiosity. Sister Maria repeated the name again. "Her name means 'to be destroyed' in Latin—an odd name for a child."

The room relaxed, understanding beginning to bridge the chasm of fear and unfamiliarity. Sister Maria continued speaking with Delenda in Coptic, asking her simple questions to help the child feel safe.

"*Delenda, Oun ek erōi en te stauros, tentawōsh?*" she asked, holding up the rope cross again. (Delenda, would you like to wear this cross?)

Delenda stared at the cross for a long moment, her small hand clinging to the ankh. At last, she placed the cross gently on the small table beside her bed, her actions careful and deliberate.

Sister Maria spoke softly, "*Hen tektanēm nai, etbe tastauros, totpe ente pekaes en Pekhristos..*" (When you are ready, dear, put on the cross, and you will put on the armor of Christ.)

Delenda looked at her, a faint glimmer of understanding in her eyes, then settled down, curling up beneath the blankets. With a final glance to ensure the child was comfortable, Sister Maria and the other nuns left her to rest, the quiet crackling of the fire bathing the small chambers in light.

Meanwhile, back in the main hall, Gerontisa Angeliki, Longinus, and Captain Theophilos gathered in a secluded corner, their faces grave as Longinus began to speak.

"The child is of a lineage steeped in the annals of history, tracing back to Cleopatra," he disclosed. "She is the last known heir of a forgotten Egyptian dynasty, pursued not for her claim to any earthly throne but for an ancient magic believed to be in her blood."

Theophilos raised an eyebrow, glancing skeptically at the abbess. Sensing his doubt, Longinus added, "Whether there is truth in this or not, I cannot say. But I can assure you those who pursue her believe it—and are willing to commit unspeakable acts to obtain it."

Angeliki's brow furrowed, her eyes reflecting concern. "And the pursuer?" she prompted, sensing the depth of the peril.

"A witch, steeped in dark arts, manipulative, and cunning. She goes by the name Skylla," Longinus replied, his voice low. "She believes the girl's blood holds the secret to eternal youth. Her pursuit is relentless and cruel, driven by a hunger for power. I have been pursuing her ever since Carthage. She has managed to elude me for years."

The abbess drew in a deep breath, the revelation settling over her. "How has she managed to remain hidden all this time?"

Longinus's countenance darkened. "Survival is a craft well-mastered by those fueled by desperation and ambition. Skylla has likely used her network to remain undetected, waiting for the right moment to strike."

He paused, his hand resting lightly on the iron staff at his side. "Ten years ago, the lands to our south were engulfed by war.

The conflict was spurred by the same dark forces that seek the child, Delenda. King Gelimer, beguiled by Skylla, waged war across the coasts of Africa and Sardinia, believing it would bring him unassailable power."

He shook his head, the memories clouding his eyes. "The Vandals, under Gelimer's command, were fierce, but their ambitions became their undoing. The war ended in a devastating battle where the Vandals were defeated, their forces scattered, and their king disgraced. We thought it was over. But Skylla… she escaped."

Gerontisa Angeliki exchanged a worried glance with Theophilos. "And now she's resurfaced, still in pursuit of her dark goals?"

"Yes," Longinus replied, his voice steady. "Over these past ten years, she has remained hidden in the wilderness of North Africa, gathering her strength. Her belief in the power of Delenda's blood has only deepened, fed by the legends of the pharaohs and the mystique of ancient magic. This woman's malevolence is unparalleled. We dare not underestimate her."

A heavy silence settled over them, each contemplating the enormity of the danger at their gates.

The abbess's voice was firm when she spoke. "We must prepare, Longinus. Not just to protect Delenda, but also to ready ourselves for the evil that may assail our people."

Longinus nodded solemnly. "Then we will need more than just our soldiers. We will call upon all our allies, both seen and unseen. And we will pray—for the Lord to guide us and shield us from the wickedness that approaches."

Captain Theophilos placed a hand on his sword hilt, his face set with determination. "If Skylla comes here, she will face more than just prayers."

Angeliki placed a gentle hand on his arm. "Violence alone will not be enough to counter such forces. We must be united—in body, mind, and spirit. This monastery has withstood many storms, both from men and from powers unseen. It shall stand through this as well."

Longinus bowed his head in agreement, his heart heavy with the duty he bore. "With your permission, I will return to Antonios."

"Granted," Angeliki affirmed, her voice full of determination. "We stand together, in the light, against whatever may come."

Back in her chamber, Delenda lay awake, clutching the ankh around her neck. She stared into the dim light of the fire, her mind far from the peace of the monastery, listening to the wind and the rain rage outside the monastery walls.

In her heart, she knew that the storm outside was only the beginning.

Chapter 9

POTHAIA

The following day, Pothitos awoke early, drawn by a desire to watch the sun rising over the Aegean coastline. Rubbing the sleep from his eyes, he perched himself on the uppermost rampart of the fortress at Kastelli. This vantage point offered an expansive view of the awakening city below. As the first delicate rays of dawn began to illuminate Pothaia, his eyes instinctively scanned the bustling city.

Below, at the docks, hardworking laborers continued the unceasing task of unloading grain from the Egyptian vessel. The rhythmic motion of their work, a familiar sight, contrasted with the tumult swirling in Pothitos's mind. His thoughts drifted back to the mysterious girl from the other evening, her image lingered like an unsolved riddle.

His gaze drifted across the bay, settling on the outline of Agio Konstantinos. The fortress-like monastery was bathed in the soft morning light. He imagined the girl there, possibly watching the same sunrise, enveloped in a world so different from his. What might she be doing at this moment? Was she looking out at the sea as he was?

As he pondered these questions, the sounds from the docks faded into a muted backdrop, the rhythmic clanking and shouting melding into a distant hum. The workers' daily chores, usually a scene of lively commerce, now seemed distant and detached, overshadowed by his growing curiosity about the girl's fate.

The docks stretched out like weathered fingers into the icy clutch of the Aegean Sea, composed of robust wooden piers and solid stone quays. These structures, built to endure the relentless sea and its salty winds, were always alive with activity. Sailors, their voices rough from shouting against the wind, maneuvered their vessels with ease. Fishermen and spongers, their hands gnarled like the ropes they wielded, hawked the day's catch, glistening fresh fish and delicate sponges basking in the sun. Merchants draped in colorful fabric haggled over goods ranging from local olives and wine to exotic spices and silks from far-off lands. The air was a tapestry woven with the scents of tar, salt, and the crisp sweetness of fresh fish overlaid with the more savory notes of spices and incense arriving from distant shores.

Not far from the chaotic sounds of the docks stood the granaries of Pothaia, ancient stone structures designed to store the city's wealth of grain. Their thick walls, which kept the interiors cool and dry, were plain except for faint remnants of older carvings, possibly depicting Demeter, the goddess of the harvest—remnants of the ancient Greeks. Inside, the granaries were divided into chambers filled with mounds of imported wheat and barley. High windows punctuated the upper sections of the walls, allowing air to circulate while shielding the precious contents from too much light. The granaries held the dominant food source for the islanders;

therefore, they were carefully guarded to ensure that the islanders never starved.

The synergy between the docks and the granaries was a finely tuned machine. As ships unloaded their cargoes, teams of stubborn donkeys and laborers bustled between the pier and the granaries. Sacks of grain were transferred swiftly from ship decks to the cool, dim interiors of the storage houses. Supervisors oversaw the operation, ensuring that none of the harvest was lost to carelessness or theft. Yet, the actual threat to their bounty was not from thieves but from a much smaller, persistent foe: rats. These rodents, ever the bane of urban and agricultural settings, constantly threatened the hardworking people of Kalymnos.

The city, well aware of the devastation that rats could unleash on grain stores, had instituted various defenses to protect the vital stores within the granaries. The smallest cracks in the walls were carefully sealed, and each breach was scrutinized by caretakers, who ensured no rat could slip through undetected.

Beneath these towering walls, the floors were elevated—a design choice that kept the grain dry and helped deter rodents from nesting directly beneath the stored supplies. The granaries were consistently swept clean, with every spilled kernel swiftly collected to prevent attracting unwanted pests.

But the true guardians of these stocks were not the humans but the cats. They prowled the perimeters of the granaries with vigilance, their presence a natural deterrent to the rodents. Occasionally, the soft patter of paws and a sudden scurry indicated the pursuit of a hunt that often ended in the shadows beneath the grain sacks.

The grain's storage was also meticulously managed. The islanders stored it in tightly sealed clay or wooden containers, sometimes reinforced with thick fabric to resist gnawing.

Despite the rigorous defenses and consistent upkeep, the granaries of Pothaia were not entirely impervious to the cunning persistence of their tiny adversaries. On the rare occasion when vigilance faltered, or nature proved too cunning, a rat or two managed to infiltrate the storage. These breaches, though infrequent, brought with them not just the threat of eaten or contaminated grain but a more insidious danger—fleas.

Unknown to the people, these fleas were tiny carriers of a disease that rooted into the rodent's fur. Once inside the granary, the fleas found themselves in an environment ripe for proliferation. The ample food supply and the warm, dry conditions of the granary provided an almost ideal breeding ground for these pests if they happened to dislodge from their scurrying hosts.

As these fleas ventured from their carriers, they often found their way into the grain. Burrowed within the stores of wheat and barley, they could survive unnoticed, their presence undetected until an unwary worker becomes a host.

Iason was starting his shift when he felt a slight sting on his forearm. He tried to scratch his arm and almost dropped a heavy sack of grain he was unloading from the Egyptian vessel.

Initially, Iason dismissed this bite as only a minor irritation. He continued his work, unaware that the flea that bit him was carrying Yersinia pestis, the deadly bacterium responsible for the plague. As he worked through the day, shifting bags and organizing the warehouse, the site of the bite began to swell, but the hardy dockworker paid it little heed, accustomed to the physical demands of his job.

Within a few days, however, Iason's condition deteriorated rapidly. He developed a high fever, and one of his lymph nodes, near the site of the flea bite, swelled to form a painful, tender bulge—a bubo. This was soon followed by severe headaches and delirium. As Iason's illness rapidly evolved, it presented symptoms unfamiliar to the people of Kalymnos. He began to develop severe pneumonia, marked by a deep, persistent cough that filled the small room where he lay with the harsh sounds of his struggle for air. With each cough, the air became tainted with tiny droplets laden with the deadly Yersinia pestis bacterium, though no one in Pothaia could yet understand the danger this represented.

The local healer Thanasis, revered for his knowledge of herbs and traditional medicine, was called upon to tend to Iason. Thanasis observed the new, troubling symptoms with concern, despite having little understanding of their underlying cause. He administered broths and herbal concoctions to ease the fever and soothe the cough. He spent long hours by Iason's side, listening to his labored breathing and feeling increasingly helpless against the relentless progression of the disease.

As the days passed, Iason's fingertips developed a blackened hue. His cough grew more violent, spewing forth a mist of infection that hung in the stale air of his room. Thanasis, dedicated to his patient, continued his care, despite the invisible threat he continually inhaled.

It was not long before Thanasis himself began to feel unwell. Initially attributing his malaise to fatigue, he soon developed a fever. Within days, a similar cough racked his body, mirroring Iason's symptoms. The illness's rapid onset in someone notable as Thanasis alarmed the island's people. The people of Pothaia had never experienced a disease so virulent. Panic began to spread through the city as Thanasis slowly succumbed to the disease.

As days turned into weeks, the disease followed the veins of trade and human movement, reaching from the granaries into the markets and homes of Pothaia. Each transaction at the market, every gathering at the local taverns, and the close quarters of residential homes became opportunities for the disease to claim new victims.

The city's physicians and healers were soon overwhelmed, their treatments futile against the swift propagation of the disease. Panic began to take root as the death toll rose, and the grim reality of the epidemic became undeniable. Desperate, the city's leaders urged people to stay in their homes and avoid gatherings, but these measures were too little or too late. The plague was not confined to the city for long; it began to creep along the paths leading to neighboring villages and towns, carried by fleeing residents, roaming animals, and traveling merchants.

As the plague ravaged the island, leaving an increasing toll of casualties in its wake, the cities, including Pothaia, found themselves overwhelmed. The usual rites and individual burials became impractical, and the grim necessity of mass graves became a frightening reality. Antonios, always a leader attuned to the needs of his people, took on the heart-wrenching task of organizing these mass burials, striving to handle the growing number of deceased with dignity under dire circumstances.

Antonios and a group of volunteers coordinated efforts to designate areas away from the city centers as communal burial sites. Understanding the emotional implications of such measures, Antonios approached the task with the solemnity needed to see it through.

Each morning, as the mist still clung to the ground, Antonios and his team gathered at the gates of Kastelli, dressed in whatever protective garments they could muster—layers of linen, herbs believed to ward off illness, and cloths wrapped around their faces. They would venture out into the city, carts in tow, to collect the deceased. The scenes they encountered were harrowing: silent city streets, homes where families had succumbed together, and bodies left in quiet despair.

The designated burial sites were on the outskirts, where the ground was dug deep and wide by those who could still wield shovels and pickaxes. Antonios oversaw the operations, ensuring that each body was handled respectfully and placed in the earth. Father Dimitri, the priest at Kastelli, offered prayers, murmuring them with weary lips—not just for the dead, but for the safety of the living. Antonios himself would often say a few words, a gesture of solace not only for the souls of the departed but for those who needed to know that their loved ones were laid to rest with dignity.

In these somber times, Antonios's role transcends that of a leader; he became a symbol of enduring strength and compassion. His presence at the burial sites, with his hands as dirty as those of any other, spoke volumes about his character. He was not an archon separate from his people but one who shared in their darkest days.

Back home, in Kastelli's fortress, Nomiki and Antonios argued each night, as she insisted that she needed to help those who were suffering. Nomiki's decision was met with protests from Antonios and Kastelli's household. They were keenly aware of the risks involved—every moment spent among the sick was a moment of potential exposure to a deadly illness. Antonios, in particular, was torn between his duty to protect his wife and his understanding of her need to act on her principles.

"But Nomiki, think of our son. You're needed here, safe with him," Antonios said with worry laced in his voice. "The risk is too great, Nomiki. Losing you…I couldn't bear it."

Nomiki, however, remained unmoved. "My heart cannot bear to sit idle while our people suffer," she replied, her voice steady. "This is where I'm needed, Antonios. I can't abandon them now."

Her determination was unshakeable, and Antonios knew no argument would sway her. Reluctantly, he conceded, arranging for the best protective measures he could. He ensured that Nomiki would always have a guard with her, that she wore layers of cloth, and that she carried herbs believed to ward off illness.

Along with the nuns of Agio Konstantinos, Nomiki worked tirelessly, tending to the sick, comforting the dying, and offering solace where they could. Her presence among the people lifted the spirits of many, reinforcing her image as a lady of the people.

As the days passed, Nomiki's bravery did not go unnoticed. Her compassion became an inspiration, rallying others to join her efforts. Encouraged by her example, the community began to organize more effectively, pooling resources to support the sick and prevent the disease from spreading further.

Yet, with each passing day, the task grew more perilous, and Antonios watched anxiously for any sign of illness in his wife. Each night, as she returned to Kastelli, he would wait for her at the gate, fearing that she would begin to show signs of sickness. Their reunion each night reminded them of the risks they faced, bound by love and duty. They found strength in the simplicity of being close, knowing whatever they faced, they would face it together.

Chapter 10

KOIMESIS

As the days turned into weeks, the emotional toll of death wormed into Nomiki's conscience. Despite her fervent efforts and the precautions taken, the disease proved pitiless and unstoppable. Her exposure to the afflicted finally exacted its toll.

One morning, as Nomiki prepared for another day at the makeshift infirmary, she felt an unfamiliar weakness. Her limbs trembled slightly, and a fine sheen of sweat covered her brow despite the coolness of the dawn. She brushed it off as fatigue; after all, the long hours were overwhelming. However, her hands shook as she sipped her sage tea, and the cup clattered slightly against the saucer. Antonios, ever watchful, noticed immediately.

"Nomiki, you're not well," he observed, his voice alarmed. He approached her, his hand reaching out to feel her forehead. It was warmer than usual.

"It's nothing, Antonios," Nomiki insisted, forcing a reassuring smile through her growing discomfort. "Just a little tired, that's all."

But Antonios, on edge from weeks of battling the disease's curse over Pothaia, knew better. "You're burning up," he said gently. "You must rest today."

Nomiki wanted to argue, to insist on fulfilling her duties, but even she could not ignore the creeping malaise tightening its grip with each passing minute. Reluctantly, she nodded, allowing Antonios to lead her back to her quarters.

Nomiki's steps faltered as they neared the corridor, her fingers briefly tightening around Antonios's arm. She never stumbled—not Nomiki, who always moved with grace. But now her breath came in shallow pulls, and she felt lethargic.

The rhythm of her morning—so often marked by ritual—unraveled in silence. She didn't speak to anyone in the household. She even walked by Pothitos without saying a word, one hand brushing the wall as though she needed it for support.

Antonios felt the tremor in her grip. He said nothing, only guided her down the passage with gentleness. When they reached their chambers, she hesitated at the threshold, blinking as though the space was somehow unfamiliar.

Inside, the air was cool and the stone walls felt damp with morning dew. What had always been a place of rest for her now seemed to press upon her from all sides.

Antonios helped her to the bed, easing her down slowly. His hands never shook, but his chest was tight, and his throat burned with dread.

Nomiki didn't speak. She stared at the window across the room, where the breeze barely stirred the curtain. For a woman who had carried so many through their suffering, her own silence was deafening.

She thought to herself, 'This is how it begins.'

"Nomiki," Antonios said as he knelt before her, "you have brought us through the worst of it. You were the strength of this house when I was consumed with my duties. Let me be your strength now."

Her eyes, usually fierce, were clouded.

"I can't abandon them," she whispered, her voice dry and brittle. "They need me. I'm the only one left who—"

"You're not abandoning anyone," Antonios said. "You're human, Nomiki. Letting yourself rest is not weakness. It's wisdom. It's love—for yourself, and for those who love you."

She looked at him for a long time, her face unreadable. Then, her eyes dropped. Her shoulders sagged.

"I'm scared," she confessed—so quietly it broke something in him.

"I know," he replied, wrapping his arms around her. "But you are not alone."

He kissed her brow and called for their son.

Pothitos stepped cautiously into the room. His small hands twisted in the folds of his tunic. "Mama?"

Nomiki reached out with a trembling hand, and he ran to her, pressing her palm to his cheek. She smiled faintly.

"I just need to rest, my sweet boy," she said, brushing his hair back. "I will be all right."

Antonios watched the exchange as a profound sadness overcame him. He knew the road ahead would be difficult, not just for Nomiki but for all of them. The illness had entered their home, and despite all their efforts, it threatened to take from him the most precious part of their lives.

Over the next few days, as Nomiki's condition worsened, the mood in the household became grim. Healers came and went, their faces melancholy and their remedies increasingly ineffective.

Antonios split his time between his duties as archon and his vigil at Nomiki's bedside, each moment he spent away from her filled him with dread.

As the symptoms intensified, the fever gave way to fits of coughing and difficulty breathing. The vibrant woman who had guided their community with compassion was fading.

Her decline quickened with each passing hour. The shortness of breath was soon accompanied by a deep, wracking cough that shook her frail body. Pothitos, kept at a distance for his safety, peered anxiously from the doorway, his young face creased with worry.

"Baba, will Mama be alright?" he asked, his voice barely audible.

Antonios stood by Nomiki's bedside as she rested fitfully. He looked back at his son with a forced smile. "We must hope and pray, my son. Your mother is strong."

But even as they spoke, Nomiki's strength waned. A healer was summoned, her face grave as she examined the archon's wife. She offered what remedies she could, but Antonios knew there was no cure.

The community of Kastelli, already reeling from the losses inflicted by the plague, watched with heavy hearts as news of Nomiki's illness spread. The archon's wife, who had been such an inspiration, was now losing the battle to the affliction she had fought so bravely against.

The air in Nomiki's chambers was filled with the scent of medicinal herbs and the quiet weeping of servants. Antonios watched helplessly as her condition deteriorated and knew he had to prepare for the worst. So he called upon Father Dimitri, the priest who had served their family and community for many years.

Father Dimitri, a gentle and pious man, arrived at the castle solemnly, carrying the tools of his trade. His slow gait and deep lines etched across his face showed the depth of his task. As he entered Nomiki's quarters, he offered a comforting smile to Pothitos, who stood just beyond the threshold of the doorway.

"Antonios, my son," Father Dimitri greeted softly, placing a reassuring hand on Antonios's shoulder. "I have come to offer the Lord's blessing to our beloved Nomiki."

Antonios nodded, his throat tight. "Thank you, Father. She needs all the peace she can find."

Father Dimitri approached Nomiki's bedside, setting down the Holy Oil, his prayer books, and the reserved Gifts. He began to prepare for the Anointing of the Sick, a sacrament meant to provide comfort and spiritual healing to the faithful. He gently took Nomiki's hand, murmuring a prayer as he anointed her forehead and palms with the Holy Oil, tracing the sign of the cross.

"Nomiki, servant of God," Father Dimitri intoned. "Receive the anointing of the Holy Spirit for healing and forgiveness. May the Lord who frees you from sin save you and raise you up."

As the priest continued with the sacraments, reciting prayers for Nomiki's soul and her journey from this world to the next, the room fell into silence. It was broken only by the sound of his voice and the quiet weeping of her husband.

Father Dimitri carefully administered the reserved Gifts, offering Nomiki the Body and Blood of Christ. Antonios knelt beside the bed, supporting Nomiki's shoulders as her lips parted just enough to receive the Gifts. Her breathing was shallow, her skin pale with the sheen of fever, but as the Holy Mysteries touched her mouth, her eyes fluttered open. For a fleeting moment, light returned to them. She met Father Dimitri's eyes and gave a faint nod of surrender.

A beat of silence passed before the priest crossed himself, then stood.

"She is near to God now," he said quietly, turning to Antonios and Pothitos. "May His mercy envelop her. May you both find strength in the days ahead."

Antonios nodded, eyes fixed on Nomiki. Pothitos lingered in the doorway, unsure.

"Come, my son," Father Dimitri encouraged gently.

The boy hesitated, then stepped forward. He reached the bedside with cautious steps and placed a trembling hand on his mother's. Her fingers twitched weakly in return.

Father Dimitri continued the prayers, his voice low. Antonios and Pothitos joined in, their voices trembling.

When the prayers ended, Father Dimitri laid a hand on both of their shoulders. "You are not alone."

Yet when he left them, they felt alone.

With the quiet threatening to overwhelm him, Antonios knelt again at Nomiki's side. He brushed a damp strand of hair from her forehead. He leaned closer, his voice barely audible.

"You gave us everything," he said softly. "Your strength… your heart. Thank you, my love."

Nomiki's breath caught in her throat. A pause. Then another breath, lighter now, fading.

Pothitos climbed onto the bed's edge and kissed her forehead. "I love you, Mama," he whispered, tears slipping down his cheeks.

Her eyes opened once more, finding them both.

A final glance, full of warmth and something more—release.

Then, a sigh. So quiet it might have gone unnoticed if not for the stillness that followed.

Antonios stared, his hand pressed against her cheek. No rise. No fall.

He bowed his head, tears spilling without restraint. Pothitos clung to him, sobbing into his tunic.

After a long silence, the boy lifted his head and looked at her.

"She looks like she's sleeping," he said softly.

Antonios nodded, his voice hoarse. "That's why we call it Koímēsis," he said. "The falling asleep. Because for those who love God… this isn't the end."

Pothitos blinked, processing his words. He nestled against his father again, saying nothing. They stayed that way, wrapped in grief and one another.

The oil lamp flickered.

Somewhere outside, a night bird called once, then fell silent.

In the stillness, surrounded by the memory of Nomiki's courage and the scent of sage, the two remained.

Later that evening, a deep brooding settled over Antonios. The once-vibrant halls of Kastelli, filled with his wife's laughter and warmth, now resounded with a hollow, mournful silence that mirrored the void in his heart. Antonios found himself wandering through these halls at odd hours, lost in his grief.

His responsibilities as archon demanded his attention—decisions needed to be made, the affairs of the state required his guidance, and the plague still needed to be combatted—but these tasks now felt insurmountable without Nomiki by his side. Her counsel had always brought him clarity and strength; without it, each decision became a mountain to climb, each problem a reminder of his loss.

Antonios's demeanor changed perceptibly. Where once there had been a confident leader, sure of his actions and quick to offer a reassuring smile, now there was a man shrouded in perpetual angst. His face, once thoughtful, was now carved with lines of sorrow; his eyes, once bright, now dimmed with suffering.

The staff of Kastelli noticed the change. Conversations would hush as he passed, his presence casting a dark undertone. Close friends and advisors tried to reach out, but Antonios withdrew, isolating himself in his sorrow. He shunned company, preferring the solitude of his private chambers or the quiet of the castle's ancient library, where he lost himself in scrolls and texts, seeking refuge in the stories of the past.

Pothitos, unable to grasp the depth of his father's grief, felt the change acutely. He missed the laughter and the warmth of his parents together, and he struggled with the frightening change in his father. The boy tried to reach out, offering small gestures of affection, but was met only with a distracted nod.

As midnight approached, a storm gathered over Kastelli. Antonios stood at a tall window in the great hall, watching as lightning illuminated the darkened seascape. The howling wind and the crashing waves seemed to vocalize his inner anguish.

"I should have protected her," he muttered to himself, a refrain that had become all too common in his moments of solitude. Guilt gnawed at him, adding to his sorrow. He felt he had failed in his most fundamental duty—not in his role as archon, but as a husband. Nomiki had been a constant presence at the infirmary, caring for the sick, her compassion as infectious as the disease was deadly. Perhaps he could have insisted more firmly; he could have prevented her exposure.

Having observed Antonios's struggle from afar, Father Dimitri chose this moment to approach him. The old priest moved quietly, standing beside Antonios at the window, sharing the view of the stormy night.

"Antonios," he began softly, careful not to startle him, "grief is a heavy cloak, and you wear it alone too often. Nomiki's spirit and love were a light for us all. She would not wish for you to drown in this darkness."

Antonios turned to look at Father Dimitri, his eyes weary. "How does one find the light again, Father, when each step takes you deeper into the dark?"

Father Dimitri placed a gentle hand on Antonios's shoulder. "By remembering that the dawn always follows the darkest part of the night. You honor her memory not by mourning her loss but by living the virtues she embodied. She lived for others, Antonios. Perhaps, in doing the same, you might find your way back to the light."

Chapter 11

DAMOS

The day of Nomiki's funeral dawned gray and heavy; the skies above the island of Kalymnos formed a leaden shroud, mirroring the sorrow that blanketed the town. In the early morning, a solemn procession gathered outside the castle, where Nomiki's body lay in state, draped in white and surrounded by a sea of flowers: lilies for purity, roses for sorrow, and sprigs of lavender for peace. Their scents mingled in the cold morning air.

The castle gates opened slowly, and the bier holding Nomiki emerged, carried by six of the household's most trusted guards. Their steps were measured, and their faces were sullen under their ceremonial helms. Father Dimitri led the rest of the procession, his black robes flowing, a large wooden cross held aloft, chanting prayers in a resonant tone that carried over the gathered crowd. Gerontisa Angeliki and the sisters of the monastery of Agio Konstantinos followed close behind. Delenda walked among the nuns, dressed in black, her head uncovered.

Antonios walked directly behind the bier, stoic but visibly shaken, clutching a single rose. Beside him, young Pothitos clung to his father's hand, his small face pinched with grief as he struggled to hold back tears. Every few steps, he glanced at the bier as if expecting his mother to rise and comfort him.

As the procession wound through the cobbled streets toward the church, townspeople joined, their sobs drowned out by the bells from churches across the island. Incense burned along the route, its smoke formed a veil over the mourners.

The arrival of emissaries from neighboring islands added gravitas to the occasion. Robed in the formal attire of their respective lands, they wore symbols representing their homes —a caduceus from Kos, two deer from Rhodes, and an eagle for Patmos. They joined the procession, their faces reflecting the deep respect Nomiki had commanded across the region.

The church's interior was bathed in the light of hundreds of candles, their flames flickering against the opaque windows. The bier was set before the altar, draped in black velvet. The congregation filled every corner, a sea of mournful faces, while outside, those unable to find room stood in respectful silence.

Father Dimitri began the service, his voice breaking the silence. The sweet fragrance of incense lingered as censers were lit throughout the nave, their smoke rising in plumes that mingled with the candlelight. This incense, a symbol of prayers ascending to heaven, enveloped the congregation.

"Kyrie eleison," Father Dimitri intoned, calling upon the Lord for mercy. The congregation joined in the chant, their voices rising and falling in waves, filling the church with deep sorrow for Nomiki's passing.

The service continued with the singing of psalms and hymns, their melodies soothing the congregation. The chanters, positioned near the iconostasis, sang the memorial hymns. The mournful lamentations conveyed that Nomiki's soul was now in God's care.

Father Dimitri approached Nomiki's body and censed the bier, the smoke curling around Nomiki's body— a final gesture of sanctification.

As the service drew to a close, Father Dimitri delivered a eulogy that captured the essence of Nomiki's life. "Nomiki was not only a devoted mother and wife," he began, his voice breaking, "but she was a servant of the Lord, living her faith through acts of kindness and charity. Her life was a testimony to the power of grace, and her love touched each of us here."

As Father Dimitri spoke, Pothitos looked up at his father, seeking reassurance. Antonios squeezed his son's hand and spoke, "Your mother loved you more than anything, Pothitos. She watches over us, even now." Pothitos felt a surge of emotions— pain and anger interwoven, clawing at his heart. The world around him seemed to whirl; the stability he had known with his mother's presence was now cruelly torn away. His mind reeled from his loss, and the finality of the funeral rites offered little comfort.

The church, usually a sanctuary of peace, now felt stifling. The prayers and hymns, meant to soothe, only dulled the edges of Pothitos's anguish. He tried to focus on his mother's peaceful figure lying before the altar, but his vision blurred, the edges darkening as a wave of dizziness washed over him.

Then, in his moment of utter disorientation, his eyes locked with that of the girl whose arrival had stirred quiet curiosity among the villagers. Her eyes, a striking shade of emerald, seemed to pierce through the fog of his emotions, enchanting him with a calm intensity.

Something unspoken passed between Pothitos and the Egyptian girl in those few seconds. The turmoil within him ebbed as if her deep green eyes were a balm to his frayed nerves, offering a tranquility he hadn't expected. Her look, full of understanding, conveyed a reassurance, soothing him.

As suddenly as it began, the connection broke when the girl looked away, perhaps aware of the depth of the link they had shared. Yet the moment lingered for Pothitos. A steady warmth filled him, in contrast to the tumult that had wracked him only moments before. He exhaled deeply and looked at his father, Antonios, who regarded him with concern. Pothitos squeezed his father's hand silently.

As the final prayers were spoken, the congregation stood together, their voices joining in the traditional Greek Orthodox funeral hymn, "Αἰωνία ἡ μνήμη" (Aionia e mnimin), meaning "May your memory be eternal." The haunting melody filled the church, evoking a profound sense of loss and eternal continuity central to the Orthodox faith.

The nuns led the hymn, their rich voices resonating deeply. The melody was a solemn chant, weaving through the mourners. The hymn spoke of remembrance and the soul's journey beyond this life, a reminder of the Christian belief in resurrection and eternal life.

"May her memory be eternal," the nuns sang, their voices backed by the deep ison from the chanter, holding them to the proper tone. The congregation joined in, each voice adding to the prayer, their words a tribute to Nomiki's memory.

As the hymn progressed, tears flowed freely among the mourners. Sobs occasionally broke through their singing as they invoked God's mercy and peace for Nomiki. The hymn's lyrics encapsulated their deep love and respect for her, as well as their prayers for her peace in the afterlife:

"Memory eternal, memory eternal,

may her soul dwell where the righteous rest."

The church sat in silence after the hymn concluded, the final notes fading with the chanter's deep ison. The power of their unified singing left a sense of peace among the congregation, as if their voices had carried some part of their sorrow away.

As the hymn faded, the priest stepped forward to give the final blessing, marking the end of the ceremony. The congregation gradually moved outside, where the final rites would take place. They slowly processed through the island's interior to the ancient Roman village of Damos, Nomiki's childhood home.

As they moved through the heart of Damos, the procession passed public fountains, their waters murmuring—a quiet backdrop to the steady, rhythmic beat of footsteps on cobblestone. The fountains, once places of lively conversation and laughter, now reflected the disheartened faces of the townspeople in their shimmering waters.

The route led them past the unused baths, imposing and silent structures. The usual hum of activity had stilled in respect for the day's task. Artisans and traders, who on any other day would be bustling about, stood with heads bowed as the procession passed the workshops lining the market. The clink of the blacksmith's hammer was silent; the weaver's loom paused mid-weave. Today, their crafts serve as a quiet tribute to the life that had touched every corner of Damos.

As the procession left the town center, the path grew steeper, winding toward the hills where the burial grounds awaited. Its silence punctuated by the high stone wall that had enclosed it for centuries. This hallowed ground, overlooking Damos, offered a final resting place, surrounded by the land's natural beauty, with hills gradually blending into the mountains in the distance.

Nomiki's burial site, veiled under the shade of ancient olive trees, held generations of her family. It was a revered spot where the roots of the trees and the family ran deep.

The grave was an open crypt, with sections designated for each family member. It was a dignified place, lined with stone and marked by simple plaques bearing the names of those who had passed. Today, it would receive Nomiki, adding another chapter to the family's history.

As was the custom, before Nomiki's body was placed in the crypt, the bones of her previously buried family members were carefully and respectfully exhumed. This practice, a part of the island's traditions, reminded the mourners of the connection between the living and the deceased, symbolizing the ongoing presence of the ancestors in their lives.

Each set of bones, wrapped in ceremonial cloths, was gently handed to the waiting family members. With solemnity, Antonios received the remains of Nomiki's ancestors, holding them with reverence. The scent of incense mingled with the earthy aroma rising from the open tomb as each family member took a moment to honor their departed loved ones.

Pothitos watched as his father and other relatives performed the tradition of kissing the bones. It was a gesture of respect and love, a personal farewell to each soul that had once animated the now-lifeless remains. After a moment of silent prayer, Antonios kissed Nomiki's father's wrapped bones and carefully placed them back into the deeper recesses of the crypt to make room for Nomiki.

Finally, it was time to lay Nomiki to rest. Ornamented with flowers and draped in a cloth embroidered with the family crest, her body was slowly lowered to rest among her ancestors' reinterred bones.

Standing beside Pothitos, Antonios once again placed his hand on his son's shoulder, squeezing gently. Together, they watched as each family member took a handful of earth and cast it into the open crypt, the soft thud of soil marking the finality of the burial. Suddenly, the overwhelming silence was broken by a shout from outside the graveyard walls.

"Antonios," thundered a callous voice.

The shouts of Halikos shattered the serene atmosphere. His arrival was unexpected and dramatic; he rode on a horse into the cemetery flanked by a cadre of armed guards, their presence unsettling against the backdrop of mourners dressed in black and gray.

Halikos, a man of imposing stature and stern demeanor, dismounted with a flourish, his cloak billowing behind him. His face was set in a mask of fury as he marched directly toward the gathered family by the gravesite. His voice boomed, cutting through the murmurs and the gentle rustling of the olive leaves.

"This ceremony must cease," Halikos demanded, his eyes scanning the crowd until they fixed on Antonios. "A curse has fallen upon us; brought by the girl you harbor in your lands. She is a graeae, a bringer of plague and death!"

The mourners recoiled, shock and confusion rippling through them as they absorbed the sudden intrusion and his accusations. Antonios, still by his wife's grave, turned to face Halikos, his grief momentarily overridden by a surge of protective anger.

"Halikos, you disrupt sacred ground at my wife's funeral," Antonios said, his voice steady despite the rising tension. "This is neither the time nor the place for such baseless accusations."

"There is nothing baseless about that beast; she brings doom to all who shelter her!" Halikos continued, pointing at the Egyptian girl. "I demand her surrender, lest the wrath she carries consume us all!"

The mourners around Antonios huddled in fear and uncertainty. The girl had indeed been a figure of quiet speculation, her arrival troublingly coinciding with the onset of the plague. Yet many had seen her gentle grace, which seemed at odds with the dark portrait Halikos painted.

Pothitos, standing beside his father, felt a rush of uncertainty. His memory of the girl's calming demeanor at the church returned to him, contrasting sharply with the violent accusations now hurled her way.

Father Dimitri stepped forward, raising his hands in a gesture of peace. "Regent Halikos, we are gathered here for a rite of passage, not in a court of blame. Matters of disease and death are for the wise to discuss in council, not for accusations in a time of grief."

Halikos glanced around, staring harshly at the mourners, many of whom looked away, their discomfort tangible. "Then let it be known," he declared loudly, "that the hospitality you extend to this harbinger of doom will bring you nothing but sorrow and ruin. If I must, I will take this matter into my own hands. I will not allow the safety of one cursed child to outweigh the lives of many."

The mood pulsed with apprehension as he strode toward the girl, who stood slightly apart from the mourners, her figure fragile against the backdrop of grave markers and olive trees. The community members, still gathered around Nomiki's grave, turned their attention to the unfolding drama, their earlier sorrow momentarily eclipsed by a sudden sense of fear.

Halikos stopped just a few feet away from the girl, disdain on his face. With a swift movement, he drew his sword, the metal gleaming ominously under the overcast sky. The sharp sound of steel sent a shiver through the crowd, and a gasp rose from the onlookers.

Before Halikos could advance further, Gerontisa Angeliki stepped swiftly between him and the girl. Her presence, usually calm and peaceful, now formed a formidable barrier. She spread her arms wide, her eyes locked on Halikos's, her expression stolid.

"You shall not harm this child," the abbess declared, her voice carrying a surprising strength that broke the silence. "If you seek blood, you will have to strike me down first."

Standing just behind Gerontisa Angeliki, the girl clutched the nun's robes, her eyes wide with fear, yet fixed on Halikos as if trying to understand the source of this aggression. The standoff seemed to suspend time as the crowd gaped in silence.

A voice suddenly called out from among the onlookers filled with conviction. "The Lord will strike you down, Halikos, if you harm a hair on a servant of God!"

Halikos turned slightly to locate the speaker, a grim smile playing on his lips. "You forget, good people of Kastelli," he replied loudly, his voice dripping with contempt. "I serve the old gods, and it is the mighty Zeus who ensures my victory. Your Christian threats mean nothing to me."

Despite his words, the abbess's resistance and the crowd's growing defiance gave him pause. Their commitment to protect the girl presented a problem he had not anticipated.

Seeing Halikos's momentary hesitation, Antonios stepped forward, his fortitude hardened by the threat to the innocent child. "Halikos, look around you," he said, gesturing to the crowd. "These are your neighbors, your fellow leaders, united in protecting the innocent. Will you spill blood on this sacred ground against all moral law?"

The men stood face to face for a few anxious moments, Halikos's sword still drawn as his eyes scanned the faces of those arrayed against him. The grumble from the crowd grew, a chorus of disapproval filling the cemetery.

Finally, with a snort of disdain, Halikos sheathed his sword. "This is not over," he warned, his attention lingering menacingly on the girl before sweeping across the crowd.

With that, Halikos remounted his horse and rode briskly away, his guards following close behind, leaving a troubled crowd in his wake. The abbess turned to the girl, wrapping her in a protective embrace, while Antonios and the others gathered closer. They were fully aware that Halikos's retreat was not the end, but the beginning of a greater struggle.

Antonios knelt beside Pothitos, gently grasping his son's hands. "Do not fear, son. We will stand by what is right, as your mother always did," he pronounced, even as Halikos's ominous threats loomed over them.

Chapter 12

BEARING THE CROSS

In the weeks following his mother's funeral, Pothitos's daily life underwent a profound transformation. The once familiar rhythms of his days, filled with his mother's presence, were now consumed by heartache.

Antonios, despite his own sorrow, tried to fill the void Nomiki had left behind. After speaking with Father Dimitri, he made an effort to spend more time with Pothitos. Despite these attempts, Pothitos retreated into solitude, finding comfort in the quiet ramparts of the castle or the secluded garden paths where his mother had once walked with him.

Pothitos's sorrow often turned to despair—a gnawing ache that made the most straightforward tasks feel impossible. Once joyful under his mother's tutelage, his studies now felt hollow. The hand-scribed Bible they had read together lay untouched on the shelf as though waiting for her return.

In solitude, Pothitos sought comfort in nature—a connection his mother had nurtured in him since childhood. He spent hours in the gardens or wandering the edges of the cliffs, where the rustling leaves and birdsong gave him fleeting respite. But even in nature's peace, his bitterness ate at him, a turmoil he could not escape.

Pothitos's grief soon took new forms. His quiet sorrow gave way to bursts of anger and frustration, a drastic change from his boyish nature. He lashed out at those closest to him—his father, the household staff, even his friends. These outbursts were brief but fierce, leaving him guilt-ridden and more isolated than ever.

Antonios, deeply concerned about his son, asked Father Dimitri to hear his child's confession, hoping the priest could provide some type of guidance. Though reluctant, Pothitos obeyed, knowing his father hoped the priest's words could ease his pain.

Confession took place in the quiet of Kastelli's chapel, where the cool, quiet interior protected him from the outside world. Father Dimitri greeted Pothitos with his usual gentle smile, but his eyes were wise, noting the tension in the young boy's posture.

Inside the chapel, the atmosphere was tranquil. Candlelight flickered gently against the stone walls, illuminating the mosaics of saints that watched over this holy place. Father Dimitri stood near the altar, dressed in a simple clerical tunic.

"Pothitos," Father Dimitri addressed him warmly. "I am glad you have come. We are here to bring you peace and to help you heal."

Pothitos nodded, swallowing the lump in his throat as he approached a secluded corner of the chapel near a small icon of Christ Pantocrator.

Father Dimitri turned Pothitos to face the icon, as was the penitent's tradition, and said, "Let us begin."

The priest took his place slightly to the side of the boy. "When you are ready, you may speak your sins, and together, we will seek the Lord's mercy for healing and renewal," he instructed.

Pothitos silently stared at the icon of Christ, then averted his eyes.

"My child," Father Dimitri interjected, his voice inviting, "your heart carries a heavy burden. Confess to the Lord, and together we will seek His mercy."

Pothitos, standing stiffly, looked at the flickering candles on the altar. When he spoke, his voice carried an edge of bitterness that startled even himself. "What is there to say, Father? Talking won't bring her back. Nothing will."

"You're right," Father Dimitri said, his tone measured. "Words cannot bring her back. But they can help us find a way through the darkness."

"Pothitos, my dear boy, it is often in our darkest hours that we must cling to our faith the strongest," Father Dimitri continued. "It is like a lantern in the night, guiding us through our sorrow."

Pothitos shifted uncomfortably, refusing to look upon the image of Christ in front of him. When he finally spoke, his voice was laced with annoyance. "But why, Father? If faith is supposed to protect us, why didn't it protect my mother? Why am I left with nothing but this... anger?"

Father Dimitri nodded. "Faith does not shield us from loss or pain, Pothitos. It offers us a way to understand, accept, and, in time, find peace. Your mother's journey was hers, and your journey through this pain is yours. Both are held in God's hands."

"But where is my peace?" Pothitos's voice rose, trembling with emotion. "It's like a storm with no end."

The priest reached out, placing his sun-spotted hand over Pothitos's. "Peace comes slowly, often so slowly we do not notice its approach. You are in the midst of the storm now, but it will not rage forever. Let yourself feel this pain, Pothitos—it's the price of loving deeply."

Pothitos pulled his hand back, crossing his arms tightly as his eyes dropped to the icon. "Talking about it, praying about it—it doesn't change anything. She's still gone, and I'm still here. Alone."

Father Dimitri sighed, a soft sound of empathy. "Yes, she is gone from this world, and that is a truth you and many who loved her must live with. But talking, Pothitos, doesn't change the past—it shapes how you carry it forward. It can make you stronger, even when you feel weakest."

Pothitos was silent, his young face twisting as he fought back tears. Father Dimitri watched the faint change in the boy's posture—how his shoulders loosened, if only slightly—as he seemed to find a small measure of comfort in the words.

"Pothitos," Father Dimitri continued, his voice firm but kind. "There is a teaching in our faith about bearing one's cross. Each of us, at some point in our lives, must pick up and carry our cross. This," he said, pausing to look at Pothitos, "this sorrow you feel, the loss of your mother, is your cross."

"It may seem unbearable now," the priest continued, "and for good reason. The cross was not meant to be light. It symbolizes the challenges we face and the sorrows we endure. But remember, Pothitos, that carrying your cross also teaches you. It shapes you into the person you are meant to be."

Father Dimitri's bearded face leaned closer, conveying the seriousness of his message. "Your mother carried her crosses too. She did so with grace and strength. She taught you, loved you, and shaped you with her virtues. Now, this pain, this loss—it is your cross. How you carry it and move forward with it will define much of your life to come."

Pothitos raised his eyes, meeting those of the priest's. His voice was almost too soft to hear, "How do I carry it, Father? How did my mother carry hers?"

Father Dimitri smiled softly, his face full of warmth. "She carried it with faith, my child. With the belief that her struggles had meaning, that her life's challenges were not just obstacles but opportunities to grow closer to God. She found her strength in her love for you and your father, serving others, and trusting God's will."

He touched Pothitos's shoulder, giving it a soft pat. "You begin by doing what you are already doing—by recognizing the pain, letting yourself feel it, and then deciding to stand up each day, no matter how heavy it seems. And you will not be alone on this journey. Your father, your friends, this community, and I will help you carry this cross when you need us."

"When you are ready, you may speak your sins, and together, we will pray for forgiveness and guidance," Father Dimitri instructed with an air of finality.

Pothitos took a deep breath, his eyes turning to the omnipotent image of Christ Pantocrator in the icon. "Father, I confess that I have been angry, terribly angry, since my mother's death. I've spoken harsh words to those who only wished to comfort me, and I have very dark thoughts," Pothitos began, his voice trembling slightly with his admission.

Father Dimitri listened intently, his look one of understanding, without judgment. "It is natural to feel anger, Pothitos, especially in the face of such loss. What matters is recognizing these feelings and learning to rise above them."

"I know, Father, but it's hard. Sometimes it feels like the anger is all I have left of her," Pothitos confessed, his eyes filled with tears.

"This powerful anger is not the bond that ties you to your mother. Your love for her and her love for you—these are the true connections that endure," Father Dimitri responded.

"I also need to ask for forgiveness for doubting my faith and being angry with God during this time," Pothitos added, his voice now steadier.

"Doubt is but a part of the journey to deeper understanding. You are young, and your path to faith will have its trials. What is important is that you keep walking the path, keep seeking the truth," Father Dimitri reassured him.

Pothitos took a moment to gather his feelings. "I…I…also have dark thoughts… about the girl, Delenda. I can't stop thinking that maybe the rumors are true, that she is a graeae, the cause of all this evil. What if she must... what if she must die for us to be safe?" His voice trailed off, the implication of his words lingering.

Father Dimitri's countenance grew troubled as he listened to the young boy's thoughts. He paused for a moment, choosing his words carefully. "Pothitos, it is a dangerous path to let fear and rumor guide our actions. Like any of us, Delenda is a child of God, deserving compassion and justice, not condemnation without cause."

"But how can we be sure? How do we know she's not what people say she is?" Pothitos pressed on, his brow furrowed with confusion.

"Look to your heart, Pothitos, and to the teachings of Christ," Father Dimitri replied gently. "We are taught to love, not to condemn. We are taught to seek truth, not to surrender to baseless fear. Have you seen with your own eyes any act from Delenda that would warrant such dark suspicions?"

Pothitos shook his head, the conflict evident on his face. "No, Father, I haven't. But the timing of her arrival, the deaths..."

"Correlation is not causation, my child. It is easy to blame misfortune on the outsider, the unknown, but it is not the way of righteousness. We must guard against the darkness in our own hearts, the quickness to judge, the readiness to harm," Father Dimitri explained.

"What should I do, Father? I am lost, and these thoughts disturb my peace," Pothitos admitted, his shoulders slumped in distress.

"Pray, Pothitos, for wisdom and for peace. Find the truth through kindness and understanding, not through fear and suspicion."

As their conversation drew to a close, Father Dimitri retrieved a small, ornately embroidered sash—a stole used specifically for the sacrament of confession—and draped it over Pothitos's head, signifying the young boy's submission to God's mercy and the church's intercessory role in forgiveness.

"Pothitos, my son," Father Dimitri began. "The Lord, who pardons all your iniquities, heals all your ills, and redeems your life, calls us to repentance and promises mercy."

With the stole resting gently over Pothitos's head, Father Dimitri raised his hands in blessing and recited the prayer of absolution: "My spiritual child, you have made your confession to my humble person, although I, a humble sinner, have no power on earth to forgive sins, for God alone forgives. Nonetheless, we recall that after His resurrection, our Lord Jesus Christ said to His Apostles, 'If you forgive the sins of any, they are forgiven them; if you retain the sins of any, they are retained'; encouraged by these divinely spoken words, I am bold enough to say that whatever you have said to my humble and lowly person, and whatever you have failed to say, whether from ignorance, or forgetfulness, or whatever it may be, may God forgive you in this present age and in the age to come. May God Who, through Nathan the Prophet forgave

David when he confessed his sins; Peter when he wept bitterly for his denial; the harlot who shed tears upon His feet; the Publican as well as the Prodigal: may this same God forgive you, through me a sinner, everything both in this age and in the age to come; and may He make you stand uncondemned before His dread judgment seat. Through the grace of the Holy Spirit, through my insignificance, you have been forgiven. Having no further care for the sins you have confessed, go in peace."

As he spoke these words, Father Dimitri's hands moved in a deliberate motion, tracing the sign of the cross over Pothitos's head, marking the final act of the sacrament. This gesture was a seal of the forgiveness granted, and a blessing meant to strengthen Pothitos as he continued his spiritual journey.

"Go in peace, Pothitos, and may the grace of God guide your steps away from darkness and toward His eternal light," Father Dimitri concluded, his voice filled with an unshakeable conviction of God's enduring love and mercy.

Pothitos bowed, feeling the weight of the stole lift from his head as Father Dimitri removed it. Touched by the grace of the sacrament, he felt a renewed sense of clarity and purpose. With his heart lighter than when he had entered, Pothitos made the sign of the cross on himself, mimicking the priest's motions.

Pothitos quietly thanked Father Dimitri and was about to leave the chapel when the priest called him back.

"Tomorrow, your father will convene a council to decide on Delenda's fate," Father Dimitri informed him.

Pothitos nodded in acknowledgment.

"I'll be present at the council," the priest continued. "There will be a proposal for you to begin training as a Byzantine soldier, sending you to Constantinople for your education. However, I intend to suggest an alternative."

He paused briefly, ensuring Pothitos was attentive, and said, "I will recommend that you train here, under Longinus, and join the Ierí Frourá. In this role, you will grow to be trusted with the guardianship of the monastery and everyone inside."

Father Dimitri smiled sympathetically as he concluded, "Tomorrow, the council will also determine your fate."

Chapter 13

THERMA

The next day, the council convened at the Therma bathhouses, a site chosen for its neutrality, tranquility, and healing. It was a multi-hour trek across the arid island for Antonios and his entourage, and by the time they arrived, they were tired and hungry. The bathhouses, renowned across the region, were a masterpiece of Roman engineering. Heated by volcanic activity deep beneath the earth, their mineral-rich waters bubbled through intricately carved stone channels. Natural light streamed through high windows, illuminating the pools of varying temperatures and imbuing the ancient mosaics and stone columns with a serene glow. It was here, amid the soothing warmth of the springs, that the leaders sought to resolve the political tensions gripping the island of Kalymnos.

As the weary travelers approached, an opulent, obese man greeted them with a broad smile and a boisterous laugh. Aristides, the regent of Panormos, was well-known for his love of indulgence and his flair for ceremony.

Draped in a luxurious robe embroidered with golden threads, Aristides moved through the gathering with surprising grace for his stature. Rings set with vibrant gemstones glimmered as he gestured expansively toward the abundant feast. "Welcome, friends!" he called, his voice warm and rich, much like the wines he favored. "Come, partake of the earth's generosity! Here, no soul leaves unsatisfied."

The main structure of the bathhouse was supported by robust stone columns and arches, allowing the mineral-rich steam to waft freely through the large, open atrium. Now weathered with age, the mosaic floors still retained scenes of dolphins and sea creatures, recalling the legendary connection between the springs and the old gods.

An image of a mythical beast dominated the mosaic floor. From the waist up, the beast resembled a maiden. Her pale, haunting features were not unlike the foam of the sea. However, this semblance of humanity was a cruel jest; extending from her torso were six long, sinewy necks, each crowned with a dog's head, mouths bristling with rows of razor-sharp teeth. Below, her form dissolved into a mass of twisting, serpent-like tails, one of which coiled menacingly around a ship, snapping its hull in two.

Within the bathhouse, pools of varying temperatures invited visitors to immerse themselves in the ritual of transitioning between hot and cold waters. The streaming sunlight cast soft beams that danced on the rippling surfaces and suffused the space with tranquility. The atmosphere seemed to cause time to slow.

At the heart of this magnificent room stood a masterpiece of architecture: a central chamber that epitomized the elegance of the Therma bathhouses. Its walls, crafted from gleaming white marble, seemed to radiate purity. Every surface bore intricate carvings; delicate patterns etched with extraordinary accuracy into the stone. Marble pillars rose from the mosaic floor, their bases and capitals carved with motifs of vines, flowers, and fictional creatures. The reflection of the chamber in the water accentuated the marble's natural veining and lent the chamber a mythical quality.

At the center of the marble sanctuary stood a platform laden with the earth's bounty, a sight to delight any visitor fortunate enough to behold it. Silver trays and polished ceramic bowls overflowed with fresh and preserved fruits—figs bursting with sweetness, pomegranates glistening like rubies, and grapes hanging in lush, enticing clusters. Olives, freshly plucked from the island groves, gleamed in the soft light, accompanied by clay pitchers of olive oil and jars of golden, thick honey.

Nearby, bunches of dried nuts and dates waited to sustain weary travelers. Loaves of bread, baked with herbs and coarse salt, lay in neat rows alongside cheeses wrapped in fig leaves. For refreshment, pitchers of cool spring water, fragrant wine, and jugs of zythos stood within easy reach.

Bundles of Mediterranean herbs filled the air with an invigorating, comforting scent. Bay leaves, oregano, and thyme mingled with the soft fragrance of jasmine and lavender, producing a heady aroma that wove through the chamber.

Amongst this scene of abundance stood a fountain carved from alabaster. Its basin brimmed with clear spring water that bubbled gently over the rim and cascaded into smaller pools below. This tranquil trickle formed a calming soundtrack for the feast.

Antonios was the first to arrive, his face grim as he surveyed the gathering hall. Soon, others trickled in: Father Dimitri, representing the spiritual interests of the community; Anastasia, the astute governor of the neighboring island of Kos, her beauty rivaled only by her diplomatic prowess; Longinus, the commander of the Byzantine garrison; Angeliki, the head of the monastery of Agio

Konstantinos with Theophilos, the captain of the Ierí Frourá in tow; and representatives from each of the historical demes of Kalymnos. The only empty seat, conspicuously draped in Kalymian blue, was reserved for Halikos, the representative from Orkatou. His absence was more than a snub—it was a calculated act of defiance that left Longinus muttering about Orkatou's growing influence on the island. "He thinks himself untouchable," Longinus whispered, his tone betraying unease. "Mark my words, Antonios, this will not end here."

Aristides mingled among the guests as they arrived, gesturing toward the attendants serving the food and drink. The attendants, scantily dressed in flowing silks and delicate jewelry, moved gracefully among the visitors, pouring wine and offering trays of ripe fruits and fresh bread. Their warm and inviting smiles encouraged the guests to savor the carefully prepared feast.

Aristides directed the newcomers toward the tables with jovial enthusiasm, laying a firm hand on their backs and pointing out the most sumptuous displays. He took pride in describing each delicacy: "Try these figs—freshly picked! And the pomegranates? Sweet as the nectar of the gods!" His laughter was buoyant and contagious as he watched the guests savor each morsel.

Upon entering the opulent marble chamber, Father Dimitri and Gerontisa Angeliki could not ignore the sight of the scantily dressed servants moving among the guests. Their faces betrayed little of their discomfort, but their tightly clasped hands and exchanged glances spoke volumes.

Father Dimitri, robed in the austere black habit of his priestly office, surveyed the scene before lowering his eyes in silent prayer. His lips moved soundlessly as he prayed for patience and guidance. Walking with deliberate dignity, he avoided eye contact with the attendants who offered him fruit and wine.

Angeliki stood in her simple monastic habit as she regarded the attendants with quiet disapproval. Her usually calm face tightened slightly as she watched the attendants pour wine and pass trays among the guests. With a subtle nod, she gestured for Father Dimitri to join her in a more secluded corner of the chamber, where the two exchanged hushed concerns.

Aristides noticed their hesitation and approached them with his characteristic joviality. "Ah, Father Dimitri! Gerontisa!" he called, his belly quivering with laughter. "You look troubled, my friends. Why so melancholy? Tonight, we feast in good company, yes?"

Father Dimitri met Aristides's debauchery with patience. "These are dangerous times, Aristides," he said firmly. "A spirit of modesty would better reflect the seriousness of our meeting."

Angeliki nodded, her voice carrying authority. "We are here to discuss matters of grave importance. Perhaps the revelry could be tempered out of respect."

Aristides let out a hearty laugh, raising his arms in a gesture of mock disbelief. "But this," he said, waving toward the scantily dressed servants, "is all the rage in Athens! They say it shows progress, Father."

Father Dimitri maintained his composure, his eyes never moving from Aristides's face. "Perhaps Athens is not the best model," he replied. "Let us remember our higher calling and guide this council with virtue."

Aristides shrugged with an indulgent smile, his mirth undiminished. "Ah, well, I shall yield to your wisdom for now. But do take a fig, Father—it's as sweet as forgiveness!" With a flourish, he offered a tray of fresh figs, which the priest politely declined.

As the other guests relaxed and indulged in the plentiful wine, enjoying the soothing warmth of the baths, Antonios paced back and forth like a caged lion, clearly ill at ease. His intense stare was due to a mix of frustration and anger that left no room for amusement. He seemed ready to pounce on anyone who dared cross him.

Flickering lamplight skewed his features as he strode along the polished marble floor, his steps rebounding softly against the chamber's walls. Occasionally, he paused, glaring into the atrium where the guests basked in luxury and laughter before resuming his relentless pacing.

His hands alternated between being clasped behind his back and drumming against the hilt of his sword in nervous anticipation. The chatter and laughter that filled the room caused him increased angst. His eyes darted toward each burst of revelry, barely masking his impatience.

Now and then, Antonios halted, his head turning sharply as he assessed the chamber and its faces. His gaze swept across the room like a predator's, studying each guest for any sign of disloyalty or dissent. None dared meet his eyes for long, quickly looking away or nodding respectfully.

In truth, Antonios was not displeased with the purpose of the gathering but with the carefree atmosphere that pervaded it. The sumptuous feast, the wine, and the baths seemed to mock the seriousness of the council's decisions. This responsibility bore down on him, and he was eager to begin deliberations shaping the island's fate.

As his pacing continued, Aristides, still cheerful from the day's revelry, offered a cup of wine to the archon. Antonios waved him away impatiently, his countenance warning that now was not the time for merriment.

Aristides chuckled and retreated, leaving Antonios to resume his prowling. Despite the baths' warmth and the abundance of wine, a chill seemed to settle around Antonios as he continued to pace, tension radiating from him like a taut string ready to snap.

Aristides resumed orchestrating the scene like a maestro, ensuring every guest was satisfied before they visited the baths. He encouraged them to sample the spring water, honey, and cheeses, his enthusiasm making even the simplest fare seem extraordinary. He raised his voice above the murmur of conversation and the gentle splashing of the hot springs. "Friends, our feast is not yet over!" Aristides boomed, his deep tone carrying across the chamber. "Behold the final indulgence—a parade of delights to sate your every craving!"

At his command, a trio of young boys began strumming lyres as dancers emerged, swaying gracefully as they entered the marble atrium. Each carried a tray laden with colorful desserts— honey-soaked pastries glistening under the streaming sunlight, sweet almond cookies dusted with powdered sugar, and pistachios soaked in honey.

The dancers twirled and dipped, their movements fluid and elegant as they weaved around the steaming pools where guests soaked in the healing waters. Their flowing garments shimmered with every twist and turn, catching the light and showcasing the delicacies balanced on their trays. They steadied their burdens with practiced ease, using graceful gestures to present the desserts to the guests and encouraging them to reach out and taste.

Aristides watched the scene with delight, clapping his hands in rhythm with the dance and calling out, "Do not be shy! The finest of Panormos awaits your pleasure!"

The dancers performed provocative movements in front of the reclining guests, their hips swaying and arms undulating to the rhythm of the lyre. Their laughter intertwined with the soft music drifting through the air, creating an atmosphere of indulgence. Weaving in and out of the baths, the steam curled around their feet like tendrils of mist while the guests, wrapped in the warmth of the springs, clapped and cheered.

For many guests, this moment was the pinnacle of the day. They eagerly accepted the sweets, savoring the honey and almonds on their lips while the dancers continued their mesmerizing performances.

In contrast, Antonios moved to the recesses, his pacing slowing as he watched the dancers move among the guests. He seethed as he took in the spectacle, his impatience mounting. He knew the council would not be taken seriously amid such a display. The night drifted further from his envisioned purpose, and he was increasingly discontent with Aristides's elaborate festivities.

He turned to Father Dimitri, catching the priest's disapproving glance, and exchanged a brief nod of agreement. The revelry continued, oblivious to the tension building in the archon's chest.

At last, he could stand it no longer. He strode into the center of the chamber, his voice cutting through the room like a blade. "Enough!" The word rebounded off the marble walls, silencing the dancers mid-step. The music faltered, and the guests froze, their attention drawn to Antonios's face, marked with fury.

"Is this why we are here?" he demanded, his voice rising with each word. "To revel in decadence while our island faces division and peril. We did not travel from the corners of Kalymnos to be entertained like children or swayed by trivial pleasures!"

He walked slowly across the atrium, his eyes scanning the startled faces of the guests, who now sat in uncomfortable silence. "Our people look to us for guidance, for common sense, for unity. How can we lead them if we fail to conduct ourselves with dignity?"

He pointed directly at Aristides, who stood wide-eyed, startled by the sudden tirade. "Aristides, I understand your desire to please, but this display undermines the seriousness of our meeting. We are here to decide the fate of our island, not to indulge in fantasies. If we cannot focus on the task at hand, how can we expect the people to follow us?"

Antonios's words stung as the silence deepened, broken only by the faint ripple of water in the baths. The guests lowered their heads in shame, their earlier laughter and revelry replaced by an uneasy quiet.

Father Dimitri and Angeliki nodded in approval, their faces reflecting relief at seeing someone voice their discomfort. Aristides bowed slightly, his ordinarily genial demeanor now tempered by Antonios's scolding. Clapping his hands, he signaled the dancers to withdraw. They left the atrium swiftly, their trays of desserts abandoned at the table.

Antonios drew a deep breath, his chest rising and falling as he composed himself. He turned back to the assembled guests and said firmly, "Let us return to the purpose of this gathering. There is no time to waste. We have work to do and decisions to make."

The anxious atmosphere remained as Antonios convened the council around a long, polished table. Aristides, still visibly shaken by Antonios's reprimand, tried to compose himself, though his fingers tapped nervously on the table. Father Dimitri and the abbess near each other, their faces implacable, while the other regents shifted in their seats.

Longinus remained standing, his staff resting against the polished marble table. With a smooth movement, he unfurled a parchment before the council members. The edges of the document curled back with age. Delicate ink strokes formed a detailed script that carried the signature of Emperor Justinian.

Longinus cleared his throat, and the room fell silent. "There is one matter to address before we begin," he said. "With the passing of Nomiki, the deme of Mesos now falls under the rule of Antonios, as stated in the agreements between their families." He held up the parchment for all to see, the official seal of

Constantinople still intact. "This document confirms that Antonios is now the rightful ruler of Mesos and its surrounding territories."

A murmur spread through the chamber as the proclamation's significance set in. The deme of Mesos, a prosperous region rich in resources, sat strategically at the heart of the island. Its acquisition significantly bolstered any ruler's authority, and with it now under Antonios's control, his power was undeniable.

Aristides leaned back, his fingers interlaced over his belly as he digested this new reality. "Then it is settled," he said, nodding thoughtfully. "Antonios is now the most powerful man on the island."

Father Dimitri nodded solemnly. "This newfound authority comes with great responsibility. We trust you will rule with justice and forbearance, Antonios."

Anastasia regarded Antonios coolly. "Your influence is paramount now. The fate of Kalymnos hinges on your ability to unite the people during these troubled times."

Standing reverently at the head of the table, Antonios spoke with confidence. "I accept this responsibility with humility. Let this be a time for unity and strength. We must put aside our differences and work together to protect Kalymnos from further division."

Longinus rolled the parchment carefully and placed it back into its protective case. "The empire stands with you, Antonios," he said firmly. "Your authority is unquestionable, and together, we will secure the future of Kalymnos."

With that, the council acknowledged Antonios's newfound position, each member pledging their loyalty to the archon of Kalymnos. Antonios addressed the tense room, "We have come here to discuss the actions of Halikos, who disrupted the sanctity of Nomiki's funeral and threatened a child under our protection.

Such behavior cannot be tolerated if we are to maintain the peace and order of our island. A suitable punishment must be decided."

Aristides leaned forward, tapping the table before speaking. "Halikos's actions were troubling, yes, but we must acknowledge that many believe Delenda to be a witch—a graeae. Her presence coincided with the outbreak of disease, and rumors have spread like wildfire. Some even believe she should be sacrificed for the greater good."

The sound of agreement coursed through the room as several regents nodded, acknowledging the fears and superstitions circulating among their communities. Aristides continued, "The people demand action, Antonios. They believe the girl has cursed us, and Halikos, for all his faults, has voiced their concerns."

Anastasia tapped her fingers thoughtfully against her chair's armrest before speaking. "You cannot ignore the will of the people. They fear Delenda's presence, and Halikos has used this fear to bolster his power. If you dismiss the rumors outright, you risk alienating those you seek to protect."

Father Dimitri shifted uncomfortably in his seat. "We cannot give in to superstition and barbarity. Delenda is but a child—innocent in all this. The teachings of Christ implore us to protect the most vulnerable among us."

Angeliki nodded in agreement as she spoke. "The girl sought sanctuary at our monastery. If we allow her to be sacrificed for the sake of unfounded fears, we condemn ourselves as well as the child."

Longinus spoke next, his tone authoritative. "A sacrifice will not solve our troubles. It will only divide our people further and give Halikos more power to sow dissent. Instead, we must hold Halikos accountable for his actions and ensure that the girl remains protected."

Antonios listened intently, his face inscrutable. When all the voices had been heard, he stood and exhaled momentarily before addressing the council. "I understand the fears of our people, but we must not let those fears lead us into error. Halikos will be absolved for his actions, as forgiveness is central to Christianity. In return, we will continue to protect Delenda. She will remain under the guidance of the sisters at Agio Konstantinos, and we will increase the numbers of the Ierí Frourá around the monastery."

He looked directly at Aristides. "We will address the fears of our people with common sense and education. They must see that Delenda is not the source of our troubles but a victim of them."

As the meeting neared its conclusion, Father Dimitri rose to make one final recommendation. The dimming light cast long shadows across the marble chamber as the priest adjusted his robes and addressed the council.

"In these uncertain times, the youth must be prepared to shoulder the burdens of leadership," he began, his voice steady yet earnest. "Pothitos, the son of Antonios and Nomiki, stands on the cusp of adulthood. He carries the blood of his parents and will one day lead with the insight and strength they embodied."

Antonios nodded slightly in acknowledgment, and Father Dimitri continued. "I propose that Pothitos be trained for the Ierí Frourá under the guidance of Longinus and Captain Theophilos. He will gain the martial skills, moral fortitude, and strategic acumen our island desperately needs through their tutelage."

Longinus listened thoughtfully as he weighed the proposal. After a moment of contemplation, he tilted his head in approval to the priest. "I will gladly accept this task. Pothitos shall receive my guidance and that of Captain Theophilos. The Ierí Frourá will instill in him the discipline and dedication required to defend our island."

Theophilos stood and pledged his support as well. "Pothitos will be trained thoroughly. He will learn the way of the sword, the shield, and the virtues that guide us."

Antonios said a silent prayer and crossed himself before saying, "I accept your recommendation, Father. Pothitos shall undergo this training and become a part of the Ierí Frourá."

Chapter 14

THE SACRED WATCH

The sun was still low in the sky as Pothitos approached the stone courtyard where the Ierí Frourá, the Sacred Watch, assembled daily. Situated outside the protective walls of the monastery of Agio Konstantinos, the training grounds overlooked the island's rocky terrain and the distant sea beyond. The monastery, a weathered but enduring structure, had stood watch over this section of the Kalymian coast for three centuries. The air here was filled with the scent of olive groves and wild herbs; the tranquil hum of monastic life clashed gently with the rhythmic drills of the soldiers.

Longinus awaited Pothitos's arrival as he leaned on his staff. His posture was stern, and the faint scars of old battles were visible across his weathered face. Beside him stood Theophilos, much younger but tapping his foot impatiently.

The Ierí Frourá was a carefully selected cohort drawn from the finest warriors of the Byzantine garrison and the household fighters of local demes. Veterans who had faced the savagery of war firsthand stood alongside younger men hardened by relentless training. They were a brotherhood, bound by trust and duty, dedicated to guarding the sacred sites of Kalymnos from marauding pirates and those who clung to forbidden beliefs.

Scattered across the island, these warriors held positions of strategic importance, ensuring that the most vulnerable and revered places were guarded against those who sought to pillage them. They were stationed in and around the monasteries, where monks and nuns sought solace. They kept vigil at the shrines and ancient churches, where relics of the past were safeguarded from those who would defile them. They stood as guardians at the fortified monasteries, where pilgrims came to worship, and along the coastal cliffs, where raiders often landed to plunder.

The Ierí Frourá served as a physical barrier and a symbol of faith in a time of fear and uncertainty. Their presence at these holy places reassured the people of Kalymnos that their heritage and beliefs would not be lost to the malice of those who worshiped the old gods.

Pothitos entered the training grounds, escorted by Antonios and Father Dimitri. The morning sun had only just begun to break through the haze when the men of the Ierí Frourá assembled just outside the walled courtyard of Agio Konstantinos, their armor glinting in the light. Pothitos looked on in wonder, his heart racing as he saw his new brothers-in-arms, each one clad in the distinct attire that marked them as the elite.

Longinus raised his staff, calling the men to attention. Their helmets, crafted from the finest steel, caught the first rays of sunlight, illuminating the engraved crosses that decorated their brows. White plumes rose proudly from the tops of their helmets, swaying gently in the morning breeze.

Their bodies were protected by lamellar cuirasses, the metal scales overlapping in complex layers that allowed strength and flexibility. The scales, made of iron and bronze, clinked softly as the men shifted. Each breastplate bore the engraved symbol of the cross. Their knees and shins were protected by greaves etched with religious symbols. Draped over their shoulders were deep blue cloaks fastened with gilded clasps shaped like crosses. Their capes billowed as the men stood at attention, the rich color contrasting with the earthy tones of the stone courtyard.

Each warrior carried a spatha at their waist, the double-edged blade honed to perfection. The hilts of the swords were inlaid with detailed carvings and inlays depicting saints and scenes from biblical battles, while the pommels bore the unmistakable emblem of the cross. The men also carried round wooden shields reinforced with metal rims and wrapped in leather. The shields had been painted with an image of the Chi-Rho standing out boldly against the polished wood.

In their other hands, many held spears with long, leaf-shaped heads that tapered elegantly to sharp points. The shafts were decorated with strips of fabric in the colors of the Ierí Frourá, their blue and white ribbons fluttering softly in the morning air. The cavalry warriors also carried barzoubas, a mace with spiked heads hanging from their belts. Every man had a small, curved dagger sheathed at his waist, the blades hidden beneath the folds of their cloaks.

Theophilos stepped forward, raising his sword in salute to the men. "Brothers," he began, his voice steady and commanding, "we stand here as defenders of the faithful, shields against the darkness. Your armor is your faith, and your swords are your conviction. Let no force of this world or beyond break your spirit."

With those words, the soldiers straightened, their chests rising with pride. Longinus raised his hand to command silence, and the courtyard fell into an expectant hush.

"Pothitos." Longinus's voice rang out, "you stand here today as a son of the demes Mesos and Pothaion, prepared to take your place among the Ierí Frourá. Your training will be arduous, but your spirit will be tempered by the fires of discipline."

He gestured to Theophilos, who stepped forward to address the young man. "Your mother, Nomiki, served this island with great courage. Your father leads with unwavering dedication. Your legacy is strong, but you must now forge your own path."

The soldiers surrounding them watched intently as Theophilos laid the flat of his blade on Pothitos's right shoulder. "The Ierí Frourá will challenge you, but it will also mold you into a warrior worthy of defending our lands."

Pothitos stood at attention as he listened intently. He felt a sense of pride swell within him as he moved to take his place among the Ierí Frourá, his eyes locked on the solemn faces of his fellow guards. But something else caught his attention from the corner of his eye—a faint movement that stirred among the shadows of the fig trees. Pothitos turned his head slightly, peering into the gloom beneath the tangled branches. There, amidst the shade, he noticed the familiar figure of the girl with emerald eyes.

She stood almost motionless, partially obscured by the leaves, staring intently at the assembled warriors. Her vivid and piercing eyes seemed to glow in the shade, like two jewels in the darkness. They held an enigmatic depth that sent a shiver down Pothitos's spine as if she were silently observing and understanding more than she let on.

Pothitos felt drawn to her momentarily, as if the intensity of her gaze compelled him to move closer. But then, Longinus's voice boomed through the courtyard once more, snapping his attention back to the other soldiers of Ierí Frourá. He straightened his posture, holding his spatha firmly in his grip, yet he couldn't shake the sense that those eyes were still watching him intently.

Antonios suddenly stepped forward, raising his son's face to meet his own. "Your journey begins here, my son. Listen well to Longinus and Theophilos, for they will guide you as you become a warrior."

After he spoke, the abbess stepped forward with a quiet grace. Her habit flowed gently in the morning breeze as she approached the assembly. The men instinctively parted to let her through, their eyes downcast in respect.

With her worn yet steady fingers, she grasped the cross hanging from her neck and spoke softly, her voice carrying through the courtyard like a breeze. "May the Lord guide you, child, in your steps as you stand against the darkness. May your heart remain righteous, allowing for discernment between good and evil. I pray your arms stay strong, wielding the sword in the defense of all that is good. For you will bear a solemn burden to protect these lands from those who seek to defile the holy."

She focused intently on Pothitos, who stood among his new brothers. She reached up and touched his head, her touch light. "Pothitos, son of Antonios and Nomiki, your journey has just begun. The memory of your mother will guide you, and the Lord will strengthen you in every step you take."

She raised her other hand over the entire Ierí Frourá; her palm extended as if casting an invisible shield of protection over them all. "In the name of the Father, the Son, and the Holy Spirit, may you guard this home of the faithful with unwavering courage. May your swords be the sword of the righteous, and may your shields be a refuge for those who seek shelter."

Gerontisa Angeliki then traced the sign of the cross in the air before them. "Go forth, Ierí Frourá, knowing that the grace of

God will protect you and guide your new brother's steps in every path."

With that, she bowed in silent prayer, and the gathered men responded with a unified murmur of "Amen." As the men departed for their posts, Pothitos prayed that he was ready for the challenges that awaited him.

As the assembly began to disperse and the men of the Ierí Frourá filed out to their duties, Pothitos glanced back toward the fig trees. The girl was gone, leaving only the gentle sway of the branches in her wake. The image of her glowing eyes lingered in his mind, creating an air of mystery over the courtyard as he prepared for the rigorous training ahead.

Antonios turned to leave, his cloak swirling gently around him. He had only taken a few steps when he heard the hurried patter of footsteps behind him. Turning back, he saw Pothitos running toward him, his sandals clapping softly with each stride.

With trepidation, Pothitos wrapped his arms around his father, hugging him tightly. The embrace was a final fleeting moment of youthful exuberance. Antonios held his son firmly, one hand resting on Pothitos's back and the other gently gripping the back of his helmet.

"Pothitos," Antonios said softly, his voice warm, "I love you, my son. I am proud of you, more than words can say."

Pothitos looked up at his father, eyes brimming with tears. He felt a swell of pride, hearing the much-needed affirmation from the man he respected most.

Antonios looked on the verge of tears, but holding his emotions together, he said, "The road ahead will not be easy, but you will make your own way with courage and honor."

Pothitos nodded, his chest swelling. "I will make you proud, Father."

"You already have," Antonios said with a smile, giving his son a final, reassuring pat on the shoulder before stepping back.

Pothitos turned to leave and join the Ierí Frourá, but the voice of Father Dimitri called to him. He turned back to see the priest standing in the shadows of the ramparts, his bearded face lined with concern.

"Pothitos," Father Dimitri began softly, "did you see the girl in the shadows…beneath the fig trees?"

When Pothitos hesitated, the priest's tone grew graver. "You must protect her. There are whispers, superstitions, but I sense she has a role to play—one that others may not understand. Be vigilant, my son."

Pothitos looked confused. "But Father, why not tell the others?"

Father Dimitri sighed, a deep crease forming at the edges of his lips. "Because not everyone can be trusted. I fear that some among us may have different motives, shrouded by fear or ambition."

He paused for a moment to make sure they were alone. "You can trust Longinus and your father—they have your best interests at heart and understand the importance of protecting the innocent. But be wary of others, for their purpose is not clear. They may not share the same vision for the girl's future or understand her significance."

Pothitos nodded slowly, Father Dimitri's words sinking in.

The priest continued, "Some within our ranks, despite their vows, might choose to harm the child under the pretense of protecting the monastery. They see her as a threat, a possible graeae, due to the superstitions that cloud their judgment."

Pothitos became conflicted as he absorbed the priest's words. He hesitated before responding, his voice laced with uncertainty. "Father, I admit that I am also torn. The girl... I've seen nothing but innocence in her, yet whispers and rumors seed doubt. How can I protect her when I am unsure of her nature? How can I be trusted to do what is right?"

Father Dimitri replied gently, "Pothitos, it is precisely your ability to question and to feel this conflict that reassures me. True discernment comes not from blind certainty but from grappling with doubt and acting rightly despite it."

Father Dimitri continued, "I trust you, not to be certain, but to watch carefully, to protect diligently, and to judge wisely. You must guard the girl from those who might misinterpret their duty as license to do harm. Watch over her, Pothitos, as if the very balance of our society depends on it, because it just might."

Father Dimitri continued as he smiled slightly. "I have complete confidence in you to see beyond the shadows of doubt and to do what is right. Trust in yourself as I trust in you."

Pothitos understood that he now bore a responsibility not only to the Ierí Frourá but also to protect the girl from those who might wish her harm.

"Will you do this for me, Pothitos?" Father Dimitri asked.

Pothitos looked the priest in the eye and nodded firmly. "Yes, Father. I will watch over her."

Father Dimitri smiled, a flicker of relief crossing his face. "Good. May the Lord guide your steps, my son. And may He grant you wisdom and strength."

With that, Father Dimitri gave a silent blessing over Pothitos and turned to leave. Pothitos stood for a moment, taking in the priest's words and knowing that he had a crucial role to play in the uncertain times ahead.

Chapter 15

THE ANKH AND THE CROSS

Every morning at the Monastery of Agio Konstantinos, the deep, sonorous toll of the bell broke the dawn's stillness, summoning Delenda and the other nuns to morning prayers. As Delenda joined the procession, the cool stone beneath her sandaled feet grounded her in this new ascetic life. Warm sunbeams streamed through the brisk air, brushing her face with a glow that softened the chill of the stone.

She moved quietly, her steps tapping softly in the vaulted space as she slipped into her usual place among the rows of nuns. Frescoes of biblical scenes adorned the domed chapel ceilings—their vivid saints and angels seemed to watch over the gathered sisters with penetrating eyes. As she settled into place, the sound of Byzantine chants filled the room.

The chants, sung in unison, enveloped Delenda in a tapestry of sound. Though the words were unfamiliar, their rhythmic rise and fall stirred something deep within her; a fragile connection to this new world that offered her a strange peace. It was as if the chants spoke a language beyond words, coaxing her spirit to awaken.

As she stood there, the ornate censers behind the altar released a blend of frankincense and myrrh. The rich, aromatic smoke curled upward, mingling with the faint sunlight, creating a play of light and darkness.

The smell of the incense was rich and heady, adding an atmosphere of timelessness to the chapel. It evoked a sense of spirituality, as if the smoke carried with it the prayers and confessions of those who had knelt here before. For Delenda, the scent was comforting, tying her to the familiar fragrances of Egypt.

The physical sensations, combined with the spiritual ambiance of the chants, forged a complex emotional landscape within her. Here, the thoughts of her past mingled with the promise of her present, where the gods of her old beliefs seemed to linger in the back of her mind as her faith was tested.

After the morning service, Delenda followed the line of nuns as they moved silently from the chapel to the refectory for their first meal. The refectory was a stark, functional room with low ceilings and long wooden tables arranged in perfect symmetry. The only sounds were the soft rustle of habits and the muted clatter of wooden bowls and spoons.

As Delenda settled into her place, she couldn't help but notice the contrast between this silent meal and the lively, raucous feasts of her past—filled with laughter, music, and conversation. Here, the quiet was deliberate, a space reserved for reflection rather than celebration.

Delenda picked up her spoon, her movements tentative as she stirred the barley in her bowl. The soft thud of wooden spoons on bowls seemed unnaturally loud in the stillness, and she paused, suddenly self-conscious. Around her, the other nuns ate with calm faces, embracing the silence as part of their daily discipline.

Noticing Delenda's hesitation, Sister Smaragda, seated nearby, offered her a gentle smile. "It is difficult to find comfort in the silence," she spoke, her voice barely audible. "Each meal is a chance for reflection. We listen, not to words, but to our thoughts, to the sounds of life, and to God."

Even after some time at the monastery, Delenda struggled to swallow the first few bites. The food remained bland, and she spent more time staring at it than she did eating it. Her feeling of isolation grew daily as she sat in silence, deprived of the familiar chatter, the boisterous noise, and the laughter that had once accompanied her meals at home.

Delenda felt an urge to break the silence—a word, a laugh, anything. But the disciplined atmosphere and the rows of the silent sisters restrained her. She felt alone in her discomfort, despite being surrounded by others.

As she pushed the food around in her bowl, trying to muster the will to take another bite, she became acutely aware of the noise within herself: her thoughts racing, tangled with confusion, homesickness, and creeping doubt about whether she could truly adapt to this life.

Sister Smaragda noticed her discomfort again and gently touched her arm. "I was like you when I first entered the monastery," she said, her voice full of understanding. "It takes time to adjust, but one day, this silence will soothe your spirit." Delenda nodded, grateful for the reassurance, and slowly resumed her meal. With each tentative spoonful, she turned her focus inward, trying to appreciate the food's simple nourishment and use the silence as a path to clarity.

As the sun warmed the earth, Delenda followed Sister Maria to the monastery gardens, a sanctuary bordered by stone walls. The morning air was crisp, infused with the scent of dew-soaked earth and budding flowers. At the neatly tilled plots, Sister Maria handed her a small trowel, its handle worn smooth from years of use. Their task was to plant seeds—a simple act that carried deeper spiritual meaning.

The soil was cool and slightly damp under Delenda's fingers, a harsh contrast to the sun-kissed air. She knelt beside the garden beds, carefully pressing small indentations in the earth with her trowel. Beside her, Sister Maria reached into her apron pocket and handed her a mustard seed.

Delenda held the tiny seed between her fingers, marveling at its potential—small and unassuming, yet brimming with the promise of life. Sister Maria watched her thoughtfully. "These seeds, like us, need time to grow," she said. "And like them, we must be nurtured. We plant them now, not knowing when they'll sprout, but we care for them patiently. It teaches us faith and patience—qualities the soul needs to flourish."

Delenda carefully placed the seed in the indentation and covered it with soil. The simple act resonated with her. She felt like the seed—buried in unfamiliar ground, reliant on care and time to grow in this strange, silent world.

As they planted, Sister Maria spoke of the monastic view of life's cycles. "Just as these seeds will grow into plants and bear their own seeds, we are part of a greater cycle," she said. "Our lives, our actions—even our thoughts are seeds we plant in the gardens of others. Each one bears fruit according to the care we give it."

Delenda listened as her hands followed the steady cadence of her daily chores. Sister Maria's comparison of gardening and spiritual life deepened her appreciation for this simple way of living, where even the smallest acts were filled with meaning.

"The garden teaches us many lessons," Sister Maria said, pausing to wipe sweat from her brow. "Notice how each plant needs different care—some thrive in sunlight, others in shade. Just as plants differ, so do we. Each of us needs something unique to grow in spirit. In our community, we nurture each other's strengths and support one another's struggles."

The lesson struck a chord with Delenda. In her former life, she had often felt like a plant struggling to grow in barren soil. Now, in this unfamiliar place, she wondered if the soil here might offer what she needed to flourish—in ways she had never imagined.

By the time they planted the last seed, the sun hung high in the sky. Delenda stood, brushing dirt from her knees as a sense of peace settled over her. Now it was time for her reading and writing lessons.

In the quiet afternoons at the Monastery of Agio Konstantinos, Delenda joined Sister Alexandria in the scriptorium—a room where shelves held ancient scrolls and manuscripts filled with centuries of knowledge. Pale light filtered through the musty room, illuminating dust motes that danced lazily in the air. Ink pots, quills, and parchment lay scattered across the heavy wooden tables, lending the space an air of chaotic learning.

Sister Alexandria, a scholarly nun with a deep respect for the written word, guided Delenda through her lessons. That afternoon, as they sat at a heavy oak table covered in scrolls and loose vellum, Sister Alexandria began with the fundamentals of the Greek alphabet.

"This is alpha," she said, her finger tracing the shape of the letter on a scrap of vellum. "Can you write it?" Her voice was encouraging, her eyes watching Delenda attentively.

Delenda leaned over the vellum, her hand trembling slightly as she held the quill. The ink felt heavy on the tip, and as she mimicked Sister Alexandria's movements, her initial strokes were hesitant. But as she progressed, her confidence grew, and soon the letter alpha stood somewhat crookedly on the page. "I never knew letters could hold so much power," she admitted, looking up at Sister Alexandria with awe.

"They do," Sister Alexandria responded with a nod, her eyes twinkling. "Each letter, each word, is more than a sound or a mark. They are the vessels of thought, history, and the soul. And through them, you may create a new way for others to see the world."

Encouraged by Sister Alexandria, Delenda dipped her quill into the ink again, this time with less trepidation. As they moved through the letters, forming syllables and then words, Delenda felt as though she was unlocking a secret language.

Sister Alexandria then selected a scroll from the shelf, one of the scriptures, and laid it out before them. "Now, let us read together," she suggested, pointing to a line. The script was elegant but complex, and Delenda followed along as Sister Alexandria read aloud.

The words they spoke were about faith, love, and charity. Themes that transcended the boundaries of all ethnicities and touched the core of her existence. As they discussed the text, Delenda understood how these ancient teachings could relate to her own life experiences and struggles.

"Words are bridges, Delenda," Sister Alexandria explained as they tidied up the scriptorium. "They connect us to the past, to others, and to ourselves. Here, in this monastery, they help us connect to something greater than ourselves." With those words, the bells rang for Vesper Service.

The bells of the Monastery of Agio Konstantinos tolled again, calling the nuns to gather for the Vespers Service. This evening prayer marked the transition from day to night, a time to reflect on the day's work and to seek spiritual guidance in the presence of the Lord.

Delenda, alongside the other nuns, made her way to the chapel, a space transformed by the fading light of dusk. The setting sun no longer illuminated the narrow windows, and in their place, candles were lit, their flames small but fierce against the encroaching darkness.

As Delenda took her place among the younger nuns, she felt a tentative sense of peace settle over her. The familiar chanting of the Vespers Service began, and she joined in, her voice a quiet addition to the chorus of prayers. The Greek phrases, though still somewhat unfamiliar in parts, flowed more easily from her lips.

The service was structured around a series of psalms and hymns, each selected for its themes of protection, guidance, and the beauty of creation. The nuns' voices melded into a single, harmonious current of sound, rising and flowing through the vaulted space like a river of devotion.

As the chanting continued, Gerontisa Angeliki moved through the aisles, swinging a thurible that released curling clouds of incense. The sweet, resinous scent filled the air, mingling with the warm glow of candlelight to create an otherworldly atmosphere.

Delenda found herself deeply moved by the interplay of light and dark, scent and sound. The candles, with their flickering flames, seemed to her like bonfires of hope in the darkness, their light a symbol of the enduring presence of God even as night fell.

Her fingers found their way to the familiar ankh hidden beneath her robe. A wave of anxiety washed over her. She wondered if any of the nuns noticed her gesture, and if they did, what they made of it. Did they see it as a rejection of their teachings? A sign of her divided loyalties? The potential for misunderstanding haunted her, eclipsing the peace she sought in her new spiritual environment.

After Vespers, Delenda wandered the monastery grounds, the cool night air brushing against her face. Tonight, the abbess joined her, sensing her unease.

"You are far from home, child," the abbess said softly. "And yet, I sense you are searching for a home in spirit—here, among us."

Delenda paused as she looked to the horizon where the dark sea met the moonlit sky. "I miss my home," she said, her voice trembling. "The people, the temples… even the gods I used to pray to. But here, there's… something. I don't know what it is yet, but I feel like I'm beginning to find a home."

Gerontisa Angeliki nodded, understanding Delenda's feelings. "That is good," she responded warmly. "Faith is not about forgetting where you come from. It's about carrying your past with you as you walk the path to where you are meant to be."

Encouraged by Angeliki's words, Delenda took a deep breath, the cool air filling her lungs. She hesitated, her fingers brushing the ankh beneath her robe, then spoke in a voice barely above a whisper. "Gerontisa, I still wear this," she admitted, drawing out the looped cross on its cord. The faint moonlight caught the polished metal, making it glint softly. "I worry what the others would think… if they saw me reach for it."

The abbess listened intently, her eyes reflecting the moonlight, wise and patient. "My child, your journey here is yours alone—it is not for others to judge the steps you take, nor the pace at which you take them," she advised. "This symbol represents a part of your history and your connection to a life that has shaped you just as much as the life you are making here."

"I pray that one day I can carry the cross you wear," Delenda murmured.

"Faith, my child, is like a cross," Angeliki said. "It is not a mere adornment, nor is it always a comfort. More often, it is a weight we choose to carry—a burden we bear willingly because it shapes who we are."

Delenda listened intently, the silhouette of the cross atop the chapel visible in the distance, a reminder of the truths she sought but had not yet fully embodied.

"The cross we bear can sometimes chafe, weigh us down, or even bring us pain. But it is also a source of strength, a constant reminder of our commitment to walk a path of righteousness and love," Angeliki continued, her hands clasped in front of her as if holding an invisible cross of her own.

"This monastery, this life of prayer and service, is our way of bearing that cross. Each of us has come to it by different roads, and we each feel its pull differently," she said, glancing toward the chapel. "And just like the physical cross worn by many around their necks, the spiritual cross we carry is not meant to be hidden away. It is a sign of our journey, visible, not as a mark of burden, but as a badge of courage and devotion."

"Thank you, Gerontisa," Delenda said softly, her voice steadier now. She let her hand fall from the ankh, feeling an ease come over her.

Gerontisa Angeliki nodded, the faintest smile softening her lined face. "Go in peace, Delenda," she said. "Bear your cross with dignity—it is within you, even now. Let it guide you as you grow into this life, as you find your place among us, under God's watchful eyes."

Delenda stood in the garden as Gerontisa Angeliki's footsteps faded into the stillness. The monastery's moonlit walls rose around her, blending with the vast darkness of the night. She reached again for the ankh but stopped halfway, letting her hand fall. Instead, she turned toward the chapel, where the distant cross stood silhouetted against the stars.

Chapter 16

FORGED IN FAITH AND STEEL

Pothitos trained under the vigilant eyes of the Ierí Frourá. Their encampment was strategically placed outside of the monastery to maintain the nuns' cloistered peace. This separation was a daily reminder of their duty to protect without intruding on the sanctity of monastic life. The physical distance underscored their role as silent watchers, ensuring that the prayers of the nuns were never overshadowed by the harsh realities of martial existence.

Each day at the break of dawn, Pothitos and his fellow recruits assembled in the clearing that served as their training ground—a natural amphitheater bordered by rough cliffs that amplified the clink of their swords and the stern commands of their leaders. Under the guidance of Theophilos, the tactician, Pothitos was instructed in the art of warfare and the virtues of faith.

The mornings started with a series of intense physical drills designed to push the recruits to their physical limits. Theophilos, who believed that the body's endurance was a mirror of the spirit's resilience, supervised these sessions with a critical eye. The recruits, clad in light armor, would line up for sprints, their feet kicking up dust as they raced across the rough terrain. Afterward, they tackled obstacle courses—climbing wooden barriers, crawling under nets, and moving under the strain of their armor, which made every movement a challenge.

After morning calisthenics, climbing exercises followed. The rocky facades surrounding their camp provided the perfect challenge. Pothitos, his hands and feet finding purchase on the rough surfaces, learned to conquer his fear of free-climbing the dangerous cliffs. The climb became a mental battle against the instinct to look down or doubt his grip.

As the day progressed, the focus shifted to mastering Byzantine weapons. The clang of metal rang out as Pothitos and his peers practiced with the spathion—a heavy, double-edged sword requiring both strength and exactness. Manolis, their weapons master, demonstrated proper stances and techniques, emphasizing balance and the fluidity needed for controlled strikes.

Manolis, known for his formidable skill and demanding methods, helped shape new recruits into defenders of the empire's sacred sites. Burly and broad-chested, with muscular arms forged by years of wielding Byzantine weapons, he carried himself with an intimidating presence. His sun-darkened skin and thick, grizzled beard completed the image of a fearsome instructor. When his calloused hands were not holding a weapon, he could be found twirling a bagledi made from polished goat horns.

Despite his intimidating presence, Manolis's eyes showed a mischievous intelligence, especially when joining in the sparring matches against the younger recruits. He moved with surprising agility for a man of his size, which made him even more formidable.

As the weapons master, Manolis was responsible for the training of all recruits in the handling of traditional Byzantine weapons. His knowledge extended beyond melee weapons to include archery and the use of the akontion, a javelin favored for its effectiveness in small skirmishes.

His teaching style was direct and unforgiving, relying on learning through doing. He often threw recruits into grueling drills without warning, barking, "The battlefield doesn't afford the luxury of time!" Yet, for all his harshness, he was deeply committed to his recruits' safety and success, ensuring they mastered the skills needed to protect themselves and the treasures they were sworn to guard.

Next came training with the kontarion, a long spear essential to Byzantine infantry. Pothitos practiced thrusting and parrying with the spear, learning to move in sync with his fellow recruits as they formed a phalanx—a formation designed to break enemy lines while shielding its soldiers.

In individual combat drills, Pothitos learned the importance of positioning, agility, and accuracy. Manolis, who personally oversaw his training, often reminded him, "A soldier's strength lies not just in his weapon, but in reading his opponent. Each battle is a conversation—you must listen with your eyes and respond with your sword." Relentless practice honed Pothitos's ability to anticipate his sparring partners, exploit openings, control the duel's rhythm, and conserve his strength for decisive strikes.

Training intensified when the recruits were organized into formations, mirroring the tactical group battles they might face. Theophilos led these drills, focusing on the phalanx—a formation that harked back to ancient times but remained highly effective.

"Unity is strength," Theophilos would declare as he paced in front of the rows of shielded men. "Together, you are a fortress; divided, you are merely stones waiting to be toppled." During these drills, Pothitos learned how his role fit into the greater whole. Each shield guarded not only its bearer but also his neighbor, while their spears created a bristling wall of defense against cavalry or infantry.

Afternoons were punctuated by shouted commands from their instructors; each call driving recruits to perfect their form. The metallic clang of spathions clashing against training shields and the whoosh of kontaria slicing through the air created the soundtrack for their training.

Their preparation extended beyond the physical. Evenings brought lessons on the empire's history, the significance of their sacred duties, and discussions on theological virtues, led by Stavros. He stood as a poignant figure among the monks and recruits of the Ierí Frourá. Despite his advancing years, Stavros's stature retained the vigor of his warrior days, and he moved with the calm assurance of a man commanding respect. His presence reflected a seamless blend of the monastic and the martial, a transition from soldier to scholar-monk.

Stavros bore the scars of past battles—witness to his years in service to the Byzantine Empire. His most striking feature was his left eye, clouded and blind from a skirmish on the eastern frontiers. The injury ended his military career but marked the beginning of his spiritual journey. Despite this, his remaining eye was sharp and perceptive, often giving the impression it saw more than two eyes could. His once-dark hair had turned silver and was tied in a knot behind his head, in the typical monastic style. His gray beard, thick and unruly, framed his stern yet wise features.

Stavros wore the plain robes of a monk, which belied the disciplined strength still coursing through his broad shoulders and sturdy frame. A rope belt hung around his waist, holding a small, worn leather pouch of cherished scriptures. His voice, though softened by age, carried the resonance of a born leader. It was this voice that drew the recruits to him, eager for his stories and lessons—a blend of historical chronicles, theological insights, and philosophical musings.

Each night, Pothitos and his fellow recruits gathered around the central fire, their sweat-soaked tunics replaced with clean robes. The camp's atmosphere shifted from the intensity of combat training to honing their knowledge. Here, Stavros took center stage, molding the minds of the recruits with knowledge, just as their bodies had been sharpened with swords and spears.

He began each session with lessons on the Byzantine Empire's rich history—its emperors, territorial expansion, and the pivotal battles that shaped their civilization. He spoke of Constantine the Great, who founded Constantinople and established Christianity as the empire's religion, and of Justinian the Great, whose current reign was marked by the reconquest of former Roman territories and the codification of Christian law.

These historical lessons were not mere stories—they were reminders of the legacy the Ierí Frourá was sworn to protect. "We are the heirs of this history," Stavros often said, his voice soft in the twilight. "Our swords defend not just land, but our empire's story. Each stone, each relic at the Monastery of Agio Konstantinos and beyond, is imbued with the divine. You are the wardens of more than places; you guard the cornerstones of our faith."

Stavros shared stories of past incursions—sacred texts desecrated, holy sites defiled—emphasizing the constant threat from those who sought to undermine the Christian order. "Your vigilance safeguards our spiritual heritage," he told them.

As the night deepened, Stavros guided the discussion to the theological virtues each guardian must embody. "Faith, hope, charity, justice, prudence, temperance, and fortitude. These are not mere ideals," he said, his voice steady. "They are the pillars upon which you must build your lives as guardians."

He also spoke of the balance between justice and mercy; the strength found in temperance, and the courage required to maintain fortitude in the face of adversity. "You are the bridge between heaven and earth," Brother Stavros reminded them. "What you do in service of the Watch reflects upon you in heaven. You must uphold the legacy that has been entrusted to us through the ages to ensure an unbroken lineage from the Apostles to each of the faith's hierarchy."

As the days unfolded into months, Pothitos grew into his role, the rigorous training molding his body and the spiritual teachings shaping his mind. He found camaraderie that extended beyond drills and sparring, standing shoulder to shoulder with four other recruits from different regions of Kalymnos, all united by a solemn duty to the Ierí Frourá.

There was Georgos, a robust and quick-witted archer from the neighboring island of Pserimos, known for his strategic acumen. Alongside him was Domianos from Mesos, the hometown of Pothitos's mother, a swordsman whose quiet strength and thoughtful demeanor belied a fierce commitment to their cause. Then there was Yiannis from Panormos, whose vibrant personality and prowess in close combat brightened the rigors of their daily regimen. Lastly, there was Panormitis, an outcast from Panormos and Orkatou. Being the illegitimate child of Aristides and a Christian slave belonging to Halikos, he was shunned by the other young soldiers.

Pothitos, Georgos, Yiannis, and Domianos formed a close-knit brotherhood, united by challenges and respect for each other's position in life. However, integrating Panormitis into this tight group was marked by tension and suspicion that simmered beneath the surface of their camaraderie.

Panormitis, a quiet and thoughtful boy, excelled in defensive tactics and scripture. He was raised in hiding by his mother until he became old enough to join the Ierí Frourá. As a child in Orchiros, his mother's conversion to Christianity made him an outcast. Here, his presence at the camp was viewed with distrust, especially by Pothitos, who harbored a deep-seated suspicion toward anyone from that side of the island.

Suspicion lingered during group exercises and strategy sessions. Though Panormitis's suggestions on defensive formations were often brilliant, Pothitos and the others resisted his input, questioning his loyalty and motives. "How can we trust someone whose own people disowned him?" Pothitos muttered to himself.

That evening, the air at the training camp buzzed with excitement for the upcoming simulated night raid. The recruits gathered around Stavros, who outlined their mission calmly. As they huddled together, each member's personality brought a distinct energy to the group.

Yiannis, ever the life of any gathering, clapped his hands together with a grin. "Let us show them what we're made of!" he roared. His enthusiasm was infectious, bolstering the spirits of the group.

Georgos, taking the lead as usual, began assigning roles with an authoritative tone. "Pothitos, flank on the right with me. Yiannis, your energy will serve us well at the front. Domianos, cover our rear," he directed, each order thoughtfully placed to suit their strengths.

Panormitis stood slightly apart, observing the initial formation layout sketched in the dirt with a stick by Georgos. The lines and arrows indicating their movements seemed too rigid and offered no flexibility to adapt. Panormitis spotted a potential flaw that could leave them vulnerable to an ambush.

Clearing his throat gently to catch the attention of his peers, he stepped forward, pointing to a section of the diagram. "If we adjust the rear guard to fan out slightly wider," he began, his voice carrying a careful inflection to avoid sounding too assertive, "it would give us a better chance to react to any flank attacks. It's a more dynamic defense... allows us to pivot faster based on where the threat materializes."

His suggestion hung in the air as all eyes turned toward him. Pothitos, already skeptical of Panormitis, narrowed his eyes slightly, his glance shifting between the proposed change in the diagram and the man who suggested it. The rest of the team, though initially hesitant, looked on with curiosity, weighing the merits of the strategy against their preferences.

Georgos, also a strategist at heart, bit his lip as he considered Panormitis's words. He stepped closer to the diagram, tracing the current formation with his finger before considering the adjustments Panormitis had suggested. "Show me," he said finally, a single phrase that granted Panormitis not just the floor but a tentative trust to elaborate.

Panormitis, encouraged by Georgos's interest, crouched down beside the diagram. With a small branch, he began adjusting the lines, his movements concise. "By expanding our rear guard like this," he explained, his finger drawing arcs that suggested a more spread-out approach, "we cover more ground and reduce the risk of being outflanked. It also puts us in a stronger position to counterattack if we're pressed."

Pothitos frowned, muttering, "I, for one, do not trust this outcast." Though quiet, his words didn't escape Stavros's sharp glance.

Without a word, Stavros pulled him aside and said, "Remember, Pothitos, a soldier's worth is measured by his actions, not his past. Wisdom often comes from where we least expect it—watch and learn."

A bell sounded as the last daylight faded, plunging the training grounds into darkness. Only the intermittent glow of torches lit the perimeter. The recruits crouched in their positions, hearts pounding, senses sharpened by every rustle of the night breeze.

Panormitis, stationed with Georgos at the center, watched the shadowy tree line where the 'enemy'—their instructors—waited.

As minutes ticked by, the recruits moved slowly toward the tree line, watching for any signs of the assault. But it materialized not from the front as expected, but from the left flank. A group of instructors, smeared in camouflage and moving with stealth, emerged from the darkness, aiming to exploit what they believed was a vulnerable spot in the recruits' defense.

Panormitis's voice was calm but urgent as he quickly relayed instructions to Yiannis and Pothitos, who were positioned nearest to the threat. "Shift left, reinforce that side. Remember the drills—cover and move, cover and move!"

Panormitis's strategic placement of the forces prevented the recruits on the left flank from becoming isolated. As the 'enemy' approached, thinking they had the element of surprise, they found themselves facing a well-prepared defense.

Pothitos and Yiannis moved quickly, repositioning themselves to form a tighter, more formidable line. Shouts rang out, and wooden swords clashed against shields, their sounds filling the night air. Instead of buckling under pressure, the young soldiers remained staunch, their movements synchronized and deliberate.

At a critical moment in the drill, Panormitis signaled to Yiannis and Pothitos. The two feigned a retreat, stumbling back as if overwhelmed by the 'enemy's' advance. The move lured the instructors deeper into what they believed was a crumbling line.

The retreat was a calculated maneuver orchestrated by Panormitis. As the instructors advanced, expecting an easy victory, they were suddenly outflanked. Domianos, who had stealthily circled the battlefield, burst from his cover in a perfectly timed flank attack. His swift and silent approach caught the instructors completely off guard.

The sudden counter maneuver threw the 'enemy' into disarray, their formation breaking under the unexpected assault. Wooden weapons clashed loudly against shields as the recruits pressed their advantage. The instructors, seasoned warriors, quickly recognized the recruits' strategy. Pinned by the feigned retreat and encircled by the flank maneuver, they had no choice but to concede. Acknowledging the effective execution and the clear victory it had secured for the recruits, Stavros raised his hand, signaling the end of the exercise.

The field fell silent, broken only by the heavy panting of the participants in the cool night air. Exhilarated by their success, the recruits gathered around Panormitis, clapping him on the back and praising his leadership. Even Pothitos, who had doubted him, nodded and offered a reluctant pat on the back. "Seems I was wrong about you. Good job tonight."

Panormitis smiled faintly, his demeanor remained steady despite the praise. "We all bring something different to the table. Together, we are stronger."

Stavros watched the exchange with a knowing smile, pleased to see respect taking root among the recruits. "You see," he said, his one good eye twinkling in the firelight, "judgment often obscures truth. True warriors judge their comrades by courage and heart."

Chapter 17

DRUMBEATS OF WAR

Shortly after Pothitos arrived for training with the Ierí Frourá, the tranquility of the monastery was shattered when Halikos arrived at the gates. The peaceful atmosphere gave way to the jarring clang of armor, as rumors of impending conflict spread like water seeping through the cracks in stone, filling the monastery's halls.

Halikos arrived with fifty soldiers, their presence menacing against the monastery's timeworn walls. Their dark armor gleamed like obsidian, and their steady march sent the sound of boots striking the earth reverberating through the courtyard—a drumbeat of war.

The creaking gates swung open, and Theophilos strode out, flanked by his own men. The look on their faces betrayed their sense of purpose, though the younger recruits showed flickers of apprehension in their eyes. Theophilos stood tall, his broad shoulders and steady gait cutting a commanding figure as he advanced to meet Halikos in the open courtyard.

Halikos's voice cut through the air like a blade. "Theophilos," he said with authority. "You stand in the way of the inevitable. This monastery—and the fiend within—will be mine. Stand aside, and no blood will be spilled today."

Theophilos took another step forward, his hand tightening on the hilt of his sword. "You overestimate your reach, Halikos, and underestimate our determination. The Ierí Frourá will defend this ground—and all within it—with our lives. You will not pass these gates."

The soldiers on both sides tensed, hands gripping weapons, ready for the command to engage. Though greater in number, Theophilos's men seemed unnerved by the hardened warriors facing them.

Pothitos stood near the back of the recruits, his hands clammy against the smooth wood of his spear. His stomach churned. His training flashed through his mind like fragments of a broken mosaic—stances, drills, maneuvers—but none of it seemed enough. In that moment, the lessons he'd struggled so hard to master felt like paper shields against the iron tide of Halikos's force.

Halikos took a step forward, his hand tapping the pommel of his sword. "You are a fool, Theophilos," he growled, his voice laced with menace. "This is your last chance. Surrender or face the consequences." His soldiers shifted behind him, their shields rising slightly in unison.

Theophilos drew his sword, the blade slicing through the air as he raised it in defiance. "We will not yield—not now, not ever. If it is a fight you seek, then a fight you shall have."

Suddenly, the heavy gates of the monastery creaked open once more, and from within emerged Gerontisa Angeliki, accompanied by Aristides. Her calm demeanor silenced the courtyard as effectively as any weapon.

"Now, now, gentlemen," Aristides calmly called out. "Must we always meet like this? Surely, there is more that unites us than divides us."

Halikos and Theophilos turned to face him, their weapons still drawn, but their bearing remained cautious. The soldiers held their positions tentatively.

Aristides continued, "Here I was, pledging my people's allegiance to these devoted sisters, only to find you two squaring off yet again." He let out a low chuckle, but the warmth in his tone carried an undercurrent of authority.

"Halikos and Theophilos," he said, spreading his hands as though to unite them. "You two are ever at odds. But we are fellow countrymen, not barbarians. We're all sons of Kalymnos, and we all want what is best for our island. The blood of our countrymen should not be spilled here—not today."

Aristides's words seemed to have an immediate effect on Theophilos. Theophilos had always taken pride in his ties to Panormos, his homeland, and the thought of brotherhood with his fellow countrymen stirred something deep within him. His grip on his sword relaxed, and he nodded in agreement. "Aristides speaks wisely," he said steadily. "We are stronger together than apart. Perhaps there is a way to find common ground."

Halikos, though still cautious, was intrigued by the unexpected intervention. "And what do you propose, Aristides?" he asked, his tone less aggressive but still guarded.

Aristides grinned confidently. "I propose we sit down and discuss our grievances. There is much we can accomplish if we work together. The island is facing threats from beyond our shores, and we cannot afford to be divided."

The abbess nodded in agreement. "Let us seek a path of peace and cooperation," she urged. "For the sake of our people and our future."

The strain in the courtyard eased as the leaders considered the proposal. The soldiers, sensing the possibility of peace, began to lower their weapons, though their posture remained alert.

Aristides continued, his words painting a vision of camaraderie. "We all have a stake in this land. Let's ensure its prosperity and safety by standing together. What say you, Halikos?"

Halikos, after a moment of contemplation, slowly sheathed his sword. "Very well," he conceded. "Let us talk. But only us three men. No need for the peace-loving sisters to attend. Know this, Aristides—my trust is hard-earned and easily lost." The keen edge in his words lingered, a warning beneath his agreement.

Theophilos, seeing an opportunity for peace, followed suit and sheathed his own weapon. "I am willing to listen," he said. "For the good of our people."

Aristides looked kindly at the abbess and asked, "Is there somewhere peaceful where the three of us— Theophilos, Halikos, and I—could meet alone?"

Gerontisa Angeliki's response was gruff, her eyes fixed sharply on Halikos. "Anything for a chance at peace," she said. "I will show you the way and leave you to discuss matters best settled among men."

From his vantage point, Pothitos watched the leaders disappear into the monastery, his body still coursing with adrenaline. The standoff had shown him how fragile peace could be, and how the actions of men like Aristides might decide the fate of their land. Despite his distrust of Halikos, Pothitos soon realized that whatever was discussed that day behind closed doors led to seven years of peace amongst the people of Kalymnos.

Chapter 18

TWO PATHS, ONE HEART

Time at the Monastery of Agio Konstantinos flowed with a stillness that seemed untouched by the chaos of the outside world. It was the year 545 AD, and across the Aegean, rumors of war and the aftershocks of the great plague stirred unease. But here, in this cloistered haven amongst the cliffs of Kalymnos, the tolling of bells, the rustle of robes, and the unchanging rhythm of prayer and labor marked life. For Delenda, the weeks stretched into months, and the months into years, each dawn was heralded by the same chimes summoning her to matins. At first, the monastery felt alien to her—a place of strange tongues and stranger customs. Yet, over the next seven years, the unfamiliar chants of the nuns softened into melodies she deeply revered.

Delenda's transformation from stranger to familiar face in the monastic community deepened. In her free time, she found herself drawn to the gardens, where thyme and oregano perfumed the air, and only the hum of bees broke the silence. Over time, the

Greek tongue, once a clumsy stranger to her lips, became as natural as the prayers she spoke at dawn. Her accent softened, her speech grew sure, and when she chanted the Akathist Hymn in harmony with her sisters, her voice carried the same intonation as theirs.

In the dimly lit scriptorium, where the faint scent of ink and parchment mingled, Delenda's hands worked steadily, tracing the elegant arcs of the Greek alphabet. These letters, which had once seemed indecipherable symbols, now flowed from her quill with grace. "Alpha… beta… gamma," she murmured under her breath, the rhythm of the words soothing. Each stroke of her quill was a bridge to the ancient scholars of Constantinople and the Desert Fathers whose words filled the monastery's libraries. Sister Alexandria, seated nearby, often paused her own work to watch Delenda with pride as her student transcribed passages from Coptic to Greek.

Despite her growing integration into the community and her acceptance of its rituals and language, Delenda's identity remained a muddled pool of her past and present. The ankh necklace, a slender loop of silver that hung discreetly around her neck, lay against her skin—a constant reminder of her roots and the life she had once known. It was more than a totem; it was a bridge to her past, to the memories of her homeland and the gods of her ancestors, which she was not ready to abandon entirely.

Her attachment to the ankh occasionally drew curious looks from the other nuns, but most had come to accept this aspect of Delenda as part of the mystery that surrounded her arrival. Even in her acceptance of new beliefs, Delenda represented a confluence of faiths—a living example that belief was an individual journey.

In the afternoons at Agio Konstantinos, the monastery's bells would chime the hour for daily Vespers. Delenda, dressed in her coarse robe of unbleached wool, made her way along the stone paths. She walked quietly to the chapel, her robe brushing against the herbs and flowers of the garden, and Pothitos, momentarily released from the duties of the Ierí Frourá, joined the community for prayer. Their glances would meet fleetingly, an unnoticed exchange amidst a sea of bowed heads.

These encounters were brief but electric, charged with an intensity neither dared to fully acknowledge. On the eve of the celebration of Saints Constantine and Helen, the amber light of dusk spilled through the chapel's narrow windows as Delenda and Pothitos entered the narthex to light their candles. The flickering glow of the flames streaked across their faces as they placed their candles into the white sand. When their hands brushed—so briefly it might have been accidental—a spark ignited in Pothitos's chest, a startling flutter of his heart. His breath caught, his cheeks flushed, and though he quickly withdrew his hand, his eyes locked with hers. Delenda's faint smile, poised and knowing, held a confidence that left him momentarily unmoored. That moment was a shared secret, delicate yet unspoken, that deepened the bond between them.

In honor of the celebration of Saints Constantine and Helen, the soldiers were invited to a communal meal held outside of the monastery gates. As the congregation dissolved into the quiet hum of the evening, Sister Maria's attention fell on Delenda and Pothitos. The soft interplay of glances between them did not escape her notice. After the meal ended and the nuns cleared their wooden plates, she placed a firm but gentle hand on Delenda's arm and drew her aside. Her voice, low and steady, carried the insight of decades spent in service. "Your heart is heavy, child," she said. "Remember, peace comes in many forms, and sometimes the gardens we wander are secrets even to ourselves. Trust what the Lord reveals in His time."

Delenda nodded slowly, shifting her attention to where Pothitos stood. She blushed and lowered her eyes as she caught his glance. Sister Maria smiled and said, "The monastic life is not for everyone, my dear. Sometimes we must follow our hearts."

While Delenda found peace in the rhythms of monastic life, Pothitos's days were a storm of discipline and sweat. His training with the Ierí Frourá left little room for idleness. The sharp clang of swords filled the training grounds each morning as he sparred beneath the stoic watch of his superiors. Shouted commands mingled with the coarse laughter of soldiers; their camaraderie forged in the fires of grueling drills. Yet, even among this brotherhood, a shadow of unease lingered. Whispers surfaced during moments of rest, carried like smoke on the wind. "The foreigner," some muttered, their voices low as they cast sidelong glances toward the monastery. "What gods does she serve? And why does she still wear that pagan token?" Though no one dared to speak openly against her, their words reached Pothitos all the same, stirring a quiet anger he could not easily quell.

Despite the murmurs of distrust among his comrades, Pothitos often recalled the words of Father Dimitri, spoken on the morning of his assignment seven years ago. The elder priest had stood before him in the quiet shade of the monastery's gates, his weathered hands clasped over his staff. Father Dimitri had said, his voice firm yet kind, "You must guard the girl from those who might misinterpret their duty as license to do harm. Watch over her, Pothitos, as if the very balance of our society depends on it, because it just might."

Father Dimitri's charge had taken root in Pothitos's conscience like a seed planted in fertile soil. Each test of martial skill during training bolstered his determination to be the shield Delenda might one day need. But protection, he realized, was not just a matter of guarding against visible threats. Suspicion, though silent and insidious, could wound just as deeply. Pothitos remained attuned to the undercurrents surrounding her. Yet, his vigilance was not born solely of duty. Over the years, his watchfulness had deepened into something more—an unspoken emotion that he dared not name but could not deny.

His attraction to the girl did not go unnoticed. Some soldiers respected his preoccupation. Others, however, viewed it with skepticism, wondering if the growing bond between him and Delenda clouded his judgment. These suspicions added a layer of complexity to his life there, challenging him to navigate the fine line between personal feelings and professional duties.

As the sun set each day, Pothitos found himself reflecting on Father Dimitri's words. He understood protecting Delenda was more than a duty; it was a test of his own integrity. In the quiet of the evening, when the clash of swords had faded, and the chants of evening prayers drifted from the chapel, Pothitos felt the pressure of his responsibilities settle around him like a cloak. He knew his actions could either bridge the gap of misunderstanding around Delenda or widen it, and he was determined to lead with honor.

Amongst the rumors of suspicion, there were moments of grace when Pothitos's and Delenda's paths crossed. In the dim stillness of the chapel, as soldiers and nuns bowed their heads in prayer, or in the fragrant expanse of the monastery's gardens, their brief interactions created a mosaic. Over the years, each passing glance was like a small pebble—together, they formed a masterpiece.

During these seven years, the monastery's gates often creaked open to welcome travelers; pilgrims seeking blessings, merchants delivering supplies, and emissaries bearing news from distant lands. Yet, among these visitors, none came as often or with such purpose as Antonios. But time had left its mark on the once vigorous leader. His broad shoulders now bore a slight stoop, and threads of silver wove through his dark hair. His stride, though still steady, had slowed, and his countenance carried the toil of years spent navigating both political turmoil and personal sacrifice. Yet his spirit remained unbroken, his mind sharp with the clarity of a man accustomed to seeing through the fog of doubt. His visits seemed to bring an air of urgency, as though some unseen storm gathered beyond the monastery's hills.

On each visit, Antonios and Pothitos walked along the monastery's pathways, the sounds of chirping birds rising in the warm air. These strolls, though fatherly in appearance, were often filled with troubling news. Antonios spoke of the unrest spreading across Kalymnos and the surrounding islands. Drought and failed harvests had fueled a quiet rebellion in neighboring Leros, which threatened to spill over to Kalymnos. Threats of defection to the old gods had grown louder, stoked by Halikos, who promised the rebellious salvation through the forgotten ways.

"They say the Christian God has abandoned them," Antonios said one evening, his voice laden with frustration. "And some… some point to Delenda as the cause. They call her a sign of God's displeasure." His words lingered in the air, and though Pothitos said nothing, his hand instinctively tightened on the pommel of his sword.

Pothitos walked in silence beside his father, the faint crunch of gravel underfoot filling the spaces between Antonios's words. He understood the precarious balance his father maintained—not just in defending the people, but in keeping Kalymnos from tearing itself apart. A leader's burden, his father often called it. But this was no simple political unrest. The whispers of rebellion were laced with something far more volatile: fear. Fear of Delenda, fear of what she represented, and fear of change. And as Pothitos rubbed the hilt of his sword under his palm, he could not help but wonder how long the peace on the island would hold.

"It's not just about faith, Baba," Pothitos replied, his own experiences at the monastery lending him a unique perspective.

"It's about fear. People fear what they do not understand, and Delenda... she's different. They do not see how she has grown, how she has accepted our ways. They only see what they are told by Halikos."

Antonios nodded as the setting sun painted his aged features in hues of amber and gold. "Yes, fear is a powerful tool, and Halikos wields it with a cunning hand. But we must stand firm, my son. We must show them that there is strength in our faith, that it can withstand storms and doubts."

As they turned back toward the monastery, Antonios's footsteps slowed as he finally came to a conclusion. "Perhaps it's time I address the people," he said, half to himself. "Remind them of the promises we've made—not just to protect our own, but to honor those who walk the path of transformation as well. Delenda's journey is not a threat. It is proof of what faith can do. If they could see what I've seen, the strength she's found, the devotion she's shown..." His voice trailed off, thoughtful. "But words will not be enough. Actions, my son. They must see us act with honor, even when they do not."

Another frequent visitor over the years was Longinus. Ever the stalwart figure, the warrior was a constant reminder of the dedication and strength required of those who served within the Byzantine Army. His visits, though draped in the warmth of familiarity, carried undercurrents of pressing concerns. As a trusted figure whose experience spanned not just military exploits but also deep political insights, Longinus brought with him not only news from the sprawling reaches of the Byzantine Empire but also exotic treats and curiosities from Constantinople, which he shared generously.

Lengthy discussions held behind the thick stone walls of the monastery's private chambers marked each of Longinus's visits. These meetings, attended by Father Dimitri, Stavros, Angeliki, and, increasingly, Delenda, were intense and hushed. Longinus, usually a man of stoicism, showed signs of concern during these gatherings. His shoulders tensed as he unfolded maps across the table and spoke of reports of unrest and political shifts that threatened the stability of regions vital to the Empire.

One morning, Pothitos was surprised when Longinus and Antonios showed up at the gates of the monastery together. During this visit, they walked through the quiet gardens. The air felt stagnant that day, as there was no wind, and the scorching Mediterranean sun beat down on their heads. Their ears were filled with the distant sound of the nuns' chants, and the faint aroma of incense could be detected rising from the chapel.

Longinus broached the subject of Delenda with tactful grace, his voice low. "Pothitos, your dedication to your duties has never been in question," he began. "Yet, there are musings among the other soldiers—concerns regarding your attentions toward Delenda. She has indeed grown into a woman of considerable beauty and grace."

Antonios nodded in agreement. "She is beautiful, no doubt, and her spirit has a strength that is rare," he added. "But remember, she has not yet taken the sacrament of baptism. She remains outside our faith officially, and this can complicate matters, especially given her past and the superstitions still lingering about her."

Longinus clasped his hands behind his back, pausing to let his words sink in before continuing. "Your role, Pothitos, is to be a guardian of all things sacred, both the relics and the people within these walls. Any perceived favoritism, especially toward someone whose status among us is still... delicate, could undermine your authority and the trust placed in you by the community."

Antonios looked toward the monastery's chapel, where a sliver of light escaped onto the path. "And there are those who might view your closeness to Delenda as crossing a line—a line that not only defines professional boundaries but also touches upon the deeper, more contentious currents within our community."

Pothitos listened intently, his respect for both men showing. The warning was clear, and he began to grasp the broader implications of his actions. "I appreciate your guidance," he replied earnestly, his voice calm despite his turbulent emotions. "I assure you both, my commitment to my duties remains absolute. Delenda's welfare is indeed among my responsibilities, but I will remain vigilant in maintaining the balance required of my position."

Longinus gave a slight nod, satisfied with the young man's response. "That is all we ask, Pothitos. Remain vigilant and remember that your actions reflect not only on your honor but on the stability of our entire community."

As they continued their walk, the conversation shifted to other matters of state and strategy, but the words exchanged flittered out of Pothitos's mind as his attention was suddenly drawn elsewhere.

The sky, a clear expanse moments before, grew gradually quiet. Unnatural dimness crept across the heavens, as though an unseen hand were drawing a veil over the sun. The warmth of the day drained away, replaced by a sudden chill that prickled along the skin. The gardens, so alive with light and color moments before, fell into an eerie half-darkness, their shadows stretching unnaturally long. Even the birds fell silent, the absence of their voices magnified by the faint, rhythmic crash of waves against the distant cliffs. Unease spread throughout the monastery, the nuns pausing mid-step to stare at the darkening sun, their faces pale and tense. The air felt drained of life—an impending doom that all could feel.

Antonios stopped mid-sentence, his eyes also lifting to the sky. His voice, when he spoke, carried a note of dread. "The heavens themselves mark this day," he said. "Such signs are rare, and in our ancestors' times, they were seen as portents. We must consider what message is being sent to us."

As the darkness blotted out the sun, a sudden, piercing scream penetrated the supernatural silence, echoing off the monastery walls and cascading through the valley. The birds took to the sky in a cacophony of panic, their screeching calls adding to the sense of disarray.

Longinus, standing a few paces away, turned his head slightly and spoke a single word, "Delenda."

Chapter 19

BENEATH A BLACKENED SUN

The serene atmosphere of the monastery, already strained by the darkening of the sun, disintegrated further once news of Delenda's disappearance spread through the corridors and courtyards. The rumors spread quickly throughout the monastery, each retelling creating a greater sense of fear amongst the sisters.

Pothitos felt a cold dread wash over him as he caught snippets of hushed conversations about Delenda. Sister Maria was said to be the last to see her, just as the sun was eclipsed by the moon. Without a second thought, Pothitos bolted toward Sister Maria's quarters, his boots striking the cobblestones in a frantic rhythm. Grim possibilities swarmed his mind, each one more disturbing than the last. Longinus and Antonios followed close behind. Normally calm and deliberate, Longinus now limped at an unsteady, urgent pace, struggling to match the desperate speed of Pothitos.

Sister Maria intercepted the trio near the sanctuary, her voice trembling. "Brothers," she began, bowing her head slightly before continuing. "Delenda is missing. The last time I saw her was just as the sun was plunged into darkness. She was with three young soldiers. Their haste was strange, and Delenda… she was silent. Something felt wrong."

Pothitos felt a surge of panic, his heart sinking. "Which soldiers? Speak clearly," he responded quickly.

"They were Panormitis, Georgos, and Yiannis," Sister Maria replied, her hands wringing nervously at her sides.

Without a moment's delay, Pothitos raced off. The sound of his steps seemed to beat in time with his racing heart, each thud a drumbeat of dread.

Longinus and Antonios, struggling to keep up, fell behind. "We must find her quickly," Longinus said breathlessly.

"This disappearance under such strange circumstances—as the sun darkened—it is no mere coincidence," Antonios murmured.

As they moved through the corridors, time seemed to stand still, the usual sounds of prayer and daily life drowned out by the burst of the activity. The nuns stepped aside as the trio made their way through the monastery.

When Pothitos reached Delenda's quarters, the sight that greeted him confirmed his worst fears. The door stood ajar, and inside, the room bore clear signs of struggle. A chair lay overturned, a shattered vase littered the floor, and Delenda's Ankh—its clasp broken—lay discarded nearby. Pothitos's eyes swept the scene, cataloging every detail. Then his eyes froze upon a faint trail of blood leading toward the door, suggesting a struggle that had spilled out of the room and into the corridors. His mind raced with possibilities, each more disturbing than the last.

The blood trail led to the scriptorium. The air was thick with the scent of incense and a faint, underlying trace of something metallic—blood, perhaps—a smell that seemed entirely out of place. Pothitos felt a tightness in his stomach as he prepared for the worst. The fear of what he might discover battled with his duty to remain ready for action.

He drew his spatha as he slowly opened the door to the scriptorium. The sight that befell them was chilling. The foreboding smell of copper suffused the atmosphere. The room lay upended, scrolls scattered across the floor with pots of ink strewn across the parchment, blotting out the once pristine letters. The black ink merged with deep red blood, forming a swirling pattern on the floor. Amongst the pooling blood, Yiannis lay motionless on the floor, his uniform stained crimson, his throat cut by a brutal, decisive strike.

As Pothitos stood stunned, staring at the ghastly scene, Longinus moved calmly toward Yiannis's body. Kneeling beside the fallen soldier, he carefully checked for any signs of life. His fingers, steady despite the chaos, pressed against the cold flesh of Yiannis's neck, while his ear strained for the faintest sounds of a breath.

Longinus's face remained impassive, but his quick, methodical checks conveyed no hope of survival for the fallen soldier. After a moment, he sat back on his heels, his complexion paling with the finality of his findings.

"There is no heartbeat," Longinus said gravely, rising slowly. His eyes scanned the room for any clues that might explain the violent episode.

He stared at Pothitos, his look conveying sympathy. "We need to secure this area and search for Panormitis and Georgos immediately," he stated authoritatively.

"Panormitis took her... Georgos must have gone after them," Pothitos murmured.

Longinus declared, "The sun darkens, and blood is shed in a monastery. This is blasphemy. We must hasten. We need to find Delenda."

The sun had already reemerged from behind the moon as Longinus, Pothitos, and Antonios began their search through the rugged landscape that bordered the monastery grounds. Challenging terrain, including steep inclines and rocky paths, wound through thorny wild shrubs and native olive trees. The trio moved cautiously, their eyes scanning for any sign that might lead them to Panormitis.

The trail they followed was subtle, almost imperceptible at times. It was Longinus, a skilled tracker, who first noticed the irregularities on the path—slight disturbances in the underbrush and broken branches that suggested someone had passed through recently, and with haste. Pothitos, fueled by anger, kept close behind them.

As they ventured further, the path led them to a more secluded area, where the foliage began to thin. As Longinus pushed the underbrush aside, he revealed a cave entrance partially concealed by overhanging rocks and thick branches. The dim entrance looked menacing, a contrast to the open sky behind them.

Longinus paused, signaling for quiet. He whispered to Pothitos and Antonios, "This could be it. Stay alert." His voice carried a note of caution.

They approached the cave slowly, their senses heightened. The air grew cooler as they neared the entrance, the musty smell of damp earth and stone emanated from within. Pothitos felt a chill of anticipation and dread at what they might find inside.

Longinus took the lead, drawing a small blade from his belt. He used the sharp edge as a tool to part the thick webs that veiled the entrance.

The trio moved further into the cave and the dim interior slowly came into view. It was larger inside than they had expected, with natural columns of stone supporting the rough ceiling. As they approached, the muffled sounds of labored breathing reverberated faintly from within the dim recesses of the cave. Longinus signaled for quiet. They moved deeper into the cavern, beyond where the last vestiges of light reached. Antonios halted abruptly, his boot catching on something soft. Letting his vision adjust to the darkness, he saw Panormitis sprawled on the cave floor, his uniform in tatters. He lay there, savagely beaten, fading in and out of consciousness.

"Panormitis!" Pothitos's voice bellowed angrily through the cave as he spotted the injured soldier. He rushed forward, his initial relief at finding Panormitis, quickly overtaken by fury. "What have you done? Where is Delenda? Tell me!"

Panormitis, pale and barely coherent, tried to focus on Pothitos's looming figure but couldn't muster the strength to speak. Seeing his friend in such a dire state only fueled Pothitos's anger and suspicion of betrayal. He lunged forward, fists raised, ready to shake the truth out of him.

Antonios quickly stepped between his son and Panormitis, his hands firmly on Pothitos's chest. "Pothitos! Control yourself! This is not the way we will handle things," he admonished his son.

Longinus joined Antonios, his presence reinforcing the need for calm. "Stand down, Pothitos. We need him breathing if we're to learn where Delenda is," he ordered.

Pothitos, caught in the grip of his father and Longinus, gradually relaxed his fists, panting from the adrenaline and emotional tumult. His heart pounded with mixed emotions—anger, fear, and an overwhelming sense of urgency.

With a strained effort, Panormitis lifted his head slightly, his voice weak. "I... I tried to stop them," he gasped, the effort to speak visibly paining him. "Georgos... he took her, against her will. I tried to stop him."

Doubt passed over Pothitos's face, his anger shifting to confusion. "Why should we believe you?" he demanded, his voice harsh.

Longinus knelt beside Panormitis and offered him a flask of water, pressing the edge onto his lips. "Explain everything, Panormitis. Where did Georgos take her? What exactly happened?" Longinus insisted.

Panormitis took a small sip, each swallow a struggle, and continued, "Georgos... he claimed he had orders from someone powerful, from outside... They…they are planning something dark. I tried to reason with them, to turn back, but he wouldn't listen. Forgive me… I killed Yiannis!"

"You did what? Who else is involved?" Pothitos interjected.

Panormitis's eyes rolled back as he tried to speak, but his strength failed him, and he slumped back, unconscious.

Antonios, releasing his grip on Pothitos, turned to Longinus with a grave look. "Dark forces are at work here. We need to act swiftly, Longinus. If Halikos or one of his followers are involved, the implications could be far-reaching."

Longinus nodded solemnly. "I'll get Panormitis back to the monastery. We need to ensure we get his testimony."

He then turned to Pothitos and Antonios. "You two must pursue Delenda's trail while it's still fresh. Find where Georgos has taken her. We are short on time."

Despite his old injuries, Longinus carefully lifted the battered soldier. The dim light outside of the cave mirrored the dark uncertainty that had settled in Pothitos's heart. The revelations from Panormitis, though fractured and incomplete, hinted at a conspiracy that stretched beyond anyone's expectations. It suggested deeper, more malignant intents that threatened not just Delenda, but the stability of their entire island.

"We must move with haste, son," Antonios said, his voice urgent. "Georgos has a head start, but he cannot have gone far. Every moment we delay risks Delenda's life."

Chapter 20

PREY IN THE DARK

Delenda stumbled over the uneven ground, her hands bound tightly in front of her, forcing every movement to be slow and deliberate. Georgos gripped her arm hard enough to bruise her skin. He dragged her through the rocky terrain that was barely discernible as a path, leading her toward an isolated stretch of the coastline.

The moon hung low in the sky, its waning crescent shining pale light over the gnarled cedars of Kalymnos. Every few steps, Delenda's foot snagged on a root or loose stone, and she would falter. Georgos hissed in irritation and jerked her forward roughly.

"Keep moving. We don't have all night," Georgos growled, his voice a harsh sound that broke the muffled rustle of leaves and chirp of cicadas. His eyes darted through the shadowy trees, watching for torchlight and listening for anyone who might be following. His other hand hovered near the worn leather hilt of his spatha. With every yank from Georgos, the ropes he bound her with cut deeper into her wrists.

As Delenda staggered through the dense undergrowth, her shallow breaths carried the sharp bite of the night air drifting inland from the Aegean. Despite her predicament, a defiant spark burned within her. Her mind flickered with frantic thoughts of escape. She scoured her surroundings, noting anything she could use to her advantage. The dense thickets that might offer concealment. The steep drops that could hinder her captor's progress. Something… anything. However, Georgos's iron grip and the deepening darkness of the wilderness stifled these fleeting aspirations as quickly as they arose.

"Stop dragging your feet," Georgos snapped as he yanked her forward with increasing force. His impatience was tangible, driven by the fear of armed pursuers descending from the monastery atop Kalymnos's hills. He suddenly slowed their pace as the path beneath them began to descend precipitously toward the unseen shoreline.

Delenda, her heart hammering against her ribs, mustered the courage to resist. "Why are you doing this?" she gasped, her voice raw with exertion and despair. "What do you want from me?" Her questions hung in the air, unanswered, swallowed by the rustling leaves and the distant roar of the ocean.

In a moment of desperation, Delenda planted her feet against a jutting boulder and pulled back with all her strength. Her resistance caught Georgos off guard, and he faltered, his grip loosening for a heartbeat. She tugged her bound wrists, wrenching her arm with such force that pain shot through her shoulders. But Georgos recovered with a snarl, his grip tightening like a vice. He shoved her forward so hard that her knees buckled against the sharp, uneven ground.

"We don't have time for this," he growled, his face close to hers, and his expression contorted in anger. "Move, graeae, or I will see you beg for mercy before the end."

Despite the threat, Delenda's spirit wasn't easily quelled. Her mind worked feverishly, weaving and reweaving plans of escape. She noticed the changes in the terrain and the sound of the waves growing louder, signaling their approach to the shore. She cataloged each detail, turning over each possibility in her mind.

As they approached a steep cliffside, the sound of waves crashing against rocks reached her ears. It was a warning of imminent danger ahead. The terrain evened out once again allowing Georgos to quicken his pace. He seemed like a man who was running out of time.

Suddenly, they broke through the tangled cedar grove, and the vast expanse of the Aegean spread out before them, its surface shimmering faintly under the crescent moon. Below the cliff, half-hidden in the recess of a rock formation, a small dromon waited. Its sails were furled, and its low deck rocked with the gentle rhythm of the night tide. A handful of figures moved like ghosts in the gloom, preparing for a swift departure.

Georgos's grip bit deeper into her arm as he began to steer Delenda along a narrow trail that zigzagged down the cliffside. "Almost there," he hissed as he leaned close to her ear. Delenda let out a cry as she stumbled to her knees. "Cry out, pagan. There's no one but your false gods to hear you now and they are as silent as your grave will be."

The roar of waves crashing against the sharp rocks below grew louder with every step, the salty mist drifting upward to sting their eyes. The path steepened, its uneven stones shifting treacherously beneath Delenda's bare feet, each step threatening to send her tumbling into the abyss. Georgos's pace quickened. Every glance over his shoulder revealed a man driven not only by fear of pursuit but also by some darker urgency.

Delenda's adrenaline surged as they approached a narrow pass. It was here that the cliff dropped steeply into the violent, foam-laced waters of the Aegean below. Delenda could make out the faint glimmer of moonlight spreading across the sea far below.

It was here, at the edge of captivity and a faint promise of freedom, that Delenda made her choice. Her bound hands trembled, but she stopped abruptly, digging her bare feet into the gravel of the path, defying the sharp pain of stones ripping the flesh of her feet.

"Move!" Georgos hissed, his patience snapping as he jerked her arm. But Delenda, summoning her last ounce of courage, twisted her body violently toward the cliff. Caught off guard by her resistance and their position near the edge, Georgos slipped, his boots sliding on the loose rock.

With a reckless energy, Delenda pulled on Georgos's arm, exploiting his momentary loss of balance. She acted instinctively, not calculatingly, driven by her raw need to survive. The sudden shift in weight was too much for him to recover. Georgos flailed, trying to pull back, but it was too late. With a cry torn from her throat, Delenda threw herself over the cliff, the force dragging Georgos with her into the darkness.

The descent was a fleeting, dizzying blur—the chill of the night air whipped around them as they plummeted toward the sea. Moonlight streaked through the darkness, a fleeting glimmer before the cold, bracing waters closed above them. Delenda's impact into the sea hit like stone, the brutal cold ripping the air from her lungs.

The frigid waves clawed at her, pulling her deeper into the depths. Panic surged throughout her body, but her need for air won out. She swiveled, kicking her legs to break free of Georgos's grasp.

Her bound hands thrashed uselessly, each flailing stroke a desperate bid to rip her way toward the surface.

Georgos, weighed down by his armor, struggled against the suddenness of their immersion. His movements were sluggish, the armor threatening to drag him deeper into the depths. Seizing on his disorientation, Delenda kicked her legs wildly, propelling her upward toward the faint shape of the rocks above.

Her lungs burned like fire as she surfaced, gasping and spluttering, the taste of salt on her lips. The surrounding sea was a tumult of waves, driven by the night wind, each swell a challenge to her frantic efforts to stay afloat. Her eyes, stinging with saltwater, focused intently on the blurry shapes of the half-submerged rocks that promised safety. Each kick was a battle, her muscles burning with effort. Her mind singularly focused on the silhouette of safety that seemed agonizingly close yet inordinately far.

Delenda managed to claw her way onto the rugged rocks that jutted out of the sea. Each breath of air she sucked in felt like a small victory, the sea raging below her, its waves slamming against the rocks and spraying her shivering form with icy water. Barnacles tore at her palms and knees, but their razor-sharp edges were her only sanctuary against the relentless pull of the Aegean.

Her bound wrists throbbed with a pulsing pain as she struggled against the coarse rope cutting her skin. The rough rocks, though painful, became her unwilling allies. Bracing herself against a protruding edge, she pressed the rope hard against the sharp surface. Each motion was agonizing, her shoulders aching from the awkward angle, but fear fueled her efforts to grind the bindings against the rock's abrasive edge.

The task was excruciatingly slow, each motion deliberate. Balancing unsteadily on the slick, uneven rocks, she had to fight the constant threat of slipping back into the sea. The saltwater soaked her wounds, sending fresh spikes of pain with every wave, but it also hardened the rope's fibers, making them grind more effectively against the stone.

At last, after what felt like endless torment, the rope frayed, its damp, salt-stiffened fibers snapping with a final, satisfying rip. Her wrists, rubbed raw and slick with blood, were free. Relief coursed through her, but it was short-lived. The relentless waves continued their assault, tugging at her legs. She pressed herself against the rocks, gasping for air, her trembling hands clutching at the rough edges for stability.

Delenda managed to scramble higher onto the rocks, seeking a more secure foothold. She eventually wedged herself into a narrow crevice, her body contorted to fit the uneven curves of her refuge. Here, the rocks shielded her from the worst of the wind and waves, though icy sprays still lashed her face, mingling with the tears of relief which streamed down her cheeks.

Huddled in this crevice, Delenda waited, listening intently for any sound of pursuit or rescue. Her heart thundered with dread as sounds of Georgos's voice rose above the crashing waves. The chill of the night air seeped into her bones, but she dared not move, clinging to the stone as she waited for what the night would bring.

Beneath Delenda, the increasingly desperate sounds of Georgos careened through the dark, tumultuous night. His armor, designed for the rigors of battle, now betrayed him in the relentless grip of the sea. His voice called out sporadically, each sound becoming more muted as he struggled against the engulfing waters. His armor, now waterlogged and mercilessly heavy, clung to him like chains, pulling him deeper into the sea's cold embrace.

From her crag, Delenda watched in silence as Georgos's figure floundered against the overpowering sea. She shuddered as his strength faltered. His labored movements, the frantic splash of his arms, and the inexorable drag of his armor toward the depths made her tremble—not with cold, but with the unsettling impact of witnessing the merciless hand of death.

Delenda's grip on the slick, cold rocks tightened, her knuckles white with exertion and cold. She knew she could not move, could not risk drawing attention to herself. So, she waited, her body tensed for flight at any moment, her mind racing with plans of escape should the opportunity arise.

Slowly, the signs of Georgos's struggle faded. His splashes became weaker, his desperate cries swallowed by the endless roar of the sea. The sea, indifferent and eternal, washed over the place where he had struggled to stay afloat, erasing him with a cruel finality.

Unsure of what to do next, Delenda crouched low among the rocks, her shivering form pressed into the stone. The salt spray stung her open wounds, each droplet a biting reminder of her ordeal. With cold seeping into her bones, the rhythmic crash of waves against the cliffs became a grim, unfeeling lullaby. The terror of the night's events clung to the recesses of her mind, as persistent as the damp chill that made her ache.

Delenda exhaled slowly, her legs trembling as her body shook from adrenaline and cold. The reality of what she had witnessed—her captor engulfed by the sea's relentless grasp—consumed her mind. The enormity of her escape mingled with exhaustion, leaving her dazed and confused. As the hours stretched on, she stayed tucked into her rocky haven. The sea whispered tales of escape into her ears, but her mind urged her to wait for the dawn and the chance to reclaim her freedom.

Chapter 21

OATHBREAKER

Delenda awoke with a sharp, stabbing pain in her shoulder as the midday sun scorched the rocky landscape around her. Squinting against the glare, she caught sight of a Bonelli's eagle—its tawny plumage streaking the sky as it climbed back into the heavens. The creature had mistaken her for carrion and had raked its talons across her skin, leaving raw, bloody trails.

The eagle's assault jolted Delenda back to the harsh reality of her battered body. Bruises blossomed across her arms and legs, reminders of the previous night's desperate escape. Scrapes marked her skin where serrated rocks had torn at her during her flight, each wound evidence of her survival.

Despite the agony coursing through her, Delenda exhaled shakily, relief mingling with the sting of her wounds. The beating left her battered yet alive. Shifting her weight gingerly, she scanned her surroundings: the rocky outcropping that provided her shelter, the cliffs towering above, and the calm sea stretching beyond.

Vulnerability pressed upon her like a heavy hand—a reminder that even here, among Kalymnos's wild beauty, she was prey.

Delenda rubbed her throbbing shoulder and shifted into a painful crouch, her body aching. The hues of dawn had given way to the harsh brilliance of midday, the sun striking the water with an unrelenting glare. She crept to the edge of the outcropping and peered below. The Aegean Sea, wild and unforgiving in the dark, now lay calm, its waves rolling lazily against the rugged coastline of the island.

Scanning the horizon, Delenda gasped at the sight of the boat—a dark silhouette against the glittering expanse of the Aegean. It bobbed ominously at anchor as a figure emerged, striding deliberately along the shoals. The sunlight struck the scales of his lorica squamata, the segmented armor worn by the Ierí Frourá—guardians whose loyalty once brought her comfort but now filled her with dread. His steps were steady, his posture betraying a mission that tolerated no failure.

Her heart began to beat wildly again as she observed two other figures moving rapidly from the opposite direction. As they drew closer, Delenda noticed that one of them also wore the familiar armor of the Ierí Frourá, while the other was clad in simple linen and leather. The trio converged near the waterline, their meeting point a blur of motion.

Delenda's thoughts churned. Were these men her rescuers, or the architects of her suffering? The Ierí Frourá's armor gleamed with authority, yet its polished sheen offered no reassurance. Every step they took seemed calculated, every glance laden with intent.

From her perch, Delenda squinted to catch the meaning behind their gestures. The wind carried only fragments of their voices—snatches too faint to decipher. Every pause, every sudden movement, unnerved her. Whatever they debated, it revolved around her—or worse, her fate.

Delenda moved carefully, her torn skin brushing against the slick stone. Each movement brought a new sting, but the need to understand the figures below outweighed the pain. Risking exposure, she crept closer, her shallow breaths barely audible over the sound of the waves. The new vantage point brought their features into sharper focus—and with them, a flicker of recognition.

She exhaled as she recognized Pothitos, his familiar frame exuding an intensity she had always trusted. Relief surged through her, so sudden and fierce it threatened to unsteady her. Beside him stood Antonios, who seemed to be leading the conversation. The two conferred with a third figure, whose back remained turned to her.

Delenda watched as Pothitos gestured emphatically toward the sea and then back toward the shore, possibly outlining a search pattern or strategizing their next moves. Antonios nodded in agreement, pointing in the opposite direction. With their attention focused elsewhere, she made a split-second decision to reveal herself.

Her appearance on the rocky outcropping was a striking contrast against the backdrop of the Kalymian coastline. Her clothes, torn and stiff with salt, clung uncomfortably to her body, and her dark hair whipped around her face in the sea breeze. The marks of her struggle were evident: scratches marred her arms and face, and her wrists were crusted with dried blood. Her skin bore the pallor of exhaustion and stress, and despite the warmth of the midday sun, a shiver racked her body. Her eyes, usually bright and alert, now held a haunted look, wide and red-rimmed. She allowed a name to escape her lips.

"Pothitos," Delenda rasped, her voice cracking with fear. The sound snapped Pothitos out of his tense focus. He turned sharply, his eyes widening as they met hers.

"Delenda!" he shouted, relief breaking through his stern visage. Straightaway, all three men ran headlong into the surf.

As the men drew closer, Delenda's relief curdled into dread. Her eyes locked on the soldier at the rear— Theophilos. The recognition hit her like a blow. He wasn't there to rescue her; he was the architect of her abduction. The memory of his voice commanding the three youths flashed through her mind. Panic clawed at her chest as the realization settled like a stone in her stomach.

Delenda's panic gave way to urgency. She opened her mouth to shout a warning, but her voice came out weak, rasping against her parched throat. "Theophilos!" she croaked, the sound swallowed by the rhythmic crash of the waves. She tried again, her desperation mounting, but the words barely carried across the wind.

Theophilos's head snapped toward her, his calculating eyes turning sharp and predatory. In one fluid motion, he drew his spatha, its steel flashing in the sunlight. Antonios, unarmed and distracted, turned too late. Theophilos lunged, aiming a killing blow at the back of his neck.

Delenda froze; horror etched into her features. Her wide eyes met Antonios's in a split second of silent warning. Understanding flashed across his face, but too late. Theophilos's blade arced downward. Antonios turned just enough to avoid the fatal strike, but the spatha bit deep into his shoulder, grinding against the bone with a sickening scrape.

The force of the strike sent Antonios reeling. He staggered back, his boots slipping on the wet, uneven rocks, and crashed into the shallow surf. The cold shock of the seawater jolted his body, but it was the warmth spreading across his left side—the rush of blood billowing into the waves—that told him how grave the wound was.

Pothitos stood in shock for half a heartbeat as the blade struck home. Terror flared in his chest, quickly swallowed by a searing rage. With a sudden move, he unsheathed his spatha, the hilt cool in his grip. His training surged to the forefront, his movements purposeful, his fury honed into a single, deadly focus: Theophilos.

"Theophilos!" Pothitos's voice thundered, bouncing off the cliffs and cutting through the crash of the waves. Betrayal burned in his tone, laced with the fierce clarity of battle. He closed the distance between them in measured strides, his sword angled ominously forward.

"Why, Theophilos?" Pothitos demanded, his voice a low growl. "What treachery is this?"

Theophilos straightened, his lips curling into a thin, mocking smile. "It's beyond you, boy," he said, his voice almost casual. "There are forces at work here that you cannot begin to comprehend. Delenda isn't just some pretty face for you to look at. She is the key—a map—to power you can't even imagine."

Pothitos advanced another step, his sword unwavering as the waves crashed behind him. "You swore an oath, Theophilos!" he shouted, his voice breaking through the wind. "You've betrayed everything you once stood for!"

Theophilos smirked, his eyes glinting with cold amusement as he raised his blade. "Blind as ever, Pothitos," he said, his tone biting. "This plan was set long before you or your father had any part to play. You were both pawns, shackled by your petty notions of loyalty."

Pothitos momentarily faltered, confusion and betrayal swirling within him. The revelations shook him to his core, challenging everything he believed about his mentor and the trust he had placed in Theophilos.

"And you would spill innocent blood for power? Betray those who trusted you?" Pothitos countered, recovering his composure.

Theophilos laughed, a cold, unsettling sound that mingled with the wind. "Innocence is a luxury we cannot afford in the pursuit of greatness. You will understand, eventually. Either you stand with me, knowing the truth, or you fall as a naïve fool."

Theophilos moved first, his spatha cutting through the air in a vicious arc. Pothitos stepped into the attack, steel meeting steel with a clang that bounded across the rocky shore. The force of the strike sent a jolt through Pothitos's arms, but he held firm, his stance steady.

The two men circled each other with fervor, their blades weaving patterns of the reflected sunlight across the rocky shore. Each move was calculated, every feint a test of the other's reflexes. Theophilos lunged, his sword striking low, but Pothitos parried, deflecting the blow with ease.

The rhythmic clash of blades continued to send vibrations up Pothitos's arm, but his attention never faltered. Theophilos fought with the diligence of a seasoned warrior and with each strike he pressed his advantage. Yet with every exchange, Pothitos found himself reading the man's movements, sensing the shifts in his weight, the slight flickers that telegraphed his intentions.

Theophilos narrowed his eyes, his strikes growing more deliberate as he tested Pothitos's defenses. He feinted left, his blade cutting sharply toward the young man's exposed flank. But Pothitos, his body primed by years of training, shifted just in time. Theophilos's blade whistled past, and Pothitos countered with a swift thrust that forced the older man to retreat, his boots skidding on the wet rocks.

Theophilos slipped, his footing seeming to falter, but the move was calculated. With a predator's cunning, he swept low, his blade arcing toward Pothitos's legs. The younger man shifted back instinctively, his heel catching on a slick stone. He staggered, his sword slipping from his grasp as he threw out a hand to steady himself. For a moment, he was exposed.

Theophilos lunged, his blade poised to strike the defenseless Pothitos. But before he could deliver the blow, Antonios surged forward from the water, his face pale. Ignoring the blood soaking his shoulder, he grasped Theophilos's leg with all the strength he could muster. The sudden tug threw Theophilos off balance, his momentum driving him forward. He toppled, crashing into the surf with a sharp gasp.

Pothitos scrambled to his feet, his hand closing around the hilt of his fallen spatha. The rush of adrenaline steadied his grip as he advanced, his steps quick and purposeful. Before Theophilos recovered, Pothitos drove him onto his back, the point of his blade pressing into the hollow of the older man's throat. His chest heaved, his pulse a deafening drumbeat in his ears, but his sword hand did not waver.

"Antonios! You dog. You do not know what you do!" Theophilos grunted, the sand and salt clinging to his face. Anxiety laced his voice as he lay pinned under the young warrior's blade.

Antonios leaned heavily on one arm, blood dripping into the surf beneath him. He managed a faint, grim smile. "You've forgotten your lessons, Theophilos," he rasped, his voice laced with pain. "Never underestimate an old soldier."

Pothitos pressed the blade harder, the steel dimpling Theophilos's skin. He swallowed hard as he stared down at the man who had once been his mentor. "It's over," he said, his voice low and cold. "Who gave you the orders? What power is worth all this blood?"

Theophilos tilted his head slightly; a slight smile crossing his lips despite the blade pressing against his throat. His voice remained calm and deliberate. "You've only just scratched the surface, boy," he spat. "Do you truly believe this was all my doing?"

"Fear, Pothitos," Theophilos continued, his voice low. "It blinds us. It binds us. It breaks us. The tale of the witch—Delenda's curse—was ripe for manipulation. Your friends? They were eager fools, primed to believe anything. The whole island was already whispering of ill omens. All it took was a nudge in the right direction. And then the sun darkened… everyone was so distracted… there was no better time to execute our plan."

He paused, gauging the impact of his words on Pothitos and Antonios, then continued, "Georgos and Yiannis—they were bored, disillusioned with their lot. I gave them purpose, I promised them power. Panormitis…" He paused, the smile fading from his face. "He was… different. Skeptical, cautious. And when he learned the truth—that the girl wasn't just being relocated to another island but offered up for a greater purpose—he faltered. His betrayal cost us time."

Theophilos's voice dropped, his words turning colder. "Panormitis made the mistake of growing a conscience. When he tried to stop us, Yiannis turned on him in the scriptorium, buying Georgos enough time to take the girl to the cave. But Panormitis tracked us down, stubborn as ever." He exhaled, a hint of annoyance crossing his features. "When he arrived, he left me no choice. A well-placed rock ended his heroics. I left him for dead in the cave, while Georgos took the girl to the shore and I readied the boat."

Pothitos's knuckles whitened around the hilt of his spatha, his stomach churning at the ease with which Theophilos described murder and betrayal. Beside him, Antonios leaned heavily on his good arm, blood still pooling at his side, his eyes clouded and unfocused.

"And now, here we are," Theophilos said, his voice calm, almost resigned. His eyes fixed on Pothitos, the defiance in them undimmed. "You think you've won, but all you've done is delay the inevitable. There are others—more powerful, more determined— others who believe, as I do, that what lies with the girl can change the course of history. They won't stop, and neither will I."

Delenda cautiously made her way through the shallow surf to Pothitos, who still held Theophilos at sword point. As she reached his side, her presence seemed to give Pothitos a newfound strength.

From the direction of the anchored boat, a commotion rang out. Five figures emerged, their strides quick and purposeful. The heavy thud of armored boots on stone carried across the shoreline, growing louder as they advanced. At their head was Halikos, his eyes burning with fury. Behind him, three soldiers rushed forward with drawn swords. Their intent was clear—death.

But it was the figure trailing just behind them that drew a cold gasp from Delenda and an unsteady glance from Pothitos. A woman, clad entirely in black, moved with poise, her feet barely seeming to touch the ground. Her presence seemed spectral, her features obscured by a veil that fluttered slightly in the sea breeze. Everything about her felt menacing, almost evil.

As they closed the gap, Halikos shouted, his voice carrying over the waves. "You cannot protect her forever! She is the key to my ascension, my return to glory!" His words were punctuated by the brandishing of his sword, pointing accusingly at Delenda.

Antonios struggled to his feet and picked up Theophilos's discarded spatha. He gripped the weapon with his right hand, its balance unfamiliar but no less deadly. Blood dripped steadily from his wounded shoulder, soaking the rocks beneath him, but his stance was firm. He moved to Pothitos's side, his frame braced like a shield. Behind them, Delenda lingered, her wide eyes darting toward the advancing reinforcements. Theophilos, taking advantage of the chaos, shifted slightly, attempting to inch away.

"Stay where you are," Pothitos growled without looking at Theophilos, his attention fixed on the approaching enemies.

As the reinforcements neared, Antonios, his breath labored and his shoulder aflame with pain, realized the grim odds they faced. "Take Delenda and run, Pothitos!" he barked, his voice carrying desperation. Pothitos hesitated, his sword trembling in his hand, torn between duty and loyalty to his father.

"I can't leave you, Father—" Pothitos began, his voice cracking with anxiety. But his words were cut off.

"This is an order, Pothitos!" Antonios barked, his voice breaking under the strain, but no less commanding. "Go, while you still can!" Pothitos gave a reluctant nod and turned to Delenda.

With a swift motion, Pothitos withdrew his sword from Theophilos's throat. Theophilos, a look of relief crossing his face, pulled himself up into a seated position. Without missing a beat, Pothitos seized Delenda's wrist, his grip firm as he pulled her toward a narrow path leading inland. She swayed, but kept pace, her mind in shock from fear.

Pothitos turned back, his chest tightening at the sight of his father. Antonios stood tall despite the blood staining his tunic, his wounded arm trembling as he raised the stolen spatha. He spoke no word as he stepped past Theophilos, his blade plunging into the traitor's chest. The traitor crumpled, lifeless. But Antonios did not falter. He turned, bloodied, yet unbroken, his stolen blade rising to meet Halikos and the oncoming tide.

Pothitos gripped Delenda's hand as they sprinted along the shoreline, his eyes scanning for a path to safety. The uneven rocks tore at her feet, but she pushed forward, her fear overcome by the sheer will to survive.

The sounds of battle erupted behind them—steel clashing, men shouting, and the ceaseless roar of the waves. Pothitos's chest tightened with every step, but he refused to look back. The final image of his father, bloodied, standing alone against the oncoming tide, was seared in his mind.

Chapter 22

BROKEN BROTHERHOOD

Panormitis's broken figure stood out against the unblemished linens of the infirmary bed where he lay recovering. The room carried a sense of oppression as Longinus and two trusted members of the Ierí Frourá stood nearby. The monastery's infirmary was modest in design, with rough-hewn stone walls lined with shelves bearing jars of dried herbs, salves, and clay vials. Slivers of sunlight slipped through narrow, barred windows, throwing angled shadows across the cool floor and illuminating the pained expression on Panormitis's face.

Longinus loomed over the bed, his formidable presence dominating the humble surroundings. He leaned forward slightly, hands clasped behind his back, his countenance dark as he prepared to hear Panormitis's account. Flanking him, two Ierí Frourá guards stood like statues, their faces carved with concern but their stances taut with readiness. One of the guards was a familiar face, Domianos. He had taken no part in the abduction of Delenda and now his silence felt like an unspoken judgment to Panormitis. Domianos remained impassive, his eyes fixed straight ahead, even as his former friend tried to make eye contact.

When Panormitis began to speak, his voice, though faltering from weakness, carried an unmistakable tone of sincerity. Each word painted a vivid story of the betrayal that had unfolded in the confines of the monastery. Longinus's eyes never left Panormitis, his face unflinching as he absorbed every detail of the rebels' plot.

Panormitis drew a shallow breath, wincing as the dull throb of pain flared with each small movement. "They were convincing," he began haltingly, "speaking of looming danger and of unseen enemies." His eyes flickered, distant with lingering doubt. "I trusted Theophilos —until we reached the scriptorium."

Longinus's disposition shifted, his stoic mask briefly slipping to reveal a flicker of shock. That Theophilos, the Captain of the Guard, could devise such treachery seemed almost unthinkable. Longinus had not only fought beside him, but he trusted him with the secrets that surrounded Delenda.

Panormitis continued, his voice faltering as if the memories themselves sapped his strength. "Once we took hold of her, it all changed. Their demeanor… shifted. There was no concern for Delenda's safety—just haste and secrecy. Georgos and Yiannis tied her wrists and told me to bind her feet. I'll never forget the fear in her eyes—it froze me where I stood."

He swallowed hard, the memory vivid and painful. "I refused. I told them this wasn't right, that we needed to speak to the abbess first. But they wouldn't listen. We were not relocating her—we were abducting her. Everything about it felt wrong."

The room seemed to shrink around Longinus as the implications settled in. Theophilos's involvement was more than personal betrayal—it was a corruption of their entire creed. When he finally spoke, his voice was low, edged with a rare tremor of anger. "And Theophilos? What was his role in all this?"

Panormitis's eyes, heavy with pain and betrayal, locked onto Longinus's. "He orchestrated everything," he said. "He told Georgos it was all planned for years—that Delenda's removal from Kalymnos was necessary for peace on the island."

A deep silence hung in the room. Longinus stood motionless, the news anchoring him in place as he grappled with the revelation. Theophilos, one of his closest companions, had turned against everything they once stood for.

"He's compromised us all," Longinus finally said, his voice low and strained. "He's compromised our mission…our honor. I need to understand why. I need to understand how deep this betrayal runs."

"Continue," Longinus commanded.

Panormitis's attention drifted off to some unseen point in the past. "Once we were in the scriptorium, I tried to stop them… or at least slow them down. But Yiannis drew his spatha on me," he reflected. "It happened so fast—we exchanged blows. I didn't want to hurt him, but I had no choice."

Panormitis's voice quivered, his guilt hanging in the still air of the infirmary. "It was all a blur—steel and shadows," he said, his mind searching for answers. "The clash of our blades rang through the scriptorium. It was frantic, desperate. Yiannis was relentless, driven by some zeal I couldn't comprehend. He believed completely in what they were doing, though I still don't know what that was."

He paused, swallowing hard. The memory clearly pained him. "I pleaded with him," Panormitis cried, his voice barely audible. "I told him we were brothers in arms, that whatever was happening, it wasn't worth this. But he wouldn't listen, he just kept coming at me."

The room remained silent, each person processing the bitter reality of duplicity within their own ranks. Longinus stood motionless, his hands locked behind his back. The burden of command had never been heavier—brother against brother, and all of it under his watch.

"I had to defend myself," Panormitis said, breaking the silence. "When he faltered, his guard dropped. My blade—it found its mark before I could pull back." His voice cracked, the final word trembling with sorrow. A single tear slid down his cheek as he confronted the truth of what he had done.

Longinus stepped forward, placing a steady hand on Panormitis's shoulder. "You did what you had to do," he said, his voice firm but tempered with empathy. "You defended yourself against a threat. Yiannis made his choice, and as painful as it is, we must live with it."

He continued, "And Delenda, what happened to her?"

Panormitis's account reflected the chaos of those moments. His voice quivered as he described the scene.

"Georgos was ruthless," Panormitis said, a note of disgust in his voice. "He bound her wrists so tightly, it drew blood. Delenda was pulling back, her feet scraping against the stone floor of the scriptorium… trying to resist. But Georgos…he's strong, and he was determined."

He paused, swallowing again, the memory clearly paining him. "Her screams…Delenda's screams… rang through the monastery's corridors. Fading… fading into the distance. It was haunting. I've never felt so helpless."

Panormitis's face was etched with pain as he continued, "The fight with Yiannis slowed me down, but when it was over I followed, fear and fury pushing me forward. I tracked them to the cave. I entered cautiously but there was very little light. Delenda was there—a small figure crouched against the rocky wall. I could barely see her in the gloom."

His voice fell to a whisper. "She looked so scared. I called out to her—softly, trying to comfort her, to let her know she wasn't alone. But before I could reach her, I was struck from behind. Pain shot through my head, and then… everything went black. I hit the ground, unconscious. Helpless."

Panormitis's words came heavily and uneven, as though each thought dragged another memory to the surface. "I never saw who hit me," he said, his brow furrowed in confusion as he searched through the fractured images in his mind. "One moment I was reaching for her, and the next—I was on the ground. Pain ripping through my head. Then… darkness."

The room went silent again, each person there trying to visualize the traitorous scene Panormitis described. Longinus's face was particularly troubled as he put together the pieces of the puzzle. His mind was already racing ahead, considering the cost of failure against the duty to act swiftly.

"I don't know how long I lay there," Panormitis said, his eyes glazed over, trapped in the memory. "When I woke, the cave was silent—empty. No Georgos, no Delenda. Just flashes of what happened… fragments of the terror."

Longinus leaned closer, his voice urgent. "Did you hear anything else? Any clue that might tell us where they went?"

Panormitis shook his head slowly, frustration evident. "Maybe… before I lost consciousness, I heard something about a boat. Georgos might have been planning to take her to the coast— to escape by sea."

Longinus nodded slowly, his mind working through the implications. "This matches reports of unusual activity along the northern shoreline," he said, his tone measured. "They are most likely planning to rendezvous with a ship."

Longinus straightened. "We need to act now. Time is against us, and every moment we wait, Delenda's danger grows. We'll coordinate with the coastal patrols—search every cove, every possible landing site."

Panormitis watched as the soldiers in the room spurred into action by Longinus's commands. His revelations had set the wheels of action in motion—a chance to mend the treachery that had unfolded earlier. Just as Longinus reached the door, he turned back, looking intently at Panormitis. "One more thing," he said. "Where was Theophilos during the abduction? You've spoken of Georgos and Yiannis—but not him."

Panormitis shifted on the infirmary bed, his discomfort evident as he winced against the pain. "Theophilos …" He hesitated, his voice taut. "He was the mastermind. He wasn't there—not in the scriptorium." Panormitis paused before continuing. "He told us he had to stay out of sight—to keep his reputation clean."

"He stayed in the shadows deliberately," Longinus said, his voice edged with contempt. "Cautious. Calculating. He knew the risks of being directly tied to Theophilos's kidnapping. His position is too valuable to jeopardize—at least to him."

"He made it clear to Georgos and Yiannis," Panormitis said, his voice bitter, "that his reputation—and his place in the guard—couldn't be compromised." He paused, exhaling slowly before continuing. "Theophilos is ambitious. He has too much to lose if he's caught. He couldn't risk being seen as the one pulling the strings."

Chapter 23

A PROMISE IN THE DARK

As Delenda and Pothitos hurriedly fled the chaotic scene on the beach, the rugged landscape of Kalymnos spread out before them—a daunting maze of uneven rocks, thorny underbrush, and steep ravines that offered both cover and danger. The sun dipped low on the horizon, bathing the terrain in a fiery light, with long shadows stretching like dark fingers over the rocky expanse. Pothitos led the way, as they wound through the wild, untamed land.

Pothitos relied on his intimate knowledge of the island's geography to guide them. He chose obscure, less-traveled goat paths, their narrow, overgrown trails hidden beneath wild thrymbi and tangled shrubs. These tracks, etched into the land over the centuries by mountain goats and solitary shepherds, twisted precariously through the hills. Every step was a risk, with loose stones and hidden roots threatening to trip even the most experienced traveler.

The paths dipped into small ravines and climbed steep ridges, where ancient olive trees formed natural archways. The scent of the wild thrymbi and thyme filled the air, blending with the earthy smell of sage. Occasionally, the trail would open to a rocky outcrop, offering breathtaking views of the Aegean, its deep blue waters stretching endlessly beneath the fading sky. But these open spaces brought risk, with no cover to shield them from any pursuers.

Pothitos guided Delenda with a steady hand on her elbow, helping her navigate the duplicitous terrain. Despite her exhaustion, she moved with determination, refusing to let her fear slow them down. Her wide eyes darted ahead, scanning for dangers. Pothitos couldn't help but admire her courage.

Despite the dangers of their flight, Delenda could not help but notice the raw beauty of these secluded trails. They moved through patches of wildflowers that erupted in bursts of color against the green and gray backdrop, and through small groves of fig trees, where the sweet aroma of ripening fruit hung heavy in the air.

Pothitos paused, gesturing toward the heavy-laden branches. "We should eat," he suggested, his voice low but carrying an undercurrent of urgency. Delenda, her energy flagging from the constant stress and movement, nodded in agreement.

They moved under the canopy of leaves, where the light dappled through, illuminating the plump, purple figs. Pothitos reached up, his fingers gently coaxing the fruit from its stem, while Delenda, following his lead, picked the lower hanging figs. They ate quickly, the sweet, sticky juice a burst of flavor, its natural sugars a vital source of quick energy.

"Let's take some with us," Pothitos said, his mind always one step ahead. Together, they gathered a small cache of the ripest figs, wrapping them in a piece of cloth Delenda ripped from her clothing.

"Once we're safe, we can dry these out," Pothitos explained, tying the corners of the cloth. "They will last longer if we must remain hidden for a few days."

Behind them, the sounds of pursuit were absent, but Pothitos took nothing for granted. His training with the Ierí Frourá had readied him for combat and tactical evasion, but the reality of fleeing with Delenda was more than he was prepared for.

His mind replayed his father's last desperate command—to run. His willingness to lay down his own life for a chance for Delenda's survival. Despite the danger, Pothitos understood the task at hand, driven not just by duty but by a deep feeling that had formed between him and Delenda.

Despite her fear and the exhaustion that clung to her limbs after the harrowing escape, Delenda moved with surprising speed. Her spirit, far from being broken, seemed to burn even brighter. As they cut through the dense underbrush, she kept close to Pothitos, matching his quick pace.

"We need to reach the old mill by the dried-out river," Pothitos panted, his voice barely audible above the rustle of the leaves. The old mill, a long-abandoned structure concealed deep within a copse of olive trees, was their best chance for a temporary refuge. It had once been a lifeline for the island's villagers during harvest seasons, grinding wheat into flour. Now, its crumbling timbers stood as a relic of simpler times.

Pothitos adjusted his grip on the hilt of his sword, his other hand gently guiding Delenda over a particularly hazardous stretch of loose stones. "Just a little further," he assured her.

As twilight deepened into night, the sounds of nocturnal creatures began to rise—the distant calls of nightingales and the subtle rustle of small animals in the undergrowth. Yet, each natural sound was tinged with the threat of pursuit, turning every noise into a potential enemy, every gust of wind into the footstep of a pursuer.

Finally, the silhouette of an old mill emerged against the night sky, its weathered timbers and moss-covered stones testimony to its long disuse. Its decrepit door swung open with a creak, revealing the dark, musty interior that would hopefully allow them a brief rest.

In the hidden recesses of the ancient structure, a waterwheel stood as a relic of ingenuity, its purpose long forgotten by those who now sought refuge within its walls. The wheel, a large, circular structure made of sturdy oak and iron bindings, was designed to lift water from the river that used to run next to it. Its spokes, though worn, radiated strength, and the troughs attached to the rim were carved from solid wood, designed to scoop and carry water with each turn.

As Delenda and Pothitos settled into the dim interior, the faint moonlight filtering through the cracks in the wooden siding played across the wheel's surface, highlighting the moss that clung to its frame and the water stains that marked its long history of use. The wheel, unmoved for years, stood as a witness to the once-bustling activity that had filled the mill, now silent save for the hushed sounds of two fugitives and the constant, soothing whisper of the wind.

Pothitos, his back against the cool stone wall, watched the wheel with curiosity. "Imagine the hands that built this," he said. "Crafted with such care, meant to sustain a community."

Delenda nodded slowly. "It's beautiful, in its way," she agreed, her voice soft. "A piece of the past left behind as the world moved on."

As Pothitos scanned the interior of the mill, his instincts were on high alert, evaluating every nook and corner for potential threats or benefits. The air was cool and musty, filled with the scent of old wood and refuse. "We can stay here until dawn," he said, his voice low. His eyes met Delenda's, seeking to offer reassurance. "Then we'll move deeper into the island's interior. I know the land well—its hidden paths and safe havens. We'll find a better place to hide, further from any prying eyes."

Delenda, still catching her breath from their frantic escape, nodded in understanding, her trust in Pothitos evident. "Lead the way, when it's time," she replied, her voice filled with weariness.

Pothitos quickly set to work, securing their makeshift refuge for the night. First, he gathered several large pieces of lumber that were strewn across the dusty floor. These, he piled against the inside of the mill's only door, making a crude but effective barrier that would slow any intruders, giving them precious seconds to react or escape.

Next, he scanned the mill for anything else that could fortify their position. Finding a few smaller broken planks of wood and some rusted tools, Pothitos wedged the planks diagonally across the door, using the tools to jam them into the old, worn grooves on the mill's stone floor. Each piece was placed with careful thought, maximizing stability and obstruction.

To further secure the door, he pulled a heavy, old grinding stone—an artifact from the mill's operational days—placing it behind the door. The weight of the stone, combined with the makeshift barricade of tools and planks, created an obstruction that would make entering through the door noisy and difficult.

Once satisfied with his work, Pothitos stepped back to survey the area one last time, ensuring that no obvious weaknesses remained. Delenda watched silently, her eyes reflecting a spark of admiration for Pothitos's resourcefulness under pressure.

Delenda began to nod off, her exhaustion evident in her slumped shoulders and the pallor of her face. She sank down against one of the walls, pulling her knees close to her chest. "Thank you, Pothitos," she sighed. "For everything."

Pothitos settled beside her, his protective nature never wavering. "I made a promise to keep you safe," he said quietly. "I intend to keep it," he added. "No matter what."

The night deepened around them, filled with the sounds of the wilderness. The air was cool and fresh, carrying the scent of earth, creating a cocoon of solitude for Delenda and Pothitos as they huddled together under the shelter of the ancient mill. Their conversation, initially cautious, deepened as the stars carved arcs across the sky.

Delenda spoke about youth, her voice carrying across the quiet night. "I grew up with the Nile as my backyard," she reminisced, her eyes glinting in the dark. "In Alexandria. The city was vibrant. Full of life and color. I remember the markets…they were always busy…with spices and silks from all over the world."

She paused as she reflected on her past, "And I remember the way the light from The Pharos Lighthouse hit the Mediterranean at night most of all; it was like a blanket of gold."

Pothitos, staring blankly at the creeping shadows of the mill, found himself drawn into her tales, each detail painting a vivid picture of a world far removed from his own. "It sounds beautiful," he replied with genuine interest. "It seems a world away from the ruggedness of my home."

Fighting off sleep, Delenda continued, her voice soft, "But there was not always beauty. There was also danger, an anxiousness that you could feel even in the laughter of the marketplaces. Perhaps that's why I was brought here…."

She paused, her story trailing off as her memories seemed momentarily overwhelming. Pothitos reached out, his hand brushing hers in a gesture of comfort. "You don't have to continue if it's too much for you," he offered gently.

His words were met with silence. After a time, Pothitos turned to look at Delenda. She had curled up next to him in the crumbling shelter of the old mill, her breathing becoming slow and steady as she drifted into a deep sleep. A gentle smile played on her lips as if she was still recounting the days of her youth.

In that moment, next to her in the dark, Pothitos was enamored with her beauty. He sat next to her memorizing every detail of her face, every curve of her lips, and the smell of her hair. The sight of her in such a peaceful state brought Pothitos relief from the fear that had gripped him since their flight. As he watched her sleep so quietly, he felt a warmth spread through him. Finally, he could close his eyes and rest—just for a moment.

Chapter 24

THE RED WAVES

As dark clouds swirled overhead, the beach transformed into a battleground marked by flickers of light. Antonios, his figure silhouetted against the darkening sky, stood ready despite the pain from his injured shoulder, which hung limply at his side. Across the cooling sands, Halikos and his three soldiers approached, their leaf-shaped swords reminiscent of Byzantine dory spears.

The air was filled with sinister chants of the woman cloaked in black. Her voice, rough with age, carried the guttural cadences of ancient Greek incantations spoken in the dark places of the world. The sound, more like the wails of a banshee, melded with the crashing of the waves, creating a haunting soundtrack to the impending clash. The light seemed to fade with her every word and the swirling wind whipped sand and salt across the face of each man. As the clouds raked the heavens, the intermittent light danced around Antonios, who stood as the lone bastion against the advancing enemy.

Antonios gripped the spatha with his uninjured arm and shifted his feet in the sand. He settled into a stance that spoke of years of combat, his eyes narrowing as he faced the advancing enemy.

The first soldier lunged forward, his blade slicing through the air. With a deft sidestep, Antonios avoided the thrust, his own sword arcing upwards in a blur of deadly motion. His riposte was swift, the blade of his sword catching the underside of the soldier's arm, slicing through sinew and bone. With a grunt of pain, the soldier faltered, losing his grip on his weapon. Antonios didn't hesitate; he completed his maneuver with a powerful thrust that sent the man staggering backward, collapsing onto the sandy beach as a dark crimson stain spread like spilled wine across the earth.

The fight's momentum didn't pause—Antonios immediately turned to face the next assailant, his mind calm and his movements calculated. The air reeked of the smell of freshly spilled blood.

The second soldier barreled forward; his weapon sliced through the air with a menacing swoosh. Antonios ducked low under the sweeping blade. The move brought him within arm's reach of his attacker, into a range where the longsword offered no advantage.

In one fluid motion, Antonios pivoted on the balls of his feet, his own spatha jolting forward. The soldier's wide swing exposed his side—a mistake Antonios promptly exploited. Driving his sword forward, the blade slipped past the soldier's chain links and sank deep into his chest. The impact halted the man's momentum, his eyes widening in shock and pain as he looked down at the blade protruding from his armor.

There was a moment when time seemed to slow, the sound of the battle fading into silence. Antonios looked into his opponent's eyes—a fleeting connection between warriors. Then, with a sharp tug, he ripped his blade free; the action accompanied by the dreadful sound of metal scraping against bone. The soldier's knees buckled, and he fell forward onto the sand, his body convulsing as his life slipped from him.

Halikos prowled the edges of the fray, his movements predatory. Dressed in a short lamellar cuirass of interlocking leather and darkened metal plates, Halikos carried himself like a man who had survived dozens of battles. His eyes, gleaming in the light, remained fixed on Antonios, watching intently for any sign of faltering in the older warrior's defenses. Halikos moved deliberately, like a seasoned hunter circling his prey, waiting for the perfect moment to strike.

Every now and then, Halikos feinted, testing Antonios's reactions, his sword-tip darting forward like the tongue of a snake, quick and menacing. Yet, Antonios, despite his visible weariness and the slick blood that stained his arm and side, met each feint with a parry. The pain from his injured shoulder gnawed at him and each shift of his stance weakened his guard, yet he refused to falter.

Halikos's circles grew tighter, his movements more aggressive as he sensed the struggle within Antonios to hold his ground.

Antonios, chest heaving with exertion, locked onto Halikos. The sound of their swords clashing resonated sharply as they engaged in a rapid exchange of strikes and parries. Each movement was a test of endurance and will, their blades moving so fast they appeared as flashes of steel in the remaining light.

Despite the pain radiating from his injured shoulder, Antonios's experience was evident. With deft footwork, he turned each of Halikos's aggressive lunges into opportunities for his own counterattacks. His swordplay was cleverly opportunistic, exploiting the smallest openings in Halikos's guard.

Antonios steadily gained ground. He breathed through the pain, each exhalation synchronizing with a block or a strike. The salty air filled his lungs as he forced Halikos backward, step by step. His strategy was clear: to push the larger man toward the slippery edge of the surf, where the wet sand and the pull of the water might level the playing field. In the distance, the witch's voice rose; her chants a rising tide of fury as she invoked old words from ancient, long-forgotten languages.

With an unexpectedly forceful parry, Antonios redirected one of Halikos's downward strikes, using the momentum to spin his opponent slightly off balance. Seizing the moment, Antonios advanced, pressing his opponent further back. The surf splashed around the large man's boots; the foam advancing and retreating with each wave. Halikos's footing slipped on the wet sand, his swings growing more desperate as he found himself being driven deeper into the sea by Antonios's assault.

From behind, a shadow shifted—silent, patient. The third soldier, who had been biding his time, waiting for the perfect moment to strike, swung his heavy blade. The impact was ferocious, the flat of his blade crashing down on the back of Antonios's head with a sickening crunch. Pain exploded as Antonios staggered forward, blood spraying across the sand in dark streaks. His knees hit the wet ground, his fingers clawing at the earth as the world tilted around him. The taste of blood filled his mouth, and his vision blurred, darkness edging in at the corners.

Above him, Halikos's face contorted into a savage snarl as he raised his great sword high in the air. The clash of battle faded, replaced by the ceaseless roar of waves and the ragged cries of the dying. Time stretched unbearably, the killing blow hovering in the air. Antonios, bloodied and broken, tensed, waiting for a strike that never came.

Halikos's blade never fell—his moment of triumph was shattered by the sharp whistle of an arrow cutting through the air. A second whistle, then a third. The last arrow buried itself deep in Halikos's shoulder, sending a jolt of pain down his arm. His grip faltered, and the great sword slipped from his fingers, crashing harmlessly into the sand.

High above the fray, on the cliffs that loomed over the beach, Longinus appeared. A dozen archers flanked him, their bows drawn tight, arrows poised to strike.

In a single, fluid motion, the archers loosed another volley. The arrows streaked through the air, their paths marked by the sharp hiss of cutting wind. One of the arrows struck true, burying itself in the neck of the remaining henchman with a sickening thud. The man staggered, his body twisting as blood spattered the sand. He stumbled back, unsteady and desperate, until his legs gave way and he crumpled, rolling into the foaming clutches of the sea.

Halikos's head snapped up, confusion clouding his face as the tide of battle shifted in an instant. His moment of triumph dissolved, slipping through his fingers like sand. With a furious roar, he reached for his sword, but his injured hand refused to obey. His fingers twitched futilely, unable to grasp the hilt.

The witch in black darted to Halikos's side, her clawed hands seizing his arm. Her chanting had fallen silent, replaced by hurried footsteps as she pulled him toward the waiting boat. Her dark robes whipped around her in the wind as she staggered across the sand, desperate to get out of bowshot.

Halikos cast one final, contemptuous glare at the bloodied Antonios, who remained on his knees in the sand. Then, without protest, he let the witch pull him away. Together they dashed across the beach, their retreat marked by the hiss and thud of arrows striking the ground around them. Their figures grew smaller against the expanse of the shoreline, dark figures swallowed by the approaching tide as they fled toward their waiting boat.

Kneeling in the sand, his strength spent, Antonios watched his enemy retreat through a haze of pain. Each movement was anguish, every moment a fresh wave of agony. The cool surf lapped at his hands, mingling with the blood that seeped into the sand, painting the beach in dark streaks. At last, exhaustion overtook him, and he collapsed face-first into the wet earth. The waves rippled around him, washing over the marks of battle as if eager to reclaim the shoreline.

Chapter 25

BETWEEN FEVER AND FAITH

The first rays of dawn crept through the weathered planks of the old mill's ceiling, their light slicing through the night like blades. The quiet stillness of the morning broke suddenly as distant shouts echoed across the hills. "Pothitos! Delenda!" Startled awake, Pothitos bolted upright, his heart pounding as the peace of his sleep was shattered.

Pothitos turned to Delenda, dread clouding his mind as he took in her state. She lay motionless beside him, her face ghostly pale except for the bright red flush of her cheeks. Sweat slicked her skin despite the cool dawn air, and her once gentle breaths rasped laboriously in the stillness.

Pothitos's hand trembled as he touched Delenda's forehead, the searing heat of a fever burning against his fingertips. Fear churned in his gut as he scanned the crumbling mill for options. The sagging beams and piles of broken tools offered little aid. Delenda's weakened condition made immediate escape unthinkable.

Pothitos moved with haste, quickly disassembling his makeshift barricade. He rearranged their scant bedding, tucking Delenda into a dark corner beneath the broken remains of a loom, piling worn grain sacks and dry grass around her to obscure her. "I pray this keeps you safe," he whispered, though the words were more for himself.

Satisfied that Delenda was well-hidden, Pothitos scanned the dim mill for a place to keep watch. His eyes landed on the waterwheel—a towering, weathered structure whose thick wooden spokes offered perfect cover. He prayed its groaning joints would mask any sound he made.

He moved silently, his feet barely making a sound on the worn floor as he approached the wheel. Climbing into the wheel was a laborious task; the wood creaked under his weight, resounding softly in the hollow mill. Pothitos managed to wedge himself between the large wooden spokes, finding a narrow space that afforded a clear view of the mill's entrance.

From this perch, Pothitos could hear the voices much clearer now. He could even make out the sound of approaching footsteps mixing with the morning breeze. His muscles tensed as he reached for the hilt of his weapon. He adjusted his position slightly, ensuring he remained unseen while maintaining a clear line of sight. He sat in complete silence, barely daring to breathe.

The rotting doorway suddenly gave way with a deafening crash, splintering under the force of the intruders. Three members of the Ierí Frourá barged in, their boots thudding against the worn wooden floor. Pothitos sat perfectly still, praying his presence remained undetected as the dim light cloaked him in shadow.

The soldiers milled about the interior, their movements careless and loud. One kicked over a rusted plowshare, sending a metallic clang ringing through the mill. Another rifled through some abandoned grain sacks, muttering curses under his breath. Dust swirled in the pale shafts of morning light, painting their movements in a haze.

Pothitos recognized the men instantly—members of the Ierí Frourá. But their familiar faces brought no comfort. Trust no one, Father Dimitri had warned him. He held his breath, every muscle taut, prepared to strike if they came too close.

The soldiers bantered back and forth, their irritation evident.

"Are we even sure they were headed this way?" one of them questioned, kicking at a discarded tool on the floor.

"We have scoured every inch of the coast. For all we know, they are halfway to Kos by now," another replied, scoffing.

"They're probably dead already," the third added with a sneer. "They couldn't have gotten far, not with Halikos and his men after them."

The soldiers' search through the mill grew increasingly lackluster as the minutes ticked by. They shuffled debris aside carelessly, their movements lacking any real intent or urgency, accompanied by a constant mutter of discontent. "This is a waste of time," one of them grumbled, pushing aside a rusted piece of farm equipment with his boot, causing it to screech against the old wooden floor.

"Surely, if they were here, we'd have found them by now— or what's left of them," another added with a dismissive snort, peering into one of the dark corners of the mill.

"Let's get out of here and report back. No use chasing the dead," the man who seemed to be in charge decided, and with that, headed back to the shattered doorway of the mill.

They stopped to make one last cursory glance around the dim interior, the futility of their mission seeming to settle in. With a collective shrug, they turned back toward the dusty, sunlit entrance. Their footsteps dragged, their voices a low rumble of resignation, fading into a silence as they exited the mill, convinced that Pothitos and Delenda had either escaped their grasp or met a fate elsewhere.

Once the soldiers' voices had faded completely, Pothitos cautiously climbed down from his perch inside the waterwheel, the wood moaning under his weight. His palms were still sweating from the near discovery, but his immediate concern was Delenda. He hurried over to where he had concealed her among the shadows, his breath catching in his throat at the sight of her.

She lay motionless, her face drained of blood and her forehead glistening with sweat. Pothitos gently lifted her wrist and saw a red line where the rocks had cut into her skin. The sight of the wounds, now clearly infected, sent a chill through him. The infection and the stress of their ordeal were taking a severe toll on her.

Pothitos knew he had to act quickly. Delenda needed water, clean water, to cool her fever and cleanse the wounds on her wrists. His mind raced through their options. The nearest cistern was back at the monastery, but doubt gnawed at him. He didn't know if it was safe there, or if the soldiers might return. He didn't even know if his father or Longinus still survived.

For a moment, he was paralyzed by indecision, but then he looked at Delenda's face and he saw his mother's face as she lay on her funeral bier. He couldn't leave her to die. So, Pothitos decided that despite the risks, their best chance was to return to the monastery. He gently lifted Delenda, cradling her in his arms, and set off toward their uncertain future.

As Pothitos carried Delenda through the rugged terrain, he was suddenly caught off guard by the sight of soldiers in all black armor. Soldiers—but not of the Ierí Frourá. Whoever they were, they blocked the path to the monastery. Tightening his hold on Delenda, he turned sharply and fled into the thickets, branches clawing at his arms as he ran.

The terrain blurred into a haze of green and gray as he pushed his body beyond endurance. His lungs burned, each breath an irregular gasp, and his legs trembled under Delenda's weight. The sun rose higher, its unrelenting heat baking his skin until his mouth felt like sand. When his sweat dried to salt, he knew dehydration was setting in—but stopping wasn't an option.

At last, his body gave out. Pothitos staggered to a halt, his legs buckling as he sank to his knees. He gently placed Delenda on a patch of soft, wild grass, her face pale against the ground. Closing his eyes, he pressed his hands together and uttered a fervent prayer. "Show us mercy, Lord." When he opened his eyes again, a dark opening loomed before him—a cave, half-hidden by an overgrown bush. He hadn't noticed it before, but now it felt like an answer.

With trembling arms, Pothitos lifted Delenda once more and stumbled toward the cave. The cool shade inside wrapped around him, soothing the raw heat on his skin. He set her down carefully, brushing a stray lock of hair from her damp forehead, before collapsing beside her in the dust. His body was spent, but he clung to a fragile sliver of hope.

The air inside the cave was cool and still, a welcome break from the burning sun. Pothitos lay on the dirt floor, his breathing slowing as his eyes adjusted to the dimness. The cave was shallow but sheltered—enough to hide them from prying eyes. He turned to Delenda, her face wan and fevered, and he felt a pang of helplessness. She needed water, something to clean her wound, and rest—but his own limbs felt leaden with exhaustion.

Pothitos shifted uncomfortably as he lay on the cold dirt floor, a persistent ache pressing into his back. Annoyance overtook his exhaustion as he rolled onto his side, reaching behind him to clear whatever was digging into him. His fingers brushed something smooth and solid—not the rough edge of a rock, but something else entirely.

Curiosity piqued, Pothitos mustered his remaining strength and clawed at the dirt, his fingers scraping the earth to uncover an object. Gradually, a rectangular shape emerged, its edges too precise to be natural. With a grunt of effort, he freed it and brought it closer, squinting in the faint light of the cave. Dust clung to its surface, and he brushed it away to reveal intricate carvings.

As the dust cleared, Pothitos trembled at the sight of what he held. The carved image of Saint Panteleimon stared back at him, serene and radiant even in the dim light. The saint's halo gleamed faintly, and his robes, though faded, could still be seen. Pothitos traced the contours of the icon with trembling fingers.

Pothitos recognized the saint immediately: Saint Panteleimon, the healer and protector of the suffering. The icon's muted colors showed through the faded wood. The green of his tunic spoke of renewal, while the red of his cloak symbolized his martyrdom. In his hands, the saint held a small medicine box and a carved spoon, symbols of his divine gift of healing.

Clutching the icon to his chest, Pothitos imparted a trembling prayer. "Panteleimon, saintly champion and healer, intercede with our merciful God to grant our souls remission of sins. O Champion and Martyr of God, imitating the Merciful and bearing from Him the grace of healing, cure our spiritual ills by your prayers, and set free from the temptation of the eternal enemy those who ceaselessly cry out, 'Save us, O Lord'."

As he held the icon close, a faint sound broke the heavy silence—a rhythmic drip, drip, drip. Pothitos's eyes darted toward the noise. He pushed himself up, his muscles screaming in protest, and staggered toward the cave wall. The sound grew louder, more distinct, as he neared its source.

Near the top of the cave wall, he saw water trickling down, forming a small pool in a basin near the cave's ceiling. The steady drip seemed almost miraculous, given their desperate situation. Pothitos hurried back to Delenda, his hands trembling as he cradled her head and carried her closer to the water.

With painstaking care, Pothitos scooped water into his cupped hands, droplets slipping through his fingers as he brought it to Delenda's cracked lips. Her body stirred faintly, a weak murmur escaping her as her lips parted to sip the cool water. Her eyelids fluttered open for a brief moment. Her eyes were dull and glazed with fever, but the sight of them sent a surge of relief through Pothitos's chest. She was still fighting.

"We'll get through this," he spoke, his voice barely heard, as much a promise to himself as to her. He cupped more water in his hands, carefully trickling it into her mouth as she weakly swallowed. The fever's flush still burned on her cheeks, but her breathing seemed steadier. As he worked, Pothitos uttered silent prayers.

As the droplets continued their rhythmic fall, Pothitos couldn't help but glance back at the icon of Saint Panteleimon. The saint, known for his healing powers, seemed to be offering them a sign, a small miracle in their darkest hour.

Chapter 26

THE BATTLE OF KASTELLI

In the confusion that followed Antonios's fall, Halikos struck swiftly, toppling the island's watchtowers and blockading its ports. With no routes to escape or call for aid, Kalymnos lay isolated and vulnerable. Marching among his ranks were mercenaries in black armor—men with light hair and blue eyes, their pale skin a chilling contrast to the sun-darkened faces of the islanders. These outsiders gave Halikos's army a threatening edge.

Halikos's next target was clear—Kastelli, the island's heart, now vulnerable with Antonios's near death and Pothitos missing. This was his chance to claim Kalymnos, but Longinus vowed to deny him.

Placing Andreas, a trusted Byzantine lieutenant, in charge of the Ierí Frourá at Agio Konstantinos, Longinus marshaled the remainder of the Byzantine armies to Kastelli. Clasping Andreas's burly hand, Longinus said, "Keep them safe. The monastery is our last stronghold. If Halikos breaks through here, all is lost."

Andreas responded with a firm salute. "The Ierí Frourá is ready to defend the monastery, captain. We will hold the line here."

As Longinus led his forces toward Kastelli, he prepared them for a brutal battle. Halikos, emboldened by recent victories, would not hesitate to crush any resistance.

When the word of the attack on the watchtower and ports reached Longinus, he dispatched runners to rally the militia from loyal demes and summon any willing volunteers.

The response to the call of arms from the demes was meager. There was no reply from the demes of Skaliodon, Amphipetron, or Peraioton. The deme of Mesos was only able to produce a handful of sun-beaten farmers and artisans.

The majority of the soldiers hailed from Panormos. Aristides, wielding substantial influence through his vast trade fleets, controlled a substantial portion of the island's wealth. His finances allowed him to maintain a private army. Among his men were local warriors and paid mercenaries—seasoned fighters accustomed to protecting his ships from pirates.

Upon reaching Kastelli, Longinus wasted no time organizing defenses. He positioned archers along the walls, set traps in the narrow passages of the fortress, and drilled every able-bodied villager in warfare. The fortress, perched high over a rocky land bridge, offered a strategic location from which to stage a battle.

As darkness cloaked the land, Longinus stood with Aristides atop Kastelli's battlements, his eyes drawn to the distant glow of fires— Halikos was coming. Below, the defenders shuffled in uneasy clusters: farmers gripping spears like plowshares and artisans muttering prayers between calloused fingers. Longinus knew they were no formal army, and their inexperience ate at him.

Pacing along the battlements, Longinus spoke to Aristides in a low voice. "The walls will hold for a time," he began, his tone troubled. "But these men—they are not soldiers. They have the heart, but it will not match steel if the enemy breaches."

Aristides agreed, his face unreadable. "My mercenaries will hold the line where it matters, but even they can't rival Halikos's veterans. Terrain will slow them, yes, but not forever. We'll need more than just fortress walls to survive this."

Longinus focused his thoughts on their best chances to survive the upcoming battle. "Position your men along the eastern wall. The fortifications are weak there and are in need of repair. This is where he is most likely to attack. We need to hold that wall, no matter what."

Aristides nodded absently, his mind seemingly elsewhere. "Longinus, I understand your strategy, but I have a proposal that could give us an even greater advantage."

Longinus turned toward Aristides. "Speak quickly, Aristides. Time is not on our side."

"The eastern wall is indeed weak," Aristides began, "but if we fortify it too obviously, Halikos will know we've prepared there. Instead, let's use that to our advantage. Let's place the militia…the weaker men along the eastern wall. Then we can place the majority of my forces in concealed positions behind the walls. We will create the illusion of vulnerability, coax Halikos's forces in, and when they breach the wall, we will crush them from within. My men are skilled in guerrilla tactics; they can strike swiftly and brutally."

Aristides paused, looking out over his assembled men. "It's not just about winning this battle," he said quietly. "It's about sending a message. Halikos and his followers must understand that we will not yield. The spirit of Kalymians will not be broken."

Longinus considered this, nodding slowly. "An ambush from within... It could work. But it will require precise coordination."

"Exactly," Aristides continued, his voice smooth as silk. "My men will be ready to move at a moment's notice. We can create a false point of defense, lure Halikos's attention to areas on which we want him to focus. Then we can prepare our true defenses elsewhere. When his forces are committed and overextended, we strike hard and fast, cutting them down before they realize what's happening."

Longinus ruminated over this proposition. "It's risky, but it could turn the tide in our favor. You control the majority of the seasoned troops here, and you know your men better than I do. I will defer to you in this instance. Make sure your men are prepared and in position. We must communicate effectively to pull this off."

Aristides nodded, a gleam in his eyes. "Leave it to me. I'll coordinate with your officers and make sure everyone knows their roles. We have one shot at this, and we must make it count."

As the first light of dawn broke, a horn sounded in the distance, its mournful wail signaling the approach of Halikos's army. From the tree line, a dark, undulating mass emerged.

Longinus stood on the battlements, his eyes straining as he took in the sight before him. Banners fluttered above the approaching force, spreading across the land bridge which connected the isthmus of Kastelli to the rest of the island. Among the billowing banners of Orkinos, his attention fell upon a solitary red flag emblazoned with a white stallion. It stood alone, set apart from the others, fluttering defiantly in the wind. Longinus whispered to himself, "Gelimer."

Longinus noticed the lack of siege machines, typically a formidable threat in any prolonged assault. He knew that they were rendered useless by the narrow land bridge that connected the fortress to the rest of the island. He understood that Halikos would also be aware of this logistical constraint. He surmised that Halikos's time was limited. He needed to crush Kastelli quickly and decisively before word of the assault reached the neighboring islands.

From his vantage point atop Kastelli, Longinus saw that escape was nearly impossible. Only a handful of rowboats clung to the rocks below, their ropes taut against the crushing surf. Precipitous cliffs and a churning sea enclosed the fortress on all sides, save for the narrow land bridge—now seized by Halikos's forces. The very geography that once made Kastelli a sanctuary now rendered it a trap, sealing his men's fate. Yet amid the grim reality, a defiant hope stirred: the fortress walls had never been breached.

His thoughts were interrupted by a harsh slap on the back. Aristides stood beside him; his grin spread across his face. "We stand together, my friend. We fight for our homes, our families, and our future. No matter the odds, we will give them a fight they will never forget."

Longinus nodded. "Indeed, Aristides. Let's make them remember this day."

Longinus, standing atop the battlements with Aristides at his side, spoke so that the tone of his voice rose above the din of the gathered men. "We must hold Kastelli at all costs. If we lose here, Halikos will control the heart of Kalymnos. We cannot let that happen."

"We are ready," came the voice of one of the elder farmers from Mesos.

Longinus nodded, his mind coursing with battle plans and contingencies. "We must hold them here. Kastelli must not fall."

The troops and volunteers stirred, their spirits lifted by the commanding presence of Longinus, and hollered back, "We shall not fall."

Longinus rallied the defenders to their posts. "Archers, take your positions along the walls! Engineers double-check the fortifications. Every man who can fight, arm yourselves and be ready."

Aristides, never one to be outdone in enthusiasm, cupped his hands around his mouth and bellowed, "Today, we show Halikos and his lot what it means to be Kalymian! We may be farmers, sponge divers, and fishermen, but we have the heart of warriors! Let them come and see the strength of our forefathers!"

The men around them cheered, the sound rising to the sky, a defiant chorus against the impending battle.

"Steady, men!" Longinus called out. "Today, we fight not just for Kastelli, but for all of Kalymnos. Remember your homes, your families, and the land you hold dear. We fight for our future!"

Halikos's forces, laden with spear point upon spear point, surged forward. At Longinus's signal, the defenders of Kastelli braced for impact and the archers let loose their bowstrings. Arrows rained down from the battlements, finding their marks among the advancing troops. The ground trembled as the invaders closed the gap to the fortress and crashed full force into the east wall.

The arrows did little to slow the relentless advance of Halikos's forces. The defenders on the battlements resorted to pouring boiling oil over the ramparts, a last-ditch measure that sent screams of agony coursing through the battlefield. Ladders were hastily erected against the fortifications, but the defenders, driven by a fierce loyalty to protect their home, sacrificed life and limb to beat the invaders back.

The second wave of attackers came with a roar of defiance, a tide of humanity crashing against the stone defenses of Kastelli. Arrows rained down from the ramparts, striking true and felling the front ranks of Halikos's army. Longinus moved along the battlements, directing his men with tactful genius, his orders countering every move the enemy made. The defenders, galvanized by their leader's presence, repelled the assault, sending attackers to their deaths in droves under the stone ramparts.

As the third wave of attackers began their march toward the castle wall, Longinus's attention was drawn to a disturbance within the fortress. Aristides moved along the lower rampart surrounded by his household warriors. Longinus watched as Aristides unfurled a banner of black and red with the same image depicted in the mosaic floor of his bathhouse: a woman with six necks around her waist, each topped with a dog's head, her body below the waist turning into serpent-tails.

Longinus's heart sank as he realized the betrayal unfolding before his eyes. Aristides, having positioned himself at the most vulnerable section of the eastern wall, lifted the banner skyward. In response, horns began to blow amongst Halikos's army.

"Traitor!" Longinus shouted, his voice filled with fury and disbelief.

Aristides turned, his expression smug and unrepentant. "It is time to turn back to the old gods, Longinus," he called back, his voice carrying over the shouts of battle. "You were blind to it, but the time for change is now. For the Cult of Skylla!!"

And it all began to make sense to Longinus. The woman in black, Gelimer's banner waving, the Cult of Skylla, Theophilos's betrayal—it was all connected. Theophilos had been one of

Aristides's men from the start. Longinus cursed under his breath. Belisarius should have let him finish the job at Tricamarum. He should have hunted down Gelimer and the witch. But instead, he allowed them to escape, thinking they were no longer a threat.

Now the consequences of that decision were crashing down on him. Aristides, with his cunning and treachery, had aligned himself with the very forces they thought were defeated at Tricamarum. The Cult of Skylla, with its dark rituals and insidious pull, had infiltrated their ranks, turning friends into foes. Aristides's betrayal was the final piece of the puzzle, a shocking revelation that left Longinus seething with rage.

"To arms!" Longinus bellowed, his voice cutting through the chaos. "Hold the line! Do not let the traitors win this day!"

Longinus hobbled down to the lower ramparts, his sword slicing through the ranks of Aristides's men. He fought with the strength of a man possessed, driven by the knowledge that the fate of an empire rested on his shoulders.

Aristides, seeing Longinus cutting a path through his men, met him with a wicked grin. "You're too late, Longinus. The Cult of Skylla will rise again, and there's nothing you can do to stop it."

"We shall see about that," Longinus growled, lunging in Aristides's direction.

Before he could reach the traitor, Longinus was checked by Aristides's household guard, a cadre of well-trained and heavily armed warriors. They moved to protect their master and surrounded Longinus.

Longinus adjusted his grip on his weapons. With his staff in his right hand and sword in his left, he moved with the grace of a myrmidon, the Greek warriors of legend. His staff whirled in a deadly arc, striking the first guard on the temple and sending him to the ground. Without pausing, he brought his sword around in a swift, lethal sweep, cutting down the second guard who had rushed him from the left.

Another guard came at him, thrusting with a spear. Longinus deflected the attack with his staff, the sound of wood clashing against metal crashed through the battlefield. He turned inside the guard's reach, his sword finding the man's unprotected side. The guard fell with a cry, his spear clattering to the ground.

Longinus turned to face the next attacker, his movements fluid. His staff caught the guard's sword mid-swing, the force of the impact jarring the man's arm. With a swift follow-up, Longinus drove the butt of the staff into the guard's chest, sending him staggering back. In the same motion, he slashed his sword across the guard's throat.

The remaining guards hesitated, their confidence shattering in the face of Longinus's ferocity. He took advantage of their hesitation, launching into a series of relentless attacks. His staff struck one guard's knee, shattering the joint and dropping him to the ground. His sword found the heart of another, piercing through his armor with a powerful thrust.

One by one, the household guards fell before him, their defenses no match for his prowess. Longinus moved like a force of nature, each strike calculated and devastating. The battlefield became a blur of motion and blood, the cries of the fallen mingling with the clash of steel.

With the guards dispatched, Longinus turned his attention back to Aristides, who stood watching with fear. "Your men are dead, Aristides," Longinus said, his voice cold and steady. "It's over."

Aristides's grin faltered, but his eyes still burned with defiance. "You think you've won, Longinus? The Cult of Skylla is eternal. You cannot kill what we represent."

"Enough talk," Longinus said, advancing on him. "Face me."

Aristides drew his sword; a gleaming blade etched with dark runes. They clashed with a resounding ring, the force of their blows sending shockwaves through the air. Aristides fought with the ferocity of a cornered animal, his strikes wild and frenzied. But Longinus, fueled by righteous anger, fought with intense focus.

Their swords clashed again and again, sparks flying from the metal. Longinus deflected a heavy blow from Aristides, countering with a swift strike that nicked the traitor's cheek. Aristides snarled, lunging forward with renewed aggression, but Longinus sidestepped, bringing his staff down on Aristides's wrist with a bone-crunching force. The sword fell from Aristides's grasp, clattering to the ground.

Longinus pressed the advantage, his sword at Aristides's throat. "Yield," he commanded.

Aristides's eyes darted around, searching desperately for any means of escape, but found none. "You may have won today, Longinus," he hissed, venom lacing his words, "but the Cult of Skylla will rise again. Mark my words."

Longinus gripped his sword, ready to end the threat once and for all. But before he could act, Aristides stepped back toward the edge of the ramparts. The realization of his intentions struck Longinus like a bolt of lightning.

"Aristides, no!" Longinus shouted, lunging forward.

With a final, mocking grin, Aristides let himself fall backward off the edge of the ramparts. Time seemed to slow as he tumbled down the precipitous cliffs, his figure twisting and turning against the backdrop of the turbulent sea below. The waves crashed violently against the rocks, their roar mingling with the distant cries of battle.

Longinus rushed to the edge, his heart pounding. He peered down into the churning waters, where Aristides's form was rapidly swallowed by the tumultuous sea. For a moment, he stood there, his mind racing with the implications of Aristides's final act.

Longinus turned to look at the utter chaos around him and saw the destruction of his army as they retreated deeper into the fortifications. Bodies lay strewn across the battlefield, and the air was filled with the cries of the wounded and dying. The realization hit him hard—less than half of his original forces still stood.

"We can't hold this position any longer," Longinus called out to his men, his voice commanding despite the weariness in his bones. "Strategic retreat! Fall back to the inner fortifications!"

Longinus and two dozen of his bravest soldiers took up the rearguard position. They formed a defensive line in a narrow passage, buying precious time for the remaining men to escape down the slow, treacherous switchback that wound its way along the face of the cliff to the small beach at its base.

"Hold them back!" Longinus shouted, his sword and staff moving in a deadly dance. Each swing and thrust was calculated, designed to slow the advancing enemy.

The rearguard fought courageously despite the overwhelming odds. Their valor shone through as they repelled wave after wave of attackers, the narrow passage working to their advantage by funneling the enemy into a bottleneck.

But the enemy's numbers were too great, and their attacks were too fierce. Slowly, the rearguard was forced to give ground, inch by inch. Longinus could see the terrified faces of the militia making their way down the cliff, and he knew they couldn't hold much longer.

"Fall back," Longinus commanded, his voice strained. "To the path!"

The remaining defenders began to retreat, backing slowly toward the edge of the path. They fought with everything they had, their blades flashing in the dim light. Six brave men fell, cut down by the relentless onslaught, their sacrifices not in vain as they bought crucial moments for the others.

Finally, there was a break in the battle as Longinus and the last of his men reached the narrow path down. "To the boats!" he shouted, turning and limping down the switchback. The narrow path was dangerous, but it was their only chance of survival.

The switchback was a perilous descent, the path winding sharply back and forth along the steep cliff face. The defenders moved as quickly as they dared, their hearts pounding with the urgency of their flight. Longinus led the way, his eyes scanning for any sign of danger ahead.

As they neared the bottom of the cliff, the sound of the enemy's pursuit grew louder. Longinus knew they had only moments before the attackers would be upon them. He quickened his pace, urging the others to do the same.

They reached the small beach at the base of the cliff just as the first of the enemy soldiers appeared above them. Longinus turned, his sword raised, ready to defend the retreating men. "Keep moving!" he shouted. "Get to the boats!"

A few remaining warriors formed a final line, their backs to the sea, as they prepared to make their last stand. The small row boats beached on the shore were their only chance of escape.

The first enemy soldiers reached the beach, their weapons drawn. Longinus met them head-on, his sword clashing against theirs. The defenders fought with everything they had, knowing their lives were on the line.

For every man they lost, the enemy paid dearly. The beach became a fierce battleground, the sound of the dying rising up over the crashing waves. Ever so slowly, the defenders continued to be pushed back, their numbers dwindling.

Longinus knew they couldn't hold out much longer. "Get in the boats!" he shouted again, his voice carrying over the chaos. "Go now!"

They began to scramble into the boats; their faces filled with fear. Longinus and two other soldiers held the line, buying them the time they needed to board the small vessels.

Finally, with the last of the men safely aboard, Longinus turned to his men. "We fall back!" he ordered. "Into the boats!"

They retreated slowly, fighting every step of the way, until they reached the edge of the water. One by one, they climbed into the boats, their eyes never leaving the enemy. Longinus was the last to board, his sword still raised in defiance.

As the small boats pushed off from the shore, the defenders watched as the enemy claimed victory. But they had done all they could. They had bought time, and they had escaped with their lives.

Longinus looked back at the fortress of Kastelli, now swarming with enemy soldiers. It was a bitter loss, but they survived. And as long as they lived, they would continue to fight.

Chapter 27

THE CAVE OF SAINT PANTELEIMON

Delenda's recovery from the infection was a slow but steady process. In the cave of Saint Panteleimon, Pothitos dedicated himself to her care with devotion. He crafted a bed of soft leaves and grasses, ensuring she rested comfortably, and bathed her fevered brow with cool water drawn from the small recess in the cave wall. Each day, he cleaned her wounds with careful hands, watching as the red line on her arm began to fade, and her wounds slowly healed.

When Delenda had gathered enough strength, she helped Pothitos place the icon of Saint Panteleimon in a natural hollow in the cave wall. The saint's serene expression and comforting presence brought them a sense of peace. They transformed that hollow into a small sanctuary, adorning it with wildflowers whenever they could. Each day, Pothitos knelt before the icon, speaking prayers of thanks and pleas for intercession and healing.

Though Delenda's lips moved silently beside him, her attention often lingered on the icon with a look he couldn't quite read.

On cooler nights, they built small fires that cast flickering light across the cave walls. Pothitos would sit close to her, watching the light dance on her face. Her features softened in the firelight, and he found himself enchanted by her beauty. Occasionally, their hands brushed, and he would feel a heat rise in his chest.

His heart lifted with each sign of her recovery. He knew she needed nourishment, so he crafted a sling from branches and strips of cloth, using it to hunt small birds and rabbits, making sure they had enough to eat. He carefully prepared the food with herbs picked from the mountainside, and they shared these meals in gratitude. As days turned into weeks, Delenda slowly regained her color.

As her strength returned, she became an invaluable guide to the natural world surrounding their sanctuary. Her knowledge of plants, honed during her time at the monastery, fascinated Pothitos. He admired the way her voice softened when she explained the uses of wild artichoke or lavender, and how her hands moved delicately as she harvested roots and leaves.

"See this one," Delenda said, pointing to a cluster of green leaves with purple-veined undersides. "It's a wild spinach. This is safe for us to eat."

Pothitos watched intently as Delenda continued to teach him. She demonstrated how to harvest wild artichoke, carefully digging around its base to extract the roots without damaging them.

"The roots can be boiled for a tea that helps with digestion," she explained, handing him a bundle of the spiky leaves. "And the leaves can be eaten raw or cooked, giving us energy."

"This one," she said, pointing to a cluster of small, purple flowers, "is lavender. Its scent is calming, and it can be used to make a soothing tea."

They gathered the plants she identified, adding them to their growing collection of herbs. Each new discovery was a step toward self-sufficiency and survival.

They drank fresh spring water from the small pool in the recess of the cave, which seemed to have miraculous properties. The cool, crystal-clear water invigorated them, washing away the fatigue of their arduous journey.

"There's something about this water," Pothitos remarked one evening, handing her a cup he'd shaped from hollowed-out stone. "It's like it carries life itself."

Delenda nodded, a smile gracing her lips. "This is a place of miracles," she said softly. "I could feel a presence here. I feel as if something is protecting us."

As they regained their strength, their days were filled with a blend of work, prayer, and talk of their past lives. Delenda spoke of her childhood in Egypt, painting vivid pictures of the sun-drenched banks of the Nile. Pothitos was spellbound by her descriptions. He couldn't help but wonder how someone who had endured so much could still speak of her past with such tenderness.

"I used to play by the river with my friends," she reminisced, her eyes distant. "We'd race through the fields, chasing each other until we collapsed in the reeds. It was back when I felt safe."

Pothitos would sit in silence and listen to her, content to hear her stories of exotic places and hidden dangers. But one night, as the firelight flickered low, Pothitos broke a long silence. His voice was tremulous.

"I've been thinking about my father," he began, staring at the smoldering embers. "I don't think he survived that day on the beach. I can still see him… standing there as the enemy charged. He taught me everything I know… how to fight, how to love, when to show strength and when to show mercy. And I… I let him die."

Delenda listened, her eyes reflecting the dying firelight. She spoke softly, "So much loss, all because of me."

Pothitos shook his head, his hand reaching over to touch hers. "No, Delenda, it wasn't because of you. We all make choices, and sometimes, we blame others to ease our own pain. But it wasn't your fault. My father told me to protect you… to escape with you. He would expect me to stand by you, just as he stood by our people."

Delenda's eyes began to moisten. "But if it weren't for me, none of this would have happened. The invasions, the devastation—it's all because of me."

He shrugged his shoulders. "For a long time, I blamed you for the death of my mother. It was easier than facing the truth. I thought if I could pin my pain on someone, it would stop eating me alive. But… I was wrong."

Delenda nodded. "I could tell that you felt that way about me… though I never blamed you for it, Pothitos. Grief has a way of clouding our minds."

Pothitos paused for a moment before continuing his tale. "The loss of my mother... it broke me," he confessed. "When she died, I stopped believing in anything. I thought the world was cruel and hollow. Then Father Dimitri sent me to the monastery, and…" He hesitated, his eyes meeting hers. "You were there. You reminded me that the world still had beauty in it."

Delenda placed a comforting hand on his arm. "You're kinder to me than I deserve. You've lost so much because of me, Pothitos. Most people believe I am the root of all problems on this island."

"Not me," he said firmly. "I am not most people."

Delenda softly moved her hand down his arm, her hand finding his and gently covering it.

He slowly continued, "I admit… It took me some time, but I eventually realized that you were a victim, just like the rest of us. My anger was misguided and now I see that those thoughts could not be further from the truth."

Delenda slid her fingers between his and gave a gentle squeeze. No one spoke; instead, they chose to let the moment stretch on. Finally, Delenda spoke, "There's more you don't know. There are secrets about me… secrets about why Halikos wants me dead."

She reflected for a moment before continuing, her voice touched by sorrow. "I am the last of Cleopatra's bloodline. In Egypt, they call me a princess, though that title has brought me nothing but ruin. There's a prophecy, Pothitos, that an heir to Cleopatra will reclaim Egypt's throne. Because of this, powerful figures created a story that my blood carries miraculous qualities. They spread rumors that consuming it will grant eternal youth."

Pothitos listened intently, finally asking, "Is that why the lady in black was there… on the beach?"

She nodded, "Many of the old cults, such as the Cult of Skylla, believe that Cleopatra found the key to eternal youth and it was passed down to me in her blood. They think that drinking it would give the high priestess of Skylla eternal youth. This is all folly. But the lady in black… the high priestess of their cult… she believes the legend. She would do anything to obtain my blood."

Anger caused Delenda's face to flush as she spoke, "To strike fear into people, she spreads the rumor that she is the reincarnation of the mythical beast Skylla… you know… the one that was written about by Homer in *The Odyssey*."

Delenda drew a shaky breath, her fingers fidgeting with the edge of her cloak. Finally, she lifted her gaze to meet Pothitos's eyes.

"There's something else you must know," she began softly. "My bloodline… it isn't just Cleopatra's."

Pothitos leaned closer, "What do you mean?"

"One of Cleopatra's descendants," Delenda said, "married a Roman soldier long ago. They had a son named Longinus." She hesitated, watching his face.

"Longinus?" Pothitos echoed. "Like our Longinus?"

Delenda nodded. "Yes, like our Longinus. This man became a centurion, who was present at the Crucifixion of Christ. They say he was the one who thrust his spear into the side of Jesus." Her voice trembled. "But when he saw the blood and water pour forth from the wound, he believed. Right there, as the temple veil was torn in two, he converted."

Pothitos stared at her. "And this Longinus… he was your ancestor?"

"Yes," she said, glancing away for a moment. "After his death, the spear disappeared. But my family—his descendants—we are said to carry a birthmark, a sign that points to where the spear lies hidden. People call this relic the Spear of Destiny, claiming it holds unimaginable power—the power to shape the fate of empires."

Pothitos was silent for a long moment. Finally, he said, "So you carry not only Cleopatra's blood, but his as well… a lineage tied to both earthly queens and the crucifixion of Christ."

Delenda's eyes shimmered as she nodded. "It is a blessing to some… a curse to me. This is why I am pursued by so many powerful figures. This is why the high priestess of Skylla has aligned with Halikos. She promises kings and power-hungry men like him control of the spear."

"The mark. Show me," Pothitos said softly.

Delenda hesitated, glancing at him for a moment before nodding. Finally, she looked away, having made her decision. She stood up and gathered her hair, lifting it to reveal the back of her neck. Pothitos gasped when he saw the birthmark. His fingers brushed the outline of the birthmark, his touch lingering as if to memorize every detail.

It was an unmistakable image of the island of Kalymnos. The shape resembled a dragon, its head in the northwest and its tail in the southeast. His finger stopped on a small red mole in the shape of a star. It was as if he were looking at a map, and this star would be on the east coast of the island—directly within Halikos's land.

"It's incredible," he declared, his fingers trembling as they hovered over the mark. "It's like a map, a guide or something."

Delenda lowered her hair and turned to face him, her thoughts unreadable. "This is why Halikos and those like him are after me, Pothitos. They believe this is a map that will lead them to the Spear of Destiny."

Pothitos nodded. "Then we must be even more cautious. You must be protected at all costs."

For a moment she looked directly at Pothitos, and he was drawn back into Delenda's green eyes, his mind traveling back to when he first saw her in his home.

"You've been burdened with a fate you never asked for, Delenda. A life of strife and danger, all for the gain of others. It's unimaginable," said Pothitos.

Delenda sighed. "I've been running my entire life. Always looking over my shoulder, always wondering when they would find me. I never wished for any of this."

Pothitos stared at the smoldering embers of their small fire. "Most people would have given in by now."

"It has not been easy," Delenda admitted, "but friends like Longinus and you have made it bearable. You've given me hope."

Pothitos reached out and pulled her into a soft embrace. "Delenda, I can't imagine a future without you in it. Our destinies are intertwined, and I am determined to protect you. No matter the cost."

"And I wouldn't want a life without you," Delenda replied, holding him close. "Together, we'll face whatever comes."

Pothitos, taken aback by her candor, felt his heart swell. "Delenda, you've shown me a world beyond anything I've ever known. You have become a light in my darkest days."

He continued softly, "I used to think my duty was my only purpose. But now, you have become my purpose."

"And you have shown me what it means to truly live, Pothitos," Delenda said. "I never thought I could feel this way, especially after everything I've been through."

They held each other in silence for a time as Pothitos found himself marveling at her beauty. She looked back at him, and he found himself pulled in again by those deep green eyes and he couldn't hold back any longer.

"Delenda," he said, his voice trembling slightly, "there's something I need to tell you." He paused, gathering his courage. "I think I'm falling in love with you."

Delenda's heart skipped a beat. She looked up at him, her eyes wide. "Pothitos, I... I've loved you from the day I first saw you through the window of your home," she confessed. "But it seemed like a love that was never meant to be. My soul was...conflicted. I knew that if I took my vows at the monastery, we could never be married. So, I prayed that God would somehow bring us together."

"Delenda," he began, his voice trembling again, "I want to spend the rest of my days with you. I have never been so sure of anything in my life. Marry me."

Delenda's eyes filled with tears, but she gently pushed away. "Pothitos, you know I care for you deeply," she said, her voice filled with sorrow. "But we come from different worlds. Your duty is to your people, and they will never accept me as one of their own. And you must go back and take your place among them."

"My place is with you, Delenda," Pothitos said firmly. "My life is empty without you. I would rather live one day with you than a thousand years without you."

"If I stayed with you, your life would be filled with danger," Delenda said, her voice breaking. "The people will see me as an outsider, and they will never accept us."

"I don't care about that," Pothitos insisted. "I love you, Delenda. And I know that it was God who brought us together."

Tears streamed down Delenda's face as she looked into his eyes. She had hesitated for so long, fearing that converting to Christianity would strip her of her chance to be with him. But now, she realized that her love for Pothitos and her acceptance of Christ were intertwined.

She spoke humbly, "I have wanted to convert for years, but I was afraid I would be sent away from the monastery if I did not take the monastic vows. But now I see God's true providence. Now I know I must be baptized. I will be with you, truly and completely. I will take your hand in marriage."

Pothitos flushed with joy as he pulled her back into his arms, holding her tightly. "I love you, Delenda," he said, his voice choked with emotion. "We will face whatever comes together as one."

That night, Pothitos held Delenda close, the warmth of their newfound commitment wrapping around them. As dawn approached, a sharp, acrid smell permeated the air, jolting them awake. Delenda sat up, her face pale with fear. "Fire!" she exclaimed, breathless. "There is black smoke rising from the direction of Kastelli. I fear the worst."

Pothitos felt a chill run down his spine. The sight of the smoke confirmed his fears. "I have to go back," he said.

Delenda placed a hand on his arm. "Then we go together, whatever the cost."

With one last look at the cave of Saint Panteleimon, Delenda and Pothitos turned and began their journey back to Kastelli, their hearts filled with dread. Together, they dared to face the unknown, ready to confront whatever awaited them in their beloved city.

Chapter 28

BETWEEN LIFE AND DEATH

Back at the monastery, the atmosphere was filled with sorrow. The sickly-sweet odor of oils and healing herbs hung like a veil over the room where Antonios lay. Once a towering warrior, his body was now frail and wasted, his skin pale and stretched thin over his battered frame. His clouded eyes stared blankly at the ceiling, as though searching for something beyond this world. Each inhalation was a rasp of death, a painful reminder of the grievous wounds that had brought him to this fragile state. Immobile and silent, he seemed caught between this life and the next.

Around him, the nuns of the monastery, led by Gerontisa Angeliki, prayed incessantly. Their soft voices rose and fell like the rhythm of the sea, chanting Greek hymns that beseeched God for mercy and comfort. Each word was a plea, filling the air as the flickering candlelight danced on the stone walls. The room was steeped in heartache, a sanctuary for a man who had given so much in the name of duty and honor.

Angeliki knelt by Antonios's side, her hands clasping his limp, unresponsive ones. Her troubled face, lined with years of care and service, was illuminated by the dim glow of the candles. She spoke words of comfort, her voice steady despite the trembling sadness beneath it. The nuns' prayers carried on, delicate but unyielding. Yet, the ointments and soft murmurs of prayer could not mask the truth of his condition—his pain lingered, written plainly across his hollowed face.

Longinus entered the room, his steps slow and deliberate. His staff tapped softly against the stone floor, punctuating each painful limp. Dust and ash streaked his tattered cloak, speaking of the hard-fought battle he had endured. His broad shoulders, once unyielding, sagged with the news he must deliver.

As he approached the bed, the nuns' voices faltered, trailing off into a hushed silence. Angeliki rose to meet him, her eyes meeting his with an unspoken question. The only sounds left in the room were Antonios's soft breaths and the distant tolling of the monastery bell, solemn and rhythmic.

Longinus steeled himself. When he responded, his voice was low. "The situation is far worse than I expected," he began. "Kastelli has fallen to Halikos's forces. Pothaia is under his control. The demes are fracturing, and unrest is spreading like wildfire across the island."

Angeliki gasped softly, her face paling as she understood the implications. Her eyes, which so often shone with fortitude, now showed unshed tears.

"And Pothitos? Delenda?" she asked, her voice trembling. The question hung in the air, heavy with unspoken fears.

"There has been no word of them," Longinus replied, his voice rough with frustration. "It's as though they vanished into thin air. Scouts are searching tirelessly, but every trail has led to nothing."

The nuns exchanged worried glances, their prayer ropes clutched tightly in trembling hands. The fate of the two young adults they had helped raise now hung in the balance.

Angeliki's shoulders slumped when she heard the news. She closed her eyes briefly, offering a silent prayer for their safety. When she opened them again, there was a glint of determination in her eyes. "We must not lose faith," she said. "We must believe that they are out there, somewhere, and that they will find their way back to us."

Longinus nodded, his voice firm despite his weariness. "We will continue the search," he vowed. "I will not rest until they're found—until both of them are safe."

He knelt beside the bed, his knees creaking against the stone floor. Gently, he took Antonios's limp hand in his own, the once-strong fingers now frail and unresponsive. "Antonios, my old friend," he murmured, his voice soft with angst. "Your son is out there somewhere. We will find him. We will protect him, just as you protected so many."

His grip tightened slightly, as though he was willing his own strength to flow into his friend. "You have given everything, Antonios—your loyalty, your honor. Now it's our turn to repay that debt. Your son will not be abandoned. I swear it, on my honor."

For a moment, Antonios's clouded eyes seemed to flicker to life, as if the sound of Longinus's voice stirred something deep within. Though battered and diminished, a stubborn flame of the warrior's spirit still burned in him, refusing to be extinguished.

Longinus leaned closer, his voice filled with emotion. "Hold on, my friend," he implored. "Hold on."

Angeliki gently interrupted his reverie. "Who remains on our side, Longinus?" she asked. Her voice was calm, but a tremor betrayed her underlying fear.

Longinus darkened, anger flickering like embers in his weary eyes. "The betrayal of Aristides and the people of Panormos was a dagger in my heart," he said. "A wolf in sheep's clothing. He whispered poison into the ears of those closest to me. Theophilos, a man I trusted as a brother, was turned against us—seduced by promises of power and glory. He became Aristides's puppet."

He paused, his hands closing into fists. "During the battle at Kastelli, Aristides struck at the perfect moment. While we held the gates against Halikos's forces, he turned on us. His men struck from within, slaughtering my soldiers from behind. I cornered him on the battlements, but he took his own life—coward that he was. No chance of redemption. No chance for salvation."

Angeliki gasped, her horror evident. "And now?"

"We have lost most of the island," Longinus admitted grimly. "The people of Mesos and Pothaia remain with us, but the stronghold and the city have fallen. Skaliodon stands, but its warriors are few, as are those of Amphipetron and Peraioton. The ports and the watchtower are gone. We are cut off from the rest of the empire… completely isolated."

Angeliki shook her head, her voice low. "Without the watchtower, we cannot light the beacon for reinforcements. We are truly alone."

"Yes," Longinus agreed. "And the worst part is, we barely have enough men to keep the monastery walls manned. If Halikos attacks, we won't hold them for long. But we must prepare for whatever comes. And we must pray that Pothitos and Delenda find their way back. Their return could tip the balance in our favor."

"And if they have Delenda?" Angeliki asked, her voice breaking slightly.

Longinus's features hardened. "If Halikos has her…then we have already lost."

The room fell into tense silence. Antonios's labored breathing, once oppressive, now faded into the background, drowned out by their thoughts.

Longinus finally broke the silence, his voice firm. "We will fortify our defenses and ensure that every soul within these walls is ready to fight. We will not surrender this place easily. I'll marshal the remaining forces and set up a watch. And we will keep searching for Pothitos and Delenda—she is our last hope."

Angeliki nodded. "We will pray for their safety, and for the strength to endure whatever comes. We must have faith, Longinus. We must believe."

As Longinus turned to leave, he cast one last glance at Antonios, lying frail and silent on the bed. "Your son is strong, Antonios," he said softly. "He will find a way."

Chapter 29

THE RUINS OF POTHAIA

Pothitos and Delenda made their way back to Kastelli, unsure of what they would find. As they approached the stronghold, the sight that met their eyes confirmed their worst fears. The once-proud fortress of Kastelli lay in shambles, its walls breached and overrun by Halikos's and Gelimer's men. The city of Pothaia had been looted, its streets strewn with debris and the remnants of a violent conquest. Smoke still lingered in the air, witness to the destruction that had been wrought.

The scene before them was one of utter devastation. The majestic walls of Kastelli, which had once stood as an impregnable defense, were now crumbled and broken, large sections lying in ruins on the ground. Intense battle and fire had left the gates splintered and hanging loosely, the defensive towers charred and blackened. Scattered among the rubble were the remnants of the defenders' last stand—broken weapons, discarded shields, and the lifeless bodies of those who had fought bravely to protect their home.

Pothitos clenched his fists, the anger and sorrow welling up inside him. "How could they do this?" he declared, his voice choked with emotion. "My home... my people..."

Delenda placed a comforting hand on his arm, her eyes reflecting the same anguish. "You will get it back," she said softly. "You have to."

Pothitos responded, void of emotion. "We need to be careful. We can't afford to be seen. Let's find shelter and see if anyone loyal to my father survived."

They moved cautiously through the darkened alley, their movements silent and deliberate. The narrow alleys provided some cover, but a pervasive sense of danger was everywhere. They avoided the main streets where enemy patrols were most likely to be, their senses becoming more alert as they neared the center of the city.

As they crept through the labyrinthine alleys, they came across scenes of devastation that tore at their hearts. Buildings lay in ruins, and the once-vibrant city was now a ghostly shell of its former self. The oppressive atmosphere was in complete contrast to the bustling, lively city they had once known. The streets of Pothaia, once alive with the sounds of commerce and laughter, were now eerily silent. Buildings that had housed shops, homes, and gathering places were reduced to smoldering wrecks. The air was filled with the acrid smell of smoke and ash, mingled with the pungent odor of charred flesh.

As they approached the marketplace, once the heart of the city, they saw it had turned into a desolate wasteland. Stalls that had displayed colorful goods and fresh produce were overturned and smashed, their wares scattered and trampled. The cobblestones were stained with dark splotches where blood had been spilled, and the ground was littered with broken pottery, shattered glass, and utter obliteration. The remnants of a vibrant life now lay twisted and broken, a grim testimony to the brutality that had ravaged the city.

They ventured deeper into the city, passing the stadium where the true horrors of the invasion became evident. Corpses lay strewn about, some cut down in their tracks, others piled haphazardly as if tossed aside in the chaos. The sight was gut-wrenching, a reminder of the violence that had consumed Pothitos's beloved home. The few survivors they saw moved like ghosts, their eyes hollow and expressions blank. The silence was punctuated only by the occasional sob or the distant sound of collapsing structures, adding to the macabre scene.

Their journey through the ruins brought them to the church of Agia Sofia, their destination. The church stood at the far end of the city, its dome miraculously still intact despite the devastation surrounding it. Pothitos gestured for Delenda to follow him into a narrow alleyway that led toward the church. "Stay close," he whispered. "We may find safety there."

As they approached, they saw that the heavy church doors were slightly ajar, letting light filter into the dim interior. Delenda peered through the gloom to see dust filtering through the sliver of light, highlighting the crucifix on the main altar. She looked back at Pothitos and said, "It seems deserted."

Pothitos carefully pushed open the heavy wooden door, the creak of the hinges sounding unnaturally loud in the stillness. They slipped inside, closing the door behind them. It took a moment for their eyes to adjust to the dim interior. The familiar scent of incense and the soft glow of candlelight were missing, replaced by a cold silence.

"We need to find someone," Pothitos said quietly, his eyes scanning the empty pews. "Anyone who can help us."

They moved deeper into the church, their footsteps tapping softly on the stone floor. As they approached the altar, a figure emerged from behind the iconostasis, a dark shape advancing on them within the bleak surroundings. The figure stepped into the diffuse light, revealing the weathered face of Father Dimitri. His eyes, filled with sorrow, widened in surprise as he recognized them.

"Pothitos? Delenda?" he spoke, his voice trembling. "Thank the Lord you're alive!"

Pothitos felt a surge of relief at the sight of the old priest. "Father Dimitri, we've been hiding. We were betrayed by Theophilos and were unsure of who we could trust. So, we ran and hid in the caves until we saw the smoke rising from Kastelli. When we saw it, we knew things were not right…we knew that we had to return."

He paused for a moment to look around. "Tell me, what has happened here?"

Father Dimitri sighed deeply. "Halikos's forces have taken the city. When your father was struck down, there was no one left to unite the demes. We were betrayed by those we thought were loyal. Many of our men were killed, others captured. Halikos has allowed the church to remain as a sign of solidarity with the people, but it's only a matter of time before they destroy everything."

Pothitos's voice broke with heartache. "My father... so it is as I feared. He is dead."

Father Dimitri allowed a brief smile to cross his lips. "No, my child, he lives." Seeing Pothitos's eyes light up, he waved his hand in caution as he continued, "But he is just a shell of his former self. Right now, he is being kept safe and comfortable by Longinus within the walls of the monastery."

Pothitos stared hard at the priest and remained silent for a long time before speaking, "How bad is he?"

Father Dimitri replied with honesty, "He will most likely survive, but I do not believe he will ever regain his ability to speak, let alone lead the people."

Pothitos responded, "I must go to him."

"I'm afraid that's impossible," replied the priest.

Pothitos protested, but he was silenced as Father Dimitri pressed on, "The monastery, our last refuge, is under siege by the former king of the Vandals, Gelimer. The nuns have enough supplies and enough fresh water in the cistern to last for many months, but the enemy has camped around the monastery and there is no safe approach."

Delenda spoke, "Gelimer… were those the men who were with the witch Skylla on the beach? Were they the soldiers we saw in the dark armor?"

Father Dimitri nodded. "Anyone deemed a threat to King Halikos has been executed by those men. I have hidden as many survivors and outlaws in the catacombs as I could. But it continues to become increasingly dangerous for me to do so. I was allowed to continue my ministry in the church, but only with the understanding that I must calm the people and convince them to accept the new regime. But I fear they are watching me… it is only a matter of time before my true purpose is discovered. The church will be destroyed and me along with it."

Pothitos said, "We must do something. We can't just give up."

Father Dimitri sighed deeply. "I know, my child. But we must be cautious. The situation is dire, and we need to be strategic in our actions. But most of all, we must keep the two of you safe. The entire island is looking for Delenda. We could hide you in the catacombs with the rest of the survivors, but I'm afraid that word will get out that you are here. The fewer people that know, the better."

Pothitos responded, "We have no need to hide here. We could go back to the mountains if needed. We've learned to survive there. We would be safe for the time being." Pothitos paused and looked up at Father Dimitri with hope. "Father, there is something we must do before anything else. Delenda and I... we want to get married. But for that to happen, she must be baptized."

Father Dimitri's eyes widened in surprise, then his face softened. He looked at Delenda, who nodded her agreement. "I see," he said, his voice gentle. "Your love for each other is great, and it is a light in these dark times."

Delenda stepped forward, her voice steady. "Father, I have wanted to convert for a long time, but I was afraid. Now I know it is the right path. I wish to be baptized and join Pothitos in faith and in life."

The priest looked at her quizzically before asking her, "Delenda, what baptismal name do you choose?"

She looked at Pothitos for a moment, before speaking, "I would be honored to take the name of your mother... Nomiki... If you would allow it."

Pothitos nodded to the priest. A smile showed on his lips.

Father Dimitri nodded solemnly. "Very well. Then we will do it here and now, in the name of the Lord. You will be baptized by economia due to the extreme circumstances brought upon us by Halikos." He called for the sexton of the church, Suzanna. She was a young lady with unblemished skin, light hair, and greenish-blue eyes. Her head was covered by a shawl, and she was instructed to take Delenda to the back of the church. The priest also asked Suzanna to stand as a Godparent to Delenda. She agreed resolutely. Delenda and Suzanna waited in the nave of the church as Father Dimitri prepared his vestments and sacraments.

As Father Dimitri returned, Pothitos stood watching the scene. Father Dimitri began the baptismal rites, his voice rising in the quiet of the church. He started by lighting a candle, symbolizing the light of Christ. He then made the sign of the cross over Delenda's head. "In the name of the Father, and of the Son, and of the Holy Spirit, Amen."

He then turned to Suzanna and asked her to hold a baptismal garment he retrieved from behind the iconostasis, a white robe symbolizing purity and new life in Christ.

Turning back to Delenda, Father Dimitri began the exorcisms, a traditional part of the Byzantine baptismal rite. He raised his hand and commanded, "Depart from her, every unclean spirit. Depart from her, every evil power. Depart from her, every phantom and encounter of the devil."

Father Dimitri continued, "Do you renounce Satan, and all his angels, and all his works, and all his services, and all his pride?"

"I do renounce them," Delenda replied firmly.

Father Dimitri then asked her to spit three times on the ground, symbolizing her rejection of Satan and all his works.

"Have you united yourself to Christ?" Father Dimitri asked.

"I have united myself to Christ," she responded.

"Do you believe in Him?" he asked.

"I believe in Him as King and God," Delenda said.

"Then repeat after me…"

Together with Suzanna, she recited the words of the Nicene Creed.

With that, Father Dimitri led Delenda to the baptismal font. He took the water and prayed over it, invoking the Holy Spirit to sanctify it. He then immersed her in the water three times, saying, "The servant of God, Nomiki (Delenda), is baptized in the name of the Father, Amen. And of the Son, Amen. And of the Holy Spirit, Amen."

He helped her to stand and wrapped the white baptismal garment around her. "Receive this white garment, which you will wear unblemished before the judgment seat of our Lord Jesus Christ, that you may have eternal life. Amen."

Father Dimitri then anointed her with Holy Chrism, saying, "The seal of the gift of the Holy Spirit, Amen." He made the sign of the cross with oil on her forehead, eyes, nose, mouth, ears, chest, hands, and feet.

Finally, he placed a black rope cross around her neck. "Receive this cross, the sign of your faith, a shield against the adversary, and a token of your baptism."

Father Dimitri then led Delenda and Suzanna around the font three times, chanting prayers and hymns, symbolizing her new life in Christ and her commitment to walk in His ways. The service concluded with the rite of Holy Communion.

With the baptism complete, Father Dimitri placed his hands on Delenda and Pothitos's heads, blessing their engagement. "May God bless this coming union and guide you both in His light. Go forth together, in love and faith."

Delenda and Pothitos stood, their hands clasped tightly together, feeling a profound sense of peace and unity. "Thank you, Father," Pothitos said, his voice choked with emotion.

Father Dimitri smiled warmly. "It is my honor. However, the marriage will have to wait until tomorrow. You must get your affairs in order, and I will have to prepare for the ceremony. The fewer people that know about this, the better. One night from now, meet me after sunset in Damos, at the Church of Christ in Jerusalem. I still have some people loyal to me and your mother in that city."

Chapter 30

THE CHURCH OF CHRISTOS

The Church of Christ in Jerusalem stood as a testament to the ancient builders' resourcefulness, constructed three centuries prior from the ruins of an ancient Temple to Apollo. Its transformation from a pagan temple to a Christian sanctuary symbolized the profound shift in the religious landscape of Kalymnos. Approaching the church, one would be struck by the grandeur of its facade. Detailed stone carvings adorned the entrance, depicting scenes from the Bible and the lives of saints. The main entrance, framed by grand archways supported by columns, invited the faithful into the church with a sense of awe.

Inside, the central nave stretched out, flanked by two narrower aisles. Rows of columns separated the nave from the aisles, their marble surfaces polished smooth by centuries of touch. These columns, salvaged from the original Temple to Apollo, bore the characteristic fluted design of Doric style, their sturdy forms lending an air of timeless strength to the structure. The columns rose to support a high, wooden-beamed ceiling, forming a vast, open space often filled with the sound of prayers and hymns.

The floor was a stunning mosaic, a tapestry of vibrant colors and intricate designs that told stories of both the natural and divine. Images of gazelles and camels, symbolizing the exotic lands of the East, roamed across the tiles. Fish, representing the bounty of the sea and early Christian symbolism, swam amidst the patterns. A leopard, its form graceful and powerful, prowled through the mosaic, embodying both danger and majesty. These images were interwoven with geometric patterns and religious symbols, fashioning a floor that was not just a surface but a work of art.

At the end of the nave stood the apse, a semicircular recess that housed the altar. This altar, too, was crafted from the ruins of the ancient temple. Doric pillars, repurposed and reshaped, formed the base of the altar. Their fluted shafts and simple, austere capitals spoke of the temple's original grandeur while now serving a new purpose. The altar was a focal point, a place where the divine met the earthly, richly decorated with religious symbols and artifacts.

High above, clerestory windows allowed natural light to filter into the church, producing a heavenly glow that shifted with the movement of the sun. These windows, consisting of translucent alabaster, diffused the light and created an atmosphere of serenity. The light illuminated the frescoes and mosaics that covered the walls, depicting scenes from the Bible and the lives of saints, their colors vivid and lifelike.

Surrounding the apse was an ambulatory, a walkway that allowed processions and movement around the church without disturbing the central area of worship. This space was lined with more columns and arches, creating a sense of depth and perspective that drew the eye toward the altar.

Within the vestibule, a large baptismal font stood, intricately carved and decorated with complex mosaic work. It was used for the sacrament of baptism and served as a reminder of the church's role as a place of rebirth.

The exterior of the church was equally impressive, set within a courtyard that was once part of the temple grounds. Pathways led to the entrance, flanked by gardens that provided a tranquil space for reflection and prayer. The Church of Christ in Jerusalem was more than a building; it stood as a symbol of the enduring power of faith, transforming the ruins of a pagan temple into a sanctuary of Christian worship, rich with beauty and history.

Tonight, the ambiance of the church was quiet and intimate. This ancient church, built from the remnants of a once-grand temple to Apollo, now served as the setting for a clandestine wedding, one that carried with it the aspirations and dreams of two souls united by fate.

The evening sky outside was a deep indigo, with a full moon casting a silvery glow over the landscape. The church, nestled amidst the ancient ruins, stood like a sentinel, its weathered stones and grand arches told tales of transformation.

As the stars began to shimmer in the sky, Father Dimitri prepared the church for the ceremony. The priest's hands moved with practiced ease, setting up the necessary items with a sense of solemnity.

Inside the nave, the flickering light of beeswax candles produced a warm glow, forming dancing shapes on the mosaics that covered the floor. The images of camels, fish, and leopards seemed to come alive under the soft illumination, their vibrant colors and details reflecting the artistry of ancient craftsmen.

Delenda and Pothitos stood near the entrance, their hands clasped tightly together. Delenda's eyes sparkled with a combination of excitement and nervousness, while Pothitos's face was set with love. They had come a long way to reach this moment, overcoming countless obstacles and dangers, and their bond had only grown stronger with each challenge.

Delenda was a vision of serene beauty, her hair gilded with sprigs of wildflowers woven intricately into her dark locks, symbolizing new beginnings and highlighting her natural beauty. She wore a simple white robe, its pristine fabric glowing softly in the candlelight, cinched at the waist with a belt woven from palms, signifying purity and humility. The black rope crucifix given to her during her baptism hung at her neck. Pothitos, standing beside her, looked equally solemn and handsome, his eyes filled with love.

Father Dimitri approached them, his appearance serious. "Are you ready, my children?" he asked.

Delenda nodded, her grip on Pothitos's hand tightening. "Yes, Father. We are ready."

The priest smiled, his eyes reflecting the warm radiance of the candles. "Then let us begin."

Suzanna stepped forward to act as the koumbara, or the sponsor of the marriage. She held the stefania, the wedding crowns, in her hands, their delicate filigree shining in the candlelight. Suzanna's presence added a sense of support, her role as koumbara symbolizing the joining of families and the blessings of the church.

Father Dimitri led the couple to the center of the nave, where the altar had been set up with a richly embroidered cloth. On the altar were the Holy Gospel, a cross, and the wine and bread meant to symbolize the Eucharist. The scent of incense filled the air, mingling with the faint aroma of beeswax and creating an atmosphere of reverence.

The ceremony began with the chanting of hymns, their melodic strains resonating through the church. Father Dimitri held up the wedding crowns, blessing them with the sign of the cross. "In the name of the Father, and of the Son, and of the Holy Spirit, Amen."

He then placed the crowns on Delenda's and Pothitos's heads, Suzanna assisting by holding them steady. "The servant of God, Pothitos, is crowned unto the handmaid of God, Nomiki (Delenda), in the name of the Father, and of the Son, and of the Holy Spirit, Amen."

"The handmaid of God, Nomiki (Delenda), is crowned unto the servant of God, Pothitos, in the name of the Father, and of the Son, and of the Holy Spirit, Amen."

The stefania symbolized the glory and honor bestowed upon the couple by God, marking the beginning of their new life together. The priest then took a long, white ribbon and tied the crowns together, signifying their unity and the unbreakable bond of marriage.

Next came the exchange of rings. Father Dimitri held the rings up, blessing them with the sign of the cross. "The servant of God, Pothitos, receives this ring in the name of the Father, and of the Son, and of the Holy Spirit, Amen."

He placed the ring on Pothitos's right hand, then took the other ring. "The handmaid of God, Nomiki (Delenda), receives this ring in the name of the Father, and of the Son, and of the Holy Spirit, Amen."

He placed the ring on Delenda's right hand, completing the exchange. The rings, meticulously carved by Pothitos from the pits of peaches that grew on a tree near the cave where they had been hiding, symbolized their mutual commitment and the eternal nature of their union. Each ring was a labor of love, representing the couple's resilience and the sweetness of their future.

Father Dimitri then led the couple in the Dance of Isaiah, a ceremonial walk around the altar that symbolized their first steps as a married couple. Holding a lit candle in each hand, Delenda and Pothitos followed the priest around the altar three times.

As they completed the dance, the priest led them to the altar, where they shared the Common Cup. This was symbolic of the Eucharist and represented their unity with each other and with God. The solemnity of the ceremony was underscored by the love in their hearts, an elation that radiated from their faces. They were finally together, united not only by their love but also by their faith, ready to face whatever challenges the future might hold, side by side.

After the ceremony, Father Dimitri raised his hands in a blessing, his voice full of heartfelt emotion. "My children, today you have pledged yourselves to each other before God and have become one in His eyes. I implore you now to consider the path ahead. The world is fraught with danger, and the battles to come are fierce and relentless. Seek peace and tranquility in your union. Find solace in each other and live a life away from harm."

Delenda's eyes welled with tears, moved by the priest's words. She looked at Pothitos, her heart aching at the thought of more strife. "Father, we wish for peace, but the world will not leave us be."

Father Dimitri stepped closer, his expression earnest. "There is wisdom in knowing when to fight and when to find refuge. You have endured much, and now, as husband and wife, you deserve a life of peace."

Pothitos's face hardened. "Father, the danger for Delenda will never end. Our enemies will not cease their pursuit. Now that we are joined in marriage, we will fight this battle head-on. No more hiding."

Delenda squeezed his hand, a silent plea in her eyes. "Pothitos..."

He turned to her and spoke softly. "First, I will see my father at the monastery, whatever the cost. Then, I will return to lead our people to victory. This is our destiny, Delenda. Together, we will face whatever comes."

Father Dimitri sighed deeply, placing a hand on each of their shoulders. "If this is your choice, may God grant you strength and courage. Remember, you fight not just for yourselves but for the future of those who depend on you. Go with my blessing but know that my prayers are for your safety and peace."

Pothitos nodded, gratitude evident on his face. "Thank you, Father. We will honor your words and carry your blessing with us."

As the newlyweds left the church, the night sky stretched above them, filled with stars. Together, they stepped into the unknown, united in purpose and fortified by their marriage vows.

Chapter 31

A SAINTS BLESSING

The moon hung low over the hills, bathing the rugged landscape surrounding the monastery of Agio Konstantinos in a ghostly light. Shadows stretched long and deep, providing the perfect cover for Pothitos and Delenda as they approached the edge of the monastic community, where Gelimer's forces had laid siege. The distant clamor of the entrenched war band—muffled shouts, the clatter of steel, and the dull thud of the siege engines in motion, reached their ears.

Agio Konstantinos, with its towering walls and formidable defenses, had long been a bastion of resistance. The Ierí Frourá had repelled countless assaults, but now, as supplies dwindled and faith waned, the siege threatened to break their spirits. For Pothitos and Delenda, sneaking past the invader's encampment was a near-impossible task. Yet, they were driven by a higher purpose—a mission to reach Pothitos's father.

Clad in dark, weather-worn cloaks, the couple moved silently through the rocky terrain. Pothitos led the way, scanning the horizon for signs of movement. Delenda followed closely, her heart pounding in her chest. The night was their ally, its darkness concealing their approach, but they knew that one wrong move, one misstep, could spell their doom.

Ahead of them, the invader's camp sprawled across the mountainside, a sea of tents and makeshift fortifications illuminated by the flickering glow of countless torches. The enemy soldiers were vigilant, their patrols frequent and thorough, but the sheer size of the encampment worked in the couple's favor. Pothitos had spent the last few nights observing the patterns of the patrols, noting the moments when the watch was most vulnerable, the gaps between shifts that they could exploit.

As they reached the outer edge of the camp, Pothitos raised a hand, signaling Delenda to stop. They crouched low behind a cluster of boulders, their eyes fixed on the nearest patrol—a group of five soldiers trudging along the perimeter, their armor clinking softly as they stepped. Pothitos watched them intently, counting the seconds until they passed out of sight. He knew they had only a brief window before the next patrol arrived.

When the soldiers disappeared around a bend, Pothitos grabbed Delenda's hand, and they moved stealthily, darting from one shadow to the next. The ground beneath them was uneven, strewn with rocks and loose soil, but they moved with stealth, their steps barely disturbing the earth. With each passing moment, the camp appeared closer. The sounds of the soldiers' murmured conversations and the occasional crackle of a fire grew louder in their ears.

They reached the first line of tents, slipping between them like wraiths in the night. The smell of cooked meat and the acrid stench of sweat and smoke filled their nostrils, but they pressed on, their goal clear in their minds. Pothitos led them through a labyrinth of canvas and rope, his memory guiding them along the safest route, away from the central fires where the officers gathered.

As they traversed the edge of the camp a sudden shout froze them in their tracks. Pothitos pulled Delenda into the cover of a nearby tent, holding his breath as a pair of soldiers strode past, their conversation punctuated by harsh laughter. Delenda pressed her back against the rough fabric of the tent, her heart hammering in her chest. She could feel Pothitos's tension beside her, his muscles taut, ready to act if they were discovered.

But the soldiers moved on, oblivious to the danger that lurked mere feet away. Pothitos exhaled slowly, a silent prayer of thanks passing through his lips. He glanced at Delenda, their eyes meeting in the darkness, and she nodded, her silent affirmation giving him the acknowledgement to continue.

They continued to skirt the fringes of the camp, careful to avoid any clusters of soldiers. The eastern border of the encampment, where the siege lines were thinnest, was their goal. There, they found a narrow pass that led up the mountainside to the monastery of Agio Konstantinos. But between them and the pass lay the most dangerous part of their journey—Gelimer's forward guard, a heavily fortified position where any intruders would be quickly spotted and cut down.

Pothitos knew they wouldn't be able to sneak through the entrenched guards this time. They were too vigilant. They needed a distraction, something to draw the soldiers' attention away from the pass long enough for them to slip through unnoticed.

As they approached the forward guard's position, Pothitos's mind raced, searching for a solution. And then he saw it—a stack of barrels, filled with oil. He glanced at Delenda, his plan forming in an instant.

"Stay here," he said, his voice barely a murmur. "I'll create a diversion. When you see the flames, run for the pass and don't look back. I'll be right behind you."

Delenda's eyes widened with fear and concern. "Pothitos, no—"

"There's no other way," he cut her off. "We must reach the monastery." He handed her a vial that they had filled with the miraculous water from Saint Panteleimon's cave. The glass vial, given to them by Father Dimitri, was cool in her hand. "Get this to my father. This may be his only chance."

She hesitated, but she knew he was right. She nodded, though her heart screamed in protest. "Be careful."

He squeezed her hand one last time, his touch lingering as if he wished to imprint the sensation in his memory. Then, with a final glance, he slipped away, his figure melting into the dark as he moved toward the barrels.

Delenda watched him go, her pulse quickening with each passing second. She concealed the small vial of water beneath her cloak. She prayed silently, her lips moving without sound, beseeching God to protect Pothitos and guide them both safely to the monastery.

The time stretched into what felt like an eternity. Delenda's eyes darted back and forth, scanning the camp for any sign of movement, any hint of danger. And then, in the distance, she saw it—a sudden burst of light, followed by a billowing cloud of smoke. Flames licked at the night sky, the orange glow spreading quickly as the fire took hold. Shouts erupted from the entrenched guard's position as the soldiers scrambled to contain the blaze, their attention diverted exactly as Pothitos had planned.

Delenda didn't hesitate. She sprang from her hiding place, her feet barely touching the ground as she sprinted toward the pass. The path was narrow and hazardous, winding up the mountainside with steep drops on either side. But Delenda was fueled by adrenaline, the urgency of her mission, surpassed only by her fear.

Behind her, the sounds of chaos grew louder—the crackle of flames, the frantic orders of officers, the clatter of weapons. But there was no time to look back, no time to wonder if Pothitos was following. She focused on the path ahead, her breath coming in sharp bursts as she pushed herself to move faster, climb higher.

The pass was steep, the rocks slick with dew and loose underfoot. But Delenda pressed on. Reaching the monastery meant hope. Delivering the water meant life.

The path wound upward, the air growing cooler as she ascended. The night sky seemed to close in around her, the stars above like distant, unblinking eyes watching her every move. Her legs burned with the effort, her lungs aching as she forced herself onward. But the thought of Pothitos kept her going. She couldn't fail him. She couldn't fail their people.

Finally, after what felt like an eternity, the dark outline of the monastery loomed ahead. Its stone walls rose up from the mountainside like a citadel against the night. The sight of it filled Delenda with a surge of hope.

She reached the entrance, her hands trembling as she banged on the heavy wooden door. For a long moment, there was no response, and Delenda was filled with anxiety. She banged again, harder this time, desperation creeping into her actions.

Suddenly, the sound of clattering armor and the scrape of steel on stone broke the stillness. From above, a stern voice called out, "Hold your arrows!"

Delenda froze. She glanced up and saw shadowy figures lining the walls above her, bows drawn, arrows aimed directly at her. For a terrifying moment, the world stood still.

The same voice called out again, this time with authority, "Who goes there? What is your business here?"

The voice belonged to Stavros, his monk's robes replaced by the colors of the Ierí Frourá. His silhouette was imposing against the starlit sky.

Delenda swallowed hard, gathering what remained of her strength. She stepped back to ensure she could be fully seen by the guards above. "It is Delenda," she called up, her voice firm but tinged with the exhaustion of her journey.

"I bring blessed water from the cave of Saint Panteleimon. Pothitos sent me ahead to deliver it to his father. We need the monastery's protection, and I must speak with Longinus immediately."

There was a pause, then Stavros leaned over the parapet to get a better look at the figure below. Recognition flashed in his eyes, and he softened slightly. "Delenda?" he called down, a note of surprise in his voice. "It's been too long since you walked these grounds. You've come in a dangerous hour."

Delenda's legs trembled with fatigue, but she managed to stand tall. "I know, Stavros. But we have no other choice."

Stavros hesitated, his eyes scanning the darkness beyond her, searching for another figure. "And Pothitos? Where is he?"

Delenda's voice faltered for a moment, her fear almost overwhelming her. "He… he stayed behind to create a distraction so I could reach the monastery. He said he would follow, but I've seen no sign of him."

Stavros muttered under his breath, lines of worry showing on his face. The news that he was still out there, possibly in danger, did not sit well with him.

"Open the gate!" Stavros ordered, his voice laden with urgency. "Let her in, quickly!"

The heavy wooden gate unlocked with a groan of wood on stone. Delenda felt a rush of relief as the gate opened enough to allow her entry.

As she stepped through the gates and into the courtyard, Stavros descended the stone steps to meet her. The torches mounted along the walls cast a quivering light over his features, revealing a man worn by years of battle and duty. He was clad in the heavy armor of the Ierí Frourá, the symbol of the cross emblazoned on his chest.

Stavros grasped her shoulders with both hands, his grip firm but not harsh. "You're safe now, Delenda. But you look exhausted. Come, sit for a moment. We'll find Pothitos."

She sat and accepted water that was handed to her, drinking deeply, the cool liquid soothing her parched throat.

As she drank, Stavros turned to one of the guards. "Prepare a search party. Pothitos must be found and brought back to the monastery. He could be anywhere between here and the enemy lines, and we need him alive."

The guard saluted and hurried off, while Stavros remained at Delenda's side, his eyes never leaving her face. "You've been through a great ordeal, Delenda. But you're safe now. Longinus will be glad to see you."

Delenda lowered the empty vessel, her voice steadier. "I'm not concerned about my safety. It's Pothitos… and our people I worry about. The witch Skylla and her allies will stop at nothing to destroy us all."

Stavros nodded grimly. "You're right to be worried. This siege will not end easily. These warriors are relentless, and they will stop at nothing to crush our resistance."

Delenda spoke softly, "I need to speak with Longinus and see Antonios. Pothitos sent me ahead with this."

She brandished a small vial of water and continued, "This water healed me some time ago, and I believe it could heal Antonios as well."

Stavros motioned for her to follow. "Come with me. Longinus will want to hear this firsthand. And I'll prepare Antonios's quarters for a visitor."

Delenda rose to her feet and followed Stavros through the dimly lit corridors of the monastery, the familiar scent of incense and stone filling her senses. Memories flooded back—of the time she had spent here, learning from the nuns, finding peace in the quiet sanctity of the monastery. But now, those days seemed far away, overshadowed by the looming threat of war.

"It's been many months since you and Pothitos disappeared," Stavros ventured, his voice low. "We all feared you were both dead."

Delenda felt a shiver run through her at his words. The memories of those harrowing days came rushing back—of the kidnapping, the narrow escapes, the nights spent hiding in the wilderness with Pothitos, always on the run, always just a step ahead of their enemies.

"We nearly were," she replied, her voice trembling as she relived the terror of those days. "There were times when I thought we wouldn't make it. But Pothitos... he was always so strong, so certain that we would survive. He kept me going, even when I wanted to give up."

Stavros glanced back at her smiling. "Pothitos is a remarkable man. His father raised him well, with the kind of conviction and courage that few possess. But you, Delenda... you've been through more than anyone should ever have to endure, and yet you're still here. That speaks volumes about your own strength."

Delenda managed a small, weary smile. "I've had no choice, Stavros. We all do what we must to survive."

Stavros nodded in agreement, his focus returning to the path ahead. "True. But that doesn't make it any easier."

As they approached the large, carved wooden door that led to Longinus's quarters, Stavros paused, turning to face her fully. "Before we go in, Delenda, you should know that Longinus... he took your disappearance hard. He was like a father to you, after all. He feared the worst when we lost contact with you and Pothitos. Seeing you alive... it will mean more to him than you can imagine."

Delenda's heart tightened at the mention of Longinus, the warrior who had been her protector and mentor during her early years in Egypt. He had taught her to defend herself, how to survive in a world that was often unforgiving and cruel. He was the closest thing to a father she had known, and she could only imagine the pain he must have felt when he thought she was gone.

"I've missed him," Delenda admitted, her voice soft. "He's been in my thoughts every day."

Stavros gave her a reassuring nod before pushing open the heavy door. "Go to him, Delenda. He needs to see that you're alive."

The door creaked as it opened, revealing a room bathed in candlelight. The walls were lined with ancient texts and scrolls, the shelves heavy with the knowledge of centuries. A large wooden table dominated the center of the room, strewn with maps and manuscripts, evidence of the ongoing struggle against their enemies.

Longinus stood near the table, his broad back to them as he pored over a parchment, his long, graying hair falling around his shoulders. The years had added to his stature, making him appear even more formidable than Delenda remembered. His presence filled the room with an air of authority, the kind that could only come from a life dedicated to both spiritual and martial discipline.

Hearing the door open, Longinus turned slowly, his eyes narrowing as they adjusted to the light. At first, he didn't recognize her, his mind still focused on the realities of the maps before him. But then, as his gaze settled on Delenda, his expression changed.

For a moment, it seemed as though the world had stopped, leaving only the two of them in that room. Longinus's eyes widened in disbelief. The parchment in his hands slipped from his grasp, floating to the floor like a leaf carried by the wind.

"Delenda..." he said, his voice cracking with emotion.

Delenda felt her own tears welling up. "Longinus... it's me. I'm here."

A strangled sob escaped the old warrior's lips, and in an instant, all the fortitude that had held him together seemed to crumble. He hobbled across the room with quick strides, enveloping Delenda in a hardy embrace, his powerful arms trembling as he held her close. Delenda clung to him, her tears flowing freely now, soaking into the fabric of his robe.

Longinus wept openly, his relief evident. "I thought I'd lost you," he choked out. "I thought... God had taken you both from me."

Delenda buried her face against his chest, feeling the familiarity of her father figure. "We survived, Longinus. By God's grace, we survived. Pothitos is still out there, but he'll make it. I know he will."

Longinus pulled back slightly, his hands on her shoulders, his eyes scanning her face as if to reassure himself that she was truly there. His expression was one of gratitude, the lines of worry and despair softening as the reality of her presence sank in.

"You've grown," Longinus said, his voice filled with affection. "You've been through so much, and yet you've come back to us. I always knew you were destined for great things, Delenda, but this... this is a miracle."

Delenda wiped away her tears, a faint smile forming at her lips. "This water is the miracle, Longinus," Delenda continued, her voice steadying as she recounted the events that had brought her here. "We found it in a cave along with an icon of Saint Panteleimon. This water healed me when I was gravely ill. Pothitos and I knew we had to bring it here, to you and to Antonios. It may be the only thing that can save him now."

Longinus's eyes softened as he nodded. "Saint Panteleimon's blessings are rare, but powerful. If this water healed you, then it truly carries the Saint's grace. Antonios has been growing weaker by the day… this may be the answer to our prayers."

He gently took the vial from Delenda's hand, cradling it as if it were a fragile relic. The liquid within seemed to glow faintly, the light reflecting from the torches on the wall. Longinus stared at it for a long moment, his thoughts turning inward.

"Our enemies are closing in on us," he said quietly, more to himself than to Delenda. "They can sense our vulnerability."

"Longinus," she said gently, "Antonios needs this water as soon as possible. Can we go to him now?"

Longinus looked up, nodding. "Yes, of course. Time is of the essence. Antonios's condition has worsened, and we cannot delay any longer."

He handed the vial to Delenda with great care. "Keep it safe, Delenda. You and Pothitos have already risked so much to bring it here. We must see this through together."

Delenda clutched the vial close to her chest, feeling the coolness of the glass against her skin. "I will, Longinus. I'll do whatever it takes."

The path to Antonios's quarters was a winding one, taking them deeper into the heart of the monastery. Delenda's mind was clear about the task ahead, but she couldn't help feeling a flutter of anxiety in her chest. She anticipated the toll that the injury had taken on Antonios, and she feared what she might find now.

As they reached the end of the hallway, Longinus paused at a door wrought with iron bands. He turned to Delenda, his appearance serious. "Antonios has always been a man of great strength, both in body and spirit. But these past few months have weakened him more than any of us could have imagined. Be prepared, Delenda… he may not be the man you remember."

Delenda nodded, steeling herself for what lay beyond the door. "I understand, Longinus. But we must believe that this water can heal him, just as it healed me."

Longinus offered her a small, sad smile. "Faith is what sustains us, Delenda. And you have shown more of it than anyone else I know."

With that, he pushed open the door, revealing the small room. The atmosphere was smothered with the scent of burning herbs and the faint odor of illness. A single oil lamp flickered on a bedside table, shining a feeble light over the figure lying on the narrow bed.

Antonios, once a man of vitality, now looked frail and diminished. His skin was pale and drawn, and his eyes were glazed over. His silver hair, once a crown of sageness, now lay limp against the pillow, and his once-clear eyes were dull and empty.

Instinctively, Delenda turned away from the sight. This was the man who had once ruled over the people of this island. Seeing him so weakened was almost unbearable. She took a hesitant step forward, the vial from St. Panteleimon clasped tightly in her hand.

Longinus moved to Antonios's side, his voice gentle as he spoke. "Antonios, my friend, Delenda has returned to us. She has brought something… something that may save you."

Antonios's eyes fluttered open, and for a moment they seemed unfocused, as if he were struggling to understand where he was. But then his unfocused eyes found Delenda, and maybe some recognition flickered in his tired eyes.

Delenda knelt beside the bed, taking Antonios's hand in hers. "Antonios. I'm here. And so is Pothitos. We brought something for you—miraculous water from the cave of Saint Panteleimon. It saved my life, and we believe it can heal you as well."

Longinus, standing at the foot of the bed, nodded to Delenda, his eyes urging her on. She uncorked the vial carefully. The scent of it filled the air, sweet and pure, like myrrh.

Delenda dipped her fingers into the vial, then gently touched them to Antonios's forehead, tracing the sign of the cross. "In the name of the Father, and of the Son, and of the Holy Spirit," she said, her voice trembling with emotion.

Antonios closed his eyes, his breathing slowing as if he were sinking into a deep, peaceful sleep. Delenda then put the vial to his lips and poured the water into his mouth. For a moment, Antonios could only gasp. He managed to swallow the cool liquid and immediately fell into a deep sleep.

Delenda could sense something shifting, a presence in the room that was comforting, as it was powerful. It felt as if the very spirit of Saint Panteleimon was interceding with the Lord for them.

For several long moments, the room was silent, the only sound the soft crackle of the oil lamp. Delenda remained kneeling beside the bed as she prayed silently for the miracle she so desperately sought.

Finally, Antonios's eyes opened again, and there was a clarity in them that had not been there before. He took a deep, steady breath, the color slowly returning to his cheeks. His hand, clasping Delenda's, felt stronger.

"Delenda," he stammered, his voice faint.

Longinus, who had been standing silently at the foot of the bed, crossed himself in disbelief. He stepped forward, placing a hand on Antonios's shoulder.

"Antonios?" Longinus asked rhetorically.

Antonios nodded slowly, his eyes closing once more as he drifted into a peaceful slumber. Delenda remained by his side, her hand still holding onto his.

As the room settled into silence, Longinus gently touched Delenda's shoulder, motioning for her to rise. "Come, Delenda," he said. "Let him rest. We'll stay close by, and we'll be here when he wakes."

Delenda hesitated, reluctant to leave Antonios's side, but she knew Longinus was right. Antonios needed time to heal, and they needed to prepare for the challenges that lay ahead. She carefully laid Antonios's hand back on the bed, her fingers lingering for a moment before she finally stood.

Chapter 32

THE PROMISE OF TOMORROW

Time seemed to stretch endlessly as Delenda and Longinus knelt in prayer, their words mingling with the tolling of the monastery bells. Delenda's thoughts were consumed with Pothitos. Her mind raced with fears of what might have befallen him. Each minute that passed without news felt like an eternity, and she prayed fervently, her hands clenched together so tightly that her knuckles turned white.

But then, just as the fear threatened to overwhelm her, the door to the chapel creaked open. Delenda's head snapped up, her heart leaping in her chest as she turned to see a familiar figure step into the nave.

Pothitos stood in the doorway, his cloak torn and singed from the fire he had set, but his eyes were bright. His chest rose and fell rapidly as he recovered from his escape, but there was no mistaking the relief in his face as he saw Delenda waiting for him.

"Pothitos!" Delenda cried, rushing to his side. She threw her arms around him, holding him tightly as if to reassure herself that he was really there, that he had made it through the enemy's camp unscathed.

Pothitos returned her hug, his hands trembling slightly as he held her close. "I'm here, Delenda," he murmured, pressing a kiss to the top of her head. "I told you I'd be right behind you."

Tears of relief streamed down Delenda's cheeks as she pulled back just enough to look into his eyes, her hands still clutching the front of his tunic. "I was so worried," she cried, her voice choked with emotion. "I prayed for you, every moment."

Pothitos smiled gently, brushing a tear from her cheek. "And I felt those prayers, Delenda. They brought me back."

Word spread like wildfire through the monastery that Delenda and Pothitos had returned, alive and safe. The news brought a wave of relief to the weary soldiers and nuns, who had feared the worst. The cloister, usually quiet and solemn, buzzed with conversations. Everyone sought to catch a glimpse of the two who had defied death and returned with a miracle in their hands.

Gerontisa Angeliki was among the first to come and see Delenda. Her gentle face was lit with a rare smile as she held Delenda like a long-lost daughter. "My child," she said, her voice quivering, "we have prayed for your safety every day since you left us. To see you here again, and with Pothitos by your side… it is truly a gift from God."

Delenda smiled through her tears, the warmth of Angeliki soothing the raw edges of her nerves. "I never stopped believing, Gerontisa. Your prayers carried me through the darkest nights."

Sister Maria and Sister Despina, two of the nuns who had been close to Delenda during her time at the monastery, followed closely behind Angeliki. They hovered nearby, their eyes wide with awe. Sister Maria, always the more outspoken of the two, reached out to touch the hem of Delenda's cloak as if to reassure herself that her friend was truly standing before her.

"You've come back to us," Sister Maria exclaimed, her voice filled with wonder. "We never stopped praying, Delenda. Not for a single day."

Sister Despina nodded fervently, her usually quiet demeanor giving way to a broad smile. "The Lord has brought you both back to us. We knew He would."

Even the old warrior monk Stavros ventured out of his quarters to see Delenda and Pothitos. His one good eye was sharp and clear as he regarded the couple standing before him. Stavros had been a mentor to Pothitos in his youth, teaching him the discipline of the mind. Now, seeing the young man standing strong and proud, with Delenda at his side, the old monk's face softened with approval.

"You've done well, Pothitos," Stavros said, his voice gravelly but strong. "Your father will be proud to see the man you've become."

Pothitos inclined his head respectfully, a look of deep gratitude in his eyes. "Your teachings have guided me more than you know."

As the soldiers and nuns gathered around, marveling at the couple's return, their attention was soon drawn to the black rope cross that Delenda wore around her neck. The necklace was formed by a series of knots tied together to form the image of a cross. Each knot was tied during the recitation of the Jesus Prayer. This cross symbolized the commitment she had made amid great peril.

Sister Maria was the first to comment, her eyes wide with astonishment. "Delenda, that cross… it's beautiful. Have you been… baptized?"

Delenda exchanged a glance with Pothitos before turning back to the gathered sisters and soldiers. "Yes," she said, her voice filled with emotion. "And afterwards, Pothitos and I pledged our lives to each other before God. Father Dimitri married us."

A silence fell over the room as the sisters stared at her with their mouths agape. The monastery had always been a place of quiet contemplation and spiritual dedication, where the bonds of marriage were rare but deeply respected. To hear that Delenda and Pothitos had been joined in holy matrimony brought a sense of delight to the community.

Antonios, who had recovered enough to walk, had been listening from the doorway. His face, though still pale from his illness, was lit with a beaming smile as he made his way into the room. "Married?" he repeated, his voice filled with delight. "This is the best news I've heard in a long time."

Delenda turned to Antonios, rushing to his side, taking his hands in hers. "Yes, Father. We are married, and we are here to stay."

Antonios's eyes glistened with unshed tears as he looked at the newlyweds standing before him. "I am overjoyed, Delenda. Pothitos, you have made a fine choice. The two of you together… it gives me hope for the future, despite all the darkness that surrounds us."

The news of Delenda and Pothitos's marriage spread throughout the monastery, filling halls with a sense of unity. Even in the face of the constant threat from Gelimer's men, who were lurking beyond the monastery walls, the community found solace in the presence of the new couple and the promise of a future they represented.

However, the threat outside the walls was never far from anyone's mind. Gelimer's forces, ruthless and relentless, had been making attempts to breach the monastery's defenses. Though they were always beaten back by the skilled and vigilant Ierí Frourá, the constant danger kept everyone on edge. The soldiers and nuns knew that a full-scale assault was only a matter of time, and they prayed fervently for the strength to withstand it.

Days passed, and life within the monastery resumed its rhythm, albeit with the ever-present threat of the siege. Delenda and Pothitos found a sense of peace in their new roles as husband and wife, even as they prepared for the battles to come. They spent their days helping with the monastery's defenses, tending to the wounded, and offering comfort to those in need.

But soon, Delenda began to notice a change within herself. It started with a persistent fatigue that she couldn't shake, no matter how much she rested. She found herself struggling to keep down food, her appetite waning as a constant nausea took hold. At first, she dismissed it as the lingering effects of her journey, but as the days turned into weeks, her condition only worsened.

It was Gerontisa Angeliki who first noticed the subtle signs. The elderly abbess had a keen eye for such matters, having cared for countless women over the years. She observed Delenda's pale complexion, the way she often paused to catch her breath, and the frequency with which she excused herself during meals.

One evening, as Delenda sat with her in the garden, Gerontisa Angeliki gently took her hand, her wise eyes searching Delenda's face. "My dear, have you considered that you might be with child?"

Delenda blinked in surprise, her heart skipping a beat. The thought had crossed her mind in passing, but she had been so focused on the dangers around them that she hadn't allowed herself to fully consider it.

"With child?" Delenda repeated, stunned.

The abbess nodded, her smile kind but serious. "The signs are there, Delenda. The fatigue, the nausea… these are common in the early stages of pregnancy. You must take care of yourself, for the sake of the life growing within you."

Delenda's mind raced as she processed the abbess's words. If she was indeed with child, it would change everything. The stakes were even higher now—not just for her and Pothitos, but for the new life they had created. Elation and fear surged through her, and she found herself at a loss for words.

"I… I didn't realize," Delenda stammered, her hand unconsciously moving to rest on her abdomen. "What do I do, Gerontisa?"

Angeliki's grip on her hand tightened, her voice gentle. "You must take care of yourself, Delenda. Rest whenever you can, eat what you're able, and listen to your body. This child is a blessing, but you must be careful, especially in these dangerous times."

Delenda nodded, her mind still reeling. "I'll do my best, Gerontisa. But… how do I tell Pothitos?"

The abbess smiled softly, her eyes filled with warmth. "Tell him with love, my dear. This is his child too, and he will be overjoyed to hear the news. The two of you will face this together, as you have faced everything else."

That night, as Delenda lay in bed beside Pothitos, she found herself unable to sleep. She listened to the steady beat of his heart, feeling the warmth of his body next to hers. The knowledge that she might be carrying his child filled her with a sense of awe.

Finally, she couldn't keep it to herself any longer. She turned to Pothitos, gently waking him with a soft touch on his shoulder. He stirred, blinking in the dim light, his eyes focusing on her with concern.

"Delenda?" He said, his voice thick with sleep. "What's wrong?"

She stuttered, her heart pounding in her chest. "Pothitos… I think… I think I might be with child."

For a moment, there was only silence as Pothitos processed her words. Then his eyes widened in surprise, his hand instinctively moving to rest on her abdomen. "With child?" he repeated, his voice filled with wonder. "Delenda… are you sure?"

She nodded, tears welling up in her eyes. "Gerontisa Angeliki thinks so. I've been feeling ill for weeks now, and she noticed the signs. It's early, but… I think it's true."

Pothitos stared at her blankly. Then, without warning, he pulled her into a tight embrace, burying his face in her hair. "A child," he said, his voice full of emotion. "Our child, Delenda."

She clung to him, tears of relief streaming down her face. "Yes, Pothitos. Our child."

Pothitos pulled back slightly, just enough to look into her eyes. His appearance was serious, but there was a deep, unwavering love in his eyes. "We will protect this child, Delenda. No matter what. We will find a way to survive, to live in peace, for the sake of our family."

Delenda smiled, her heart swelling with love for the man she had married. "I believe you, Pothitos. We will find a way."

As they held each other in the quiet of the night, the looming threats outside the monastery walls seemed momentarily distant. For now, they had each other, and the promise of a new life growing within Delenda gave them the strength to face whatever challenges lay ahead.

Chapter 33

THE MAP TO DESTINY

As the siege continued over the next few months, the signs of Delenda's pregnancy became unmistakable. Her once slim figure began to round, her belly swelling with the life growing within her. The other sisters in the monastery, particularly Gerontisa Angeliki, Sister Maria, and Sister Despina, took special care of her, ensuring she received plenty of rest and nourishment. Despite the enemy soldiers entrenched outside of the monastery walls, the sight of Delenda's growing belly brought a rare and much-needed delight to the community. Her condition was a reminder that even in times of darkness, life could still flourish.

Pothitos felt a new sense of purpose. He had always been driven by his love for Delenda, but now that love extended to the unborn child whom they both anticipated with trepidation. Pothitos became even more protective of Delenda, making sure she was never far from his side and that her every need was met. But as Delenda's condition progressed, so too did the challenges facing the besieged monastery.

The monastery had always been a place of resilience, its walls sheltering those within from the chaos outside. But as the siege dragged on, a new threat began to creep into their lives. The food supplies, which had been carefully rationed to last through the siege, were found to be infested. Worms and rot spread through the grain stores, and much of the monastery's food spoiled beyond use. The discovery sent a wave of fear and uncertainty through the community. The soldiers and nuns had already been on half rations, and now, with much of their remaining food tainted, starvation became a real and imminent danger.

Antonios, who had almost fully recovered thanks to the hallowed water from Saint Panteleimon's cave, immediately called for a council. His strength had returned, and with it, his clarity of mind. Longinus, Stavros, and Gerontisa Angeliki all gathered in the small chamber that served as their meeting place. Pothitos was also present, standing close to Delenda, who sat beside him, her hand rested protectively on her swelling belly.

Antonios spoke first, his voice tinged with concern. "The situation is dire. The infestation has destroyed a good portion of our food supply, and what little remains is insufficient to sustain us through the year. We must consider our options. If we stay here, we will eventually starve."

Longinus frowned deeply. "Escape seems the only viable option, but the enemy is at our doorstep. Gelimer's forces are relentless, and the walls of this monastery, though strong, cannot hold them indefinitely. We are outmanned and outmatched. To attempt a breakout would be suicide."

Gerontisa Angeliki added softly, "Our people are weak with hunger. To escape in such a state would mean leaving behind those who cannot keep up. We would lose many along the way."

Stavros nodded grimly. "It is true. We are surrounded, and the enemy has cut off all means of escape. Even if we could find a way through, the journey would be full of hazards."

A deep silence fell over the room as the strain of their predicament settled on everyone's shoulders. The threat of starvation was just as lethal as the swords of their enemies, and the thought of fleeing only to fall into the hands of Gelimer's men filled them all with dread.

Pothitos, remaining quiet until now, suddenly spoke up, his voice filled with a spark of hope that cut through the gloom. "Escape is not the answer," he said firmly, his eyes burning with conviction. "We cannot run from this fight, not now. If we flee, Gelimer and Halikos will pursue us to the ends of the earth. They will not stop with Delenda—they will come for our child, for all of us. No, we must stand and fight. We must unite the demes and defeat them once and for all."

His words hung in the air, challenging the despair that had begun to settle over the council. Delenda looked up at Pothitos. He was right, they could not run forever. Their enemies would never allow them to live in peace, not as long as they posed a threat to their ambitions.

Antonios considered Pothitos's words carefully before speaking. "You speak the truth, Pothitos. But how can we expect to defeat such a force? We are vastly outnumbered. We are a small group against a mighty army."

Pothitos spoke with conviction, "There is one thing that could tip the scales in our favor—the Spear of Destiny. If the legends are true, it holds the power to turn the tide of any battle. With it, we could rally the demes, unite our people, and strike down our enemies. Gelimer and Halikos would be powerless against us."

At the mention of the Spear of Destiny, a murmur ran through the room. The spear was a relic shrouded in mystery and legend, said to be able to command armies with its power. But it was also a relic that had been lost for generations, its location unknown to all but the most learned scholars.

Gerontisa Angeliki spoke with caution, her voice laced with skepticism. "The Spear of Destiny is a myth to many, Pothitos. Even if it does exist, finding it would be like searching for a needle in a haystack."

Longinus spoke with reluctance. "We have a map."

Gerontisa Angeliki, her voice filled with incredulity, responded, "A map… to the spear that touched our Lord and Savior? Where? How?"

Longinus's gaze settled on Delenda as he replied, "Delenda is the map. She bears a birthmark—one believed to reveal the location of the Spear of Destiny. This is the reason Gelimer and Halikos relentlessly pursue her."

Antonios's eyes widened in shock, and he exclaimed, "Longinus, this power was within our reach all this time? Living amongst us, and you withheld it? Think of the lives that could have been spared! I remember when Delenda first arrived. You showed me that mark, and you told me it was a sign of her royal lineage."

Longinus's voice remained calm but firm as he responded, "What I said was true. Everything I did was to protect her, to protect all of you. Imagine the devastation that could have followed if word had spread about a weapon like this. Power of this magnitude corrupts even the most pious."

He looked around the room, meeting the eyes of each person. "Finding the spear is a perilous endeavor, but given our circumstances, it may be our only option."

The room fell quiet, broken only by the shuffling of feet and the exchange of uncertain glances. Finally, Pothitos spoke up, his voice finding confidence. "Longinus is right. I've seen the birthmark with my own eyes. It's more than just a symbol—it's a map of our island, and it points to the spear's location in Halikos's lands."

Gerontisa Angeliki's face clouded over with concern as she interjected, "But Halikos's lands are vast and heavily fortified. We wouldn't even know where to begin our search."

Antonios nodded in agreement, his tone carrying a note of disappointment. "Gerontisa Angeliki is correct. We don't have the luxury of time or resources for such a quest. Every day we spend searching is a day closer to starvation—or worse, to our defenses being breached."

Pothitos's fists clenched, his irritation palpable. "We must try. If we do nothing, we are condemning ourselves to a slow death. But if we find the spear, we have a real chance—one that could end this war once and for all. I refuse to let my child be born into a world ruled by the likes of Gelimer and Halikos. We owe it to the future to fight for a better world."

The room was steeped in contemplation. The task before them was monumental—finding the Spear of Destiny in the heart of enemy territory seemed an impossible mission. But the alternative, surrendering to a fate of death and despair, was equally dire.

Then, from the doorway, a voice broke the silence. "I know where to begin."

All eyes turned toward the source of the voice. Emerging from the shadows of the corner was Panormitis. The room fell into a hushed silence as he stepped forward, commanding attention. Panormitis had recovered from the ordeal in the cave, his once-weakened form now strong and steady again.

Panormitis approached Pothitos, his voice filled with remorse. "Pothitos, before anything, I must apologize—for falling into Theophilos's trap and for all that followed."

But Pothitos closed the distance between them, pulling Panormitis into a firm embrace. "No, my friend," he said, his voice wavering with emotion. "It is I who should apologize. I doubted you when I shouldn't have. I will always be grateful for how you protected Delenda."

As they stepped back, Pothitos finally felt a degree of optimism. "Tell us what you know, Panormitis."

Panormitis nodded, his voice gaining strength as he recounted what he had seen. "In one of the churches in Halikos's lands, I remember a mosaic. It depicted a spear—one that matches the descriptions of the Spear of Destiny. My mother raised me in that region before I joined the brotherhood here. I know the terrain well, and I believe I can guide you to that church safely."

A ripple of surprise swept through the room. Panormitis, who had always been a quiet and stern figure, was now offering them a lifeline—a chance, however slim, to find the relic that could save them all.

Longinus, ever the pragmatist, regarded Panormitis with deep thought. "If you are certain of what you've seen, then this may be our best chance. But you must understand the risks, Panormitis. Halikos's lands are crawling with soldiers. If you are caught, it could mean death."

Panormitis met Longinus's stern eyes without flinching. "I understand. But if there is even a chance that this spear exists, then we must take it. We have no other choice."

Antonios looked to Longinus, then back to Pothitos and Panormitis. "Then it is settled. If Panormitis can guide you, Pothitos, then I believe this is the path we must take."

Pothitos agreed. "I will go. We cannot let this opportunity slip away."

Gerontisa Angeliki, who had remained silent for much of the discussion, finally spoke. "This is a dangerous route, but it is also the only one that offers us a chance at victory. Go with our blessings, Pothitos, and may the Lord watch over you. We will pray for your success and your safe return."

Delenda, who had been listening intently, took Pothitos's hand in hers, squeezing it tightly. "You must find the spear and bring it back to us. And when you do, we will end this threat forever."

With the decision made, the council began to plan the mission in earnest. Supplies were gathered, routes were discussed, and prayers were offered. Pothitos, accompanied by Panormitis and a small group of trusted warriors, would set out at first light, venturing into the heart of enemy territory in search of the Spear of Destiny.

As the council dispersed, Delenda stayed behind, her thoughts heavy with the knowledge of what lay ahead. She watched as Pothitos prepared for the journey; her heart filled with dread.

"Pothitos," she stammered, her voice catching in her throat. "I can't bear to think of you going and not knowing when you'll return."

He reached out, taking her hands in his. "Delenda, I will return. I swear it. But there's something I need you to do for me while I'm gone."

She nodded, her grip on his hands tightening as she waited for him to continue.

"I want you to keep a brazier burning on the topmost parapet of the battlements," Pothitos said, his voice firm. "As long as that flame burns, I'll know that all is well here, that you're safe. But if I ever see that the flame is out, I'll know you're in danger. It will be a signal to me, and I'll come back to you as fast as I can."

Delenda's eyes filled with tears at the thought of him worrying about her while he faced such dangers on his journey. But she understood the importance of his request, the need for some connection between them, even when they were miles apart.

"I'll do it, Pothitos," she promised, her voice trembling with emotion. "I'll keep the flame burning, no matter what. You'll always know that I'm here, waiting for you."

Pothitos gently cupped her face in his hands, his thumb brushing away a tear that had escaped down her cheek. "You are my strength, Delenda. Knowing that you and our child are safe will keep me going. I will not let anything keep me from coming back to you."

Delenda nodded, tears filling her eyes. "I know you will return to me, Pothitos. I have faith in you."

Pothitos looked into her eyes. "I will return, Delenda. I promise you that. And when I do, God help our enemies."

And with that, Pothitos and his companions set out on their quest, leaving the safety of the monastery behind.

Chapter 34

PALIO PANAGIA

The journey to Halikos's land was laden with danger, every movement uncertain. Panormitis, Pothitos, and a few trusted soldiers set out on this perilous trek, knowing none of them may return. They moved cautiously, their senses heightened by the constant threat of discovery. The island, once their familiar home, now felt like a labyrinth of potential traps and hidden dangers.

As they ventured deeper into the island, the beauty of Kalymnos unfolded before them. The valley that stretched out before them was an arid expanse, which was dotted with olive trees that swayed gently in the breeze. The sea, a deep sapphire blue, shimmered in the distance, meeting the horizon. It was a sight that could have inspired peace, but for them, it was a reminder of what was at stake.

Their journey was slow and deliberate as they navigated the island's diverse terrain. The paths they followed were narrow and winding, often no more than goat tracks carved into the rocky slopes. The higher they climbed, the more hazardous the path became. Any misstep could mean a life-threatening fall, but Pothitos and his companions moved with the ease of the goat herders who grew up in these lands.

Foraging and hunting along the way, they sustained themselves on the island's bounty—wild herbs, berries, and the occasional hare or bird caught with Pothitos's slingshot. Each meal laid bare their dependence on the land and their vulnerability in this rugged environment. Nights were spent huddled around small, carefully concealed fires, their conversations hushed as they kept a watchful eye on the darkness that surrounded them.

After a few days of arduous travel, the group reached the highest peak on the island, a place where the air was thin and crisp, and the earth seemed to touch the sky. The path to the summit was barely a path at all, more suited to the nimble hooves of goats than the weary feet of men. The wind whipped around them as they ascended, its cold bite whipping their exposed skin.

At the peak of the rugged path, the group came upon the small chapel dedicated to the Prophet Elias, a simple yet striking edifice that seemed to emerge organically from the rocky landscape. The chapel's whitewashed walls gleamed against the darkening sky. The structure was unpretentious, built with stones that appeared to have been hewn from the mountain it sat upon, its edges softened by time and weather.

The chapel's roof sloped gently, giving the building a quaint, welcoming appearance. A single wooden door, weathered by the elements, stood at the entrance, its surface embellished with elaborate carvings of crosses. Above the door, a small bell hung in a simple wooden frame, its chimes clinking softly in the mountain winds.

Inside, the chapel was equally humble. The floor was made of rough-hewn stone, smoothed by the countless pilgrims who had knelt and prayed there over the years. The walls were covered with faded frescoes, their colors muted but still vibrant with the stories of saints and angels. A small altar, blocked from view by the iconostasis, stood at the far end of the chapel.

In the entryway stood an icon of the Prophet Elias, his figure draped in a robe of deep purple, the color of royalty and the divine. Kneeling upon the rugged, barren ground of Mount Horeb, he gazed upward, his face a portrait of reverence and fervor, his hands raised in supplication and reverence. Above the Prophet Elias, amidst a whirlwind of celestial flames, a magnificent chariot emerged. It was no ordinary vessel but a divine chariot of fire, blazing with the glory of the heavens. Seated within this fiery spectacle was a figure surrounded by the swirling tongues of flames, who represents the divine presence, a manifestation of God's power and mystery. The chariot, adorned with intricate details and engulfed in flames, symbolizes not just the divine transportation but also the bridge between the earthly and the heavenly, between man's existence and God's realm. The wheels of the chariot, caught in the eternal dance of the flames, signify the movement of the divine through the world, a constant presence that guides and governs the cosmos. This icon, set against the simplicity of the rocky Mount Horeb, alluded to the moment when the divine touched the mortal, when sacred revelations are bestowed upon the chosen.

The group, awe-struck by this icon and weary from their journey, decided to rest here for the night and gather their strength. Despite its small size, the chapel offered a sense of peace and shelter from the elements. The air was cool and fresh, carrying the scent of wild herbs that grew in the cracks between the stones.

Pothitos knelt before the iconostasis. His knees pressed into the stone floor as he bowed his head, his thoughts turning to those he had left behind and the road that still lay ahead. He prayed for strength to carry on, for the forbearance to lead his men safely, and for the protection of those he loved.

As he prayed, the others in the group also took a moment to reflect. Panormitis stood near the door, his hand resting on the hilt of his sword as he looked out at the vast expanse of the valley below. The soldiers, all seasoned men who had seen their share of battle, stood in reverence, their heads bowed in silent prayer.

As the others prayed and tended to their gear, Pothitos walked to the edge of the peak and looked back toward the monastery of Agio Konstantinos. The sky was dark now, and the moon was waning. In the distance, far below, he could just make out the faint glimmer of light from the brazier that burned on the tallest tower of Agio Konstantinos—a small, flickering flame that stood as a symbol of faith and resilience. It was a connection to the life he had waiting for him, a reminder of what he was fighting for.

"Can you see it?" Panormitis asked, coming up beside him, his voice quiet.

Pothitos nodded, his eyes still fixed upon the distant light. "Yes, it's still burning. It feels so far away now, but it's there."

Panormitis placed a hand on his shoulder. "That light will be there, Pothitos. It will guide us back when this is all over."

Pothitos smiled faintly, the comfort of Panormitis's words settling in his heart. "Let's hope so," he said, turning back to face the path ahead. "We still have a long way to go."

Pothitos awoke to the first light of dawn, casting a golden hue over the mountain peak they had just conquered. Panormitis stood overlooking the valley below. As Pothitos approached, Panormitis turned to him and said, "This was my homeland before Halikos's pagans drove out the Christians. This is our destination."

Following Panormitis's gaze, Pothitos beheld the valley cradled within the mountainous expanse of Orkatou —meaning "land of the orchards." The valley, a verdant oasis amidst harsh, stony cliffs, thrived with life. Here, the earth's bountiful gifts flourished under the Mediterranean sun, crafting a beautiful basin clutched by the arid mountains.

The valley was a patchwork of green, a living tapestry that pulsed with the wealth of Orkatou. Olive trees, their ancient trunks twisted and gnarled, stood in orderly rows, their silvery leaves shimmering in the morning light. Their branches, laden with emerald-like fruit, promised of a rich harvest. Between the olive groves, the orchards burst with the colors of the season—figs, pomegranates, peaches, and mandarin oranges painted vibrant splashes against the deep green backdrop, their sweet fragrances mingling in the air.

Dotted across this lush landscape, small pagan temples rose from the hilltops. The local people revered a pantheon of deities, believing their favor was crucial to the valley's agricultural prosperity and the protection of their homeland.

Among the hills, encampments of Halikos's men—his pagan warriors—were scattered, their fires flickering in the early dawn. A deep, narrow inlet from the sea carved its deep blue tendril into the valley and was a lifeline that sustained the community. This waterway, vital and ever flowing, connected the valley's inhabitants, with small, agile boats gliding across its surface, carrying goods and people.

Panormitis extended his arm, pointing across the valley to a small, weathered church, its walls crumbling and seemingly abandoned. "That is Palio Panagia," he said, his voice marked with a mix of nostalgia and sorrow. "It was the church I grew up in. This was before Halikos outlawed Christianity and forced our people to return to the old gods. This is where we must go."

He paused, lost in his thoughts, as memories resurfaced. "I remember a mosaic on the floor," he continued, his tone softer, "depicting a spear. As a child, I often found myself staring at it, thinking it seemed strangely out of place amidst the other sacred images."

The descent down the mountain proved as arduous as the climb had been, if not more so. The rocks shifted beneath their feet, threatening to send them tumbling with each step. The unforgiving terrain demanding every ounce of their focus. Each footfall had to be carefully placed, every handhold methodically chosen, as the steep slope plunged toward the valley below.

Adding to the challenge was the constant need to avoid Halikos's encampments, which dotted the landscape like silent sentinels. Panormitis's intimate knowledge of the local paths became their lifeline. He led the way with ease, guiding them along narrow, hidden trails that kept them far from the prying eyes of the enemy soldiers. They passed like shades, slipping silently through the rugged terrain until, at last, they reached the valley.

Once within the valley's folds, Panormitis led them with a surefooted grace, weaving through the maze-like alleys lined with grapevines, the heavy clusters of fruit dangling temptingly above. They moved quietly, their footsteps muffled by the soft earth beneath. The mingled scents of lemon and mandarin from the groves tantalized them as they passed through, the citrus fragrance a bittersweet reminder of the land's abundance.

Twice, they encountered villagers along their route— simple folk who, upon spotting the group, quickly retreated into their homes, closing their doors.

At last, they reached the far side of the valley, where the land began to rise once more into the foothills of the mountain. They scrambled up the rocky grade, the church of Palio Panagia midway up the slope. The ancient structure, weathered by time and neglect, stood like a solitary guardian over the valley—a symbol of the past that Panormitis could not leave behind. Their journey had brought them full circle, from one side of the valley to another.

Clearing debris from the crumbling doorway, Panormitis pushed aside the remnants of what had once been a proud threshold, leading the way into the vestibule of the ruined church. The air inside was thick with dust, a suffocating reminder of years of neglect. Sunlight filtered through the shattered remains of windows, burnishing fractured beams of light that danced upon the broken stone floor. The once-majestic nave now stood in silent decay, a haunting image of the past.

At the center of the nave, the mosaic Panormitis had spoken of remained intact, a solitary survivor amidst the ruin. The mosaic's tiles, though covered in dust and grime, still glimmered faintly, as if resisting the passage of time.

But the rest of the church had not fared as well. Marble pillars, once soaring, lay toppled and broken, their majestic forms reduced to rubble scattered across the floor. The altar, once the centerpiece of Palio Panagia, had been desecrated beyond recognition. The sacred relics that once adorned it were either stolen or defiled—golden chalices looted, and once-pristine cloths now shredded and stained with dark, unidentifiable marks.

The frescos on the walls depicting the saints and the life of Christ, were defaced, the images now scarred by deep gouges and crude symbols etched by pagan hands. In places, the plaster had been chipped away entirely, exposing the rough stone beneath, as if the very foundation of the church had been violently torn at by those who sought to erase its sanctity.

As Panormitis stood amid the devastation, he felt a deep sorrow, his memories of the church's former glory clashing painfully with the reality before him. This was not merely the ruin of a building; it was the desecration of something deeply personal, a violation of the sacred ground where he had once communed with the Lord.

Pothitos placed a comforting arm around Panormitis's shoulders, gently pulling him back from the brink of sorrow. "I'm sorry," he murmured, his voice heavy with empathy.

Panormitis shook his head, his attention still on the surrounding devastation. "Me too," he replied with sorrow. Then, with a deep breath, he straightened. "Let's do what we came for."

Panormitis instructed the other soldiers to stand guard outside. As they left, the church fell into a deep silence, broken only by the faint rustling of the wind through the broken windows. Panormitis knelt beside the mosaic, his hands trembling slightly as he began to clear away the debris. Dust and grime had settled over the stones, dulling the colors and obscuring the image beneath. But with each careful swipe of his hand, the ancient design began to emerge, like a memory being slowly unearthed.

As the last of the dirt was wiped away, the image took form—an elegant depiction seemed to shimmer in the dim light. The Virgin Mary was seated in a cave, her serene face radiating strength. She pointed with her right hand toward something unseen, while her left hand rested gently on a rock beside her. Her eyes, tender and contemplative, were cast downward, gazing into a small pool of water at her feet.

Next to the pool lay the figure of a Roman soldier, his body laid out as if in eternal rest. His eyes were closed, and his arms were folded across his chest in a pose of solemn dignity. In the pool of water lay a spear, its head shining gold and from its tip spouted blood which mixed with the water. The detail of the scene, the careful rendering of the spear, spoke of an artist who had captured more than just a likeness—there was a reverence here, a story etched into the stone.

Below the mosaic, an inscription was carved in ancient script: "Kieria Psili." The words hung in the air, their meaning elusive but laden with significance. Panormitis stared at the image, his mind racing as he tried to piece together the puzzle that lay before him. This was more than just a relic of the past—it was a message, a connection to something deeper, something they had come all this way to uncover.

Panormitis's eyes widened with sudden excitement as he repeated the inscription aloud, "Kieria Psili! I know this place!"

He turned to Pothitos, his voice brimming with promise. "It's a small cave near the summit of this mountain. Legend has it that the Virgin Mary once stopped there to drink from a small pool of water. She placed her hand on a stone, and the imprint of her hand remains there to this day."

Panormitis's eyes shifted back to the mosaic, his mind sifting through the possibilities. "Maybe there's some truth to the story after all," he continued, his voice hushed, as if speaking the words aloud might make them real. "Perhaps someone traveling with her—someone entrusted with guarding her—left behind the spear of the original Longinus."

He paused, the significance of his own words settling over him like a revelation. The mosaic, the inscription, the cave—it all seemed to point to a hidden truth, a piece of history that had been buried in myth and memory. If the spear of Longinus, the very weapon that had pierced the side of Christ, truly lay hidden in that cave, then they were on the brink of a discovery that could change everything.

"We must go there, Pothitos," he urged, his voice firm. "If the spear is there, we cannot leave it behind. It must be found, for the sake of everything we've fought for."

Chapter 35

THE BELLY OF THE BEAST

Panormitis and Pothitos burst out of the small church, adrenaline still flowing with the thrill of the revelation they had just uncovered. But the moment they stepped outside, their exhilaration was shattered by the gruesome sight that awaited them. Most of their small band of soldiers lay dead, their throats brutally slit, and their bodies carelessly strewn across the narrow path leading up to the church. The ground was soaked with blood, the dark stains seeping into the earth, and the air—once filled with the promise of discovery—now stank of the stench of death and despair.

As the two men stared in stunned horror, the sound of footsteps shuffled ominously around them. Slowly, they lifted their eyes from the grisly scene, all their senses prickled with dread. Emerging from the foliage of the surrounding trees were two dozen of Halikos's men, their faces as cold as the steel of the blades in their hands. At the forefront of this sinister assembly stood a woman dressed in black, her presence as chilling as the death that surrounded them. In her grasp was the last of Pothitos's men, his face pale with terror as she pressed a sharp knife to his throat.

"Did you really think you could enter these lands without being discovered?" she sneered, her voice dripping with cruel amusement. "You fools!" She took a deliberate step closer, her eyes narrowing with malice. "Now, tell me why you are here and what you've learned, or you will suffer the same fate as your companions."

Pothitos nodded toward the captured soldier. "Let him go," he said, his voice steady despite the fear coursing through him. "He knows nothing of our plans."

The woman's lips broke into a wicked smile, a flicker of dark amusement dancing in her eyes. "You," she hissed, her voice like poison. Her beady eyes searching Pothitos's features, as she extended a long, sharp-nailed finger, pointing it directly at him as if marking him for death. "You were with Delenda on the beach, weren't you?"

She stepped closer, her face twisting with a perverse delight. "I have a use for you, boy," she threatened, her voice low and menacing, sending an involuntary shiver down Pothitos's spine. "I'm gonna use you to help me get my Egyptian princess. We are gonna have fun together, my boy," she promised, her words laced with a sickening sweetness. "But first, we must soften you up a little… let you watch your friends die… slowly."

With that, she threw back her head and let out a laugh—a sharp, piercing sound that sliced through the air like the screech of a predatory bird. It was a laugh devoid of any humanity, filled with the promise of pain and suffering beyond imagination. The men surrounding her shifted eagerly, their weapons drawn, eyes gleaming with anticipation as they prepared to carry out her sadistic command.

She cackled, "Take them away."

Guards roughly separated Pothitos and Panormitis and threw them into different cells in a makeshift prison, leaving the fates of both men uncertain. Pothitos's cell was a cold and damp tomb carved deep into the earth. The only light came from a small, high window at ground level, through which he could occasionally glimpse the boots of passing guards. The sparse cell offered little comfort—just a bucket in the corner and walls that seemed to close in on him.

Sitting on the hard ground, Pothitos stared up at the dim light filtering through the window. He wondered what he could do now, how could he possibly ensure Panormitis's safety. The silence amplified his fears. For the first time, he felt the creeping tendrils of despair in the pit of his stomach.

The creak of the door swinging open abruptly interrupted his thoughts. Two of Halikos's men stormed into the cell, their intentions dark. Pothitos tensed, instinctively backing away, but there was nowhere to run. They lunged for him, and he fought back, his despair fueling his resistance. But it only took a few brutal strikes from the pommels of their swords to subdue him. Each blow sent shockwaves of pain through his skull until his vision blurred, and he tasted blood in his mouth.

They dragged Pothitos, blood streaming from a gash above his eye, out of the cell, his boots scraping on the stone floor. The world swayed around him; a chaotic blend of pain and confusion clouded his mind as he was hauled to the center of the encampment. They forced him front and center; his vision slowly cleared, allowing him to focus on the scene before him.

Panormitis knelt a short distance away, his hands bound tightly in front of him, his face bruised. But it was the massive bronze statue that dominated the space—a life-sized bull, its mouth gaping wide in a terrifying semblance of a roar. They had bored out the statue's nostrils into holes, and beneath it, someone had stacked a pile of dried wood.

Pothitos's heart sank as he realized what was about to happen. His mind reeled, struggling to comprehend the horror unfolding before him. A commotion broke out nearby, and he strained to focus, his head still spinning from the earlier blows. Through the haze, he saw one of his fellow Ierí Frourá soldiers, barely conscious, being dragged toward the bull. The large, hinged door on the side of the statue was wrenched open, revealing the hollow interior, and with a sickening finality, the soldier was shoved inside.

"No!" Pothitos screamed, lurching forward in a desperate attempt to stop them, but before he could get far, a powerful kick to the back of his legs sent him crashing to the ground. Someone pushed him into a kneeling position, his body trembling with pain and helpless rage.

From the shadows, Skylla emerged, her presence as cold and malevolent as the bronze bull itself. Her dark eyes gleamed with pleasure as she surveyed the scene. "I see you're ready to pray to my gods now," she mocked, her voice dripping with cruel satisfaction. She laughed—a chilling, hollow sound that coursed through the camp.

"Tonight, we sacrifice to the gods to ensure our victory," Skylla declared, her voice rising with fervor. The words hung in the air like a death sentence. With a cruel smirk, she added, "Don't worry my boy, your time will come. Your companion will be next, and once I have my sweet little princess, I have something very special waiting for you."

The wood beneath the bronze bull was lit and slowly stoked, the crackling flames licking higher as they hungrily devoured the dry wood. Waves of intense heat radiated outward, distorting the scene before Pothitos's eyes and making the air shimmer. The belly of the bull, once a dull, lifeless metal, gradually began to glow a deep, malevolent red, as if the statue itself were coming to life, possessed by the fury of the gods.

As the heat surged, steam began to billow from the bull's nostrils and gaping mouth, twisting upward like ghostly puffs of smoke. The transformation was terrifying, the once cold bronze now blazing with the light of the fire beneath. The soldiers surrounding the statue watched with satisfaction, their faces illuminated by the growing inferno.

Inside the bull, the screams of Pothitos's fellow soldier began to pierce the air—high, desperate cries of agony that seemed to resonate from deep within the metal beast. The structure of the bull amplified the tortured sounds, transforming them into the terrible bellowing of a beast in pain. The mournful, monstrous cries reverberated through the camp, bouncing off the stone walls and chilling the blood of all who heard it.

Pothitos struggled against the hands holding him down, his body thrashing in vain as he tried to block out the horrifying sounds. But there was no escape from the reality of what was happening, no way to close his ears to the screams of his comrade being tortured within the fiery belly of the bull. Each amplified shout sent a fresh wave of horror coursing through him, each one a cruel reminder of the fate that awaited them all if they did not find a way to escape.

Skylla, standing at the edge of the ritual, watched the spectacle with a look of perverse delight, her satisfaction growing as the bull's cries grew louder, more animalistic. The heat of the flames danced in her eyes, reflecting the terror she had unleashed.

Pothitos struggled with helpless fury as he fought against his captors, but their grip only tightened, forcing him to remain on his knees. The sight of Panormitis, bound and kneeling beside him, only deepened his despair. His friend's life was hanging by a thread, and the witch's taunting words danced in his mind—his time would come, and there was nothing he could do to stop it.

The bull's bellowing grew louder still, the cries of the dying man inside merging with the eerie, animalistic sounds emanating from the statue. It was a nightmarish symphony of suffering, designed to break the spirit of anyone who heard it. The steam continued to pour from the bull's nostrils, thick and suffocating.

And through it all, Skylla's laughter rang out—sharp, cruel, and triumphant—drowning out the last of Pothitos's protests as the ritual reached its terrible crescendo.

Pothitos was eventually dragged back to his cell, the rough hands of Halikos's men leaving bruises on his arms and shoulders. The screams from the ritual still echoed faintly in the distance, a haunting reminder of the horrors he had witnessed. But as he was thrown back onto the cold, hard floor of his prison, it wasn't the screams or the sight of the fiery bronze bull that haunted him most—it was the smell. The nauseating, sickly sweet stench of burning flesh which clung to him, filling his nostrils, seeping into his skin, and embedding itself deep in his mind.

He curled up on the floor, his body aching, his mind teetering on the edge of madness. Every breath he took was tainted with that smell, that terrible smell, and no matter how hard he tried to push it away, it lingered, tormenting him even as he drifted into a restless, fitful sleep.

In his dreams, the smell followed him, choking him, as visions of flames danced around him. He saw faces twisted in agony, heard screams that reverberated through his skull, but it was the smell—the unbearable, suffocating smell—that kept pulling him back into the nightmare.

Suddenly, he was jolted awake by a noise outside his cell. At first, he thought he was still dreaming, still trapped in that frightening vision, but then he heard a voice—faint, urgent, and familiar.

"Pothitos, wake up… hurry, wake up!"

His name, repeated with increasing desperation, cut through the fog of his exhausted mind. Was this another trick of his imagination, or was someone truly calling to him? Sore and bone-tired, he forced himself to focus, blinking away the haze of sleep.

"Pothitos, hurry! I don't have much time!"

This time, he recognized the voice—Panormitis. His heart leapt. How could Panormitis be here? How could he have escaped?

"How?" Pothitos croaked, his voice hoarse from screaming.

"During the execution, a childhood friend of mine recognized me," Panormitis said urgently. "He snuck me the key to my cell door. Hurry, take it!"

Pothitos heard the clatter of metal on stone as Panormitis tossed the key into his cell. He scrambled forward, his hands shaking as he grasped the cold key. Every second felt like an eternity as he rushed to the metal bars, desperately shoving the key into the lock. But when he tried to turn it, the key wouldn't budge.

His heart pounded in his chest as panic set in. He tried again, twisting the key with all his strength, but it refused to turn. The lock remained stubbornly shut, as if mocking his efforts. Sweat dripped down his forehead, mixing with the dried blood on his face as he tried again and again, each failed attempt driving his desperation higher.

"Please, no…" Pothitos stammered frantically, the smell of burning flesh still clinging to his senses, feeding his terror. He twisted the key once more, his heart skipping a beat, but the lock held firm.

The sound of footsteps outside the cell made his heart stop. A guard had heard him, and now there was no time left.

"Hey, who's over there?" the guard's voice barked, rough and suspicious.

Pothitos froze, his blood running cold as he heard the guard's approach. But before he could respond, Panormitis's voice cut through the tension.

"Sorry, I have to go! Someone's coming. I'll be back with help!" Panormitis called, his voice filled with urgency.

Pothitos heard Panormitis's footsteps fading away, swallowed by the dark corridors of the prison. He was alone again, clutching a key that didn't fit, surrounded by the stench of death, and haunted by the knowledge that time was slipping away.

As the guard's steps grew louder, Pothitos backed away from the door, hiding the key in his palm. The cell fell into silence once more. Escape had been within his grasp, only to be snatched away by a cruel twist of fate. Now, all he could do was wait, hope dwindling with each passing moment, as the gloom closed in around him.

Chapter 36

TWIN FLAMES IN DARKNESS

Days had long since lost their meaning for Pothitos. The passage of time, once marked by the rising and setting of the sun, had dissolved into an endless blur of darkness and pain. When he first arrived in the prison, he had at least been able to see a sliver of sky from the high window in his cell. The faint light that trickled in provided him with some connection to the outside world, a reminder that there was still life beyond the stone walls that confined him. But after the guards discovered the key Panormitis had given to him, even that small comfort was taken away, plunging him into a new depth of despair.

The discovery of the key was a turning point, the moment when the fragile thread of hope he had clung to was violently severed. The guards had descended upon his cell like a pack of wolves; their faces warped with rage. Pothitos barely had time to comprehend what was happening before he was dragged out into the harsh daylight, his protests falling on deaf ears. The beating that followed was brutal and relentless, designed not just to punish him, but to break him. They whipped him at the post until his back was a raw, bloody mess, each lash searing pain deep into his flesh. Every strike was accompanied by a cruel taunt, a reminder that he had dared to defy them, dared to hope for escape. He had dared to dream of freedom, and for that, they would make him suffer.

After the beating, they dumped him into a new cell—a dank hole in the ground, so small that he could barely crouch, let alone stand erect. The stone walls were cold and damp, and the stench of rot and decay permeated every fiber of his being. The ceiling was low, and every movement made his body ache. There was no window, no light, just the oppressive weight of the earth above him, pressing down on his spirit. It was a place designed to break a man's spirit, to crush any remaining shred of hope, and to force him to confront his own insignificance in the face of overwhelming power.

Pothitos lost track of time in that hole. Hours turned into days, days into weeks, each one blurring into the next as he struggled to maintain his sanity. The darkness was absolute, unrelenting. It was as though the world had forgotten him, as though he had been buried alive. His thoughts often drifted to Delenda and the child she carried; the only anchor he had left to the world of the living. He clung to the belief that she was still alive. The idea that she was out there, somewhere, enduring her own trials, kept him from succumbing entirely to despair. If they had killed Delenda, surely they would have killed him as well. The fact that he was still breathing, no matter how painful that breath might be, meant that she was likely still alive. He prayed that she was being protected, even as he knew that prayer was a flimsy defense against the reality of their world.

The outside world was little more than a distant memory, a place he could no longer reach. Occasionally, a guard would toss rotted food and dank water into the hole, the only sustenance

Pothitos received. The food was barely enough to keep him alive, and each sip of water tasted of mold and filth. He would force himself to eat and drink, knowing that survival was the only way to keep the possibility of seeing Delenda alive again. His bucket of excrement was raised out of the hole on a rope every few days, the only interaction he had with the world above. It was a degrading existence; one designed to strip him of his humanity.

Despite the isolation, there were moments when sounds from the camp above reached him, pulling him from the depths of his despair. On occasion, he would hear the bellowing of the Brazen Bull—a terrifying reminder of the fate that awaited those who defied Halikos's men. The smell that accompanied those bellows was like a ghost that lingered in the corners of his mind, a specter that haunted him every moment, awake or asleep.

But even as he suffered, his thoughts remained with Delenda and the child. He imagined her in the safety of the monastery, cared for by the nuns, as she awaited the birth of their child. He pictured the child—whether boy or girl; he did not know—being born into a world of violence and strife, but also into a world where love still existed, where hope had not been entirely extinguished. He imagined the warmth of the monastery, the quiet prayers of the nuns, the soft cries of his newborn child. It was a fantasy, but it was all he had to cling to.

As time wore on, Pothitos found himself slipping further into despair. The physical pain was constant, but it was the psychological toll that weighed heaviest on him. His thoughts began to spiral, doubts creeping in like tendrils at the edges of his mind. What if Delenda was dead? What if the child was born only to be captured or killed? What if everything he had fought for had been in vain? What if his faith, once a source of strength, was nothing more than a delusion? These questions gnawed at him, eroding the resolve that had once seemed unbreakable.

The darkness of the cell became a reflection of his own inner turmoil, a physical manifestation of the despair that gnawed at his soul. The walls seemed to close in on him more with each passing day. He felt as though he was suffocating, drowning in the blackness that surrounded him. The God he had once prayed to seemed distant, indifferent to his suffering. The justice he had believed in seemed a cruel joke, a lie told to comfort the weak.

And yet, even in the darkest of moments, there were small flickers of light. Memories of Delenda's smile, the sound of her laughter, the feeling of her hand in his—these were the things that kept him from surrendering entirely to the darkness. He held onto them with fierce determination, refusing to let them be taken from him, no matter how much the world outside his cell sought to break him. He remembered the way she had looked at him, the way her eyes had shone with love and trust. He remembered the way she had spoken of their future, of the life they would build together. These memories were his lifeline, the only thing keeping him from drowning in despair.

Meanwhile, back at the Monastery of Agio Konstantinos, the atmosphere was equally bleak. The nuns and the remaining Ierí Frourá soldiers were growing increasingly desperate as the time passed without word from Pothitos. The once-bountiful food supplies had dwindled to nearly nothing, and every day was a struggle to find enough to eat. Foraging parties, led by Longinus, ventured out into the surrounding wilderness, but they often returned empty-handed, harried by Halikos's men who were constantly patrolling the area. The enemy was always close, always watching, always waiting for the chance to strike.

Delenda's presence at the monastery had been a source of comfort for many, her strength and resilience a flicker of light in the gloom. She had become a symbol of hope, a reminder that life could still flourish, even amid war and death. But as her pregnancy advanced, the strain began to show. Her belly swelled with life, and with it came the anxieties and fears that accompany childbirth. The nuns did their best to care for her, but they, too, were haunted by the uncertainty of the times. Childbirth was dangerous under the best of circumstances, and in a world beset by war and famine, the risks were even greater.

Despite their fears, the nuns did everything in their power to make Delenda comfortable as her time drew near. Gerontisa Angeliki and the others tended to her day and night, soothing her worries and helping her through the bouts of pain that came with the final stages of pregnancy. They brought warm water into the infirmary, prepared clean linens, and did everything they could to create a nurturing space within the walls of the monastery.

But fear was always there, lurking in the background. Many mothers and children did not survive childbirth, and the harsh conditions of the monastery only increased the risk. The nuns prayed fervently for Delenda's safety, but they knew that prayer alone might not be enough. They knew that death could come for her, as it had come for so many others. They understood that the life she carried within her could be snuffed out before it had even begun.

The day finally came when Delenda went into labor. The monastery was filled with the sounds of her screams. As the contractions intensified, the nuns rushed to her side, doing their best to comfort her. The hours dragged on, filled with pain and fear, as Delenda struggled to bring her child into the world. Each scream from Delenda sent fresh waves of anxiety through those waiting outside.

Outside the infirmary, Antonios paced the hallways, his face etched with worry. Longinus stood by his side, offering what comfort he could. The men were helpless in the face of what was happening, forced to wait as the women tended to Delenda. The waiting was torture, each moment stretching into an eternity. Adding to the sense of impending doom were the sounds of the encampment outside the monastery and the distant shouts of men.

The labor was long and difficult, the hours stretching into what felt like an eternity. Delenda's screams grew weaker, the effort of childbirth taking its toll on her already exhausted body. The nuns worked tirelessly, their hands moving with practiced skill as they guided Delenda through the ordeal. The life of both mother and child hung in the balance, and there was nothing they could do but continue to fight.

Finally, after what seemed like an eternity, the sounds of a crying baby broke through the tension. The relief was like a wave of hope washing over those waiting outside. Sister Alexandria emerged from the infirmary; her face flushed with exertion but shining with exhilaration. In her arms, she cradled a small, squirming infant, its cries filling the air with life.

"It's a boy!" she exclaimed, her voice ringing with triumph. "He will be named after his father's father, Antonios Pothitos, following tradition."

The news brought a wave of relief to those waiting. Antonios, overwhelmed with emotion, sank to his knees, tears streaming down his face. Longinus placed a comforting hand on his shoulder, the two men sharing a moment of gratitude. The birth of a son was a blessing, a sign that life would continue, that hope was not lost.

But the relief was short-lived. Delenda's screams continued with renewed intensity. The nuns inside the infirmary exchanged worried glances, their joy at the birth tempered by the realization that the danger was not yet over. Exhausted, Delenda's screams faded as childbirth took its toll on her. Finally, an unnerving silence enveloped the monastery.

And then, just as hope seemed to be slipping away, Sister Maria burst through the infirmary door, her face alight with astonishment.

"It's also a girl!" she exclaimed, her voice trembling with emotion. "There are twins—two children!"

The news sent a ripple of shock through the monastery. Twins were rare, and in these harsh times, the birth of two healthy children was nothing short of a miracle. The nuns crowded around the newborns, their exhaustion forgotten in the face of such a blessing.

Delenda, despite her weakened state, managed a tired but radiant smile as she held her children for the first time. "This child was brought to us by the angels," she spoke, her voice filled with awe. "Her name shall be Angeliki Nomiki."

The birth of the twins brought a renewed sense of optimism to the monastery. Despite the hardships they had endured, despite the losses and the uncertainty that surrounded them, life had found a way to continue.

But even as the nuns celebrated the miracle of the twin's birth, the threat of war loomed large. The enemy was still at the gates, and the monastery was still under siege. The battle was far from over, and the future remained uncertain. But for now, in this moment, there was joy. There was life. And that was enough.

For Pothitos, still trapped in his dark, dank hole, the hope that had kept him alive was now more crucial than ever. He did not know that his children had been born, that Delenda had survived. He did not know that life had trampled on death, that hope had triumphed over despair. But deep within him, he felt a stirring, a sense that something had changed. He did not know what it was, but he knew that he must hold on. He had to survive. He had to return to his family.

And so he held on, clinging to the memories of Delenda. He held on, refusing to let the darkness consume him. He held on, knowing that even in the darkest times, there was still light. And one day, he knew that light would lead him home.

Chapter 37

THE LONG ROAD FROM GEHENNA

One cold evening, Pothitos sat in his damp hole, his body aching from neglect and abuse. The familiar, harrowing sounds of the Brazen Bull resounded above, the tortured screams of another victim being amplified into a nightmarish roar. The pitiful cries cut through the still air like a knife, making Pothitos wince. He could feel the vibrations from the infernal statue even in his underground prison, each agonized bellow shaking him to his core. The smell of burning flesh wafted down through the cracks in the earth, choking the already stale air. Pothitos had long since learned to endure the stench, but tonight it felt especially suffocating, perhaps because he was at the very edge of what his body and mind could endure.

As he huddled in the corner, trying to distance himself from the horrors above, he heard an unexpected sound—a rope being lowered into his hole. His heart skipped a beat, confused by this break in routine. The bucket of filth was typically raised and emptied in the mornings, when a sliver of light would sometimes spill down into the pit, marking the start of another bleak day. But tonight, the sound of the rope sliding against the rough stone filled him with an unexpected sense of alertness.

With a sudden burst of adrenaline, Pothitos grabbed the rope. He yanked it with all the strength his emaciated body could muster. To his shock, the guard holding the other end of the rope was caught unawares and came tumbling down into the hole with a heavy thud. The guard groaned, stunned from the fall, and in that moment of disorientation, Pothitos's instincts took over.

Without a second thought, Pothitos threw himself at the guard. His hands, calloused and raw from captivity, seized the rope with a fierce tenacity. He wrapped it around the guard's neck, pulling it tight as he pressed his knee into the man's back, using his weight to anchor him down. The guard, realizing his peril, began to struggle, thrashing wildly in the confined space. But Pothitos, driven by a primal urge to survive, held firm. His bony fingers dug into the rope, pulling it tighter and tighter until the guard's thrashing became weaker, his breath coming in desperate, wheezing gasps.

Pothitos felt the man's trachea crush under the pressure, heard the sickening crack of cartilage and bone giving way. The guard's body went limp, his eyes rolling back into his head as his life drained away. Pothitos didn't release the rope, not until he was certain the man was dead. He couldn't afford to take any chances. He could feel the rapid thumping of the guard's heartbeat slowing, then ceasing altogether. Pothitos finally let go, his hands trembling with exertion and shock. The body slumped to the ground, lifeless.

The hatch above him had been left open, and for a moment, Pothitos simply stared at it, the possibility of escape dawning on him. His heart pounded in his chest, a wild excitement surging through him. After so much darkness, so much confinement, he had been given a chance—perhaps his only chance—to escape. He couldn't squander it.

Wasting no time, Pothitos clambered up the rough-hewn rock wall, his limbs weak and unsteady, but driven by sheer willpower. His fingers scraped against the jagged stone, tearing at the skin, but he hardly felt the pain. Every muscle in his body screamed in protest, but he forced himself to keep moving, inching closer to freedom. As he reached the top of the hole, he hauled himself over the edge, collapsing onto the ground in a heap, his chest heaving as he gasped for air.

The camp was uncannily quiet, except for the sounds of distant revelry and the screams from the Brazen Bull. The guards, it seemed, were all preoccupied with the execution. There was drinking, shouting, and the clinking of metal as the men celebrated their grotesque spectacle. No one had noticed the open hatch, the missing guard, or the frail figure now lying on the ground, half-dead, but determined.

Pothitos forced himself to his feet, his legs trembling beneath him. He had been hunched over for so long in the cramped confines of his cell that standing upright was an agonizing challenge. The faint evening light, though fading, was blinding after months of darkness, and it took several moments for his eyes to adjust. The cool air stung his skin, a polar difference to the damp and musty environment he had grown accustomed to.

He scanned his surroundings, trying to gather his thoughts. To one side, the sounds of laughter and celebration grew louder— the guards completely absorbed in their gruesome entertainment. On the other side, there was only desolation, a stretch of empty land leading into the wilderness of the surrounding mountainside. Freedom lay in that direction, but so did the unknown.

Unable to fully stand erect and with his vision still impaired by the light, Pothitos hobbled away in the direction of desolation, moving as fast as his emaciated body would allow. His heart pounded in his chest, fear and optimism battling within him. He was weak, his body a mere shadow of what it once had been, but his spirit—though battered—was not yet broken.

Every step was a struggle, his legs threatening to give out beneath him. His bare feet, calloused and cracked, lurched over rocks and debris, but he pushed forward, knowing that to stop now would mean certain death. His thoughts were jumbled, each one sparking memories of how close he had come to losing his life in that hole. The screams from the Brazen Bull grew fainter as he put distance between himself and the camp, replaced by the rustling of leaves and the distant cries of nocturnal animals.

The mountains loomed ahead, a foreboding mass of rocks and crevasses. It was a place of danger, a place where he could easily lose his way, but it was also a place where he might find refuge, where he could hide from his pursuers. He had no plan, only the instinct to survive. The thought of Delenda and their child fueled his desperate flight. He didn't know if they were alive, didn't know if he would ever see them again, but he knew that he had to try. He had to keep moving, had to keep fighting, if not for himself, then for them.

Pothitos glanced back over his shoulder and saw the campfires of Halikos's men flickering in the distance. He turned away from the horrors he was leaving behind. The fear spurred him on, giving him the strength to continue. He focused his attention back on the path ahead, putting one foot in front of the other.

The mountains soon swallowed him, the valley forming a canopy that blocked out what little light remained. The forest was silent, save for the occasional rustle of leaves or the distant hoot of an owl. It was a different kind of darkness here—less oppressive, less suffocating, but still frightening. Every shadow seemed to move, every sound was a potential threat.

Pothitos pushed onward, his body screaming for rest, for relief from the torment he had endured for so long. But there could be no rest, not yet. He knew that Halikos's men would soon discover his absence, and when they did, they would come after him with a vengeance. The knowledge kept him moving, kept him from collapsing in exhaustion.

Finally, after what felt like an eternity, Pothitos found himself in a small clearing. The moon had risen, leaving a pale, silvery light over the landscape. He fell to his knees, his body trembling with fatigue, his mind a whirlwind of thoughts and emotions. He had escaped the camp, but what now? Where could he go? How could he survive in the wilderness with nothing but the rags on his back?

But even as these questions swirled in his mind, Pothitos felt a glimmer of hope. He was free. For the first time in as long as he could remember, he was no longer a prisoner, no longer confined to that hole. He had escaped the clutches of Halikos's men, had survived when so many others had not. That was something.

He knew he couldn't stay in the clearing for long. The wilderness, with all its dangers, was the only place he could hide, the only place where he might have a chance of evading his pursuers. Pothitos forced himself to his feet once more, his legs shaking beneath him, and staggered toward the heights. The darkness swallowed him up, but this time, it was a darkness he chose, a darkness that might just lead him to freedom.

As he disappeared deeper into the mountains, the sounds of the camp faded into the distance, replaced by the whistle of the wind through the night and the soft crunch of loose pebbles underfoot. The night was still young, and the journey ahead was still fraught with danger, but for the first time in what felt like an eternity, Pothitos felt the faint stirrings of hope. And as long as he could keep moving, if he could keep fighting, there was a chance that he might find his way back to the life that had been stolen from him.

Chapter 38

KYRIA PSILI

When Pothitos finally stopped to rest, the exhaustion hit him like a hammer. His legs trembled beneath him, muscles quivering with fatigue, and each breath clawed at his throat as though the very air was trying to choke him. The sharp mountain winds cut through his threadbare clothes, chilling him to the bone, but the cold was nothing compared to the weariness that threatened to drag him down into the earth. He was high up in the mountains now, far above the cell he had been confined to, and the thought flickered in his mind that perhaps he had escaped death only to climb into the realm of Hades.

But Pothitos was not dead – not yet. He forced himself to look around, taking in his surroundings with a soldier's instinct for survival. The peak of the nearest mountain loomed above him, a jagged silhouette against the night sky. The world stretched out before him, vast and unforgiving, but there was something almost peaceful about the desolation. Up here, far from the horrors of the battlefield and the prison he had clawed his way out of, he felt a strange sense of clarity.

An idea wormed its way into his mind, stubborn and persistent. If he climbed higher, if he could just reach the summit, perhaps he would be able to see the flame still burning at Agio Konstantinos in the distance. The thought of that flame, of the brazier that had stood as a beacon for so long, stirred something deep within him—a need to know, to see with his own eyes that the fire had not been extinguished, that Delenda was still safe.

Pothitos gritted his teeth and pushed himself to his feet, summoning every last scrap of fortitude he possessed. His body protested with every step, his muscles screaming in agony, but he ignored the pain. He had endured worse. He had survived the unspeakable. This was just one more trial, one more mountain to conquer.

The climb was brutal. The rocks were sharp, and the thin air made every inhalation a battle. But Pothitos had been forged in the crucible of war, and he knew how to push through the pain, how to force his body to obey even when it wanted nothing more than to collapse. Slowly, painstakingly, he made his way to the highest point of the mountain, his eyes fixed on the summit as though it were his final goal in life.

At last, he reached the peak. Pothitos stood on the pinnacle of the mountain. He turned in a slow circle, scanning the horizon in all directions as he sought to orient himself. The stars were cold and distant, but familiar to a man who had spent so many nights under the open sky. He found the North Star, steady and unwavering, and from there he turned toward the east.

And on the horizon, he saw it—a faint, flickering speck of light, barely visible in the darkness. But it was there. The fire still burned.

Relief flooded through Pothitos, so powerful that it brought him to his knees. That distant, burning speck was proof that the monastery had not yet fallen, that Delenda was still safe within its walls. He had feared the worst, that the flames would have been snuffed out by the enemies that pursued him, but the light still burned, defiant and enduring. Then he finally allowed himself to rest.

Dawn bled across the horizon, a faint line of light that slowly devoured the night. Pothitos woke with a start, the remnants of his restless sleep clinging to him like cobwebs. His body was a mass of aches and pains, every muscle protesting as he forced himself to sit up. The cold had seeped into his bones during the night, and now, in the harsh morning light, he felt the full weight of his exhaustion. His throat was dry as old leather, and a gnawing hunger twisted in his belly—a hunger so fierce it felt like it might consume him from the inside out.

For a moment, he sat there, staring blankly at the ground, his mind struggling to shake off the fog of sleep. Then, like a jolt of lightning, the memories of the previous day came flooding back. The escape, the climb, the flame he had seen on the horizon. The thought of it drove him to his feet, every step a battle against the stiffness in his limbs.

He made his way back from the peak of the mountain, driven by the need to see, to know what lay below. The air was sharp and biting, but it cleared his head as he crested the ridge. And there it was—the valley he had escaped from, sprawling out before him like a nightmare made real. Far in the distance, he could make out the clustered tents and makeshift homes of Halikos's troops, the encampments that had held him prisoner for so long. Smoke curled lazily into the sky from the center of the camp, and Pothitos couldn't help but wonder if it came from the Brazen Bull, claiming yet another poor soul in its fiery belly.

The sight of it made his stomach turn, but he forced himself to stay focused. He had escaped, but he was far from safe. His mind, despite the hunger and thirst that gnawed at him, began to turn to the practicalities of survival. He needed food, water, and a way to keep moving. Standing on this mountain, staring at the enemy camp, would do nothing to keep him alive.

His eyes scanned the landscape, searching for anything that might sustain him. And then he saw it—a grove of cactus plants, their spiny arms reaching toward the sky. He knew enough about the wild to recognize the promise those plants held. The fruits they bore, prickly pears, were edible, and the thick, fleshy leaves stored water, enough to quench his burning thirst if he could get to it.

But first, he needed a tool. He searched the mountainside for a sharp rock, his eyes combing through the loose stones and boulders until he found one that would serve his purpose. It was a rough thing, toothed and unpolished, but it would do. He knelt by a larger, harder rock and began the arduous task of grinding the edges of the stone, working it against the unyielding surface until it began to take on a sharper edge.

It was slow, painstaking work, and his hands soon bore fresh cuts and scrapes, but Pothitos pressed on, driven by the knowledge that his survival depended on this crude blade. Time slipped by unnoticed, the sun rising higher in the sky as he worked. Finally, after what felt like hours, he held up the rock and examined his handiwork. It was far from perfect, but the edge was sharp enough.

He made his way to the cactus grove, moving with the caution of a man who knows he is still in enemy territory. The prickly pears hung heavy on the plants, their bright, red skin dotted with vicious-looking spines. Pothitos used the sharpened rock to slice through the stems, careful not to impale his fingers on the barbs. Once he had gathered several of the fruits, he set to work peeling them, slicing away the outer layer with quick, efficient movements. The succulent flesh beneath was a welcome sight, and as he bit into the first one, the sweet, tangy juice burst across his tongue, a balm for his parched throat.

He ate slowly, savoring every bite, feeling the strength returning to his limbs with each mouthful. The juice dripped down his chin, sticky and refreshing, and he could almost feel life flowing back into his body. When he had eaten his fill, he turned his attention to the cactus leaves. He used his makeshift knife to slice into the thick green pads, prying them open to reveal the water stored inside. It was bitter, tasting of earth and sap, but it was water, and it was enough to keep him going.

Rested and with his thoughts beginning to clear, Pothitos found himself dragged back to the night when he and Panormitis had been captured. The memory was like a blade, sharp and cutting, thrusting him back into the confusion of that fateful moment. They had been on the cusp of something—a discovery, a revelation that had danced just out of reach, like a riddle in the dark. But what had it been? What had they been so close to uncovering?

The riddle gnawed at him, and then, like a dam breaking, the memories came rushing back with a force that nearly caused him to keel over. The cave… Kyria Psili. Panormitis had spoken of it with such urgency, the importance of finding the Spear of Destiny—Longinus's spear, the weapon that had pierced the side of Christ, a relic of unimaginable power. Pothitos had forgotten in the fog of pain and despair, but now the memory surged through him, clear and vivid, as though Panormitis were speaking the words in his ear once again.

But with the memory came sorrow, a deep and aching sadness that settled like a stone in his chest. Panormitis, his companion, his brother in arms—surely, he must be dead. If he had lived, he would have returned with a rescue party. Panormitis would never have abandoned him. Pothitos could see his friend's face in his mind's eye, the determination that defined him. The thought that Panormitis might be gone, that his bones lay somewhere unmarked and forgotten, was almost too much to bear.

But Pothitos knew he couldn't let the sorrow overwhelm him. He was close—he had to be. The cave, the one Panormitis had spoken of so many moons ago, must be nearby. He stood and looked around, scanning the barren landscape with a soldier's eye. The mountains stretched out before him, harsh and unforgiving, offering no clues. It was a desolation of impassable stone and for a moment, doubt gnawed at him. How could he possibly find the cave in this wilderness?

He climbed back over the far side of the mountain, his eyes narrowing as he searched the horizon. And then, in the distance, something caught his attention—movement, small but distinct. A goat, moving with the sure-footed grace of its kind, was picking its way up into the mountains, following a narrow, almost invisible trail that wound through the rocks.

Pothitos watched, his breath catching, as the goat paused and turned to look at him. For a moment, their eyes met, and Pothitos felt a strange sense of connection, as if the animal were beckoning him, urging him to follow. Then, without a sound, the goat turned and continued on its path, disappearing into the side of the mountain, as though the earth itself had swallowed it whole.

For a heartbeat, Pothitos stood frozen. He had been a soldier for too long to ignore an omen when it presented itself, and this felt like a sign—a sign from God, from fate, or perhaps from Panormitis, guiding him to the place they had sought.

Gathering what little strength remained in his battered body, Pothitos set off after the goat, following the faint trail that wound up into the mountains. The path was narrow and exposed, but he pressed on, driven by a willpower that had been rekindled deep within his heart. The wind howled through the peaks, but Pothitos barely heard it. His mind was focused on the path ahead, on the dream that perhaps, just perhaps, he was being led to the very place that might hold the key to everything, the cave of Kyria Psili, the resting place of the Spear of Destiny.

He pressed on, climbing higher into the rugged mountains until he reached a narrow fold in the rock. Before him loomed a sheer precipice, a vertical wall of stone that seemed to block his path. The rock face was intimidating, smooth and unyielding, and for a moment, Pothitos hesitated. Was this the way the goat had taken? He wasn't quite sure. But then he heard it—the faint tinkle of a bell somewhere above, carried down to him on the wind. The goat was there, just out of sight, and with that sound came relief.

Pothitos scanned the sheer rock wall more closely, and there, hidden amongst the shrubs clinging to the edges of the cliff, he spotted a series of narrow slits cut into the stone. They were like steps, rudimentary and worn, as if some ancient hand had carved them into the mountainside. A makeshift staircase, inviting him to climb.

With a grunt of effort, Pothitos grasped the first handhold and began his ascent. The rock was cold under his fingers, and the narrow ledges offered little in the way of security, but he climbed steadily, his muscles straining with the effort. One slip could send him plummeting to his death, but he pushed the thought aside, focused only on each step, each handhold, driving himself upwards.

Finally, Pothitos hauled himself over the edge of the abyss and found himself staring at a small cave nestled into the mountainside. The entrance was dark, almost foreboding, but as he steadied himself, he noticed something—a scent, faint but unmistakable, wafting from the cave's depths. It was the rich, heady odor of myrrh, so strong it seemed like a blessing.

Pothitos hesitated for only a moment before plunging into the darkness of the cave. There was no time to second-guess his decision; his instincts screamed that this was the place he had been searching for, the cave that Panormitis had spoken of. The air inside was cool and damp, a sharp contrast to the biting wind outside, and it took time for his eyes to adjust to the near-total blackness. But Pothitos was no stranger to the dark; after months spent in that pit, he could navigate even the most impenetrable gloom.

He moved cautiously, feeling his way along the slick, damp walls with outstretched hands. The cave floor was hazardous, the rocks wet and uneven, and more than once he stumbled, his head brushing against low-hanging stalactites. Each time he lost his footing, he caught himself, forcing down the rising panic that threatened to overwhelm him. He had come too far to fail now.

As he pressed deeper into the cave, Pothitos realized it was divided into three chambers. To his left was a small alcove, barely more than a pocket in the rock; ahead of him lay a broader chamber, its boundaries lost in the darkness; and to his right, high up on the cave wall, was a narrow crevasse, just wide enough for a man to crawl through. He explored the first two chambers quickly, but they held nothing of interest—just more damp rock and dripping water. He returned to the narrow crevasse, and he knew, with a certainty that settled in his bones, that his goal lay there.

Pothitos approached the slippery wall and began to climb. It was a slow, grueling ascent, the rock offering little purchase, and he had to wedge himself into the narrow gap to keep from slipping back down. The stone scraped at his skin, tearing at his clothes, but he paid it no mind. He crawled on his belly, inching his way through the crevasse, his elbows and knees bruising against the irregular stone. Finally, the passage opened into a slightly larger chamber, where he could almost sit upright.

The scent of myrrh was overpowering here, so strong it took his breath away. Pothitos paused, his head swimming from the intensity of the odor. This was it. He was sure of it. He reached out into the darkness, his hands searching the cool, damp stone of the cave wall. As his fingers brushed against the surface, he felt something—a smooth indentation, small and unmistakable. The impression of a hand, outstretched, as if reaching toward him from the rock itself.

Pothitos jerked his hand back, his heart pounding in his chest. He lifted his fingers to his nose and caught the scent of myrrh again, stronger now, more distinct. His hand was slick with an oily substance, and he realized with a shock that he had found the source of the scent. This was the imprint of the hand of the Panagia, the Virgin Mary. Reverently, he crossed himself, tears pricking at the corners of his eyes. Despite everything—the suffering, the pain, the despair—he had been guided here, to this sacred place.

Steeling himself, Pothitos plunged his hand forward again, feeling along the stone until his fingers encountered something unexpected—a cool pool of water, hidden beneath the imprinted rock. The water was deep, too deep for him to reach the bottom from his distorted position. With a grunt of effort, he shimmied his body forward, inching himself over the edge until he could drop into the pool feet-first. The cold water hit him like a shock, rising to his waist as he waded through the darkness. His hands and feet scoured the floor, searching, searching—until he touched something solid.

He gasped as he closed his fingers around the object, pulling it free from its watery grave. It was long and narrow, the metal cool to the touch, and as his hands traced its edges, he felt the unmistakable sharpness, the deadly point of a spearhead. The realization struck him like a hammer blow. He had found it. The Spear of Destiny.

Pothitos stood in the darkness, the spearhead clutched in his trembling hands, overwhelmed by the enormity of what he had uncovered. Slowly, reverently, he placed one hand back on the imprinted rock, his other holding the spearhead close to his chest. He uttered a silent prayer to the Virgin Mary, thanking her for guiding him, for deeming him worthy of this sacred relic.

The weight of the spearhead in his hand was heavy, almost unbearable, but it was a burden he would carry with honor. Pothitos knew that his journey was far from over, that there were still dangers ahead, but for the first time in a long while, he felt true promise. He had the Spear of Destiny in his hand. The tides of fate had shifted. The flames beneath the brazen bull still burned—but he now carried a fire of his own, one that could reshape the world.

Chapter 39

A FLAME ON THE HORIZON

It was night again when Pothitos emerged from the cave with a renewed sense of purpose. The spearhead, cool and heavy in his hand, seemed to pulse with a power of its own, a power he thought he could feel coursing through his veins. He had found it—the Spear of Destiny, the relic that had been lost for so long, and now it was his. The journey had nearly broken him and tested him in ways he had never imagined, but he had prevailed. He had survived. And with the spearhead in his possession, he felt as though nothing could stand in his way.

The air outside the cave was sharp and cold, a biting wind tugging at his tattered clothes, but Pothitos hardly noticed. He made his way back down the narrow, rutted path, his movements swift and sure despite the fatigue that clung to his limbs. The climb that had taken all his strength earlier now seemed effortless. The sheer walls that had loomed above him like impossible barriers were now nothing more than a passage back to the world he had left behind. He felt invincible, as if the spearhead had lifted the burdens on his soul.

At last, he reached the peak of the mountain once more, the same vantage point where he had first gazed out upon the distant horizon. He looked eastward, toward Agio Konstantinos, his eyes straining in the darkened sky. And there it was—a tiny, flickering flame, still burning, still holding out against the darkness that surrounded it. The sight of it filled him with fierce joy, a surge of triumph that washed away the memories of his suffering.

But as he watched, something changed. The flame, so bright and defiant just moments before, began to flicker. Pothitos blinked, thinking his eyes were deceiving him, but no—he could see it clearly now. The flame was flickering, weakening, as if it were struggling to hold on. His heart, which had been soaring with victory, suddenly lurched in his chest.

"No," Pothitos cried out, the word torn from his lips in a breathless gasp.

He took a step forward, staring at the distant flame, willing it to burn brighter, to resist whatever force was trying to extinguish it. But it was no use. The flame continued to dim, shrinking with each passing moment, until it was no more than a faint, trembling glow on the horizon.

Pothitos felt his blood run cold. He had seen men die on the battlefield, had watched as the light faded from their eyes, but this was different. This was his symbol, his last vestige of hope, and now it was being snuffed out before his very eyes. He could almost feel the life draining from it, the light slipping away, and with it, the promise that had kept him going through all the trials and hardships he had faced.

"Lord, please," he pleaded, his voice filled with dread. Something was wrong—terribly wrong.

The flame flickered one last time, a final, desperate gasp, and then it was gone. The brazier atop Agio Konstantinos had been doused, its light extinguished. The darkness that had been kept at bay for so long now rushed in to fill the void, and Pothitos felt it like a physical blow, a crushing weight that settled over him.

For a moment, he stood frozen, his mind refusing to accept what his eyes had seen. How could this be? He had found the spearhead, the very relic they had sought, the key to everything. But what good was it now? What good was a weapon of legend if the one he loved had already died, if the walls of Agio Konstantinos had already fallen? The questions tumbled through his mind, but he had no answers, only a growing sense of dread that gnawed at his insides.

Pothitos dropped to his knees, staring at the horizon where the flame had once burned. He had felt so sure, so certain that he was being guided, that Panagia herself had led him to the cave, to the spearhead. But now, doubt flooded his heart. Had he been too late? Had all his struggles been in vain?

He clenched his fists, his nails digging into his palms, the pain a small comfort in the face of the despair that threatened to consume him. The feeling of triumph that had filled him only moments ago had turned to ashes in his mouth.

Pothitos lifted his eyes once more, searching desperately for any sign of the flame, for any spark that might indicate that all was not lost. But there was nothing. Only darkness.

A shudder ran through him as he realized the truth. The brazier had been doused, and with it, his faith. Agio Konstantinos had fallen, or was in the process of falling, and the flame that had been their inspiration was no more.

Pothitos bowed his head, his body trembling. He had failed. He had escaped the clutches of his captors. He had found the sacred relic, but he had still failed to protect those he loved.

Delenda. The thought of her, alone and vulnerable in the monastery, filled him with a cold, hollow dread.

The flame was gone, but Pothitos knew his journey was not over. He still had the spearhead. He still had strength left in his limbs, and a fire burning in his heart, though it now burned with anguish and rage. The path ahead was shrouded in darkness, but he would walk it all the same.

With a slow, deliberate motion, Pothitos rose to his feet. The mountain wind howled around him, a mournful cry that seemed to align with his sorrow, but he stood against it. He looked once more to the east, toward the place where the flame had flickered out, and he swore an oath.

He would find Delenda. He would make his way to the monastery, even if it meant walking through the Gehenna itself. He would use the spearhead, the relic he had fought so hard to obtain, and he would make those who had extinguished the flame of Agio Konstantinos pay for their sins.

Pothitos turned his back on the desolate peak, his mind set, his heart hardened by the knowledge that the time for hope had passed. Now was the time for action. The time for war. And with the Spear of Destiny in his hand, he would carve a path through the darkness, even if it led to his death.

Chapter 40

THE KNOCK AT THE GATE

The attack came without warning, a sudden, brutal onslaught that shattered the fragile peace of the monastery. It was well before dawn; the sun had yet to pierce the sky. The nuns and soldiers of the Ierí Frourá had been on high alert for weeks, knowing that the forces of Halikos, Gelimer, and Skylla were gathering in the surrounding lands. But even with this knowledge, nothing could have prepared them for the fury that descended upon them.

The first sign of the attack on the monastery was a small boulder that sailed over the high walls, arcing through the pale dawn light before it crashed down among the olive groves. The thud it made was dull, almost innocuous, but it was a herald of what was to come. A brief stillness followed, a moment when the world seemed to hold its breath, and then the air was filled with the sound of creaking wood and snapping ropes, as more boulders were launched from the mountainside.

The rocks came in quick succession, peppering the fortress walls and gates with relentless thuds. They weren't large enough to breach the walls— Halikos's men had dragged light trebuchets up the steep mountain paths under the cover of night, but these were not siege engines designed to shatter stone. They were a distraction, a nuisance, meant to keep the archers off the walls, to sow chaos and fear within the hearts of those inside.

Longinus stood among his troops, his temple pulsing as he watched the boulders bounce harmlessly off the thick stonework. His men, the Ierí Frourá, were seasoned warriors, men who had faced death a hundred times before, and they did not flinch at the sight of stones falling from the sky. But they knew what this meant. The enemy was here, and this was only the beginning.

One of the smaller boulders struck the brazier that had burned high on the monastery wall, the flame that Delenda had kept lit for Pothitos. The brazier toppled, spilling its contents— logs and oil—across the cold stone. For a brief, brilliant moment, the fire flared up, burning brightly as the oil caught and fed the flames. But it was a short-lived blaze, the light flickering and dying as the fire found no purchase on the stone.

Longinus watched as the flame dwindled and then snuffed out entirely, leaving behind only the blackened stain of charred wood and spilled oil. A chill ran through him, a cold dread that settled in his bones. The brazier was more than just a light—it was a symbol, a mark of defiance against the darkness that surrounded them. And now, with the flame extinguished, it felt as if a part of his soul had been snuffed out as well.

The boulders continued to rain down, bouncing harmlessly off the thick walls, but the real damage was already done. The archers had been forced to take cover, their vantage points now exposed and dangerous. Halikos's men had bought themselves time, time to bring up their heavier weapons, time to plan the next phase of their assault.

Longinus knew the enemy was patient. Halikos was a man who would not rush headlong into battle without evaluating every option, without ensuring that victory was within his grasp. The boulders were a warning, a signal that the real fight was about to begin. And when it did, it would be fierce. He looked at the men around him, their faces grim. These were men who had fought together, bled together, and they would hold this place to the last breath. But even they could not deny the unease that had settled over the monastery with the extinguishing of that flame. The walls still stood unbroken, but the brazier's light was gone.

As suddenly as the rocks had started flying, they stopped. The sudden silence was as jarring as the bombardment itself, leaving a ringing in the ears of every man and woman within the monastery walls. For a moment, it seemed as though the world had paused. The defenders of Agio Konstantinos, tense and exhausted, allowed themselves a fleeting sigh of relief. It was a respite, however brief, and they took it with the wary gratitude of men who knew the storm had only just begun.

But no sooner had they caught their breath than the rocks began again. With a crack of wood and a hiss of stone, the trebuchets unleashed another volley, the boulders arcing through the sky to crash down against the fortress walls. The pattern repeated itself in cruel, unrelenting cycles. The bombardment would cease, sometimes for hours, sometimes for only minutes, lulling the defenders into a false sense of calm. And then, just as they began to hope that it might be over, the assault would begin anew. The sky filled with the whistling of stones and the ground shook under the impact.

Day and night, it continued, a merciless dance of stone and silence that ground the nerves of the defenders to raw edges. Sleep became an impossible luxury, the constant tension, the anticipation of the next strike keeping every soldier and nun on edge. They took turns at the walls, but even those who lay down to rest found no comfort. Their eyes would close, but their minds would remain alert, listening for the next barrage, the next thud of rock against stone.

The boulders were small, yes, too small to shatter the thick walls, but they were deadly in their own way. Every strike was a reminder of the enemy's presence, a reminder that they were surrounded, isolated, with no likelihood of reinforcement. Every crash sent dust and debris raining down on the men below, and though the walls held, the men did not always fare as well.

Occasionally, a boulder would find its mark, striking a soldier who had been just a heartbeat too slow in seeking cover. The results were devastating. An arm shattered here, a leg broken there, men who had fought in a dozen battles brought low by a single, unthinking stone. The nuns worked tirelessly, splinting limbs and binding wounds, their hands stained with blood. But not all injuries could be mended.

Delenda saw it herself, on the second night of the siege, when a warrior—Nikitas, a man of stout heart and quick wit—was struck down by a rock that came out of the darkness with the speed of a viper. The boulder crashed into his skull with a sickening crack, and the man crumpled to the ground, his bow clattering from his hand. They carried him from the walls, his face a mask of blood. But there was nothing to be done. He was dead before dawn.

It was a death that sent a ripple of fear through the ranks. These men were warriors, men who had faced death many times, but this was different. This was not a death in the heat of battle, a death met with sword in hand and courage in the heart. This was a death that came in the stillness, a death that struck without warning, without honor. The fear of it crept into their minds, gnawing at their spirit like a rat in the night.

And yet, they held the walls. Despite the terror, despite the exhaustion, the men of the Ierí Frourá kept their posts, their eyes ever watchful for the next attack. The nuns, too, did their part, moving among the wounded with efficiency, offering prayers and comfort where they could. They were no strangers to suffering, and their presence, their calm in the face of the storm, gave the soldiers a thread of hope to cling to.

Delenda herself felt the weariness seeping into her bones, a heaviness that seemed to drag at her every step. Her muscles were sore from holding her children, her eyes stinging from the tears she cried for Pothitos. She stopped wondering long time ago whether he still lived and had accepted that she would raise her children alone. The memory of the extinguished brazier haunted her, the image of that flickering flame, now gone, a constant reminder of the promise that she made to Pothitos to keep it alight. She knew, as did every person within those walls, that this was merely the prelude. The real assault had not yet begun, and when it did, it would be with a wrath they could scarcely imagine.

But for now, they endured. For three days and three nights, they persisted. The boulders kept coming in bursts that shattered stone and bone alike, but the walls of the monastery held firm. The men, though battered and bruised, stood their ground, their eyes scanning the horizon for the first sign of the true assault.

And when the silence came again, as it inevitably did, they did not allow themselves a respite. They knew that Halikos, Gelimer, and Skylla were out there, waiting, planning, and that when the next blow fell, it would be one from which they might not recover.

It was still dark when the assault finally came. Halikos, the warlord whose name had become synonymous with terror, led the charge. His men, a savage horde, crashed against the monastery's walls like a relentless tide. They carried torches and battering rams, their war cries booming through the halls like the howls of wild beasts. Halikos himself, clad in his blackened armor, strode at the forefront, his sword pointed menacingly forward as he urged his men onward.

From the east came Gelimer, the cunning chieftain known for his ruthlessness in battle. His forces were smaller in number, but no less deadly. These were men who moved like a shade, striking swiftly and silently before melting back into the shadows. They carried bows, their arrows tipped with poison that could fell a man in seconds. Gelimer, with his hawk-like features and cold, calculating eyes, directed his troops without mercy. He had laid siege to many fortresses in his time, and he knew exactly how to exploit every weakness in a stronghold's defenses. His archers took their positions on the ridges surrounding the fortress walls, their arrows raining down on the defenders from above. The poison-tipped shafts finding their marks, striking the soldiers and nuns who remained in the monastery's courtyard. The defenders tried to shield themselves with their cloaks and shields, but the arrows seemed to come from everywhere at once, each one carrying death on its tip.

By Gelimer's side was Skylla, the witch whose very name inspired dread. She moved through the ranks of his followers like a wraith, her presence as chilling as the night wind. Dressed in flowing black robes, her pale face framed by wild, dark hair, she seemed more a creature of the underworld than of the earth. In her hands, she carried the tools of her dark craft—talismans of bone, and an ominous-looking dagger. Skylla's eyes burned with hatred as she prepared to unleash her wickedness upon the monastery.

Inside the monastery walls, the defenders of Agio Konstantinos scrambled to prepare for the coming onslaught. The nuns, their faces pale, moved through the corridors, arming themselves with whatever they could find—knives, staffs, even the heavy candlesticks from the altar. They had taken vows of peace, but they were ready to fight to protect their home and the lives within it. Gerontisa Angeliki, the eldest among them, led them with a calm born of faith, her hands steady despite her heart pounding with fear.

The soldiers of the Ierí Frourá, though few, were determined to make their stand. They knew the monastery's defenses better than anyone, and they positioned themselves at the weakest points, ready to repel the invaders. Longinus moved among them, offering words of encouragement. He had fought in many battles, but none had felt as important as this one. He knew that the fate of the monastery, and of those within its walls, rested on the outcome of this battle.

As the first wave of attackers reached the courtyard, the walls exploded into chaos. The battering rams thundered against the gates, each blow sending tremors through the wood. Archers continued shooting their volleys of arrows over the walls, their deadly shafts finding targets among the defenders. Screams of pain and fury filled the air, mingling with the crack of wood and the roar of the invaders.

The invaders were relentless. They surged forward, their sheer numbers overwhelming the fortifications. The gates began to buckle under the force of the battering rams, and soon they splintered, the heavy wood giving way with a deafening crack. The enemy poured into the courtyard, a flood of steel and fire that swept over everything in its path.

Longinus led his men with a ferocity born of desperation. They met the enemy at the courtyard gates, their swords flashing as they cut down the first attackers to breach the walls. Blood flowed freely, staining the stones red as the battle raged. They were outnumbered and outmatched, but they fought with the strength of those who have nothing left to lose.

Inside the monastery, the nuns and the remaining soldiers retreated to the inner sanctum, the last refuge within the ancient walls. They barricaded the doors, their eyes glistening with tears for the final stand. The cries of the wounded carried through the corridors, the sounds of the carnage that was already unfolding. The sacred relics that had been the heart of the monastery were gathered together, the nuns praying desperately for a miracle, for some divine intervention that might save them from the terror that had descended upon them.

Delenda huddled in the corner of the makeshift infirmary, clutching her newborn twins close to her chest. The sounds of battle outside sent shivers down her spine. She looked into the faces of her children, their innocent eyes wide with confusion and fear, and said a quiet prayer for their safety. She knew that the walls of the monastery, once a fortress, were now little more than a brittle shell, ready to crack under the unremitting assault.

Longinus, his armor dented and bloodied, managed to retreat into the inner sanctum before the doors were barricaded. He gripped his sword tightly in his hand. He had sworn to protect the monastery and its inhabitants, and he would not break that oath, even if it meant his life. The other soldiers, those who remained, took up positions beside him.

The doors to the inner sanctum shuddered under the force of the battering rams, each blow bringing them closer to collapse. The defenders could hear the taunts of Halikos's men on the other side, their voices filled with the promise of death and devastation. The nuns clutched their koubastinis, their prayers growing more fervent as the doors began to splinter.

And then, with a final, thunderous crash, the doors gave way.

Chapter 41

BROTHERS OF KALYMNOS

Pothitos ran through the mountain pass with the urgency of a man possessed. The spearhead was gripped tightly in his hand, its weight no longer a burden but a burning promise. He could feel its edges digging into his palm as if it were alive, pushing him forward. Every step was a prayer, every breath a plea for strength. He did not let himself think of what might await him at the monastery—the images of broken walls and dying screams that haunted his mind. There was no time for doubt. Only action.

The path wound through the rocky terrain, but Pothitos moved with speed and agility born of desperation. The scent of myrrh still clung to him, mingling with the sweat that soaked his skin, and in his mind, he could hear the sound of Delenda's voice, urging him onward, driving him forward. He knew that time was running out, that every moment he wasted brought the monastery closer to its doom.

As he rounded a bend in the trail, the sound of distant voices and shuffling feet reached his ears. He froze. A primal fear gripped him. Could it be enemy scouts? He ducked low, creeping closer, the spearhead ready in his hand.

And then he saw them—a vast, ragged band of men, surging up the mountain like a living tide. Shepherds, farmers, fishermen, men who had lived their lives amongst these mountains, who knew every rock, every tree, every hidden trail. They were armed with whatever they had managed to lay their hands on— clubs, scythes, daggers, anything that could be turned into a weapon—and they moved like a tidal wave, their eyes fixed on the distant walls of Agio Konstantinos.

At their head strode two men Pothitos recognized instantly: Vlassios, the broad-shouldered leader of the Peraioton deme, and Savvas, the wiry regent of the deme of Skaliodon. They were men of stark contrasts. Vlassios looked like the earth itself had shaped him—his hands were like shovels; his face tanned from decades under the sun. He carried an ancient axe over one shoulder, its blade nicked and worn but still deadly. Beside him, Savvas moved with the easy grace of the sea, a trident slung across his back and a net draped over one arm. His sharp features gave him the air of a man who knew the tides of both water and war.

And at the center of them all, walking with confident strides was Panormitis. The trials he had endured hardened him, his hair wild and matted, but his eyes still held that same fire, that same spirit that had always driven him. He looked like a man reborn, a warrior who had walked through the fire and emerged on the other side stronger.

Pothitos's heart leaped in his chest at the sight of his old friend. A surge of relief coursed through his body. Panormitis was alive. Not just alive, but leading an army.

For a moment, Pothitos stood frozen, thoughts coursing through his mind. He's here. They're here.

Panormitis saw him then, standing alone on the path, and a grin split his face. He raised a hand in greeting.

"I told you I would be back to rescue you!" Panormitis shouted over the advancing horde.

Pothitos let out a laugh. He allowed himself to take in the sight of his friend, of the hundreds—no, thousands—of men following him. This was not just a rescue; this was a reckoning.

"It took you long enough," Pothitos called back, his voice cracking. The two men clasped each other's forearms like brothers who had been torn apart by war and fate. "You look terrible," Panormitis exclaimed.

"I could say the same," Pothitos replied, his voice catching in his throat.

"We all look terrible," Vlassios interrupted, his voice a low rumble as he approached. "But we're still breathing, and that's more than I can say for the swine who've taken the monastery."

Pothitos looked around him at the gathered army and said, "Well… what took you so long?"

Savvas stepped up beside him. "We've been gathering the men for weeks. Every farmer and fisherman from the four demes are here. They're tired of hiding, tired of running. This is their land, and they're ready to die for it," he said.

Pothitos shook his head in disbelief and playfully shoved Panormitis. "I thought you were dead," he said.

"I thought the same about you," Panormitis replied, his voice gruff but warm. "But here we are, eh? Alive and well, ready to give these dogs what they deserve."

Pothitos nodded, a fierce grin spreading across his face. "Indeed. And we've got something they don't." He held up the spearhead, the ancient weapon glinting in the light, its edges sharp and deadly. Panormitis's eyes widened as he took in the sight of it, and for a moment, a reverent silence fell between them.

"The Spear of Destiny," Panormitis said with awe in his voice. "You found it."

"I did," Pothitos replied. "But it won't mean anything if we don't reach the monastery in time."

Panormitis's grin returned, a fierce, wolfish smile that sent a thrill of anticipation through Pothitos. "Then we'd better not keep them waiting."

Side by side, the four men turned to face the distant walls of Agio Konstantinos. The ragtag army surged forward, their footsteps thundering like a storm over the mountains. Their cries filled the air, not as soldiers, but as men reclaiming their lives.

As they neared the monastery, the walls came into view—battered and broken, scorched black by fire. The air was thick with smoke, and no defenders stood on the ramparts. Instead, a dark horde stood before the gates, their pagan war cries rising like a funeral dirge.

Panormitis felt the blood drain from his face. "Are we too late?" he uttered.

Pothitos raised his spearhead—now affixed to a solid spear shaft—high into the air, his voice ringing out over the advancing horde. "For Kalymnos!"

And together, they charged.

Chapter 42

THE BATTLE OF AGIO KONSTANTINOS

The gates of the inner sanctuary crashed inwards with a thunderous roar, the wood splintering under the relentless assault. Dust and debris filled the air, choking those who stood ready to face the enemy. The defenders knew this was it—this was the moment when everything would be decided. Longinus rallied the men around him. Antonios was at his side, sword and shield in his hand. Together, with what few warriors remained, they formed a shield wall across the open expanse between the shattered gates of the inner sanctum.

Their shields locked together with a resounding thud, creating a barrier of steel and wood, a last line of defense against the horrors that waited beyond the gates. These were the best of what was left, men who had fought and bled together, men who knew the horrors their enemy was capable of. Stavros and Andreas, veterans of countless battles, stood shoulder to shoulder with Longinus and Antonios. They all knew they were buying time, sacrificing themselves to ensure that the elderly and infirm could find refuge in the sanctuary behind them. The nuns, the children, and the wounded—they had to be protected at all costs.

But as they braced themselves for the inevitable onslaught, the expected rush of merciless pagans never came. Instead, a strange and ominous sound began to rise from the darkness beyond the shattered gates. It was a low, haunting melody, carried on the mountain air, growing louder with each passing moment. The sound was unfamiliar to some, but others recognized it immediately—an instrument of the Greek shepherd, the tsabouna, its eerie notes drawn from bagpipes made of sheepskin.

First, there was one, the mournful wail of the tsabouna reverberating off the stone walls of the monastery. Then another joined it, and another, until it seemed as if the hills were alive with the sound. The invaders exchanged uneasy glances as the music swelled, filling the air with a sense of foreboding. The melody was not one of war, but it was no less menacing for it. It was the sound of something ancient, something that spoke of deep roots and old blood, a song that had been played in these mountains for generations, long before any invader had set foot on this land.

The tension mounted as the music grew louder; the notes intertwining into a haunting symphony that filled every crevice of the monastery. And then, from the darkness beyond the gates, there came a sound that sent a shiver down the spine of every man who heard it—a defiant roar. A cry of fury and determination that seemed to shake the very earth.

Out of the darkness, they came. Thousands of them, their numbers stretching far beyond what the pagans could have imagined. Shepherds, fishermen, farmers—simple men who had lived their lives amongst the shores of this island, now rising up to defend what was theirs. They charged forward wielding whatever weapons they had—an array of scythes, clubs, and knives, anything that could be turned to killing.

At their head, leading them into the fray, were two figures that seemed to shine as the morning sun broke over the horizon, illuminating them. Panormitis led the charge; his voice raised in a battle cry that carried through the dawn. And beside him, there was Pothitos. But there was something different about him, something that made the men of the monastery pause in awe. The rays of the rising sun seemed to illuminate him with an otherworldly light. It was as if he had been chosen for this moment.

The defenders, who had been ready to sacrifice their lives to buy a few more moments of time, now found themselves swept up in the surge of new allies. The clash of steel and the cries of the wounded were drowned out as the sound of the tsabouna continued, weaving through the madness. The merciless pagans, who had been so certain of their victory, now found themselves overwhelmed by this sudden, unexpected surge of kinsmen.

The shepherds, with their curved staffs and deadly daggers, fought with the knowledge of the land in their bones, using the terrain to their advantage, outmaneuvering the invaders at every turn. The fishermen, their hands rough from years of hauling in nets, wielded their makeshift weapons with efficiency, striking down enemies with tridents and fishing spears. The farmers, whose strength came from years of tilling the rocky soil, swung their sickles with deadly accuracy, cutting through the enemy ranks like wheat before the scythe.

And through it all, Pothitos moved like a man possessed, his eyes fixed on the enemy, the Spear of Destiny held high. Every strike he made seemed to find its mark, every blow landing with a force that drove the enemy back. He fought with a singular purpose. Get to Delenda. He was no longer just a man—he was a warrior of legend.

The pagans had come expecting to crush a weakened monastery, to stamp out the last flickering flame of resistance, but they had been met instead by the wrath of a people who refused to die quietly.

The battle had reached a fever pitch. The haunting sound of the tsabouna continued like the cry of some ancient beast roused from its slumber. As the music ebbed for just a moment, a brief lull in the chaos, Antonios seized his chance. He savagely broke from the shield wall and charged forward through the maelstrom of clashing steel and bellowing men. His eyes were locked on one figure amid the swirling melee— Halikos, the butcher, the man who had brought so much death and despair to his land. This was his moment, and he would end it, here and now.

The two warriors met with a clash of swords that sent sparks flying into the air. Halikos moved with the raw power of a man who had cut down more foes than he could count. He wielded his sword with strength, a weapon honed in the fires of countless wars. Antonios felt the force of every blow reverberate through his body. His arm shook with the impact, his muscles straining under the relentless assault.

Around them, the fight raged on. Farmers, shepherds, and fishermen fought with desperate fury, felling trained warriors with nothing more than scythes and clubs. But Antonios had eyes only for Halikos, and the enemy leader seemed to know it. They circled each other like predators, each looking for an opening, each knowing that this duel would decide more than just their own fates. It was a battle for the soul of the land, for everything they had fought to protect.

Halikos attacked with the ferocity of a man who believed himself invincible. His sword whistled through the air; each swing aimed with deadly intent. Antonios parried and dodged, but he was being driven back against the monastery wall where there was no escape. Halikos, sensing the advantage, pressed forward, driving Antonios back step by step, his strikes coming faster and harder with every passing second.

Pothitos, watching from the remnants of the shield wall, saw his father being pushed to the brink. He saw despair in Antonios's eyes, the way his movements were slowing, the way Halikos was battering him down like a hammer striking an anvil. Without thinking, Pothitos moved to step forward, to intervene, but Antonios, with a sharp, commanding voice that cut through the noise of battle, stopped him in his tracks.

"He is mine!" Antonios shouted, his voice left no room for argument.

Pothitos froze, his hand slackening around the shaft of the spear he held. He knew his father well enough to recognize the finality in his words. This was not a fight for two men—this was his fight, and his alone. Pothitos nodded and stepped back, his eyes never leaving the two combatants.

Halikos, emboldened by Antonios's apparent weakness, gave a great and powerful swing, a blow meant to end it all. The sword sliced through the air with the force of a gale, a strike that would have taken the head from an ox. All along, Antonios's retreat had been a deception. As the massive blade arced toward him, Antonios moved with the speed and agility of a man half his age. He sidestepped the blow with ease, his body flowing like water around the deadly steel.

Before Halikos could recover, before he could even register that his killing blow had missed, Antonios struck. His sword flashed out, quick as lightning, and the point drove through the side of Halikos's neck, cutting cleanly through flesh and bone. The blade emerged on the other side, slick with blood, and for a moment, the two men were locked in a moment of death, their eyes meeting for one brief, final exchange.

Halikos's eyes widened in shock, the realization of his own mortality dawning in those last, fleeting moments. His mouth opened, but no words came—only a gurgle of blood as he careened to the ground, his life ebbing away. Antonios stood over him, his chest heaving, the sword still buried in his enemy's neck. He watched as the light faded from eyes, and then, with a final twist of the blade, he yanked his weapon free.

The world seemed to pause, the fighters on both sides momentarily stunned by the sight of Halikos's fall. The terror of the mountains, the man who had brought fire and sword to so many villages, was dead. The sound of the tsabouna, which had been so haunting and relentless, now seemed softer, almost mournful.

Antonios looked down at the blood-soaked ground, at the body of the man he had slain, and then he turned to Pothitos, his face lined with exhaustion but lit with a fierce pride.

"It's done," he said, his voice quiet, the moment sinking into him.

Pothitos approached, his eyes meeting those of his father's, and for a moment, they simply stood there, two warriors who had seen more than their share of death. Then, as if by unspoken agreement, they embraced, their arms wrapping around each other in a bond forged by fire and blood.

"It took you long enough to get back," Antonios sighed with fatigue.

Pothitos managed a weary smile, his hand clapping his father on the back. "Better late than never, eh?"

The sounds of the battle began to surge once more, but now the tide had turned. The death of Halikos had crushed the enemy's morale, and the invaders began to falter, their confidence crumbling with every step they took back. The farmers, shepherds, and fishermen, now emboldened by the sight of their fallen enemy, pressed forward with fury, driving their enemies back.

As the battle turned against them and the enemy faltered, Gelimer, the chieftain known for his cunning rather than his bravery, saw that the tide had shifted irreversibly. His eyes darted across the battlefield, taking in the sight of his warriors being cut down by farmers and fishermen, men who fought with a fury that could not be quelled. The death of Halikos had shattered whatever remained of their fortitude, and their lines were broken and men scattered.

Gelimer, though no coward, was not a fool. He had no intention of dying in filth alongside the common soldiers. His mind, always calculating, sought a way out. The battle was lost, but there would be other days, other wars, and he intended to live to see them. With the stealth of a man well-versed in slipping away from a fight when the winds turned against him, he began to edge toward the shadows, his eyes scanning the chaos for an opening.

Then he saw it, a narrow gap in the fighting near the northern edge of the monastery wall, where the defenders were still focused on the last pockets of resistance. If he could slip through there, he could make for a grove of trees, where he would be hidden from sight. Gelimer smiled to himself, his heart racing with the thrill of escape. The others could die here; he would live. He would rebuild, gather new men, strike again in time.

But as he moved toward the gap, he faltered. A figure stepped into view, blocking his path. It was Longinus.

The captain of the Byzantines stood waiting for him, calm and sure, his iron-rimmed staff gripped firmly in both hands. Longinus had seen this coming—he had known that Gelimer, with all his craftiness, would try to flee like he did at Tricamarum. The king had always been more fox than wolf, a man who preferred to lead from the rear and strike only when victory was assured. But

Longinus had learned long ago that a fox was no less dangerous than a wolf. Sometimes, it was more so.

Gelimer's eyes narrowed, his smile vanishing as he realized his way out had been blocked. There was no mockery in Longinus's expression, no taunting words—just the hard, cold look of a man who knew exactly what needed to be done.

Gelimer, unwilling to be caught like a rat, drew his sword. "You think you can stop me?" he snarled, his voice filled with arrogance.

Longinus didn't answer. He simply shifted his stance, planting his feet firmly on the ground and raising his staff with the ease of a man who had wielded such a weapon in battle many times before. His iron-rimmed staff was not the elegant tool of a swordsman, but a brutal, blunt instrument, designed to crush bone and shatter skulls. And Longinus knew exactly how to use it.

Gelimer, his pride wounded, lunged forward with a vicious swing, his sword slicing through the air. But Longinus, calm as ever, deflected the blow with a quick turn of his staff. The clash of steel against wood rang throughout the battlefield, but there was no power behind Gelimer's strike. It was wild, born out of fear and frustration. Longinus had no trouble swatting it aside.

Gelimer tried again, this time with a thrust aimed at Longinus's chest, but again the staff moved effortlessly, knocking the blade to the side. With every failed strike, Gelimer grew more frantic, his movements more erratic.

Longinus, his eyes never leaving Gelimer's, waited for the moment when the chieftain overextended himself, when his desperation would leave him vulnerable. It didn't take long. Gelimer, his face contorted with rage, brought his sword down in a wild overhead swing, hoping to batter his way through Longinus's defenses. But it was exactly the opening Longinus had been waiting for.

In one swift motion, Longinus brought his staff up to meet the blow, the iron rim catching the edge of Gelimer's sword, and sent it skittering off to the side. Before Gelimer could recover, Longinus swung his staff down in a brutal arc, the heavy iron-capped end aimed directly at his opponent's head.

The impact was sickening. The crack of bone careened across the battlefield as Longinus's staff connected with Gelimer's skull. The king's eyes went wide with shock as his knees buckled beneath him. He slumped to the ground, his body convulsing as his brain registered the mortal blow. Blood poured from the wound and mingled with the fragments of bone and brain matter that clung to the iron rim of Longinus's staff.

Gelimer's body twitched once, twice, and then went still. His lifeless eyes stared up at the sky, his mouth caught in an expression of disbelief. The cunning man, who had once fancied himself the king of the Vandals, now lay dead in the dirt, his life snuffed out in an instant.

Longinus stood over the body, his chest rising and falling, the staff still gripped tightly in his hands. He looked down at the shattered remains of Gelimer's skull, the blood pooling around the former king's head, and felt nothing but the cold satisfaction of a job well done.

This wasn't even a battle, Longinus thought, wiping the brain matter from his staff against the edge of Gelimer's cloak. Gelimer had been a man who thought he could win wars with schemes and treachery, but in the end, all it had taken was one blow—a single, crushing strike to remind him that all men, no matter how clever they thought themselves, bled the same.

The invaders were in full retreat, their morale shattered, their leaders dead. Longinus, his work done, turned his back on Gelimer's broken body and strode back toward the heart of the battle, where his men fought to finish what they had started. He would leave the dead to the crows.

Agio Konstantinos would stand.

Chapter 43

THE WITCH AND THE SPEAR

Pothitos and Antonios burst into the infirmary, the sound of their heavy boots was drowned out by the relentless noise of battle raging outside. But as they crossed the threshold, the chaos of the battlefield fell away, replaced by a silence that was far more terrifying than the battle outside. What Pothitos found inside was a vision from a nightmare, a scene that would be seared into his memory.

Delenda was huddled in the far corner, her body trembling, covered in blood that ran in rivulets down her arms, across her hands, and dripped from her fingertips. She was cradling two small, squirming figures—her children, their children—clutching them to her chest as though she could shield them from the evil that had invaded the halls of Agio Konstantinos. But standing over her, her face a mask of madness, stood Skylla, the witch.

Skylla's eyes blazed with an unnatural light as she sliced with her dagger over and over, the blade flashing in the dim light of the infirmary. "I will take your blood," she shrieked, her voice sharp as a razor, "and then I will take the blood of your children!"

Delenda, her strength waning, gasped in pain as the dagger severed her flesh again and again, each strike accompanied by a fresh gout of blood. Her body began to give way, her knees buckling as she slipped to the floor in a pool of her own blood, her arms instinctively trying to protect her children. But as her strength failed her, the children were left exposed, vulnerable, their cries rising into the air.

Pothitos, standing in shock at the doorway, felt his heart shatter as he took in the scene. The world narrowed to a single point—the sight of his children, their tiny bodies writhing in fear, and the wicked blade descending toward them. In that instant, all his training, all his years as a warrior, fell away. He was no longer the soldier, the seasoned fighter; he was only a father, a man who saw his children in danger and knew he had to protect them, even if it cost him everything.

With a primal roar Pothitos hurled himself forward, his arms outstretched, his focus entirely on his children. He didn't even register that there were two of them—only that they were his, that they needed him, and that he would give his life to save them.

Skylla's dagger, still wet with Delenda's blood, arced downward, aimed directly at the heart of one of the infants. But before the blade could reach its mark, Pothitos threw himself in its path, his body shielding his child from the deadly strike. The cold steel pierced his chest, driving deep into his flesh, the force of the blow stealing the breath from his lungs. The pain was immediate, a burning, searing agony that radiated through his entire body.

But Pothitos didn't care. He didn't care about the pain, didn't care about the blood now pouring from his wound. All that mattered was that he had stopped the blade. He had protected his children. With a grunt of effort, he twisted his body, wrenching the dagger free from Skylla's grip, even as he felt the blood draining from him. His vision began to blur, the edges of his world growing dark as he staggered backward, his arms reaching out desperately to touch his children.

The Spear of Destiny slipped from his grasp and clattered to the floor, the sound echoing in the blood-soaked room. Skylla's eyes darted to the weapon, her face contorting malevolently as she reached for it, believing that it had power… power that could turn the tide of the battle in her favor.

But Delenda, lying in a pool of her own blood, was not done yet. Summoning the last reserves of her strength, she crawled forward, her fingers wrapping around the haft of the spear. With a cry that was part rage, part defiance, she drove the spear forward, ramming it into Skylla's midsection.

As the spear pierced her abdomen, a terrible scream ripped from Skylla's throat. The sound was inhuman, a shriek so piercing and raw that it seemed to rend the very fabric of the air around them. The spear seemed to run through her like fire. Skylla's scream grew louder, more terrible, a sound so unearthly that it felt as though the very walls of the monastery were shaking in response.

And then they were. The ground beneath them trembled violently, the stone walls of the monastery groaning as if in pain. The earth itself seemed to rise up in fury, cracks spiderwebbing across the floor, racing up the walls as the very foundation of the building began to tear apart. Skylla's form convulsed, her body writhing.

Pothitos, now on his knees, could barely hold himself upright. His vision was fading fast, but he could still see Skylla, writhing in pain with the spearhead buried deep in her gut. He could still hear the witch's horrible scream and feel the monastery quake beneath him.

The walls of the infirmary began to crumble, great chunks of stone crashing down around them as the earth buckled and heaved. The ground split open, gaping chasms tearing through the monastery, swallowing everything in their path. Pothitos reached out blindly, his fingers brushing against the soft, warm bodies of his children, pulling them close even as the world fell apart around him.

Skylla's scream reached a fever pitch, a final, desperate cry. Windows shattered, stones tumbled through the air. Skylla's body was reduced to a crumpled heap on the cold floor, the Spear of Destiny impaled deep within her.

The earth continued to shake; the walls continued to fall, but in the heart of the storm, Pothitos held his children and Delenda close. He looked down at their faces, their tiny, innocent faces, and a tear slipped from his eye. He had saved them. He had done what he had to do.

And as the darkness closed in, as the walls of the monastery crumbled and the earth beneath him was torn asunder, Pothitos recited a quiet prayer to the Virgin Mary, thanking her for the strength she had given him, for the chance to protect his children, for the life he had lived. And then, with his final breath, he called out to his father, "Baba, save them. Save the babies."

Chapter 44

TEARS OVER TWO ISLANDS

Antonios rushed to the broken bodies of Pothitos and Delenda. The sight before him was almost too much to bear. Pothitos, his son, lay covered in blood, his arms wrapped protectively around his wife and the two infants, the children he had given everything to save. Delenda grasped onto him, her blood staining the stone floor, her face pale and serene. The room was covered in dust and the ground beneath Antonios's feet trembled as the earth continued to heave in anger.

Tears blurred Antonios's vision as he knelt beside them, his hands shaking as he pried the crying infants from Pothitos's arms. The children's wails filled the air, a sound that seemed to pierce his soul, a reminder of the lives that had been lost to save them. Antonios's throat tightened, and for a moment, he thought he might choke on his grief. But there was no time to mourn, no time to give in to the despair that threatened to overwhelm him. The earth was shattering around them, and if he didn't act now, they would all be buried beneath the rubble.

With tears streaming down his face, Antonios cradled the children against his chest, their tiny bodies squirming. He forced himself to his feet, his legs unsteady beneath him. The ceiling above groaned ominously, the cracks spreading across the stone, and Antonios knew he had only moments before the monastery collapsed in on itself.

He moved with a desperation born of pure instinct, his mind barely registering the chaos around him as he sprinted toward the entrance. The walls were crumbling, stones raining down around him, but Antonios dodged and weaved, driven by a single purpose: to save his grandchildren, his last living legacy. He reached the threshold of the infirmary just as the ceiling gave way behind him, the sound of stone crashing down, like the roar of a beast.

Antonios stumbled out into the open air, gasping, his heart still pounding in his chest. He looked down at the infants in his arms, their faces wet with tears and he knew that he had done all he could. But as he stepped outside the monastery walls, a new horror awaited him.

The ground beneath the monastery itself began to give way, the stone crumbling as the earth bucked and heaved. Antonios's heart seized in his chest as he saw the very ground where he had just stood, where Pothitos and Delenda lay, began to collapse. The cliffs, those sheer, unyielding cliffs, gave one final, thunderous crack, and the entire section of the monastery where he had just escaped from tumbled into the sea, taking with it Pothitos, Delenda, the witch, and the Spear of Destiny.

Antonios knelt on the rocky ground. His eyes searched the ocean below for any sign of Pothitos or Delenda. The waves subsided momentarily, and he thought he caught a glimpse of them.

The two star-crossed lovers, embracing each other as they were dragged to the bottom of the sea. And then they were gone.

The two infants, the last remnants of Antonios's family line, whimpered softly in his arms, their tiny bodies pressed against his chest as though they could sense the magnitude of the horror surrounding them. But Antonios could only gape at the tragedy that was unfolding below him.

Pothaia, the city he had ruled over, the city he had sworn to protect, was being torn apart by forces beyond his comprehension. The earth itself was splitting open, great fissures forming in the ground as if the very bones of the world were being shattered.

Pothaia had once been a proud and thriving place, a proud example of civilization along the Aegean coast, its people hardened by the sea and strengthened by the mountains that sheltered them. But now, it was dying. The earth, cracked and broken, was tearing itself apart, and the sea, once their lifeblood, was now their destroyer.

He helplessly watched as the ground beneath the city buckled and split, as the streets he had walked a thousand times cracked open like an eggshell. The buildings, once tall and sturdy, crumbled and sank, the stones of homes and shops tumbled into the gaping chasms. The docks, where the sponge fishermen had once brought their hauls to shore, where the sailors had brought news from distant lands, were now splintered wrecks, swallowed by the rising tide.

Then came the waves—great, towering crests of water, more monstrous than any Antonios had ever seen, rolled in from the horizon with the force of an army. The monstrous waves, towering and furious, resembling a pack of ravenous dogs, crashed over the shores with a ferocity that defied belief. They surged inland, crashing over the granaries and the markets, sweeping away everything in their path. The sea devoured the lower quarters of the city first, the shorefront homes vanished beneath the churning water. But the waves did not stop. They rose higher and higher, engulfing the city's heart, drowning the grand coliseum that had once been the pride of Pothaia. The mighty structure, where Antonios had watched countless games and competitions, where the people had gathered to celebrate and to mourn, cracked apart like a toy under a child's foot. Its walls buckled, the great stone arches collapsing in on themselves before the entire edifice was dragged into the sea's depths. The fissures that had opened in the earth widened, deepened, until they formed a vast rift that ran through the heart of the city, splitting it into two.

The land, once whole, was now divided, the city sundered into two halves that drifted apart like pieces of a broken puzzle. The eastern part of the city, where the wealthy had once lived in their grand villas, where the churches had stood in all their glory, was now separated from the western part, where the common folk had toiled and lived their simple, honest lives. The sea poured into the chasm between them, filling it with a dark, swirling current that seemed to drink in the ruins of Pothaia with a voracious hunger.

The land that had been Pothaia was no more. In its place, there were now two separate islands, uneven and raw, the wounds of the earth still fresh. The great city had been torn in two, the halves now isolated from each other by a narrow strip of sea that foamed and churned like a living thing. And in the distance, where the cliffs had crumbled, where the monastery had once stood, there was nothing but ruins and the roar of the ocean far below.

Antonios felt a hollow emptiness in his chest as he watched it all unfold, as he watched the land he had known his entire life disappear before his eyes. Pothaia, the heart of his world, was destroyed, not by an army, not by the hands of men, but by the earth and sea, forces too powerful to resist, too ancient to comprehend.

The silence that followed the destruction was more deafening than any roar of battle. The waves, having done their work, began to subside, their fury spent. The earth, having torn itself apart, finally grew still. And all that remained was the soft, steady lap of the sea against the newly formed shores, the quiet after the storm.

Antonios struggled to his feet, his legs weak beneath him, his eyes still fixed on the scene before him. He could see the remnants of the city now, scattered across the two islands like bones left after a feast. The great coliseum was gone, the docks were no more, and the streets and buildings had been reduced to rubble. Only the rocks and the dark waters remained, the final, grim witness to what had once been.

He turned away then, unable to bear the sight any longer, and reeled back from the edge of the cliffs, the two children still clutched in his arms. His tears had dried, leaving his face streaked with dirt, his heart numb with angst. He had lost everything—his son, his home, his city. And now, as he looked upon the two islands that had once been one, he realized that nothing would ever be the same again.

The infants in his arms whimpered, their tiny hands grasping at his armor, and Antonios looked down at them, his heart breaking all over again. They were all that was left, all that remained of a world that had been torn asunder. He sank to his knees again, unable to go any further, his anguish too much to bear. He wept then, wept for Pothitos and Delenda, for the city that had been lost, for the future that had been stolen from them all.

Antonios felt a presence beside him, and when he looked up, he saw Longinus there, his face as drawn and haggard as his own.

Longinus said nothing, for there was nothing to say. He simply sat down beside Antonios, his own tears flowing freely as they both looked out at what remained. They sat together in the quiet, the only sound the sea against the newly formed shores.

Chapter 45

EPILOGUE

Months had passed since the earth had torn itself asunder, since the sea had swallowed Pothaia and its people, leaving behind two islands. The land had settled into its new shape, the fury of the earthquake long subsided, but the scars it left behind were deep and enduring. The city was gone, its ruins buried beneath the waves, and the world as Antonios and Longinus had known had changed forever.

Now, they stood together on the ruined battlements of the castle of Kastelli; the wind whipping through their hair as they looked out over the new landscape that had been born in the wake of the disaster. Below them, the island of Kalymnos spread out, rugged and resilient, a place reshaped by the forces of nature but still standing, still defiant. Across the narrow stretch of water, the sister island of Delendos rose from the sea, its jagged peaks catching the last rays of the setting sun. Earlier that day, Panormitis, the new regent of Orkinos, had decreed that the island formed in the earthquake's aftermath would bear Delenda's name.

The island of Delendos was a tribute to the woman who had sacrificed everything, who had given her life to protect the future. It was a place of haunting beauty, the western half of its highest mountain carved by the quake into the unmistakable profile of a princess. The contours of the rock had formed into the likeness of Delenda, her face serene and regal, crowned with the silhouette of an Egyptian princess's headdress. It was as if the earth itself had sought to honor her, to immortalize her sacrifice in stone. The image was so clear, so unmistakable, that it took Antonios's breath away every time he saw it.

"It is fitting," Antonios spoke, his voice soft. "That she watches over us still."

Longinus, standing beside him, nodded slowly, his gaze fixed on the distant island. "She was more than a princess," he replied, his voice rough. "She was a guardian, a protector. And now, she guards us in death as she did in life."

Antonios's eyes lingered on the profile of Delenda, the woman who had given him so much, who had brought his grandchildren into the world at the cost of her own life. The pain was still raw, a lingering presence in his heart, but there was also a measure of peace. Delenda had not died in vain. Her children lived, and through them, her legacy would endure.

But with that legacy came danger. From the hour of their birth, each twin carried upon their palm a fragment of mystery—a birthmark unlike any other. Alone, each mark was incomplete, little more than a broken outline. Upon each hand lay half a star, its meaning obscured. Yet when their hands were joined, the fragments became whole: the islands of Kalymnos and Delendos, divided by the narrow sea. Between those islands, the broken halves of the star drew together, their lines locking as if two pieces of a forgotten seal had at last been restored. Only in that moment did the star reveal its full shape, marking the place where the Spear of Destiny had vanished into the depths. They were not mere birthmarks, but omens etched into their flesh—a sign that bound their legacy to the fate of their parents.

Both men understood what this meant. The spear was a powerful relic, one that could change the fate of nations, and it would not remain hidden forever. Others would come looking for it, and when they did, the twins would be in grave danger. It was inevitable that their existence would attract attention, that those who sought power would seek out the children who bore the mark of the islands and the star. The threat was too great to ignore, and they could not risk keeping the twins together.

"It is too dangerous," Antonios said, his voice laden with sadness. "Keeping them here together would draw too much attention. We cannot protect them both if they are in the same place."

Longinus turned to face his old friend, his expression one of understanding. "I agree," he said quietly. "We must divide the burden. I will take Angeliki with me back to Sardinia. The allies we have there are strong, and she will be safe in their care. I will raise her as my own and protect her with my life."

"And I will keep little Antonios here," Antonios replied. "He will be raised as the heir to Kalymnos, as the future archon of these lands. I will teach him everything I know and prepare him for the day when he must take up the mantle of leadership."

The two men stood in silence for a moment, the gravity of their decision settling over them like a shroud. They knew that separating the twins was the only way to ensure their safety, but it did not make the choice any easier. The bond between the children was strong and tearing them apart now would leave a scar that neither Antonios nor Longinus could heal. But it was a necessary pain, a sacrifice they were both willing to make for the greater good.

As the sun dipped lower on the horizon, deep shadows hung over the islands, Antonios and Longinus turned their attention to the west, where the last light of day illuminated the profile of Delenda on the mountain of Delendos. The sight of her likeness, her face etched in stone, brought a fresh wave of sadness to Antonios's heart.

"We will protect them," Longinus said firmly, his voice carrying a promise. "No matter what comes, we will keep them safe."

Antonios agreed. "For Delenda," he whispered. "For Pothitos. For the future of Kalymnos."

Together, they watched as the sun sank behind Delendos; the light fading from the sky, forming a silhouette of the profile of Delenda amongst the island's crags. The wind whistled through the battlements, carrying with it the scent of the sea, the sound of the waves crashing against the shores of the two islands that had once been one.

The world had changed, but Antonios and Longinus knew that they had to change with it. They had to be strong, for the sake of the children, for the sake of the land they had sworn to protect. And as the last rays of sunlight disappeared, they shed a tear for those they had lost, for the sacrifices made, and for the uncertain future that lay ahead.

But they also knew that they would face whatever came with courage and tenacity. The islands of Kalymnos and Delendos were more than just land—they were the living memory of those who had fought and died to protect them. And in the hearts of those who remained, that memory would never fade.

As the darkness fell, Antonios and Longinus stood together, watching over the two islands that had been reborn from the ashes of destruction. And in the silence that followed, they made a vow—to protect the legacy of those who had fallen, to guard the children who bore the future in their blood, and to ensure that the story of Pothitos and Delenda would be told for generations to come.

Historical Notes

The Last Prince of Kalymnos is a work of historical fiction grounded in as much authentic history as possible. Many of the characters and locations woven into the novel are not merely products of imagination, but remnants from the past.

In writing this novel, I drew from the historical geography of ancient Kalymnos but took creative liberties to serve the story. While several historical demes such as Orkatou, Skaliodon, Pothaion, and Panormos did exist in antiquity, I modified the geographical boundaries of certain demes to better serve the dramatic and thematic needs of the story. I have also taken creative liberties by fictionalizing a rift between Orkatou and neighboring demes, using this division as a symbolic and structural element in the narrative. Finally, I have adjusted the spelling of names and places, such as Telendos, to better fit the story. While inspired by real locations and traditions, this is a work of historical fiction and is an adaptation of the legend of The Princess of Telendos.

Historical figures such as King Gelimer, Tzazo, Belisarius, Emperor Justinian, and Godas once walked the earth and shaped the turbulent politics of their time. The name Longinus, given to the centurion in this story, is drawn from Christian tradition—the very soldier believed to have pierced the side of Christ, later associated with the fabled Spear of Destiny. This relic, shrouded in myth and mysticism, has stirred centuries of speculation. It is even said that Hitler himself scoured Europe in search of the spear, believing it held the power to grant world domination.

The setting of the novel is equally rich in real-world geography and legend. Carthage, the Vandal Kingdom, the Battle of Tricamarum, Grotto della Vipera, and Nuraghe Porto Pirastu were all actual events and real-world locations.

The island of Kalymnos, its regions, and the names of its ancient demes are faithfully portrayed. The city of Damos, the Castle of Kastelli, the Monastery of Agio Konstantinos, the Church of Profiti Elias, the Cave of Saint Panteleimon, the Church of Christ in Jerusalem, Kiria Psili, the Church of Palio Panagia, and the once-prosperous city of Pothaia all anchor the narrative in genuine history.

Pothaia, devastated by a powerful earthquake in 554 AD, is said to have been swallowed by the sea—splitting Kalymnos into two distinct islands, Kalymnos and Telendos. To this day, the submerged foundations of the ancient city can still be glimpsed on the sea floor, a haunting reminder of a world lost to time. Many believe that the current city of Pothia was renamed after the lost city of Pothaia.

This novel strives to honor those truths—both historical and legend—while building a story that bridges the divide between myth and memory.

Acknowledgements

First and foremost, I give all glory, honor, and heartfelt gratitude to my Lord and Savior, Jesus Christ. It is only through His guidance, strength, and grace that I was able to create this story. I thank God for the inspiration, for the doors He opened, and for the endurance to see this project through. To Him be the glory always.

I want to thank my beautiful wife Susie—This book would not exist without your patience, love, and support. You took on the weight of the household—managing every detail—so I could pour myself into this novel. Your selflessness gave me the freedom to create, and for that, I am forever grateful.

To my greatest creations, my children Peter and Michael— you are the heartbeat of my life. Your laughter, your wonder, and your joy reminded me to live in the moment, and in doing so, brought light and inspiration back into my world. You will both always be in my heart.

To my parents Peter and Angie—thank you for introducing me to the magical island of Kalymnos. Instead of urging me to sit still on the beach, you let me explore every corner, every trail, every legend hidden in the rocks and castles. That freedom planted the seeds for this story long before I ever realized it. Your love, guidance, and unwavering faith in me have been the foundation of everything I've become. You showed me, even in the darkest days, that love will always shine through. You didn't just support my dreams—you gave them life. This book is as much yours as it is mine.

To my father-in-law, Jim and my mother-in-law, Sandy—thank you for raising such an extraordinary daughter and for becoming my tireless editors-in-chief. Now I truly know how much you love me. Because only a labor of love could explain your willingness to take on the monumental task of fixing all my mistakes. Your patience, insight, and careful attention to detail helped polish what would have otherwise remained a very rough stone. I'm fairly certain more than a few red pens were sacrificed along the way, and I'm eternally grateful for your sharp eyes and even sharper wit.

To my sister Maria—thank you for keeping our family firmly rooted in the Orthodox faith. It shines through in all we do. To my Grandparents, brother-in-law Kosta, sister-in-law Lauren, nephews (Derrell, Stephen, Vlassi, Peter, Pothito, Anthony, Savvas, Christian, and Andrew), and nieces (Lexi and Maggie)—thank you for constantly feeding my imagination and cheering me on. Your encouragement and energy helped shape this story in ways you may never realize. Whether through honest critique or words of support, you helped shape every page.

To my brother Tony and my Uncle Rick—thank you for introducing me to J.R.R. Tolkien and for nurturing my love of storytelling and fantasy. The magic of words, the depth of worlds, and the thrill of imagination you shared with me continue to inspire every chapter of this book.

To the members of "The War Council" — it was in those quiet hours that the course of this book was drawn. Every battle line, every alliance, every act of betrayal or courage was contoured long before swords clashed, or banners flew. Strategy, not chaos, shaped the fate of this story. The battlefield may seem ruled by chance, but victory is born in the minds of those who gather around the map — long live "The War Council."

To Brooke and George — thank you for taking the time out of your busy schedules to do a final read-through. Without you my book would have been perilously adorned with far too many treacherous words.

I would also like to express my deepest thanks to the incredible staff of The Archaeological Museum of Kalymnos. Your generosity in allowing me to explore your collections and immerse myself in the rich history of the Kalymian people has been invaluable. Your passion for preserving the island's heritage is evident, and I encourage everyone to visit this remarkable museum — it is truly a gateway to understanding the soul of Kalymnos.

My sincere appreciation goes to the many people of Kalymnos whose kindness, stories, and spirit helped breathe life into the characters of this book. It is the people who give this island its true heart. To Thea Eleni Kardoulias — thank you for sharing your stories of Kalymnos. Though I took creative liberties in adapting them, your memories and voice were a compass in my journey. Also, a special thank you to Manolis — though our encounter was brief, it sparked reflections that will last a lifetime. Your island, your stories, and your resilience live within these pages. From the bottom of my heart—thank you all.

I would be remiss to not thank my co-pilot Chewie. I couldn't have finished this without your constant attention. The countless hours of typing with you on my lap would have been much lonelier without you there.

Finally, to my loved ones whose journeys ended too soon, your memory lights our paths forward. You molded who I am, and though time and distance now stand between us, I carry your stories, your laughter, and your love with me always.

As J.R.R. Tolkien wrote, *"I will not say: do not weep; for not all tears are an evil. But beyond the sorrow, I hold to hope — that beyond the circles of this world, we will meet again, beneath fairer skies, where no shadow falls."*